hell's FORTRESS

ALSO BY MICHAEL WALLACE

— hell's —
FORTRESS

MICHAEL WALLACE

THOMAS & MERCER

Published by Thomas & Mercer, Seattle

www.apub.com

Amazon, the Amazon logo, and Thomas & Mercer are trademarks of Amazon.com, Inc., or its affiliates.

ISBN-13: 9781477824504
ISBN-10: 1477824502

Cover design by Scott Barrie (Cyanotype Book Architects)

Library of Congress Control Number: 2014903901

Printed in the United States of America

CHAPTER ONE

Jacob Christianson was in surgery, setting a broken bone, when his brother David brought word of the invaders. A patrol had spotted them eight miles south of Blister Creek, trudging up the highway toward the southernmost gun emplacements.

He left his work to his nurses, and the two men galloped south. It was late May and the outside world was collapsing in spasms of war, famine, and disease, while the weather was more like late winter than the end of spring. Nevertheless, a certain complacency had slipped into the valley. People stared in curiosity from their porches and fields as the men thundered past.

They arrived at the roadside bunker to find Elder Smoot waiting inside behind a .50-cal machine gun. His beard trailed to his chest, gray as the unkempt hair on his head. Decades of sun and wind had tanned the skin on his hands to leather, but his arms and shoulders were still broad and powerful. His teenage son, Grover, stood on top of the pillbox with a pair of binoculars.

David jumped down from his horse and took the stairs into the half-buried pillbox, while Jacob scrambled up top to look. He grabbed the binoculars from Grover and sent the boy below.

The caravan was still a half mile down the abandoned highway. It was led by two huge hay wagons drawn by mules, their beds stuffed with possessions, like some vision from the Dust Bowl. An old Bluebird school bus followed, towed by a team of shabby horses. Figures trudged alongside. Twenty, thirty people, all on foot. They were bundled in coats, scarves, and gloves.

Smoot's voice came out hollowly from below Jacob's position. "At last it comes. The locusts have arrived."

Jacob came down to find Grover and David prying open a crate with a crowbar and unloading ammo cans. Smoot stared grimly down the barrel of the gun, his eyes and nose the only visible parts of his face over the long curly gray beard.

"What do we do?" David asked.

"Shoot them," Elder Smoot said. "Blow them away." He pulled back the breech bolt with a snick.

Jacob didn't immediately rebuke Smoot. Eight months had passed since the army pulled out. Seven months since they lost phone and Internet. All through the frigid, lingering winter, they'd stayed isolated in their desert fortress while the outside world crumbled. Jacob was supposed to be the voice of reason in the church and community, and here he was, terrified of outsiders like anyone else.

The date was May 27. A lean winter. Months of crushing isolation. Nothing but drones in the sky to remind them that the outside world existed. Keeping them prisoner.

The military had ended its occupation after Jacob's cousin drove a Winnebago packed with explosives into the heart of town and blew himself up in front of the temple, together with a number of army personnel. Since then, quarantine, mostly enforced from the sky. For months now, he'd expected them to invade, this time in greater force. Seize the grain and everything else of value in the valley.

"Jacob?" David prodded.

"Hold your fire."

Jacob went outside for another look. Two days earlier, one of the crazy weather swings brought a few brief days of springlike weather, melting the snow from the highway. It stretched south through red rock and sagebrush, like a black line painted through the desert. The caravan was taking its time. They had no fuel, of course, only animals, but that didn't explain the desultory way the refugees trudged forward, step by exhausted step.

They radiated hunger and desperation. No doubt there were sick and injured in the party, who he could help in the clinic. That didn't mean they weren't also dangerous. And armed.

"Get your wives on the radio," Jacob called in to David. "Tell them to open the armory and rouse the militia."

His brother obeyed, flipping on his radio as he came outside for better reception.

"We don't need the militia," Smoot said. "We can finish it here."

"I'm going to talk to those people. You man the gun, but do not shoot unless you hear it from my mouth. Grover, help with ammo if your father needs it.

"I don't see the point in talking," Smoot said. "We posted warnings. They ignored them."

"Maybe it's over. Maybe the quarantine is broken."

"You don't know that."

"That's why I'm going to find out."

"No good will come of this," Smoot warned. "We can't let the gentiles into the valley. They'll destroy us."

Jacob was growing annoyed. He had made his decision, but yet again, Smoot kept pushing, and always down more violent, aggressive paths.

"For all we know they're saints. Refugees from Colorado City, or one of the other polygamist communities. What happens when you shoot them all and discover they're cousins of one of your wives?"

Smoot sputtered. Jacob didn't wait for him to find an argument, but walked away from the pillbox. He left the horses where they were cropping at the grass and wildflowers that grew among the sagebrush, drew his rifle from its holster, and slung it over his shoulder. David stood to one side, speaking in urgent tones into the radio. Jacob walked to the highway and checked again through the binoculars.

The caravan had picked up pace. The refugees must have spotted the gun emplacement. Most of them appeared to be adults, but he saw at least four or five children. That was good. More likely they were families than raiders. But at least one of the men was black and a few looked Hispanic, which ruled out fellow saints. Descended from the early Mormon settlers, polygamists were invariably of northern European descent.

David joined Jacob. "I spoke to Miriam. She wants to load up the trucks and drive out with the militia. I told her to stay in town."

Jacob lowered the binoculars. "And she listened?"

"Reluctantly. You know how she is."

"Good. Elder Smoot is more than enough for me to handle. I don't need Miriam's itchy trigger finger too."

David's first wife was ex-FBI. She was only one of many hard-headed people in town, men as well as women, but in some ways she presented more challenges for Jacob than an Old Testament–style patriarch like Elder Smoot. She had her training, she was ready for the end of the world, and she was convinced she knew the will of the Lord at all times. If anyone thought that giving birth to a child would mellow her, they were mistaken. She was stronger than David, stronger than David's younger wife, Lillian, and probably stronger than Jacob, in all honesty. In all of Blister Creek, only Jacob's sister Eliza could match her will. And Eliza was in the Ghost Cliffs again, searching for a way out of the valley to reach her fiancé.

The caravan halted some fifty yards away. Maybe this was Eliza's answer. If someone found their way in, then maybe she could get out. Had the drone quarantine broken? Jacob looked into the sky, but didn't see anything. Didn't hear the familiar and hated whine of turboprop engines.

A man stepped forward from the caravan. He raised hands covered in fingerless gloves. No weapon. Stubble covered his face. Behind him, people leaned against the hay wagons, or sat on the pavement, wrapped in blankets. Faces looked out from behind steamed-over windows on the bus.

The man stopped about thirty feet away. "Is this Blister Creek?"

"Who are you?" Jacob asked.

"Name is Joe Kemp. And you are . . . ?"

"What do you want?"

"We're starving. We heard you have food."

"Who told you that?"

"Drive them off," David whispered. "We have nothing to give them."

"Or what?" Jacob asked his brother. "We shoot?"

"Yes."

It was a hard thing, a *cruel* thing. But Jacob worried that his brother and Elder Smoot were right. Helping these people would only bring more refugees. If the army had called off the drones to fight elsewhere, Blister Creek could find itself inundated with survivors from southern Utah and beyond.

Kemp started walking again. He kept his hands up.

"Hold it right there," Jacob said. "Not another step."

David lifted his rifle.

The man faltered. "For God's sake, please. We have sick children. They're dying. They said you have medicine. You have to help us."

Jacob had decided to turn them back, all of them. Now he stopped. Withholding food was one thing, but medicine?

Kemp seemed to sense the hesitation and he pressed. "Bandits robbed us in the mountains. They shot my mother in the stomach."

"Keep your story straight. Is it sick kids or an injured mother?"

"Both. For God's sake, listen to me. I'm telling the truth. She caught part of a shotgun blast. I took out the pellets, but it only got worse. I don't know what else to do."

"Took them out, how?"

"Pried them out with my fingers. She's unconscious."

"Shouldn't have done that. You probably introduced sepsis."

"Are you the doctor? Please look at her. And the children."

"I don't like this," David said.

Jacob motioned for his brother to lower the rifle, then turned back to the man. "Take off your coat. Put it on the ground."

"It's cold."

"If you want our help, you'll do exactly what I say."

Kemp obeyed. He folded the coat and set it in front of him, then stood shivering. Beneath, he wore a filthy flannel shirt.

"The scarf too. I want to see your face."

Removing the scarf revealed a gaunt face with skin stretched over sharp cheekbones.

"Now take a couple steps back."

Kemp did it. He had a lean, hungry look, and eyes that sparkled with dangerous intelligence. He stood on the balls of his feet, taut as a piano wire. He stared at Jacob, as if sizing him up. It was the look of a man who had done terrible things to survive. His pants were combat fatigues. Ex-military?

David stepped forward, searched the man's jacket, and confiscated a hunting knife. Then he stepped to the man and patted him down, but didn't turn up any other weapons. David rejoined Jacob, who told Kemp to put his coat back on.

"Listen to me carefully," Jacob said. "That concrete box behind me is fortified with a Browning M2 and enough ammo to hold off a small army. We have other defenses along the road, including mines, anti-tank guns, and ambush sites. We're not a soft target."

"I understand."

"If you disobey me, we will kill you to set an example. Do you understand?"

"Of course."

"How many people do you have?"

"Forty-seven."

"They're all here?"

"That's right. We were bigger a few weeks ago. Almost eighty when we left Las Vegas, but we left the others along the way."

"Where did you leave them, St. George? Is there a camp there?"

"No, I mean they died. A few killed by outlaws. But most fell from exhaustion. There wasn't anything we could do. The bus couldn't hold any more people—it carried our supplies too."

"So they starved to death," Jacob said.

Kemp scowled. "Nobody starved. Yes, they were hungry. Sometimes we didn't have anything for days. But we shared what we had. The trip was too much for some people. They stopped walking and wouldn't move."

"That's what starvation looks like. You die of cold or exhaustion or disease. If you were out of food, why didn't you eat your animals?"

The man shifted and looked at his feet. "We did. These ones are new. We found them in an abandoned camp. Their owners had been driven off or killed."

He was equivocating, or at most, sharing a part of it. No way was he telling the full truth. Jacob should have turned them back. But now he was involved.

"Will you help my mother?" Kemp asked. "The wound is bad. She needs help."

Jacob looked north toward Blister Creek. The town was three miles away, waiting, vulnerable. The white spire of the temple. The clean, gridded streets, laid down by his ancestors. Generations of Christiansons and Kimballs and Smoots and Youngs. Devout, convinced they were God's chosen, destined to hold out in this desert sanctuary against the forces of Satan. So much superstition and delusion. Why would God choose this place above all others? Why these people?

He might have laughed, if somehow he hadn't ended up as their leader at what appeared to be the end of human civilization. First a supervolcano in Indonesia had trashed the growing seasons of the world. Then humanity, instead of pulling together, was now tearing itself apart.

War came first to the Middle East, dependent upon the outside world for grain it could no longer provide. Starving, they'd cut off the oil. That prompted an American invasion. After that, it was just one bloody step after another until half the world was in flames, and the other half starving. Those same conflicts were playing out here in the United States, with outright civil war on the West Coast and a hundred bush wars all throughout the interior of the continent.

The sun was a fiery red ball cutting a bloody gash on the horizon. Particles of volcanic dust mingled with the ash of burning cities to leave the sky a purple bruise. It was almost dusk; Jacob had to decide.

"Okay. We'll help. Pull back to that rocky outcrop." He pointed to a sandstone hillock. "You have two nights. We will give you what food and medical care we can, but forty-eight hours from now—by sunset—you'll be on your way out of the valley."

"Thank you."

"If anyone leaves your camp, they will be shot. Tell your people. Make it clear. There will be no second chances."

"And my mother? The sick kids?"

"I'll send a truck to take them to the clinic."

"Thank you."

Jacob walked back toward Smoot and his son at the pillbox. David followed. "I hope you know what you're doing."

"I don't."

"I'm serious."

"So am I. There's no user manual for the end of the world."

"I thought there was. It's called the scriptures."

Jacob gave him the side eye. "Now don't *you* start."

"Why are you doing it? We're bursting at the seams. Eating through our food, burning up the fuel. Another year of crop failures ahead of us. Are you going to give away our medicine now too?"

"There's one thing we don't have. Information. We don't even have AM radio anymore. Who's in charge out there? Anyone? I want info."

"What good is that?" David asked.

"Is the army planning to occupy the valley again? Are there more refugees on the way? How about other towns? Are any of them holding on? Or are we alone? Sooner or later we have to find out."

"Not yet we don't. Now we weather the storm."

What had gotten into David? He sounded like Miriam, or maybe one of the older men from the quorum. One by one, Jacob's friends, family, and confidants were succumbing to the siege mentality. And now his own brother.

When they returned to the pillbox, Jacob called Smoot and his son out and let David explain the situation. Smoot glowered, but held his tongue. Jacob radioed town and got David's senior wife on the phone.

When Miriam heard that newcomers had arrived, she fired off a number of breathless questions, all of which Jacob deflected. He asked her to pass a message to Lillian to prep his clinic, then told Miriam to send a truck to haul the sick and injured into town.

"When you come, bring fifty pounds of dried peas and a hundred pounds of flour. Two gallons of cooking oil and twenty pounds of powdered milk. That should do it."

The line fell silent.

"Miriam?"

"I'm here."

"Did you get all that?"

"If you leave the granary open, the mice multiply."

"They're not vermin, they're human beings."

"Not much difference these days. You do this and the news will spread to every unprepared fool west of the Rockies. Free food. Free housing. Free medical care. Come and get it."

"They're not staying. I'm treating them at the clinic and sending them on their way."

"And the food?"

"They're starving and we're going to feed them while they're here."

She muttered something that came out as garbled static. Elder Smoot stood to one side, scowling. He'd been openly listening to the entire conversation. Hard to say if the scowl was agreement with Miriam's opinion, or disapproval that she was talking back. Both, most likely.

Jacob waited until Miriam fell silent.

"Are you done?" he asked her.

"You're the prophet. If that's what the Lord commands, I'll do it."

There was a question at the end of that. Does He? Does the Lord command?

"Good. See you soon."

Jacob cut the radio, then looked down the road through the binoculars. The refugees were turning around, a slow, sad procession moving south on the highway toward the rocky hill. Even Kemp, their leader, slumped in his jacket and scarf like a prisoner of war shuffling from one end of camp to the other, just to get a bowl of soup. They looked helpless.

They're not. They're the survivors.

Seven, almost eight months of isolation. This was not the time to let down one's guard.

CHAPTER TWO

Eliza Christianson entered the dining room and was stunned to see four thin, filthy children at the table. Strangers. The children devoured slabs of fresh bread slathered in butter, stopping only long enough to let out a series of dry, barking coughs. While they ate, Fernie wheeled herself around the table to scrub their faces with a washcloth. One of Eliza's youngest sisters followed with a bowl of steaming water, already cloudy with dirt. The girl wore a prairie dress, tight braids in her cornsilk hair, and a pinched look of disgust at having to attend to the dirty children.

Eliza could only stare.

Fernie wrung out the washcloth and looked up from her work. "We have visitors."

"Yes, I see. What? How?"

"They came up the highway from the south. Whole caravan of refugees."

"But the quarantine . . ."

"Maybe it's over."

"I was just up in the Ghost Cliffs. There's a drone circling over the reservoir right this minute."

"I don't know, Liz. I can't explain it."

"Where's Jacob?"

"In the clinic. But you can't—"

Eliza didn't wait to hear what Fernie had to say. Her heart was pounding. Eight months of isolation. Finally, the roads had cleared of snow and she could search for a way out of this valley. This prison. She had to find a way.

Jacob's clinic was in the second garage, where their father used to work on his tractors. Jacob had scrubbed it, sterilized it, and divided it into an examination room and a surgery. Boxes of medical supplies lined the walls, anything and everything he'd gotten his hands on during the first year of the crisis. Refrigerators held medications and vaccines. Two years into the crisis, some of them had reached the end of their useful life.

The electricity flowing from the reservoir and the windmills powered this room first, before any other building in the valley. Not so much as a porch light flickered on until Jacob had his power. All the surgery lights were blazing now, and Jacob stood in his scrubs, removing his mask and gloves. Sister Lillian, David's younger wife, stood by his side. She was similarly dressed.

They stood over the prone body of an unconscious woman in a hospital bed. She looked to be in her sixties. Gray, haggard. A sheet covered her lower body, and the upper half was naked, bandaged around the waist, with the orange stain of Betadine coloring the skin. An endotracheal tube threaded down her throat to force air to her lungs.

Jacob looked up and noticed Eliza. "You heard the news?" he asked.

"No. What happened? Who are they?"

"Gentiles," Lillian said. She collected syringes, tubes, bloody gauze, and surgical tools in a plastic tray. Every possible item would be sterilized and reused. "They came from Babylon."

"Las Vegas?"

"It's a regular war zone out there," Jacob said. He pulled the sheet to cover the woman's torso, then glanced at the ventilator behind the bed and shook his head. When Lillian made to leave, he told her, "Make sure those children don't see the blood. This might be someone's grandma."

The young woman carried the tray of equipment into the house. Eliza stayed near the door, knowing that in her filthy state, her brother wouldn't want her anywhere near the patient.

"How did they get into the valley? Is the quarantine broken?"

"I don't know. What did you see in the cliffs?"

"A drone. Only one, but it definitely spotted me. It buzzed overhead for ten minutes or so before disappearing to the east. I thought about pushing up the road, but I didn't like my chances."

"Good. I'd rather not see my favorite sister reduced to a crater in the pavement."

He said it lightly, but she knew he didn't like her probing the boundaries of the military-enforced quarantine. He kept urging patience, and faith that Steve knew how to keep himself alive out there. If he'd kept contact with the FBI, then surely he was safely holed up somewhere, waiting for the crisis to ease.

She didn't have to wonder what Steve would have done if the situation were reversed. When she was helping him unpack after moving to the valley, she'd come across a medal and a commendation letter from his service in Afghanistan.

She had turned it over in her hand. "What is this?"

Steve had swept it back into the box with an embarrassed shrug. He took the letter before she could read it. "Ah, it's nothing."

"Can't be nothing if they gave you a medal."

"They gave me lots of medals. Most of them were for showing up."

"Yes, but you keep that one separate. That was a Silver Star, wasn't it? That's for heroism, right? What happened?"

"A platoon of Afghan soldiers got pinned down by the Taliban in the Spin Gar Range. We dropped in and pulled their chestnuts out of the fire. Really, it's nothing." He stopped, shook his head. "No, I shouldn't have said that. Claiming it was nothing doesn't honor the guys who didn't make it. Me, I was just there, doing my job. And a little luckier than Koster and Hogan."

Steve fell silent, and Eliza regretted pushing. There was a reason he didn't like to talk about his time with the Army Rangers, and it generally had to do with his buddies who hadn't returned.

Steve cleared his throat and she caught him taking a surreptitious glance at the letter before he closed the box and then stared at a spot on the wall. "We got those Afghanis out, though. Can't say it was worth losing two buddies, but I'm glad we completed the mission."

She put a hand on his arm. "It was good of you to help those men, even if they weren't Americans."

"You never leave anyone behind. You just don't."

Now Eliza remembered those words and the way Steve's jaw had set like a block of granite when he spoke them. No, he wouldn't have abandoned Eliza to the outside world.

"Where are the rest of the refugees?" Eliza asked Jacob, who was still staring at the sick woman with a troubled expression.

"Camped south of the Moroni checkpoint. Joe Kemp—he's their leader and some sort of ex-military guy, I think—said they'd fled Las Vegas with several dozen refugees after the Californians attacked the city. Half of them died getting here."

"You're not letting them in, are you?"

"I can't."

"Good." She felt guilty as she said it, but they all knew. Their own existence balanced on the tip of a sharp and very deadly sword.

"But I couldn't turn them away either. Miriam brought some food. She's not happy about that."

"No, she wouldn't be."

"Those kids you saw inside have giardia—not cholera, thank goodness. I gave them an anti-parasitic. I'm running low, and couldn't spare it. But what could I do?"

Eliza looked at the unconscious woman. She was pale, even though Jacob must have given her blood. He had recorded the blood type of everyone in Blister Creek. One word from their prophet and every last person in town would roll up their sleeves, gentile recipient or no.

"What happened to her?" she asked.

"Shotgun blast from a distance. Moderate penetration of the obliques and rectus abdominis."

"That doesn't sound so bad. Why is she unconscious?"

"Because sepsis has invaded her kidneys and is disrupting her metabolic functions. It's Kemp's mother—he introduced an infection trying to fish out the pellets."

"That was dumb," she said.

"It sounds that way to us, but I can see why he did it. Anyway, she's the reason Kemp was in Las Vegas in the first place. Probably deserted his unit to find her—that's my guess, anyway. Bandits attacked them last Wednesday. The attackers killed two refugees, and injured this woman."

"And Kemp brought her here . . . why? How did he know about the clinic?"

"I don't know. Maybe the bandits told them. Alacrán is out there, still carrying a grudge. Could be he's spreading the news."

"Good for her that you were willing to help."

Jacob looked troubled. "Maybe it's a mistake. A bad precedent. The quarantine has helped us as much as hurt us. If it's lifting—"

"But I saw a drone."

"In the north. These people came from the south."

Again, that surge of hope, as Eliza's heart turned over in her chest. "Is that possible?"

"Let's assume they're running flights out of two bases. One is at the Green River camp. The other is Las Vegas. They've got a thousand square miles to patrol—it makes sense they'd divide it up. Only now the civil war has engulfed Vegas."

"I don't understand why they care about Las Vegas. Is it strategic?"

"Nellis is one of the biggest Air Force bases in the country. It's the staging ground for federal offensives into Southern California. If California can push the federal troops out then maybe they've got a chance of breaking free." He gave a cheerless smile. "That way they can starve to death independently."

California was always on her mind these days, and she'd given a fair bit of thought to Las Vegas, as well. It was the only real city between southern Utah and Los Angeles.

"And lucky for us too," Jacob continued. "The last thing on their mind in Las Vegas is some desert cult."

"So why doesn't the Green River military base pick up the slack?" she asked. "Or abandon their own patrols and go help Las Vegas?"

"Maybe Green River is going to send trucks to steal our grain and all they care is that we don't smuggle it out and sell it. Maybe those idiots in Salt Lake are controlling the flights. Who knows what's happening out there? War is chaos."

"If the quarantine is breaking, this is my chance. I'll go to California before things get worse. If I head west, I can cross the mountains."

"Hold on."

Eliza's mind was spinning again. "What do you think, day or night? Night. Has to be. I know it's slower, but I've got to assume the drones aren't out there with their infrared, because if they are—"

Jacob came over and put a hand on her arm. "Eliza, listen to me."

"You're not going to talk me out of this." She tried to pull free. His grip wasn't hard, but it was firm. Like when she was a girl, and Father would scoop her up.

"You'll never make it alone, not with the war, the bandits. Hundreds of miles of lawless desert."

"Then send me with help."

"How can I justify that? We can't spare anyone, you know that."

Eliza stopped struggling. "Steve is out there. And I'm going to find him. Nothing you can say will stop me. And if I have to go alone, without your help, I'll do it."

He hesitated, and in that moment she knew she had him. "You're determined?" he said at last.

"I'll crawl to L.A. on my hands and knees if that's what it takes."

Jacob let out a long sigh. "Okay, I have an idea. This could be your chance."

It took her a second to figure out what he was talking about. "The caravan."

"I'm forcing them out of the valley, back the way they came. You'll go with them."

"Have you asked them yet?"

"It's not a question of asking. They're starving. I'll bribe them with food. The kind of offer that will make Elder Smoot sputter and rage." He smiled. "And make Miriam's eyes bulge in disbelief that I'd be so generous."

She struggled with mixed emotions of hope and dread. It was really happening. "What do you know about these people?"

"Nothing. They might be bandits, for all I know. Most likely not. They're probably simple refugees. But they're the survivors—never forget that. That makes them dangerous. You don't have to do it, you know that."

"I'm going," she said quickly. "But I'm scared, of course I am. Out there alone, trying to survive."

"You'd better survive. But forget the alone part. That will never happen."

"Fernie won't let you come with me, and I—" She hesitated. "I can't ask that either. Not even for Steve."

"I know she won't. And I can't leave Blister Creek anyway. Never again until this is over. I have to hold this together. But I'll send two volunteers to accompany you across the desert. The best I can spare."

"Volunteers? How did you manage that?"

He smiled. "I haven't yet. But I'll ask, and they'll say yes. All I need is sufficient justification—I'm still working on that part."

"Who are they?"

"First, Stephen Paul Young. He's smart, loyal, and as reliable as anyone in this valley. If, heaven forbid, something happens to him, his wife Carol is strong enough to hold his family together."

"That's good. I trust him. Who is the other person?"

"Sister Lillian."

Eliza felt a tickle of misgiving at this. "She's so young."

"Only two years younger than you. And she's strong too—Lillian survived the Kimball cult. Then she's had to manage as Miriam's junior wife." He smiled. "That's almost worse."

"I'd rather have Miriam than Lillian. I could use someone ruthless. But I suppose that's too much to ask."

"Miriam has a four-month-old baby, and she's too important to Blister Creek anyway." He shook his head. "The best I can manage is Lillian. She may not be a former FBI agent, but she has trained under one."

"So have I," Eliza said. "Under *two* agents, if you count Steve. Believe me, that doesn't mean much."

"Miriam trusts Lillian. And if she does, we should too."

When Eliza thought about it, she couldn't argue with Jacob's plan. Ruling out Miriam and Jacob, what better companions could she imagine? The only other men in the valley as tough as Stephen Paul were also patriarchal jerks; she wouldn't travel with one of those. And among the women, maybe Sister Rebecca could match Lillian. Maybe not.

"When do I leave?" Eliza asked.

Jacob looked back to the unconscious woman in the bed. "As soon as I'm done with Helen Kemp. By tomorrow, most likely."

"So soon? She'll be ready to move?"

A shadow passed over his face.

Eliza put a hand on his shoulder, thinking he was frowning about her leaving the valley. "I have to do this. Steve's alive, I know he is. If there's anything good in this world, if God cares about me at all, then he has to be. Don't you think?"

"I can't answer that, Liz. The truth is, I don't know. I don't know anything anymore."

"I don't believe that. You saved those kids. And what about Helen Kemp? She'd have died from an infection if not for you." A smile crossed her lips. "Okay, so maybe God had a hand. And modern medical science. Antibiotics and all of that."

"I didn't give her any."

"What?"

His voice was flat. "She is suffering from multiple organ failure. I could have pumped her full of a broad-spectrum antibiotic, and her odds might have jumped from two percent to ten percent. She's an older woman from outside the community. I couldn't do it. Not with so many other uses for those antibiotics."

"So you . . . ?"

"Stopped the bleeding. Gave her morphine to make her comfortable." He looked down at his hands. Eliza had seen them give shots, perform surgery, milk cows, and administer priesthood blessings. When he looked up, Jacob's face seemed to have aged ten years. "I suspect she will die during the night."

CHAPTER THREE

Jacob drew Kemp around the side of the house. The Christianson children—Jacob's own, plus his youngest siblings, still living at home with their mothers—crowded the porch to stare at the stranger. Eliza walked behind. A deep frown had furrowed her face all morning.

"The children should be better soon," Jacob said. "Follow my instructions exactly. If you try to save the medication, the giardia will come back stronger than ever."

"You could let us stay. We'll work for our living."

It took effort not to agree. How could he turn these people away? He could make it work. Forty-seven mouths to feed; he'd done the math. But what about the next forty-seven? And the forty-seven *hundred* who came after them?

"You don't know what it's like out there," Kemp pressed. "Thousands dead already. Around the world, millions. Tens of millions. When I was in Iran . . ." His voice trailed off and he shook his head. "I know weapons. I fought in the war. I can help defend this valley."

"We have defenders already."

"For God's sake, don't drive us off."

"I know places you can go. I'll send you with seed to plant. There are abandoned farms and ranches. If you're careful—"

"We're not farmers. And the climate has gone to hell. If *you* haven't managed to plant anything yet this year, how are *we* supposed to raise crops?"

"I'm sorry. I'll give you what help and advice I can, but you must leave."

"Damn you, Christianson."

Jacob hardened his heart. He had to do this. They stopped in front of the side garage door, opposite from his clinic.

"In addition to the seed, I'm sending you with provisions. Three months' worth."

Kemp's eyebrows raised. "Three months? That's a small fortune these days. What's the catch?"

"The catch is you need to take my sister with you." Jacob nodded back at Eliza as he said this. "Together with two of her companions. They need to leave the valley and I want you to smuggle them out."

The man stared at Eliza, his expression unreadable. "Because of the quarantine?"

"That's right. You heard about that?"

"I heard it. I don't believe it. Sounds like a cop-out, a lame justification for why you guys won't help anyone, because they're forcing you to stay in your own little valley. But here I am, and you still won't help."

Jacob wasn't going to argue this point. "Those are my terms. Take three people out of the valley with you and you get three months of food in return."

"Why?"

"That's our business, not yours."

"Wait until you see what's out there," Kemp said to Eliza. "You'll be sorry you ever left."

"It doesn't matter," she said. "I need to get out."

"They'll travel with you a couple of days," Jacob said, "then slip away at night. That's all you need to know. What's your answer? Yes or no?"

A calculating look came into Kemp's eyes. "Tell you what, how about I smuggle them out, then return with my people? Instead of paying us with food, you let us stay in the valley and earn our keep."

"Last fall I let in several families from outside the valley," Jacob said. "They were Mormons—Salt Lake City variety, but still. My people were up in arms. If I let you in, a bunch of gentiles, a mob would drive you out. There's already grumbling. Word spread you were drinking whiskey in your camp and that scared people. People are terrified God will abandon us."

"I'll toss the liquor. We'll be Mormons if that's what it takes."

"If I let in one caravan, how do I turn away the next? And the one after that? How long until fifty thousand starving people descend on the valley?"

"I'm talking about forty-seven, not fifty thousand."

"No."

"Not even to help your sister?" Kemp looked at Eliza.

"Not for anything," Jacob said. "You must leave. Will you leave with three months of food or not?"

"You bastard."

"Is it a deal?"

"Yeah, it's a deal. Now open that door and let me see my mother."

Jacob took a deep breath and lifted the garage door with a clank of metal on metal as it slid to the ceiling. Miriam stood inside, standing discreetly to one side. She gave Jacob a nod. Some of the hardness had returned to her face. Jacob nodded back and let his eyebrows climb in warning.

Be careful, Miriam.

Kemp didn't look at her. He only stared at the bed. At the shape beneath the sheet, which had been drawn up over her head.

"Oh, my God."

"I'm so sorry," Jacob said. And he was. Deeply, numbingly sorry.

Kemp rushed to the bed and drew back the sheet to reveal the blank, gray face of his mother.

Eliza came up behind Jacob and put her hand on his shoulder. Her fingernails dug in. Warning him not to tell Kemp the truth.

"How did she—?" Kemp began.

"She was suffering septic shock when you brought her in. Her organs were failing and her blood pressure crashing. Maybe if I'd seen her a few days earlier, but it was too late."

"I killed her!"

Jacob made his way to the side of the bed. He put his arm around Kemp's shoulder, but the man shrugged him violently away. "I lost them all. My God, I lost everything. My father, my brother, my girlfriend. Her kid—only two years old—he died. I tried to save him." Tears streamed down his face and marked streaks in the road grime.

Jacob's resistance crumbled. How could he send these people away? He would let them stay. Then deal with Smoot and other members of the quorum if they raised a stink. If necessary, he'd find another way to smuggle Eliza out of the valley. Maybe the drones were going away. Maybe all they had to do was wait.

"I'll kill myself," Kemp said. "That's what I'll do. What's the point? I'll end it."

"You can't do that. Those people out there need you."

"Why, so I can kill them too? Like I killed my mom?"

Jacob took him by the shoulders. "Listen to me. You didn't kill her. You tried to help. There were no doctors, you didn't have medical training. Of course you'd try to dig out the pellets."

"How could this happen? She had an infection, I get that. But why didn't the antibiotics help? Was it really too late?"

"Unfortunately, yes."

"Tell me what did, what you tried. I have to know."

Jacob hesitated. It wouldn't do any good telling the truth, but he wasn't in the habit of making up stories to cover his own shortcomings. "Well, you see—"

Kemp must have caught the guilt in his voice. He whipped his head up. "Wait. You did try, right? Tell me you didn't give up."

"It was too late. She was suffering multiple organ failure. Her odds were less than ten percent—probably some fraction of that—even if somehow we'd been able to airlift her to a world-class hospital. Out here, in the desert, with what I've got to work with . . ."

Kemp stared him down. "So you didn't give her anything for the infection."

"It would have been throwing those antibiotics away. I'm running out. If I'd given them to your mother, other people would die."

The man stared at him in silence. Muscles clenched on the side of his jaw. He took a step toward Jacob. Before he could make another move, Miriam was at his side, her gun aimed with rock steadiness at his temple.

"Make a move and I splatter your brains," she said.

Kemp slowly swung his head to look at her. Cold fury raged behind his eyes.

"She's former FBI," Eliza said. "Push it and you'll be sorry."

His gaze swung back to Jacob. He took a step back.

"I am truly sorry," Jacob said. "Would you like to take the food with you, and take my sister and her companions? Or will you go alone?"

"Send the food. Send the people. And bring me my mother's body. I won't bury her in this valley. Before the end comes, you'll be digging up corpses for food. Mark my words."

★★★

"What do you think he meant by that?" Eliza asked as the two pick-ups rolled down the highway toward the refugee encampment. She was in the lead pickup with her brothers, Jacob and David, as well as Stephen Paul Young.

Jacob had been stewing over Kemp's curse—almost biblical in its flavor and the dread it inspired—since the man muttered it six hours earlier.

"Absolutely nothing."

"You mean that thing about eating corpses?" David asked from the back. "Miriam told me about that. Damn creepy. He's lucky she didn't shoot him."

Kemp was so unhinged after Jacob's ill-advised admission that they were escorting him back to the camp with what passed for Blister Creek's entire police department, now that Steve Krantz was gone. Kemp sat in the backseat of the other pickup truck's extended cab, flanked by Miriam and Dale Trost, formerly of the Cedar City PD, a refugee himself. Lillian drove. Jacob had radioed ahead to the Moroni checkpoint, where Smoot and his sons were back on the guns, and warned them about the situation.

"If you ask me," Stephen Paul said, "we're too lenient with this ungrateful jerk. Those kids would have died if you hadn't gifted them our precious medicines."

"It was the right thing to do," Jacob said.

"Until your own children get sick next winter and you've got no way to treat them."

"Three months of food is ridiculous," David added.

"It's not a gift," Jacob said. "We're asking him to take three people out of the valley."

"That covers their medical care," Stephen Paul said. "And the food you already gave them. If they balk, we force them at gunpoint."

"I might have saved his mother. I didn't. That's worth something."

David started to say something else, but Jacob asked them all to stop arguing. They continued in silence.

The sun squatted overhead by the time the trucks reached the Moroni checkpoint. A cloudless sky stretched from horizon to horizon, unbroken by cloud or contrail. It wasn't the brilliant blue of years past, but tinged with slate, with a reddish smear around the horizon. When Jacob's group stepped out of the truck, he was surprised to discover the air was as hot and dry as over-toasted bread. It tasted chalky. They shuffled out of their jackets and left them in the trucks.

"Maybe summer is finally here," David said. "Time to plant the fields?"

"It's one day," Stephen Paul said. "Don't get too excited."

"Go ahead," Jacob told Lillian as she rolled down the window of the second pickup truck. "We'll be there in a minute."

Smoot came striding over from the pillbox. He eyed Miriam, Trost, and Lillian as they drove off with Joe Kemp toward the refugee encampment.

Smoot stroked his beard and scowled after his daughter; like the other two women, Lillian wore jeans and a long-sleeved shirt. Over the past six months, the prairie dress had been falling out of fashion with the women of the valley; it was a look now reserved mainly for girls and elderly women. The women of Smoot's household maintained the older style, and no doubt he would have insisted that his daughter dress appropriately. Jacob enjoyed the discomfort in Smoot's face; the man wanted to speak up, but couldn't. Once he'd given her to David for marriage, he'd surrendered that right.

Smoot turned to Jacob. "Regretting it now?"

"Regretting what?"

"Not cutting them down like I suggested. I warned you—they're locusts."

Jacob felt his face flush. With Helen Kemp's body stiffening in the back of the truck, Smoot's callous words rubbed him raw.

Eliza interposed herself between Jacob and the church elder. "Now is not the time to push my brother, Elder. Get in the truck. You can help us with these supplies."

Smoot ignored her. His sons manned the .50-cal in the pillbox, and their presence seemed to bolster his recalcitrance. Today it was Grover again, plus his older brother Bill, a man with two wives and several children. Their horses grazed nearby, tethered to an iron ring on the side of the bunker.

Smoot lifted the tarp on one of the pickups to inspect the supplies beneath. "Giving away the farm, Christianson?"

"You know why."

"Yes, to chase down your sister's boyfriend. Don't know why she can't marry a righteous man of the church instead of a gentile."

"Steve Krantz is one of us now."

"Fine. *Former* gentile. He's still one man. You ever think maybe he doesn't want to come back? That Eliza tricked him into baptism and he took the first chance to run like the devil? And straight into the devil's arms, I'd say."

Eliza bristled visibly at this, but didn't take the bait. Good for her. Neither did Jacob. He reached into his truck to fetch several sheets of paper from the glove compartment. Then he called Stephen Paul over and handed him the papers.

"A list of stuff we need. I'm sending you with silver coins to buy it all, if you can. Don't go mucking around war zones and abandoned towns, but if you can get these things—especially antibiotics—it will save lives."

"Justification for a foolhardy plan," Smoot said. "We're going to risk three lives to save one, that's the bottom line."

"Where's your faith?" Stephen Paul demanded. "Brother Jacob wouldn't send us into the desert to be killed."

"And did you test that or swallow it blindly?" Smoot asked him. "Did you fall to your knees and ask the Lord if it was right to leave your wives and children?"

"Of course I did." Stephen Paul sounded shocked at the question. "The instant Jacob called to ask, I gathered my wives and we all prayed together to know the Lord's will." He gave Smoot a sharp look. "You must have heard the plan at the same time I did. Didn't you pray about it?"

"Well, no," Smoot said, sounding uncomfortable. "It was all so sudden, and I wasn't asked to go."

"But I was. So I did."

Stephen Paul had played a trump card, against which there could be no argument. The Lord had confirmed it. What greater proof could there be? Of course both elders were operating on the assumption that Jacob would never take such a dangerous step without praying about it himself first. Which he hadn't done, shamefully enough.

He was doing it for Eliza. If he didn't, she'd go off on her own, and he could never allow that. So yes, Smoot was at least partly right about the supply-gathering nonsense.

"I still say it's a fool's errand," Smoot grumbled after a long, uncomfortable pause. "But fine, let's get this over with." He called over his shoulder. "Bill, anything funny happens on that ridge, you know what to do."

"Um . . ."

Jacob made his way to the bunker and looked in the gun slit.

"What you do is you wait for my signal. Don't start shooting because something looks funny. You got that?"

"Yes." Bill didn't look at his father.

"You too, Grover."

"Yes, Brother Jacob." Smoot's younger son looked even more frightened to be obeying Jacob instead of his father.

Fortunately, Smoot didn't make an issue of it, but climbed into the pickup truck with the others. They drove slowly down the road until they caught up with Kemp and his minders, waiting in the road opposite the refugee camp.

Kemp and two other refugees retrieved the body and carried it up to their camp. Jacob waited until they were gone before he called his companions out of the trucks. They waited for Kemp to return. When he did, his face was stony and unreadable.

Jacob cleared his throat. "Does your bus have a working engine?"

"It did two weeks ago," Kemp said. "That was the last time we had fuel. It was barely enough to get us to the outskirts of Vegas. Don't know if it would still work or not."

Trost and David pulled back the tarps on the first pickup truck and hauled out plastic buckets filled with wheat and dried peas and carried them to the camp.

"Sounds like you could use some diesel," Jacob said.

He grabbed a five-gallon container and dragged it to the edge of the bed. There were four fuel containers in all.

"Where the hell did you get that?"

"We are savers. It's almost gone, but I think I can spare twenty gallons."

That was a lie. Slowly but surely they were draining the supplies Jacob's father had laid up before his death, but they still had several huge tanks hidden in the ground behind the abandoned service station.

"What about our wagons?"

"Load your people into the bus and stuff it full. The draft animals will make better time pulling empty wagons."

"Five miles an hour, maybe. And twenty gallons is nothing."

"You show up, you make demands," Miriam said. "You take our food, our fuel, and give us nothing in return. You're lucky you're not dead."

"Heaven forbid you help your fellow humans in need," Kemp said.

"Twenty gallons," Jacob said. "Five miles an hour. Five miles per gallon for the bus—isn't that about right?"

"Not quite, but okay."

"That's a hundred miles. I know a place you can go, near the abandoned marina at Lake Powell. The lake is deserted and full of fish. There's water for irrigation. Might be some old trailers to live in when winter comes."

Kemp stared. "And that's your best offer?"

"That's my only offer. You've got a chance, anyway. That's the best anyone can hope for these days."

★★★

The refugees and the men and women from Blister Creek worked together. Kemp's people were sullen at first, but they warmed when Eliza distributed mended socks and handwoven wool mittens. Children squealed with delight when Lillian produced homemade honey drops. The bus was clean of vermin, but the stench of body odor and unwashed clothing made Jacob's eyes water.

He used a funnel and the gas containers to refuel the bus, then helped Kemp fool around with the carburetor until they got the bus engine to turn over. The two men communicated in grunts and single-word sentences.

When the bus was fully loaded, the last thing Jacob and David took from the truck was a locked trunk containing fully packed saddlebags for Eliza, Lillian, and Stephen Paul. Guns, ammo, food, water purification tablets, medicine, maps—everything to carry them across the western desert to California.

Engine rumbling, the bus rolled onto the road while children piled aboard and men drove the mules and horses with their wagons into place to follow behind. A day of grazing and rest had done the animals good; they looked like they'd survive the trip to Lake Powell. Last came the mounts for the trio from Blister Creek, roped to the back of the caravan.

When they were ready to depart, Stephen Paul suggested a prayer for Eliza and her companions. Couldn't hurt. But there was no need to make it a spectacle, so Jacob called the saints to the shoulder of the road, apart from the refugees. Miriam watched from about twenty feet away, hands on her hips. Emotions churned on her face; no doubt she thought she should be going in Lillian's place, new baby or not. Trost stood inside the bus, talking over the map with Kemp, who sat behind the wheel.

Jacob folded his arms and bowed his head, but before he opened his mouth, someone shouted behind him. A rider was galloping bareback down the road toward them from the north. One hand gripped the mane and the other waved madly in the air.

"Grover?" Miriam said. "What the devil is he doing?"

Grover pounded up. "They're here. Run! Hide!"

A black speck of movement overhead caught Jacob's eye. A turbofan engine whirred. A military drone dove from the sky like a giant, swooping bird of prey. Then came a flash of light and a hiss. A missile raced toward the ground.

CHAPTER FOUR

Eliza stared in horror as the missile raced toward them. She barely had time to throw herself to the ground before the air split with a terrific explosion. A wave of heat and pressure rolled over the highway.

She lay flat while flaming pieces of wood showered down. Her ears rang. For a moment she couldn't move, as if a giant fist had punched her to the ground and knocked the air from her lungs. Her head swam, and it took a moment to regain her equilibrium. She struggled to her feet, thinking only to get off the road. Find a boulder or a gulley and cower until the attack was over.

The two pickup trucks from Blister Creek blazed. One of the refugee wagons had simply disappeared, and dead and dying animals lay strewn across the road. A horse screamed. People called out. A few feet away, Stephen Paul lay on his belly, groaning, with what looked like a shard of wood sticking out of his back. Where was Jacob?

The bus had avoided the destruction and now inched into motion. It was driving off, trying to escape.

"Eliza, stop them!"

It was Jacob, struggling to his knees behind her. His eyes looked glassy and dazed. Blood trickled from his nose.

The missile. It must have been a warning shot.

The drone had blown up one of the wagons and killed several animals. Destroyed the trucks. But no people. How easy to target people walking on the road. Or the school bus. Then it would have been a massacre.

Somewhere, hundreds of miles away, a young drone pilot sat behind a video monitor, watching them, trying to decide whether to fire a second missile. Eliza had spent months thinking of those pilots, imagining what was going through their heads, what they would do in certain circumstances. Were they growing resentful of Blister Creek, of its peaceful, isolated location, its plentiful food, while their own hometowns fell apart? And hoping that Blister Creek would test the limits they'd imposed on it, so they'd have a chance to pull the trigger?

She was suddenly certain that if the bus made a run for it, all those people would die. Trost was on board. Dozens of innocent refugees.

Miriam had also regained her feet and seemed to understand Jacob's warning at the same moment. Together, she and Eliza ran after the bus, crying for it to stop.

Grover, still on his horse, galloped past the two women. The boy was unharmed; he must have been far enough away to avoid the attack entirely. The bus was heavily laden and accelerating sluggishly, but it had already picked up enough speed that Eliza and Miriam would never catch it. Only Grover had a chance.

He pulled his horse alongside the front door of the bus, which still lay open, and grabbed for the side mirror. With an impressive feat of agility, he swung from the horse and into the bus. His mount veered away, tossing its head. Shouts came through the open windows, together with the sound of struggle. The bus slowed on the road.

"Go," Miriam said from behind Eliza.

Eliza reached the open door and swung herself inside. Kemp was driving, the wheel in one hand and a pistol in the other. Grover struggled with him for the gun. Trost lay on the ground, wrestling with two men who fought to keep him from drawing his own weapon. Eliza reached over Grover and grabbed at Kemp's wrist in an attempt to wrench away the gun.

Miriam climbed in. "Put it down!"

Kemp ignored the command. He kneed Grover back, who in turn fell into Eliza. She backed into Miriam and almost knocked her out of the bus.

"Move!" Miriam told them as she righted herself. She lifted her gun.

A woman sitting in the front row grabbed at Miriam's arm as she fired at Kemp. The blast was deafening in the enclosed space. The shot went wild and smashed into the windshield. A snowflake pattern showed where it had hit.

A teenage boy tackled Miriam. Moments later, she was mobbed by the refugees. They dragged Grover back too, but Eliza broke free before they could get her. She drew her own gun. They stopped, and she held them off as she stood in front of the door.

"Stop the bus," Eliza said. "The missile was a warning shot. They're going to kill us if we run."

Kemp ignored her. Free of his attackers, he mashed his foot on the pedal. His free hand pointed the gun at Eliza. She aimed her own weapon back at him.

From the road behind them came the telltale thump of the .50-caliber machine gun. What were they thinking? Was Bill Smoot shooting at the bus? But when Eliza glanced out the open door to see, tracer bullets were flashing skyward. Bill was trying to shoot down the drone. A terrible mistake.

Before she could snap her gaze back to Kemp, the image of destruction on the road burned into her mind like a photograph of a single, awful moment of time. Jacob and Lillian were dragging Stephen Paul from the road, Smoot crawling after them on hands and knees. A mule with an open belly staggered down the center line, its guts spilling almost to the ground. Other animals fought to free themselves from the two remaining wagons to which they were yoked.

Bill kept firing.

She didn't spot the second missile, only a flash of light followed an instant later by a concussive boom. She looked back again in time to see a fireball rolling from the bunker. When it dissipated, the bunker lay in smoking ruins.

Bill Smoot.

Eliza faced Kemp again. "Stop the bus," she said. "It's our only chance. Please, for mercy's sake."

"The hell I will."

The bus was gaining speed. The carnage disappeared behind them, until she could see nothing of the attack or its survivors, only a column of smoke still drifting higher.

The drone was still circling, she knew. Some carried two missiles. Others an array of missiles and guns. And it could always call backup. If another drone lurked over the reservoir on the north end of the valley it would reach them in moments. Eliza braced herself.

But still the desert rolled by. A minute passed, then two. Five minutes, ten. Twenty. Still they cut south along Highway 89 at speeds Eliza hadn't traveled in over a year. She glanced at the speedometer. Only fifty miles per hour. It felt much faster.

"Put down the gun," Kemp told her.

"Put yours down. Let my friends go."

"No. You first."

"Why, so you can shoot me?"

"Believe what you want," he said. "But sooner or later, one of us is going to grow tired and that's how accidents happen."

"Don't do it, Eliza," Miriam said from the floor, where refugees kept her pinned. "He's driving. You're not."

The implication was clear: shoot him. Wait until his attention was diverted, then put a hole in his head.

Eliza couldn't do that. And so she handed over the gun to one of the men holding Trost on the floor. She prepared to be swarmed, but nobody moved against her. Kemp set the gun on his lap and drove. They traveled for nearly an hour before he stopped the bus in the middle of the road.

"Get out."

"What, here?" Eliza asked.

"This is it. Forty miles. What I promised your brother."

"What about my companions? The other two are still back in the valley."

"Now you have three to keep you company."

"They're not the same people. And we don't have our horses."

"Not my problem. Walk back to Blister Creek and get them."

The refugees released Miriam, Grover, and Trost. The former police officer sported a darkening goose egg in the middle of his forehead. Grover was pale and shaking. Miriam looked ready to tear out someone's throat with her bare hands.

"What about our supplies?" Eliza asked.

"Since you're returning home, I figure you don't need them."

Miriam tensed. Eliza seized her wrist to restrain her. "Forty miles—that's going to take us three days on foot. We're not leaving without the contents of that trunk."

"I could kill you all," Kemp said. "It's what you deserve."

"In cold blood? After we gave you food and medicine?"

"My mother is dead. Her body was in one of those wagons. What's left of her now?" His voice caught. When he spoke again, the leaden tone had dropped, replaced by barely restrained fury. "This is all your doing. Your fault."

"So you *will* kill us?"

She'd said all of this in a voice loud enough to reach the back of the bus. People were muttering, and she knew that some, at least, would be thinking this over. Desperate or not, it was a tough thing to rob and murder four people.

"Bring up the trunk," he said.

They dragged it down the center aisle. Of course it was too big to carry on the road, but Eliza had planned to abandon it all along. It was only meant to keep the saddlebags safely locked away until Kemp had smuggled them out of the valley.

When it was up front, Kemp pointed at Eliza. "You have the key. Open it."

"Outside."

"No, here."

"So you can rob us?"

"I'll get it open with or without you. Use a crowbar if I have to. Open it now and I'll share out what I find."

"And steal the rest."

He shrugged.

Eliza glanced at her companions, but they would be no help. Trost looked like he was suffering a concussion. Miriam would take the hardest line possible. Grover looked on the verge of puking. She fished the key from her pocket.

When it was open, Kemp and two other men rummaged through the saddlebags. Most of the goods disappeared into the back of the bus: their rifles and ammunition, bandages, pills for sterilizing water, bedrolls, silver bullion coins, binoculars, matches, and most of the food. In the end, all that was left was a single cook set, a single box of matches, two full canteens, and enough food for maybe two meals. Eliza looked on in dismay.

"We'll never make it three days on that."

"It will take you two days, tops. And the food is a courtesy. My thanks for your so-called assistance. You could make do without."

"How are we supposed to defend ourselves?"

"Try not to get in any gunfights. Now take your crap and get off my bus."

Miriam was shaking with fury by the time the four companions from Blister Creek stood on the pavement. Eliza fought down her own anger and tried to feel grateful. They were alive.

The doors closed on the school bus. It rolled forward, slower this time now that the refugees weren't fleeing for their lives. Traveling at no more than ten miles an hour, it took a few minutes until it disappeared onto the shimmering horizon. The four of them watched until it was gone.

"They will burn when the Lord returns in his glory," Miriam said.

"They were trying to survive. So are we." Eliza let out a long sigh. "Officer Trost, are you badly hurt?"

"My head is killing me. But I think . . . think I'll be okay."

She looked into his eyes, trying to remember what her brother had said about concussions. Were his pupils dilated? Yes, she thought so.

"Grover?"

"It blew up," the boy said. "Sweet heaven, my brother. Bill."

Eliza squeezed his wrist. "You were brave, the way you rode after the bus."

"They killed him."

"I'm so sorry."

"It could have been me. I was at the bunker—I only just left. Bill sent me to warn you. I didn't know—" He stopped, swallowed hard.

"My dad, is he—?"

"He's alive. I saw him crawling off the road. Jacob is with him. He's a doctor."

A shuddering sob worked its way up in Grover's chest. For a moment he looked twelve years old, not eighteen.

"Hold it together," Miriam said. She scanned the sky.

"Have a little compassion," Eliza urged. "He just lost his brother."

"There will be time to mourn later. Right now, we've got to get off the road. For all we know, that thing is still up there. This is a crappy place to hide."

Miriam was right. They'd lost elevation as the bus tore south, and were now in the heart of the desert. Whatever crazy weather patterns had sent the monsoonal clouds spilling over the mountains the past year and a half hadn't greened this stretch of desert. Cover was spotty—sagebrush and spiny plants, with sandstone boulders dropped here and there like a giant's marbles.

A sea of sand dunes lay to the south, with clumps of grass and brush struggling to anchor the edges. Snowcapped mountains of the Paunsaugunt Plateau glimmered twenty or thirty miles to the east, with white and coral sandstone bluffs and mesas like a broken tabletop between the mountains and the highway. West lay the mountains of the Markagunt Plateau, the highest peaks of the Grand Staircase that led all the way south to the Grand Canyon. Cedar City lay on the other side of those mountains. A bent speed limit sign hummed in the wind.

They traveled west from the highway for several minutes until they found a sandstone outcrop to take shelter and assess their situation. A brown and tan gopher snake, resting in the shade, puffed itself, hissed, and vibrated its tail. Eliza started, then, seeing it wasn't a rattler, ignored it until it slithered off.

Trost touched the lump on his forehead. He looked stronger. "Sonofabitch pistol-whipped me." He looked at Eliza, his eyes clearer than they'd been. "So what, wait here until dark and then make for home?"

"The drones have infrared," Miriam said. "Daylight, darkness, it doesn't matter. If they're watching the highway, it won't matter how or when we return."

"So why did you tell us to leave the road?" Eliza asked.

"Because you have a decision to make."

Trost's scowl spread as he kept rubbing the lump. Grover also frowned, but his expression spoke of confusion.

Eliza met Miriam's gaze. "You have a baby waiting for you."

"There's no shortage of wet nurses in the valley. She'll be okay." Miriam said it casually, but her voice was tight and Eliza knew she'd struck a nerve.

"And Diego too," Eliza added. Miriam and David's adopted son had just turned twelve, young enough that he'd miss his mother when she was gone, but old enough to suffer grownup worries about her safety. "That's two kids who need their mother. And what about David? He must be sick with worry."

"Getting murdered by a drone won't help anyone feel any better. Heading west is safer."

"You know what you're saying, right? Is this what you want?"

"Doesn't matter what I want or not. We can't get home right now. So how do we make the best of it?"

"That's crazy," Grover said. "We have to find a way back. What choice do we have?"

"A big choice," Trost said. He leaned back against the eroded sandstone. "We can take our chances walking home, or we can help Eliza."

"You mean go to California to look for her boyfriend? That's crazy. The Lord is raining destruction upon the wicked. I'm not going out there. No way."

"If you go back, you do it alone," Miriam told him. "The rest of us are sticking with Eliza. Right, Brother Trost?"

"Don't answer that," Eliza told the man. "Miriam, that isn't fair. To any of you and least of all to Grover."

"If you have objections," Miriam said, "take them up with the Lord. It was His decision. He chose this company. Jacob made his vote, and God overrode him."

"That's nonsense, and you know it. Trost, tell her."

"Oh, *now* you want him to speak up. Yes, Trost, tell me. Tell us all."

"I'm not telling anyone anything," he said. "I've had one pistol-whipping and I don't need another."

Miriam turned back to Eliza. "You don't want to find Steve?"

"Of course I do. But we have no supplies. No weapons. Grover is a kid. Trost didn't ask to do this."

Miriam turned to him. "Trost, no more equivocating. Are you in or not?"

He dropped his hand from his head and rubbed instead at his walrus mustache. He looked steadily at Eliza. "Jacob rescued my daughter from Las Vegas. He gave us a home in Blister Creek. You know I don't believe in your church, but I respect your brother. And I owe him one. It's your call."

"Grover?" Eliza said.

"I told you," Miriam said. "He can go home alone—probably get scorched on the road by a drone—or he can come with us."

"That's not fair," Grover said.

"Suck it up," Miriam said. "This is your chance to be a man. To prove your worth to the Lord."

"Please stop the religious stuff," Eliza said. "I need to think clearly—that's not helping."

Miriam shrugged. "Fine. The next few years are going to be ugly, whether it's the end of the world or not. We need men and women, not boys and girls. This is Grover's chance to mature. Right now he's a boy. When we return, he'll be a man."

"*If* I return," Grover said. "What if I don't?"

"You think it's chance that took you out of that bunker?" Miriam asked. "Are you saying your brother died for some random shake of the cosmic dice? No, the Lord pulled you out for a reason. This is it."

That sat uncomfortably in the air for several seconds before Eliza cleared her throat. She already knew which way this was going to go. She was desperate to go west, to find a way across the deserts of Utah, Nevada, and California. To find Steve and throw herself in his arms. Grover was dead weight, in her opinion, and Trost wasn't quite as useful as Stephen Paul would have been, but Miriam?

Lillian would have been fine, but Miriam was a killer. Former FBI. Cold-blooded defender of the saints. Eliza felt bad for David and his children, but was suddenly more confident of her chances of getting through to L.A. If only she could figure out logistics.

"We have no animals, little food," she said. "No weapons. Everything Jacob sent with us those jerks stole."

"We tighten our belts and cross the mountains," Trost said. "When we come down the other side, we'll be in Cedar City. Assuming it's still there. I have friends in town. They'll restock us."

"Even if they're starving?" Eliza asked.

"Trust me. They'll do it."

Miriam rose to her feet and hoisted the sole remaining saddlebag, light enough it could be carried by one person, slung over the shoulder. "Good, then it's settled."

"Again, what about the drones?" Eliza said.

"They're watching the highway. North-south. We're headed west, over the mountains. Do you think we can reach the foothills by dusk?"

Miriam didn't wait for an answer, but stepped out of the rock shelter and trudged into the dusty sagebrush plain, heading west. Trost climbed to his feet and gestured for Grover to do the same. Miriam was already thirty or forty feet away and moving swiftly. Grover set out after her, but Trost waited for Eliza to move.

Eliza looked after her sister-in-law. What was it Jacob said about Elder Smoot? You can't stage-manage a grizzly? What about a lioness?

Trost gave Eliza a penetrating look. "There's a reason why your brother wanted to send Lillian instead of Miriam. And it's not just because Miriam is a nursing mother. My advice? Keep that one on a short leash."

"And how am I supposed to do that?"

"I don't know, but if you don't, this is going to be a bloodbath."

CHAPTER FIVE

Jacob lay next to Stephen Paul, who had a shard of wood jutting from the small of his back. The wagon had showered off splinters like a Gatling gun firing crossbow bolts. One of them had hit its mark. Jacob had dragged his companions off the roasting highway, then forced them down.

"Don't move." Jacob's ears were ringing and when he spoke it sounded like he was at the bottom of a well.

Stephen Paul groaned and reached back to grasp at the splinter of wood. It was the width of his thumb and as long as his forearm.

Jacob took the man's wrist and moved his hand to his side. "Leave it alone. You'll break off the tip."

Not to mention Jacob's worry that it might be nicking one of the lumbar vertebrae. That could be disastrous.

The first blast had stunned Smoot, but the elder seemed to be recovering. Now he was calling in anguish for his sons. Bill, blown to kingdom come. Grover, missing.

"My wife," David said. He lay a few feet away. "Oh, God. Please."

Lillian was blinking and stunned, but he meant Miriam, of course. She should be home nursing her child, only a few months old. Jacob never should have called her out. And now she was missing.

But alive. They were all alive except for Bill. Jacob saw them get onto the school bus, first Grover, then Eliza and Miriam. And Trost was there too, already on board before the attack started.

"My boys," Smoot said. He was trying to get up. "Dear Lord, why?"

"Stay down," Jacob said. "That's an order."

"I have to see."

"There's nothing you can do for Bill. Grover got on the bus. So did Miriam and Eliza. He's safe with them."

"We have to—" Smoot began.

"No. We don't. They're gone. There wasn't a third blast. The drone let them go. But it might still be overhead. Stay down."

What had happened on that bus? Miriam was armed. Eliza too. A fight? Why did they keep going instead of stopping? Kemp had taken an insane risk driving off like that. One more missile and dozens would have died.

The bunker kept burning. Inside, ammunition exploded like popcorn. A booming woof rumbled through the air as one of the larger crates went off. Bullets whizzed overhead.

Worse than the burning bunker were the screams of dying horses. One of them, trailing its intestines, had staggered from the road and lay gasping a few feet away, with blood foaming at its nostrils. Another had run several yards on pure momentum before collapsing.

Slowly, the bunker fire began to die as it burned up the limited fuel inside. Jacob rolled over and squinted against the sun. Nothing. No movement. No sound.

"Stay down. Don't sit up, don't draw your weapons. Nothing."

"What are you doing?" David asked.

"You too. Stay here."

Jacob climbed to his feet. He moved quickly away from the others to the highway. If the drone was lurking, he'd rather it target one person and not all five.

The pickups were burning, one a total wreck, and the other with a fire in the truck bed, where a canvas tarp provided fuel. He grabbed a fire extinguisher from beneath the seat and hosed it down until it was out. Then he retrieved a box of shells from the glove compartment and searched the highway until he found his rifle.

He went first to the horse with its intestines lying in the dirt. Flies were already dropping to lap at the blood. The horse looked up at him with its eyes rolling back in their sockets.

"I'm sorry," he murmured. He aimed at its skull and fired. Its hooves shuddered, then went still.

Next came the two horses with broken legs—shattered, really— and then a pair of mules on the highway, one of them pinned beneath another dead animal. Most of the animals had run off. He looked through the scope of his rifle and was horrified to discover his own horse a hundred yards off, on her knees. Her rib cage lay open and three splinters stuck out of her neck like spears broken off at the shaft. She was a good horse, patient and tireless, which was why he'd planned to send her into the desert with Eliza.

He'd named the mare himself. *Jenny.* Father hadn't liked it. "A horse shouldn't have a woman's name."

"Why not? You give horses male names all the time. Even the old billy goat is named Heber, after your uncle."

"That's different. We're going to call her Pear, 'cause of that patch of hair that looks like a fruit. And that's final."

Jacob never bothered with "Pear." She was always Jenny to him. The rest of the family took it up too. After a while, even Father abandoned the struggle and called her by her real name. How old was she now?

That must have been ten years ago. It had been late summer and he was home from medical school to help with the haying.

With a sick feeling in his heart, Jacob wiped his eyes, then fixed the horse's chest in his scope. The gun was a .30-06, powerful enough to bring down an elk. It would do this ugly business just as well. He squeezed the trigger. The rifle shot rolled across the desert. Jenny slumped forward, head collapsing. She didn't move. For a long time, neither did Jacob.

He engaged the safety on the rifle and slung it over his shoulder. Still nothing in the skies. No other attacks or explosions, including south along the highway where his sister and the others had disappeared in the bus. He walked back to his companions, still lying flat on the edge of the highway in the baking soil amid brush and anthills.

"Elder Smoot, come with me. The rest of you stay here."

Smoot stumbled onto the road. Jacob took his shoulder to steady him. Together, they approached the collapsed bunker. The fire was mostly out, and the ordnance had stopped exploding, but it spit an acrid smoke through holes in the wall.

Smoot shielded his face from the heat as he approached. "Bill! Are you there? Bill!"

"He's gone," Jacob said. "He never felt a thing."

"Why? Why would this happen?" He started forward. "I've got to get him out of there."

Jacob grabbed his arm. "No. We'll come back for him later when it's cooled. Now, it's time to take care of the living. I have to get Elder Young to surgery."

Smoot turned with a haunted expression. "Bill has a family. Children. Why would the Lord let this happen? Please, Brother Jacob, help me understand."

How could Jacob answer that? Platitudes? Or the truth? Bad things happened. Nobody had set off the volcano on the other side of the world that had started this whole nightmare. That was nobody's fault; it just *was*.

But with the world collapsing around him, Jacob struggled to hold on to even that. More and more it felt like the universe—or God, if you went that far—was conspiring against them. Against Jacob. No matter what he did, people kept dying. And so he didn't have an answer for Elder Smoot. Nothing that would satisfy either of them.

But Jacob had to try.

"He died defending his people."

Smoot looked him in the eyes, waiting for more.

Bill must have spotted the drone circling and opened fire. Not one chance in fifty of dropping it out of the sky. The first missile had been a warning; otherwise, why destroy an empty cart and a few animals? The second had been a response to a threat. Bill Smoot had thrown his life away. If he hadn't fired, the enemy wouldn't have either.

"We're alive because he drew the enemy's attention," Jacob lied. "Those drones carry two missiles. The first one missed. The second killed your son. It could have easily destroyed the rest of us. Or blown up that bus. Then forty-seven refugees would have died. Plus four of our own."

"Only two missiles? Are you sure?"

"Absolutely," he said, though he knew nothing of the sort. "Why do you think it left? It was out of ammo."

"But you ordered us to lie flat. Why?"

"There might have been a second drone. I had no way of knowing. We were lucky. There wasn't."

"My son. His body."

"Later. I promise."

Smoot stared at the bunker, but let Jacob draw him away. Moments later, Smoot, David, Jacob, and Lillian were carrying Stephen Paul to the remaining truck. They cleaned the ash and burned tarp from the bed, then salvaged a filthy sleeping bag and some charred clothing from one of the overturned wagons, which they used to make a bed.

"Lillian and David, ride in the back. Keep him from moving. Elder Smoot, come up front with me."

Jacob hesitated next to the driver's side door and stared south. How far had the bus gone? Should he go after them? What if that invited another attack?

Would Eliza come back? Not with the continued threat of a drone strike on the highway. Not when she'd waited months for just this opportunity. She'd forge west, going alone if she had to. But he guessed Miriam would relish the chance to accompany Eliza, baby at home or not. Miriam would try to talk Trost into joining them. Jacob had brought Trost's daughter out of Las Vegas; the man would feel obligated. That left Grover, but would the boy risk venturing back on his own with drones in the sky? No, Jacob thought not.

Eliza. Miriam. Officer Trost. Grover Smoot.

Not the group he would have sent to cross the desert and the war zones, bandits, starvation, and disease they would encounter along the way.

Let Eliza go. Trust her. You've got plenty to worry about here.

First, he had to remove the splinter from Stephen Paul's back. Then the dead animals and broken carts needed cleaning up. Then there was the recovery of Bill Smoot's charred body. What an awful task that would be.

"Are we going?" David asked.

"One second."

Something about the scene still bothered him. If the drone quarantine wasn't broken, how had the refugees approached in the first place? A momentary lapse of vigilance?

Or something more sinister?

CHAPTER SIX

Joe Kemp meant to keep driving down the highway until the school bus ran out of gas. Roll to a stop and get out. Set off across the desert. No food, no water. A day or two, then his pain would be over. His dead buddies in Iran, his dead family: all forgotten.

What about the other refugees? They could go to hell. He'd carried them too long.

His brother, Teddy, had fallen in a riot before they could escape Vegas. Trampled to death when the aid truck ran out of bread before it ran out of starving people. A week later, Teddy's wife was kidnapped and raped by roving teenagers on the outskirts of the city, then left for dead. She shot herself, leaving two kids. Then, a few days outside the city, Kemp's two nephews—ages six and eight—caught some sort of intestinal bug. The boys died three days later, literally crapping themselves to death. The bug took five other children from the caravan, plus one elderly black lady by the name of Janine.

A few days of quiet followed that before bandits attacked the caravan near the Nevada/Utah border. That's when his mother had taken the shotgun pellets that Kemp tried to pry out of her belly.

His heart was a black pit as he barreled south after kicking the four cult members out of the bus. The refugees cried for him to slow down. He ignored them and kept his foot mashed to the pedal. Mostly women and children back there. Couple of Hispanic teenagers, an old Asian dude from Santa Monica. Two vets from the Iran war, not much different from Kemp except one wheezed like an emphysema patient, his lungs burned out by mustard gas, and the other had one leg. There had been stronger men in the caravan, but they had died. Two of bronchitis. Three others in a firefight.

The refugees could make their own way now. He was done. Run the bus till it wouldn't run anymore, then he was gone. Walk across the bloody desert until he could walk no more.

Sorry, Mama. I tried.

What would she say? *Don't give up, Chipper*—that was her nickname for him. Always "don't give up," and "only quitters quit."

Guess I'm a quitter, then.

What was his alternative? Take these people to Lake Powell, like that polygamist dude said? Make some mythical Shangri-la where they could hunt and fish and grow sweet peas and tomatoes while the world burned around them?

Kemp still had an eighth of a tank of gas when he couldn't take it anymore. He pulled the bus onto the shoulder of the road and got out and bent over. It was hot and he thought he'd pass out. Gradually, the feeling subsided.

The ground was soft sand, anchored with clumps of grass and sprawling thickets of prickly pear cactus. It would have been a good place to bury his mother, had there been anything left of her to bury. He blamed the polygamists for that too. That bastard Christianson above all.

"Kemp, what the hell?" It was Tippetts, the guy with the burned-out lungs. Special delivery from the Persian First Army, extra mustard. He stood at the bus door, leaning out, wheezing.

"I'm leaving. You're on your own."

"What?" Tippetts said.

"You heard me."

"Yeah, but look."

"I know it's a desert, dumbass. I'm taking a walk, got it? Drive, stay, do what you want."

"Not that. *Look.*"

Tippetts pointed down the highway. A pair of vehicles drove side by side from the south, using both lanes. The heat radiated in waves off the blacktop, making the vehicles shimmer. Still too far to pick out details.

Military. Who else had fuel? Bandits these days were on horseback, rarely motorcycles, but never two trucks driving side by side. But what was the army doing down here? There were no towns, no bases for two hundred miles, so far as he knew. Unless they were more polygs. Could be.

He hurried back to the bus and shouted for people to arm themselves.

Kemp couldn't outrun the oncoming trucks, but he could get the bus turned across the road. Swing it wide like a battleship to present a broadside of pistols and rifles out the windows. A few volleys and maybe they'd convince the other side to find a softer target.

The bus wouldn't start. It coughed and sputtered, almost caught, then died with a cough and a gasp. He turned the key again, pumped the gas. Again, nothing. He'd turned it off without thinking, worried subconsciously about fuel, he supposed, but forgetting how much effort it had taken to get the engine running in the first place.

"Wait for my orders," he cried. He grabbed a box of shells and one of the rifles he'd taken from the polygamists, jumped out of the bus, and took position next to the front tire. What he wouldn't give for an M16, but the deer rifle was good enough. Good penetrating power, a decent scope. His hands had been working automatically as he dropped, and he had a shell chambered when he lifted the rifle to his shoulder.

Tippetts took up position with another rifle, and Kapowski, the one-legged marine, hopped down and readied his own gun.

Inside, children screamed, men shouted, women cried for ammunition to be passed forward. The windows of the bus were already lowered against the heat and weapons bristled out.

The two vehicles—military Humvees, the tan paint faded and sandblasted—rolled to a stop a hundred yards forward. They had heavy machine guns up top, armor plating all around. Kemp's throat tightened.

A voice came through a megaphone from one of the Humvees. "Put down the weapons."

"Who are you?" he shouted back.

"It won't be a fight. It will be a massacre. Now put them down."

"Could be a bluff," Tippetts said. He was so close that his wheezing was the loudest thing Kemp could hear. "They might be out of ammo."

"We still couldn't penetrate that plating."

"I know. But what are they going to do, ram us?"

"Kap, what do you think?" Kemp asked.

"I don't know," Kapowski said. "They probably know the bus is dead. Otherwise we would've run."

A long moment passed. Kemp looked through the scope. Soldiers in fatigues manned the blast shield of the mounted guns. Body armor, helmets. One of them held a megaphone and the other stared back at Kemp through a pair of binoculars.

He made his decision. "Stand down. We can't win this."

Guns withdrew into the bus. Kemp and the other two ex-military guys set down their rifles and rose to their feet. Kapowski gripped the side mirror so he could support himself on his remaining leg.

Three soldiers climbed out of the Humvees and approached slowly with M16s at the ready. Kemp still couldn't see insignia or service.

"Corporal Joe Kemp, 1st ID," he announced when they drew closer. "Honorable discharge. This is PFC Tippetts, 10th Mountain, and Corporal Kapowski, U.S. Marine Corps. The rest are civilians. What's your unit?"

The lead man lowered his weapon. "Kemp? Is that you? Sonofabitch, it is."

The man tore off his helmet and grinned. He was sunburned, a fresh scar across his forehead, but the face was familiar.

"Sarge? Oh, my God."

The two men embraced.

It was his sergeant from the Gulf, Lance Shepherd. During staging in Iraq, Shepherd had been the biggest asshole in the army, running his men relentlessly. It was like being back in basic, and dudes started calling him Old Shitbeard. Shepherd was a vet of the Afghanistan campaigns, back during the War on Terror, and had a dim view of guys who loafed around behind the lines.

When they invaded Iran and found themselves facing the Revolutionary Guards, then irregular militias, then finally old ladies in chadors ululating as they suicide-charged your position with AK-47s, suddenly the platoon had a more enlightened view of Shepherd's merits.

"You know this dude?" Tippetts asked.

"Damn straight. Sarge saved my butt in Tehran. Remember the story about the exploding donkey? That was this guy."

"Thought you signed up for another tour," Shepherd said.

"I should have," Kemp said. "But my brother needed to get out of Vegas, so I took my three Purple Heart exemption. Besides, they were going to stick me stateside. I didn't like the thought of killing Americans, know what I mean?"

Shepherd's face darkened. He hooked his finger toward the bus. "Is your brother on board this deathtrap?"

"Terry didn't make it."

"Sorry, man." Shepherd turned to his two companions. "Go back and tell them it's all right, they're good. Oh, and get Alacrán on the radio. Tell him we've got some new Rs."

"Alacrán?" Kemp said as the other two soldiers trotted back to the Humvees. "Wait, *Rs*? You're not talking about recruiting me for some bogus mission, are you?"

Shepherd ignored the questions. "So that was your bus coming out of Blister Creek this morning. Would have told the boss to recall the birds if I'd known."

"That was you? Doesn't the Air Force control the drones?" Kemp looked over the sergeant's uniform with new scrutiny. It was filthy, insignia missing. He didn't recognize the unit patch. "What's with the scorpion? Who are you with, anyway? What's going on?"

Shepherd took his arm. "Come here for a sec."

Kemp turned to Kapowski and Tippetts. "Take a look at that engine, will you? See if you can figure out what's going on."

As Shepherd led him away, Kemp looked at the man with growing suspicion. "Shoot straight with me, Sarge. What's going on?"

"So you know what happened in Las Vegas?"

"You heard me, I was in it. Big battle. Siege. Not over yet, far as I know."

"And it won't be anytime soon. We can't hold the city against the Californians. Too many battles. Supply lines stretched too far. That's why we pulled in irregular troops. You see any of them?"

The question raised bitter memories. "Yeah, I saw. Armed mobs. Irregulars held us at gunpoint while they raped our women and girls. My sister-in-law killed herself after."

"Sorry, man." Shepherd rested a hand on Kemp's shoulder. "We learned hard lessons in Vegas. I blame the general for emptying the prisons and handing out guns. In retrospect, that was a mistake."

Kemp pulled away from the man's touch. "Ya think?"

"The president is yanking us out of the Middle East. Even Saudi. The oil fields are burning anyway and there's nobody to put them out."

"That's old news. Let those ragheads eat their oil, if they can."

"The Paks and Indians are nuking each other. And what China is threatening will make Hiroshima and Nagasaki look like a couple of supersize firecrackers."

"Keep out of it," Kemp said. "That's what I say. And if California wants to slide into the sea, let 'em."

"Sure, stop the bleeding. I'm with you all the way. But what isn't so well known is that we've lost Iowa and Nebraska too. Most of Kansas. Washington, Oregon. Most of the farm states are in open rebellion."

"I get it," Kemp said. "Let the rest of the world starve. Why should they care?"

"Exactly. Only we can't let them get away with it or we'll all die. Now is the time to stop the bleeding. We don't, we'll look like Canada. Did you hear about Toronto?"

"No, what happened?"

"Never mind. We've got to cauterize the wound. Las Vegas is the place to burn it out. Fifty thousand troops—we've got to hold the line. Three more months, then we'll be stabilized in the Midwest and we can pull back."

"What about here?" Kemp asked.

"The Great Basin is finished. That idiot governor is still hanging on in Salt Lake, but the rest of these sand and mountain states are a bunch of refugee camps and crazy survivalist communities."

"Like Blister Creek."

"Exactly. It's easy enough to patrol here, if you've got the fuel and the food. If the rebellion spreads, we'll harass their supply lines. Cut them off at the knees. A thousand miles of wilderness right here, buddy. Easy enough to do, if you use the right tactics."

"Don't BS me, Sarge. What are you saying? You're part of some irregular unit?"

"For now."

Kemp narrowed his eyes. He stared at Shepherd, then looked back toward the bus. Tippetts stood in its shade, watching them. No doubt wondering what kind of deal Kemp was cutting. He wondered that himself.

"What's that got to do with Blister Creek?" he asked.

"See, we got a situation. Right here, right in the middle of no-man's-land. What you've got is a well-fortified, well-stocked group of gun nuts. A fertile valley with its own power supplies, food enough to hold out for years."

"Sounds like a problem," Kemp said.

"Or an opportunity."

"How do you mean?"

"Things are pretty lean here on the front lines. You'd think the army would keep the grub coming, but no. We've got to take care of ourselves, know what I mean?" Shepherd draped an arm over his shoulder. "You look beat, man. Come to camp and we'll toss back a couple of beers. Talk it over. What do you say?"

It sounded great. Better than that god-awful moonshine Kapowski had fixed up from prickly pear fruit, rotten bread, and what tasted like brake fluid. And the heat and the exhaustion had sapped his will to run, to hoof it across the desert until he died.

He looked at the bus. Thought about his mother. About the fundies in Blister Creek. About Christianson. Then he turned back to Shepherd.

"All right. Let's go."

CHAPTER SEVEN

Eliza was ready to collapse from exhaustion. Ahead, Miriam marched at a relentless pace across the desert. Even with her sister-in-law carrying the saddlebag with their remaining supplies, Eliza fell farther and farther behind. The others struggled even more. Trost was a good fifty feet to the rear of Eliza, and Grover, after an initial spurt of energy, was soon a speck far behind.

They followed the banks of an arroyo that cut a jagged line across the plain. Normally, these dry washes turned to sand by the end of April, but it was almost June and a muddy current still gushed down the channel. Eliza stayed back from the edge. The sandy banks were damp and could give way with a single misplaced step.

A hazy orange sun beat down. A pair of vultures rode thermals a mile overhead, seeming to study the four people struggling across the desert. Eliza wondered if they possessed the ability to detect desperation or if they were merely curious. They could hardly be underfed. It was a good time to be a scavenger.

To keep herself going, Eliza thought about Steve. His massive arms and shoulders. A collegiate hammer thrower, he was still strong enough that he could toss her in the air like she was a child. She imagined those arms pulling her close as his mouth nuzzled her neck. She would be helpless.

After another twenty minutes, when she was ready to cry for mercy, Miriam stopped and chugged water while Eliza caught up. Miriam was panting and drenched with sweat, but not gasping like Eliza. She handed over the canteen when she was done, but kept the saddlebags slung over her shoulder.

Eliza took two gulps, then turned an exhausted gaze to Miriam. "And one of us gave birth a few months ago."

"I've been exercising." Miriam reached for the canteen. "What's taking those two?"

Trost staggered up. He doubled over, wheezing. At last he straightened, and unscrewed the cap of his canteen with trembling hands.

Eliza took the saddlebags from Miriam and draped them over a clump of sagebrush. "Can I talk to you for a second?" she asked Miriam.

"I guess."

"Trost, tell Grover when he catches up that we'll be resting for five minutes. No longer."

"Five minutes," Miriam said as Eliza led her away from the wash. "But no more than that."

Eliza braced herself for a power struggle. She chose her words carefully.

"I'm sure you know that there's nobody in Blister Creek who gives me a better chance than you."

"And?"

"I'd take you over all the Smoots in the world, that's for sure."

"What are you driving at?" Miriam asked.

Eliza glanced back at Grover, finally dragging himself up to Trost's side. She let a confidential note creep into her voice. "Come to think of it, I'm not sure the Smoot we got is a net positive, if you know what I mean."

"The last thing we need is to babysit that kid. Grover is eighteen? You'd think he was eight, the way he's carrying on."

"But we're stuck with him now. At least until Cedar City. Then maybe we can dump him in town until we get back. Also, don't forget Trost. He's not as young as we are."

"No."

"Go easy on them," Eliza said. "And on me too. I'm doing my best, but I'm struggling to keep up."

"You're not the one I worry about."

Eliza put her hand on Miriam's arm and leaned in with what she hoped was a sympathetic expression. It was a gesture she'd seen Jacob use a million times in a friendly, gentle way that soothed the most savage polygamist patriarch. "We can't be fighting each other. So either I stand down and let you lead, or . . ."

"Or what?"

"Or you let me make the big decisions."

Miriam nodded calmly. "I can do that."

"You can?"

"Sure. I know what Jacob wanted. And I know he was inspired by the Lord to set you in charge. Not just here, but as president of the Women's Council."

Inspired? That wasn't exactly how it had played out. Jacob, with his spiritual doubts and his desire to give the women equal say in the community, had stood back while the women chose their own leader. Eliza had been stunned when the others selected her.

"Believe me," Eliza said, "the first time we run into trouble, I'm going to stick the gun in your hand and push you out front."

"Hah."

"But when it comes to finding our way across the desert, I need to make the decisions. I'll ask your opinion, of course." When Miriam didn't immediately respond, Eliza continued, "I've been studying maps all winter. I grew up out here. I know the best way across, I know how to survive. And as for those two—"

She glanced over her shoulder. The two men (she forced herself to count Grover in that category) were scrambling down the embankment to the water's edge. They stripped out of their shirts and undergarments and splashed their faces and torsos from the muddy stream.

"—we have to make allowances."

"Fine."

Eliza let out a sigh of relief. "Good. Now tell me, why are you driving us so hard? It's almost dark. We'll never make it over the mountains in one day. Why not pace ourselves?"

"It's those drones. Day or night, they'll be able to see us out here."

"They haven't attacked us. I've got to think we're safe by now."

"Say they fired their two missiles," Miriam said. "The first was a warning. The second destroyed the bunker. If they'd had a third, it would have wiped us out. Maybe that's what they wanted all along."

"Speculation."

"Maybe so, but tell me that's not what you were thinking." Miriam nodded. "So the drone flies back to refuel and rearm. That takes a couple of hours. Three, tops. They'll be back over this territory before dusk. How long until they find us?"

"Why do they want to kill us anyway?" Eliza asked. "Now that we've escaped the quarantine, what possible good does it do to track us down?"

"An example to Blister Creek. If we somehow make it back, the others will know the quarantine can be evaded."

"You don't know they'll attack us. You're just speculating."

"Those drone pilots are nineteen- and twenty-year-old kids," Miriam said. "Operating a joystick, playing a video game in front of a computer monitor. We got away. They want to hunt us down and win the game." She shrugged. "You're right, I don't *know* it, but I'm not willing to take a chance either."

Eliza looked toward the hills. The closest stood in a row at the feet of a higher range rising ominously at their backs.

"It's another two miles to the hills," Eliza said, "then we'll face some hard hiking to get into the forest where there's cover. I don't know that I'm up for it, and I know those other two aren't."

"We can't spend the night out here, that's for sure."

Eliza studied the terrain closer at hand. There were rocky outcrops and twenty-foot hillocks jutting here and there from the ground, but nothing that would give cover from infrared when night fell.

"What about the arroyo?" Miriam said. "The water is low. We could go down and burrow into the soft sand on the side. The ground will shield us."

"No way. It rains and we all drown. Even a little bit and those hillsides start slumping down. We'll be buried alive."

"Then we double-time it for the hills."

Eliza was afraid Miriam was right. After her effort to wrest control of the decision making, now that she had it, she saw no alternative but to go along with Miriam's original plan.

"And when we reach the hills, what then?"

"I have no idea," Miriam said. "Look for a mountain pass?"

"Some of those mountains are ten, eleven thousand feet high," she said. "Thick woods, twenty feet of snow up top. We have to find Route 14 over the top if we're going to have a chance."

Miriam looked dismayed as she scanned the foothills and range. "I have no idea where that is."

"Pretty sure we didn't reach the turnoff to Alton, which means 14 is south of us. We'll get up to the woods, then cut south until we find the highway."

"What's that road like?"

"Steep. The summit is up by the tree line. For all we know, the highway is still covered with snow after the spring we had. Wish that creep Kemp had left us a knife so I could make snowshoes."

"You can do that?" Miriam sounded impressed.

"Sure. I used to go hunting with my brothers. Jacob and Enoch taught me how. Keep an eye out for jagged rocks—something that would cut an aspen branch. Bet I could still figure out something."

Miriam looked back toward the others. "Our five minutes are long gone. Are you ready?"

"Let's go. But I want to explain our thinking to the guys first."

"Make it quick."

Grover's face sagged when Eliza gave him the bad news about reaching the hills by dark. "I don't know if I can."

"What would your father say?" Eliza asked.

He sighed. "He'd grab his bullwhip and start cracking. That old man would chase me across the desert until I collapsed from exhaustion. Then he'd toss me over his shoulder and tell me I was worse than a girl as he carried me the rest of the way."

"Is he as bad as all that?"

"You should have heard what he said when he found out Lillian was teaching me the piano."

Poor Grover. A gentle boy in a world of men. Where was the place for a boy like that in a family like the Smoots? What if you didn't want the man stuff: branding cattle, hunting, hauling wood, and eventually collecting a harem of wives?

"Come on, already," Miriam said. She was bouncing on the balls of her feet. How the devil did she have so much energy?

"Brother Trost?" Eliza said to the police officer. "You okay?"

The older man put on his shirt and fixed his cowboy hat back on his head. "I'll manage."

The four of them broke into a trot. Within minutes, Miriam had pushed far into the lead.

CHAPTER EIGHT

It was dusk before the Humvee reached its destination, a spooky abandoned town on the Utah/Arizona border named Colorado City. Kemp knew without being told that it had been another polygamist enclave. The houses were massive compounds with multiple wings, like in Blister Creek, and the chapel had a distinctly Mormon look about it: squat and brick, with no cross on the steeple. But most of the buildings had burned down, gutted vehicles blockaded all but the central streets, and coyotes trotted through brown, weedy yards. Bodies swung by ropes from utility poles. Their clothing hung in tatters, and their bodies were so picked over by crows that it was impossible to tell age or gender.

"Every once in a while some fundy creeps into town from the hills to do some looting," Shepherd explained when he saw Kemp staring.

"Isn't this their town? How do they loot their own homes?"

"Got to stop thinking like that. That world is gone."

Kemp was alone with the irregulars. The school bus had run out of gas some thirty miles to the north, and there it would remain.

Kapowski and Tippetts had stayed behind, together with the second Humvee. Shepherd didn't want the refugees coming into town. Not yet.

The Humvee turned down a street, passed two armed men in fatigues, then stopped in front of one of the remaining houses. An M1-A1 tank squatted in the yard. Grass grew around the treads and extra armor had been welded onto the front. A monster like this got what, half a mile to the gallon? Took ten gallons just to get the gas turbine engine up and running. It wasn't going anywhere. But the 120 mm cannon could blow the hell out of anything that came rolling down the road.

The house itself was two stories, with wings attached here and there and barely matching the original structure except in the olive-green siding. As Kemp climbed out of the Humvee, one of Shepherd's men yanked the garage door open and he and two others unloaded crates from the back of the vehicle. They stacked them together with crates and drums of various sizes that already packed the interior of the monster-size garage.

Across the street, a fuel or ammo dump sat beneath camouflaged netting in the space between a house and a cottonwood tree. Two men guarded it from behind sandbags. Based on vehicles and movement, it seemed that most of the houses along this street billeted troops. Still, it couldn't be a large force. Maybe a hundred and fifty men, from what Kemp could see.

He helped Shepherd carry the final crate into the garage. "Food, fuel, and weapons. That's what's going to win the war. Isn't that what you said in Iran?"

Shepherd grunted as they maneuvered it into position. "Some things change. Others don't. We've got plenty of weapons. It's food and fuel that's the devil to find. Good thing nobody else has them either."

"Except Blister Creek."

Shepherd's face darkened. "For now. Come on. Time to meet the general."

They found the so-called general inside at the table, studying a map through the dying light that filtered in through the window. He ate directly from a can of peaches, which he slid to one side when the others entered. He rose and wiped his hands on his pants. Kemp had a hard time not staring at the peaches.

"This is the new recruit," Shepherd said. "The others aren't worth spit. I left them in the dunes."

"Hold on," Kemp said. "I haven't been recruited to anything. I got three Purple Hearts and the army says—"

"Have a seat," the man said. "Go ahead, take a load off. Shep, get this man a beer."

He spoke with a slight Spanish accent. Burn scars marked his face. A general? He didn't wear a uniform. Didn't carry himself in a military way.

Kemp hesitated, but the thought of a beer won him over. He'd toss back a six-pack if he could. Blunt the memory of his mother's hollow stare. Of his two nephews, pale and dead. He sat down.

Shepherd poured the beer into a dusty glass and set it on the table. Kemp drank it down. It was warm as piss.

"Get me another. And some food."

The man retrieved an MRE from the pantry: meatloaf in gravy, applesauce cake, green beans, and a peanut butter HOOAH! bar. Kemp wolfed it all down.

When he'd finished the second beer, he felt almost human again. He sized up the general. "We going to have some introductions?"

"Is that necessary?" the man asked. "This is Shepherd, you're Kemp, I'm the general."

"You don't look like any general I've ever seen."

"You can call me Alacrán if you want. Scorpion, if you like that better. I'm not fussy about titles, so long as people do what I ask. And the sergeant here is my right-hand man. If half of what he told me on the radio is accurate, you could be number three."

"Just like that? Corporal to number three? Never heard of that rank, but whatever."

"We've got bigger things to worry about out here than ranks and army BS," Shepherd said.

"I think you're both full of crap," Kemp said. "You're not army. You're not irregulars. You're a bunch of bandits and deserters."

"Do bandits and deserters control predator drones with hellfire missiles?" Alacrán said.

"That sounds like bullshit to me."

"You came into the valley with three carts and a school bus," the man said in his accented English. "Nobody bothered you until you tried to leave. A warning shot, then the second missile hit the bunker when it started shooting back."

Kemp fell silent. He hadn't told all of that to Shepherd. And Kapowski and Tippetts had never been alone with the sergeant's men long enough to give additional details.

"Our buddies would have finished the job," Alacrán continued, "but we're short of equipment on that end. Another week or two and they'll call off the quarantine of Blister Creek—the drones will be sent elsewhere. The army has already abandoned the Green River base. Withdrawn most of the ordnance."

"There are a hundred thousand refugees in Green River," Kemp said. "What about them?"

"Like I said, abandoned."

"Left to die, in other words."

Kemp heaved himself to his feet and stumbled into the kitchen to look for more beer. He found a can sitting on the counter. He popped the top and took a swig on his way back to the table.

It was now almost dark and nobody made a move to turn on the lights. "No generators, huh?"

"Can't spare the diesel," Shepherd said.

"Kerosene for lanterns?"

"Only when absolutely necessary."

"We can sit on the porch if you'd like," Alacrán said. "Hell of a sunset out there."

"I've seen enough sunsets. Bring in a light. Now is one of those necessary times."

They were giving him enough of a leash that he felt comfortable pulling at it. They needed something from him. Otherwise, why the beer? Why the bogus offer of promotion? Why not give him the chance to join and if he turned them down, toss him out? Or worse, string him up with those poor fools dangling from utility poles.

Shepherd left and returned with a lantern. It hissed to life.

"That's better." Kemp drained the beer. "Cut to the chase. What do you want?"

"You're a smart man," Shepherd said. "A survivor. And you keep your eyes open. We want to pick your brain, for a start."

Alacrán nodded. "Right now you are the leading expert on Blister Creek, Utah. Tell us what you saw."

"Bunch of religious nuts. A zillion women. The old ones in dresses with sleeves to their wrists. A million kids each. Creepy old dudes with Stepford Wives. Some guy was ranting about the chosen people and Jesus burning the wicked. They didn't like me stepping about, that's for sure."

"And the leader?" Alacrán asked. "Did you meet Jacob Christianson?"

"Yeah." He felt his face flush at the sound of the bastard's name. "Yeah, we met."

"What's your read?"

"He's a son of a bitch. But a cool one, plays himself as some kind of saint."

"Well," Alacrán said with a smirk, "they're all saints, are they not?"

Kemp shrugged. "He's not like the rest. Come to think of it, neither are the others he keeps around him. His sister, for one. Then there's some lady with a gun who knew how to handle it. A tall cowboy dude named Stephen something. An old cop—don't think he was a polygamist at all. They're all different."

Alacrán leaned forward. "What do you mean, different? Not religious, or what?"

"Maybe they are, maybe they aren't. But they're practical. The Christianson guy is a doctor. He gave medicine to our sick kids. Could have saved my mother, but said he couldn't spare the antibiotics."

The memory of it made his face burn.

"The saint's a liar," Alacrán said. "He could have helped."

"What makes you say that?"

"Because Christianson looted the Panguitch hospital when it closed down. He's got the biggest supply for a thousand miles. He didn't *want* to help, that's all."

Kemp jumped to his feet and slammed a fist on the table. "I knew it."

Christianson wouldn't have done a thing to help if not for those people he wanted to smuggle out of town.

"Calm down, Kemp," Shepherd said. "You can't do anything about that now."

"Some polygamists jumped onto the bus when you left," Alacrán said. "Are they hiding in your group?"

"How did you know about that?"

"The drone."

Kemp sat back down. His face was still burning.

Even out of ammunition, the drone must have followed them down the highway to see what they were about. That was why Sarge came up the road in the Humvees to meet them. Alacrán had received the news and sent them out.

"Three people jumped onto the bus at the last minute," Alacrán said. "We think they were from Blister Creek."

"Four, actually. One guy was already on board."

"And are they hiding with the refugees?"

"No, I kicked them out. You should have looked while you were up there. You might have seen them." Kemp narrowed his eyes. "Wait, if your drone was following, they would have seen that."

"It ran low on fuel," Shepherd said, "and had to turn back."

"Who were they?" Alacrán asked.

"The town cop, some kid, Christianson's sister, and the lady with the gun. Former FBI, supposedly. Whatever, she knew what she was doing."

Alacrán rubbed at the scar tissue on his face and his expression darkened. "She's former FBI, all right."

"I took their gear and left them food enough to get home. But I don't think they're headed back. They were trying to get out of town all along. The Christianson woman and a couple of others. I'll bet they're headed out for . . . well, wherever."

The two other men exchanged looks.

"That's all I've got," Kemp said. "You know, don't you? Where are they going?"

"Los Angeles," Alacrán said. "To look for Eliza Christianson's fiancé. He's another FBI guy, stuck outside the valley when the government threw down the quarantine last fall. Jacob Christianson did some begging, but the army wouldn't wait."

"FBI?" Kemp thought about the upheaval and violence when California pulled away late last year. There had been bloody reprisals against FBI and CIA agents who tried to thwart the secession. "Is he even still alive?"

"We don't know," Alacrán said. "And I'll bet neither do the polygs. But they're stubborn. They'll look for him."

Kemp didn't call that stubborn, he called it loyal. He'd kill to have someone like that, someone to fight for him. A girl to come home to at night. Couple of buddies to share beers with. His mom back. His brother, his nephews. Good for the polygamists if they wanted to rescue one of their own. Then he remembered Jacob Christianson and the antibiotics, and his heart hardened.

"It will be a lot easier to take the compound if they don't make it back," Shepherd said.

"You can't toast them with air strikes?"

"Nah, we're on our own. That drone attack was our last aerial support."

"And you don't have enough men and equipment to storm the valley? Couple of tanks, some Bradleys . . ."

The two men only stared at him. Alacrán spoke first. "We have a couple of different plans going. One of them is cutting the head off the snake. If we get the top eight or ten people, the rest will fall. We can leave this hellhole and move into nicer accommodations in Blister Creek."

"How do you figure it's nicer? Same kind of town, same kind of terrain. Seems the only difference between Colorado City and Blister Creek is the people running it."

"Exactly," Alacrán said, apparently missing the irony. "All the fundies around here are dead or run off. Blister Creek has a ready-made supply of compliant labor, assuming you can get rid of a few hardened old men."

"By compliant labor, you mean women and children."

"Right, to keep things running. They'll adapt to the new regime quickly enough. And while we consolidate, we'll have all their food and their electrical supplies. And that valley is more defensible, especially with the prep these doomsday types have done."

Sergeant Shepherd leaned back in his chair. "But then we're right back to our problem. Blister Creek is a little *too* defensible at the moment. They had bunkers and mines. Machine guns, assault rifles. Probably grenades."

"And this is where I come in," Kemp said. It wasn't a question.

"This is where you come in," Shepherd agreed.

"I've got a sniper rifle," Alacrán said. "I understand that's your area of expertise."

"Eleven confirmed kills in Iran," Shepherd said.

Most of them had been ugly kills. Screaming women, children with AK-47s. An old man with an anti-tank gun.

"I did what I had to," Kemp said. "What kind of gun?"

"M40," Shepherd said.

"What variant?"

"A1. It's an older model, but in fine condition."

"I'm sure it will do. Tripod? Correct cartridges for sniping?"

"Yes."

Kemp imagined sighting Christianson through his scope. "Can you get me into the valley?"

"Not yet," Alacrán said, "but soon."

"Then what, take it easy while I wait? You got a place with AC? And central heat too."

"Like I said," Alacrán said. "Cut off the head of the snake. That's step one, and there's more to the head than just Christianson. While we work to secure your firing position on Blister Creek, you'll be going after the part of it that's out in the open."

Both men looked eager now that they were down to the nuts and bolts of it.

"You know the desert," Shepherd said, leaning forward. "You survived it. You know where you left those four—the kid, the FBI woman, the former cop, Christianson's sister. And we know where they're going."

"So I track them, locate their camp, and pick them off one by one?"

"Too hard for you?" Alacrán said.

"Like shooting jackrabbits. Assuming I can find them. And keep myself alive. It's hell out there. But I don't know—my beef is with Christianson, not these others."

"That's how you get to Christianson," Shepherd said. "Kill off his support and he'll be weak."

"So it's not really the head of the snake," Kemp said. "It's cutting off the body to get to the head."

"Quit dicking around—you know what the general meant. Are you in?"

Kemp enjoyed being needed. And of course he was turning it over. He didn't have the stomach to kill civilians, but he wasn't sure there was such a thing in this day and age. Not in Iran, not in the U.S. Could he peg them, one by one, from a distance? Yeah, he could.

"Might take a couple of weeks to get west and finish the job," he said. "Depends on where I catch them. Maybe Cedar City if I hurry. That cop will take them there first. To resupply."

"Take as long as you need," Alacrán said.

"Will we be ready to move on Blister Creek when I get back?"

"We'll make it happen," Shepherd said.

"Two conditions. Satisfy them, and I'm in."

"Name them," Shepherd said.

"First, you keep your promise. When I get back, I'm number three. No more grunt work. No more 'yes Sarge, no Sarge.' And as number three, I make the call what happens to those people up at the bus. If I come back and find them slaving around for you, some heads are going to roll."

The sergeant nodded. "You got it."

"Second, when it's time, you leave Christianson to me. He killed my mother. No long-distance sniping. I'm going to look into his eyes and tell him I offed his sister, right before I put a bullet through his brain."

The other two men exchanged smiles.

"Check the supplies," Alacrán said. "Take anything you need except fuel. We're down to a couple hundred gallons of diesel."

"Can you spare a horse?"

"Yeah, that we can spare. Can you leave first thing in the morning?"

"Why wait? I can hoof it ten miles back up the road before midnight. Give me flashlights, batteries, *two* horses—so I can push them harder—and I'll catch these bastards before they make it down from the mountains. Come on, let's go."

The other two men pushed away from the table to do his bidding. Kemp waited until they were gone, shouting orders, then wandered into the kitchen to forage. He'd travel lean and mean. He was used to that. But he'd be damned if he'd set off on an empty stomach. He found a can of peaches and pried off the lid, then guzzled them straight from the can.

CHAPTER NINE

Eliza got up at the first sliver of dawn. She'd been awake and shivering, her bladder full to bursting for what seemed like hours, waiting for daybreak. Miriam slept peacefully next to her in their makeshift bed of broken pine boughs, with more boughs serving as blankets. A few feet away, Trost snored softly while Grover mumbled in his sleep.

Eliza slipped out from beneath the branches. Her body ached from sleeping on roots and jutting stones, and her calves and leg muscles groaned, unwilling to cooperate. How far had they run yesterday? Fifteen miles?

Massaging her thighs and stretching as she walked, she picked her way through the fir trees until she reached the highway. Not a single vehicle, not a rider, nobody on foot or bicycle. The road yesterday had been like those strips of faded blacktop near abandoned mining towns, except the pavement was still black, the dividing lines still yellow and fresh. Reflectors on the shoulders warned nonexistent traffic whenever the highway curved. Here and there, culverts had overflowed and carved gullies across the road, or trees had fallen and blocked the way, but most of the time it was easy to imagine the rumble of an engine and the glow of headlamps rounding the corner. Only it never happened.

She stood in the middle of the road, listening. Thinking. Mostly about Steve, wondering if he was okay, but also about her family in Blister Creek. About the wars and the famine.

To her surprise, it was Trost who woke first. He approached from the camp.

"Five thirty-two a.m.," he said. "Pretty early to be up and about."

"You're still keeping time?"

He held up his wrist to show an old-fashioned windup Timex. "Belonged to my dad. Been ticking since the seventies."

"Are your folks still alive?" she asked.

"No. My dad died of cancer when I was a kid—he was a down-winder who caught fallout from the weapons tests. My mother passed away two years ago just when things started to get interesting."

"I'm sorry."

"Don't be. I miss her, of course, but it was a mercy that she passed when she did. All this would have terrified her."

Eliza changed the subject. "What do you figure, about fifteen more miles before we reach the summit?"

"Something like that, yeah. We've been lucky—we haven't reached the snow line yet. It's hard to say what it will look like up top, but what if the road is still covered?"

"If it is, we'll make snowshoes."

"How is the food holding up?" he asked.

"We've got a bit of jerky and some dried apricots. Enough for breakfast, then it's gone."

"I checked the snares. Was hoping to get a rabbit in the night. Nothing. Not even a chipmunk."

"We didn't have time to do it properly," she said. "Plus, no tools."

Grover roused himself next, then Miriam, the latter well rested and full of energy. They ate the last of their food and drank water from a mountain spring.

Miriam led them in prayer before setting out. After the usual stuff asking for guidance and inspiration, her prayer turned weird.

"Clear the way before our passage, oh Lord. Strike down the wicked. Burn those who strive against us. Turn their food to filth. Let their water taste of bile. Plague them with boils and fill their throats with ash. Let those who live by the sword perish by the sword."

Eliza opened her eyes. Grover had his arms folded, eyes scrunched, nostrils flaring. Trost cracked his eyes and looked curiously at Miriam. He glanced at Eliza and when their eyes met, he shook his head.

Miriam continued. "Wield us in thy hand, Lord, that we may smite thine enemies a mighty blow. That they shall tremble and flee before us. That the earth shall be cleansed in our passage. In the name of Jesus Christ, amen."

"Amen," Grover said, firmly.

Eliza looked at Miriam. "Amen? What was that?"

"I felt inspired," Miriam said. "Let's go."

"'Fill their throats with ash'?" Trost muttered for Eliza's benefit as they set out. "'Plague them with boils'? Surprised she didn't command their gonads to fall off."

They came upon the first evidence of Miriam's so-called "cleansing" a couple of hours later when they rounded the corner to discover a large cabin at the edge of a mountain lake off the shoulder of the highway. Built of logs with an A-frame roof to shed snow, the cabin looked like a rich person's vacation getaway except for the beat-up pickup trucks parked in the driveway. Clumps of snow still spotted the yard, which was dotted with aspen seedlings.

They studied the house without approaching, afraid that they'd come upon someone's mountain redoubt.

"It's abandoned," Miriam proclaimed.

"What about the trucks?"

"See that truck parked beneath the eaves? There's still snow in the bed—it must have slid off the roof during the winter. Nobody has driven out of here since last year."

"So maybe they ran out of gas?" Eliza asked.

"And that broken window to the left of the door. It got frigid last winter. It's *still* cold up here at night. If anyone were living here, they'd board it over, put a blanket up, or do something to block the drafts."

They still approached cautiously. The front door was unlocked. Eliza pushed it open and stepped back.

"Hello?" No answer.

She stepped into a foyer with a vaulted ceiling. Dirty blankets and clothes lay scattered across the floor. Muddy boot prints marked the carpets. Blankets and couch cushions were tucked into the corners where people had made beds. The furniture itself—chairs, couches, dressers—was missing, presumably burned for warmth. The others came in behind her.

"There were people here," Eliza said. "Wonder where they went."

"Not our concern," Miriam said. "Let's see if we can find anything useful."

There was no food in the pantry, nor so much as a ketchup bottle in the fridge. No power, of course. No batteries or flashlights, or even toiletries to take from the bathrooms. There was a loft over the living room, and Eliza climbed up to investigate. She found more bedding and a couple of mattresses. The loft smelled of stale sweat.

"Hey," Grover said from the kitchen. "Look what I found."

It was a hand-written note, sitting in open sight on the counter, overlooked in their first pass through the kitchen. Trost took it from him and read aloud.

"'April 3. My name is Kelton O'Reilly. I am thirty-seven years old and used to work as a web designer before the crash. The others are gone. I'm setting out for the polygamist town as soon as the storm lets up. I hear they have food. There's still three feet of snow on the highway and I'm so weak, I don't think I'll make it far on foot. All I have to eat is some pine bark and two field mice I caught in the traps this morning. But maybe I'll find a frozen deer that the coyotes haven't discovered yet. The others are in the shed.'"

Trost turned it over, but there was nothing on the other side. "That's it?"

"O'Reilly?" Grover said. "That's not one of our families. Why would he make for Blister Creek?"

"Same reason Joe Kemp and his crowd came to the valley," Eliza said. "Word is spreading. We have food and supplies."

Miriam grabbed the note and looked it over. "It won't do them any good. We're not open for business." She slapped it back in Trost's hand with a sour expression, as if she was suffering from indigestion. Then, when he made to put it back on the counter, added, "No, don't leave it here. If anyone else stumbles in, we don't want them getting ideas about Blister Creek."

He looked it over one more time before folding it and stuffing it in his back pocket. "'The others are in the shed.' I don't like the sound of that."

Eliza's stomach churned. "I hope I don't regret this, but . . . let's have a look."

They found the toolshed around back, tucked against the patio, which overlooked the small lake. Miriam threw open the doors and a foul smell roared out. They staggered back a pace and she shut the doors hastily.

"Let me see," Eliza said.

"Are you sure? It isn't pretty."

She was sure. She lifted her shirt over her mouth and nose and opened the doors. When her eyes adjusted to the dim light, she could only stare, speechless.

Bodies lay side by side on the floor, stacked two deep. Men, women, children. Maybe fifteen in all. They stared at the ceiling through glazed eyes, sunken deep behind sharp cheekbones, the skin pulled taut. The youngest child was no more than three, with blond, curly hair. So thin, like the dried-out animals you found in the desert. Only this was a child.

"What is it?" Grover asked. "What do you see?"

"Stay back, don't come in here."

A figure moved closer and she turned to tell Grover to mind, but it was Trost, with one hand covering his mouth and nose. He looked over her shoulder and made a swallowing sound deep in his throat.

Eliza shut the shed doors.

"They must have driven up in the fall," he said, "and got trapped when the weather turned."

"It snowed all winter," Eliza said. "What did the note say, April? I'm surprised they held out that long. They must have found food in the house."

"Not enough, though. O'Reilly was the last, and the only one to make it out."

"He didn't, though, did he, because we never saw him. He must have died on the road." Eliza looked at Miriam. "That's what it means to cleanse the earth. Horrible suffering. Children starving to death. Are you sure that's what you want?"

Miriam looked at the ground.

Trost pulled out O'Reilly's note and read, "'There's still three feet of snow on the highway and I'm so weak, I don't think I'll make it far on foot.'"

"Wait a minute," Eliza said. "You don't think there's still gas in those vehicles, do you?"

CHAPTER TEN

There *was* gas in the tanks, but getting to it was a different matter. First, Grover and Miriam searched the house for the keys while Eliza helped Trost siphon gas into buckets from a garden hose they found around back. They got two gallons into one bucket and about a gallon and a half into the other, all unleaded, according to the gas caps. The plan was to mix it and pour it back into whichever vehicle they could get started.

The problem was the keys, which didn't turn up. After the initial search, the four companions scoured the house. They shook every piece of clothing, lifted every blanket, checked and double-checked drawers in the kitchen. They searched the vehicles themselves, which sat unlocked, then around the house. Perhaps they were under a rock or loose paving stone. No.

A sour feeling turned over in Eliza's stomach. "We have to go in the shed and turn out their pockets. Any volunteers?"

Grover licked his lips. "I bet O'Reilly took them. So if he ever made it back he'd have the vehicles."

"Maybe," she said, "but that doesn't do us any good. Our best hope is in that shed."

"I'll do it," Miriam said.

"Are you sure?" Eliza asked.

"The rest of you stay here."

Miriam disappeared for several minutes, while the others waited, looking at their hands or staring into the distance without communicating. When Miriam returned, she looked ill. "No."

Eliza fought down her frustration. "Great. And now we've wasted so much time we'll have to stay here tonight. There's no way of making it over the pass before dark, and it will be too cold to sleep out."

She didn't want to stay in the house. After seeing all those dead bodies, the house had a creepy feeling about it. It was hard to imagine sleeping. Besides, the house was right off the highway; they'd have to keep watch in case someone else came along.

"On the plus side," Miriam said, "I found a bunch of tools in the back of the shed behind the bodies. I set them out. We could carry them for trade in Cedar City."

"That's something," Eliza said. "What kind of tools are we talking about?"

"Screwdrivers, hammers, and so on. Plus bigger stuff—axes, picks, shovels. Couple of saws. Fishing poles—nobody seemed to have used them all winter."

"The lake was probably frozen over," Eliza said. "But we could catch our supper if we can dig up worms for bait."

Trost went around the house to look at the tools while Eliza and Miriam discussed how they would spend the night. Miriam agreed about the safety of the house. If not for the possibility of catching fish to rebuild their food supplies, she was in favor of setting out and getting higher into the mountains before calling it a night.

Trost was grinning when he came back. He held a heavy toolbox.

"Forget the keys, I can hotwire us a ride."

After looking over the vehicles, he settled on an old Dodge pickup. Less computerized and easier to hotwire. It was also more sluggish after sitting in place all winter, plus they'd drained the tank, and it took a good forty-five minutes of messing around until he got it to turn over. As he fiddled with it, the other three kept busy. Grover dug up the yard looking for worms, then took the poles down to the lake. Miriam and Eliza changed out the Dodge's bald, rotting tires for better ones off the other vehicles.

It was late afternoon before they were gassed up, loaded, and ready to set out. Grover had caught three trout, which he'd cooked as fast as he caught them. As the pickup rattled up the mountain road, they shared out the fish. It was just enough to leave Eliza hungrier than when she'd started. But she felt stronger, and was relieved she wouldn't have to spend the night in the house.

Trost drove. "With any luck," he said, "we'll be down in Cedar City in time for supper."

"Which is what these days?" Miriam said. "Boot leather and toasted grasshoppers?"

"The fundamentalists aren't the only ones who prepared for the end, you know," Trost said. He sounded testy. Like the majority of Utahns, he was part of the mainstream LDS church that had given up polygamy over a hundred years earlier. "Our prophets have been warning us about a year's supply of food forever."

"They aren't real prophets," Miriam said. "They're a bureaucratic gerontocracy, but fine, whatever."

"What do you know about it?"

"Don't we have enough worries without starting a religious war?" Eliza said. "Miriam, when we get to Cedar City, act civilized, will you?"

"I know what I'm doing. I grew up among gentiles, remember?"

"Starting with calling other Mormons saints, not gentiles, for one. For that matter, don't call *gentiles* 'gentiles,' either."

"Sure, why not? Anything else?"

"Just . . . good manners, right? And if that means you keep your mouth shut, then do that."

They zipped along for the next ten minutes, making excellent time as the road snaked higher and higher. They passed through gorgeous meadows dotted with wildflowers and thick stands of aspen with their leaves quaking in the breeze. The higher they got, the more snow remained, until soon only the road itself wasn't covered with a blanket of white.

Then they were passing through a slushy film, then shifting to fuel-burning four-wheel-drive to climb through several inches of snow, then a wet, icy foot of snow that remained. They had to get out several times to push when the pickup got stuck. Another time Trost lost traction and nearly drove them off the road while the others braced themselves to go crashing over the hill and into the forest. He fought it under control at the last moment. When they reached the summit—9,900 feet, according to a roadside sign—the needle was nudging at empty.

They stopped to refill their canteens from a mountain stream and to shake off some of the motion sickness from the long, winding drive.

"That was a good day's hike right there," Eliza said. "If we'd come up on foot, we'd have been spending a night up here any way you looked at it."

"Not only that," Trost said, "we were lucky there weren't any more washouts. I hope our luck holds."

They coasted down the mountain where possible, even when it meant creeping at five or six miles an hour until they reached the next dip. Trost only nudged the gas when the road made a temporary climb. Even so, they'd only reached the foothills above Cedar City before the engine died altogether. He managed to coax out another half mile or so by coasting before the road rose a little too high to the next crest and they couldn't make it any farther. They parked the truck and got out.

The Great Basin stretched beneath a bruised sky. The opposite mountain range lay shrouded in smoke or a fine haze of dust, but the view was wide open both south and north, where the freeway sliced across the western edge of Utah. Fields shimmered green, though whether from the heavy spring rains or because people were actively planting them, it was hard to say.

Cedar City itself sat below them like a giant map. It was a Mormon pioneer town with wide, leafy streets laid out on a grid in the downtown, sprawling from there into the surrounding farm and grazing land. Or that's what it had been two years earlier. Now, block after block of the newer subdivisions to the south and west lay in blackened ruins. Houses gone, fields turned to ash. No trees. Essentially, anything that touched or drew near I-15 was gone. Nearly two-thirds of the city of thirty thousand people, obliterated.

"Good lord," Trost said. "What the devil happened down there?"

"It wasn't that way last fall?" Eliza asked.

"No, it wasn't like this at all. We were holding on—by the tips of our fingers, but managing. And look, there's not a single car on the freeway, or any of the side roads. Is there no fuel? None at all?"

"There's more traffic in Blister Creek," Grover said.

"Look, there's a rider," Miriam said. "No, two."

About a mile away and several hundred feet below, two men on horseback trotted down the road before disappearing beneath the trees that still grew on the east side of town.

"There had better be cops," Trost said with a grumble. "If I get down there and find my officers have deserted the force, I'm going to crack some skulls."

They pushed the truck to the side of the road, where they unloaded the tools salvaged from the house. These they hid in the scrub oak that lined the road.

From there, they descended into town on foot. The air smelled of a distant brush fire. It was quiet. No chainsaws, lawnmowers, trucks, or any of the other sounds you'd associate with a small town on a summer day. The houses in the uppermost foothills were abandoned, yards overgrown with weeds. Front doors hung open, with the contents of the homes salvaged—or looted, depending on your point of view. Several had burned down.

Lower still, they came upon a farmer's wide field, now given over to hand-carved wooden grave markers. Hundreds and hundreds of them marched across the field. The upper part of the makeshift cemetery showed signs of fresh digging, while below, grass had grown up around the markers. They came upon another field of fresh graves around the next bend, this one even larger.

Four men were digging graves at the end of the field, while a fifth stood at watch, armed with a rifle. Three bodies lay side by side next to the first grave, wrapped in sheets. One of the men stopped to wipe the sweat from his forehead with a gloved hand. He leaned against his shovel and happened to glance up the road. He spotted the newcomers and dove for the ground with a shout.

The man with the rifle swung it around and aimed it at the four companions. He screamed for them to freeze. They raised their hands.

The man with the rifle started to come forward, then stopped after several paces. "Dale Trost? That you?"

"Hank Gibson?" Trost said. "What the devil is going on here?"

"TB. More victims."

"What's with the chain gang?"

"Looters."

The scene shifted in Eliza's mind as they followed Trost's lead and cautiously approached the others. It wasn't a man protecting workers. It was a man standing guard over four prisoners. Chains and manacles linked them together; she hadn't noticed that at first. Their heads were shaved and they wore gaunt, hungry expressions. Two of them were kids, no older than sixteen. One of these was missing an ear. An angry gash, poorly stitched, marked its absence.

Gibson was a tall, wiry man with an iron-gray mustache. He was missing two fingers on his left hand.

He turned to the men. "Get to work, you dogs."

The prisoners returned to their labors. Picks clanked stones. Shovels tossed dirt out of the hole.

Trost gestured at the boy with the missing ear. "Who did that?"

"You steal a man's food, you join the work crew. You break into his house to do it, you lose an ear. Second time, it's a hand. Hard cases, we fit 'em with a necktie." He stuck his tongue out the side of his mouth and pantomimed raising a rope at his neck.

"Is that the law these days?" Trost asked.

"You have a better idea? These vermin are like rats. We can't keep them out."

"Did you say tuberculosis?" Eliza asked. "I've never heard of that around here."

"Third outbreak since December. We've lost hundreds already."

"Yeah, I can see from the graves," Trost said. "Though it looks more like thousands, to me."

"You can thank the army for that," one of the prisoners said. "Bombed us out. That's why we stole that food. What choice did we have?"

"Shut up and get digging," Gibson said. He turned back to the newcomers. "He's mostly right. Bandits took over the old Walmart and instead of sending in the National Guard like we asked, the government flew a couple of B-52s over and turned half the town to rubble. That made the problem worse." He looked Trost over with a critical eye. "They say you hooked up with the polygs. Looks like they're keeping you fed."

"I've been earning my keep," Trost said. "But I've still lost a good twenty pounds."

"Could have been fifty. Could have been all of it." He met Eliza's gaze, then sized up Miriam and Grover. "Is the mountain road open?"

"No, it's closed," Miriam said.

"How did you get over, then?"

"It's closed with .50-caliber machine guns," she clarified. "And land mines. Sniper rifles. Grenades."

"Yeah, I got it. You fundies take care of your own. Well, Trost, it's a good gig if you can get it."

"Who's in charge?" Eliza asked. "Is there a mayor?"

"The army came through last fall after bombing the place and arrested the mayor and the city council. When the army pulled out, the Cedar City PD declared martial law. I'm chief of police now. So that means me, I'm in charge."

"You?" Trost sounded aghast.

"What was I supposed to do? You left. Mendoza died of meningitis. Phillips and Wirtz were killed in the riots."

"What about Nielsen? Udall?"

"Nielsen is a young guy—the army drafted him when they came through and we never heard from him again. Udall disappeared. They say he ran for the hills with his wife and kids. His brother has a ranch somewhere by Price. Or maybe it was in Arizona. That makes me the last guy standing. What are you doing here anyway? These your new wives? Who's the kid?"

"We're on our way to Los Angeles," Eliza said. "We had a run-in with bandits, and we're hoping to resupply in Cedar City."

"What do you need?"

"Mostly food, but also firearms. They took everything."

Gibson grabbed a shovel from one of the prisoners and used it to measure the depth of the last grave. "That's good enough, boys. Get those bodies in the ground and cover 'em up. Looks like you earned supper tonight." He turned to the others. "Have you got anything to trade?"

"We do," Eliza said. "Good tools—axes, saws, wrenches, all sorts of stuff."

"Shovels too," Trost said. "Yours look well-used."

"We've got plenty of tools," Gibson said. "We'll take what you've got, of course—stuff wears out, there's no way to replace it. But we can't pay much. What we need is fuel. Or silver. That still has value. Got anything like that?"

"I told you," Eliza said. "We were robbed by bandits."

"Then you'd better go back to Blister Creek and get something useful."

"If we could do that, we wouldn't need your help in the first place," Miriam said.

Trost had been edging forward during this conversation and now stood close enough to Gibson to lay a hand on the man's shoulder. "Help me out here. It was me who got you that job in the first place. Don't you at least want to see the tools?"

"Tell you what," Gibson said. "Come down to the house and I'll feed you the same supper I was going to give to these fools. Two hard-boiled eggs and a bowl of oatmeal."

"How generous," Miriam said.

Eliza gave her a look and she closed her mouth.

"You have any idea what that's worth these days?" Gibson said.

"We'll take it," Trost said. "What about the tools?"

"We'll check them out in the morning. If they're any good, I'll give you enough food to see you back over the mountains where you belong. You want to come this way again, you'd better be prepared to pay your way."

By the time the prisoners had finished burying the bodies, the sun was sinking over the western desert behind a rim of red and purple fire. The distant mountain ranges were almost glowing. It was the most brilliant (and weird) sunset Eliza had seen yet.

The prisoners trudged down the highway, chains clanking together, while Gibson followed with his rifle slung over one shoulder. The four companions from Blister Creek brought up the rear.

It was still late afternoon in Los Angeles, four hundred and fifty miles across the desert. Somewhere out there, Steve was waiting. Eliza had no intention of returning to Blister Creek until she found him.

CHAPTER ELEVEN

Minutes after finishing their miserly dinner of oatmeal and hard-boiled eggs, Miriam rose from the table and said she wanted to go back and hide their tools better. They hadn't planned to leave them overnight and she said she was worried about bandits.

Eliza was suspicious of the overly casual tone in her sister-in-law's voice. "Alone? It's dark up there. Can you even find the way?"

"I'll be fine. Look, if thieves find our truck, they'll find our tools. We lose those and this jerk won't give us so much as a dog biscuit."

Gibson lived in a mansion on the bench overlooking Cedar City. A pair of Ferraris sat in the front yard like the world's most expensive lawn ornaments. They certainly weren't going anywhere. The interior of the house was posh, with cathedral ceilings and a kitchen dripping in marble. Eliza didn't think Trost's eyebrows could rise any higher to see how his former deputy had set himself up. Then the servants appeared.

But even though Gibson seemed to think of himself as some sort of overlord of the struggling town, when the last daylight faded, he did not have any lights to turn on. They ate on the deck, beneath the moonlight. Cedar City lay dark as a ghost town below them.

And when Gibson joined them for dinner, the only concession to his status was a package of stale cookies that he snacked on when they'd finished the eggs and oatmeal. He didn't offer to share.

"Stay here," Eliza told Miriam. "Maybe later we'll all go out together."

"I'm going," Miriam said. "You can come with me or hang out here, it doesn't matter."

"I'm serious. We need to stick together. Look, will you take Grover, at least?"

"What good is he going to do?"

Grover rose to his feet. "I'll keep you safe."

"What, because you think I need a man?"

"Two is safer than one," Eliza said. She wasn't worried about Miriam's safety so much as the woman's intentions. "Take him. Please."

"Fine. Come on, Grover."

"Don't go mucking around," Gibson said. "You get tempted to help yourself to anyone's property, you think long and hard about those men on the chain gang this afternoon."

Miriam fixed him with a hard look. "Weren't you one of the deputies who came with Trost to investigate Blister Creek a couple of years ago after the chemical weapons attack?"

Gibson stammered. "Well, yes."

"You saw what we did, and you still want to pick a fight?"

Gibson fell quiet until Miriam and Grover were gone, picking their way around the wraparound deck instead of going back through the house. "Damn it, Trost. What kind of game are you playing here?"

"No game," Trost said.

Eliza leaned across the table. "We're not enemies, Mr. Gibson."

"Doesn't mean we're friends either."

"As far as I know, Blister Creek and Cedar City are the only towns left standing in southern Utah. Why can't we help each other out?"

"So you're planning to share your food?" Gibson asked. "That's right, I know what you're sitting on. Word is spreading fast. Soon everyone will know."

"We don't have to share food to help each other," she said. "We can keep the mountain passes open. Spread information. Guard the roads north and south against bandits. When things quiet down, we can trade."

"I don't think so. I see what you're trying to do."

Trost snorted. "And what's that? You think we want to take over or something?"

"Why not? Everyone else does."

What a paranoid fool, Eliza thought. Anyone could take Cedar City at any time. It was right on the freeway, exposed to the desert on three sides. But why would they want to? All it meant was more mouths to feed. More desert wilderness to fight over. The town had little food and poor prospects of growing their own.

She had to get Gibson off this aggressive stance. "You can share information, though. That's free, right?"

"Yeah, I guess."

"We lost our last AM station in the spring," she said. "Did India and Pakistan ever go to war?"

"You didn't hear?"

"No," Trost said. "What happened? It didn't go nuclear, did it?"

"That's *all* it was. Between the famine and the fuel shortages they didn't have the ability to fight a ground campaign. Pakistan tried a sneak attack. India wasn't fooled. For two weeks they went back and forth nuking each other's cities."

"Sweet heavens," Eliza said.

"Pakistan hit the Indians with about three dozen bombs before they ran out," Gibson continued. "India kept up the war for another two weeks before exhausting themselves. India landed about a hundred nukes. Nobody knows the exact number—news is scarce these days from that part of the world."

The horror of it made Eliza's head swim, her stomach clench. "How many died?"

"Maybe thirty million in India. It's too big and Pakistan's arsenal was too small to finish the job. But they'll get their revenge. India is starving. Thirty million is just a start."

Her mouth was dry. "And Pakistan? How many died?"

"All of them."

"There were two hundred million people in Pakistan," Trost said. His voice was flat and heavy. "Surely not all."

"Close enough. Have you seen the sunsets? Volcanic ash and fallout. Bet we're getting a nice dosage of radiation all the way over here."

"What about Japan and China?" Eliza asked. "Are they still fighting?"

"Yeah, but the Chinese haven't gone nuclear. Guess they know it would blow back in their faces. They tried to land a huge army in Kyushu. The navy didn't make it across. A million men bobbing around in the Sea of Japan. The Chinese government is admitting to a hundred million dead from the famine. It's probably worse than that. You heard about Europe?" Gibson added.

"You mean the revolution in Britain?" Eliza said.

"Germany and Italy now too. Spain is one big refugee camp. By the time they started turning away the Moroccans it was too late. In fact, about the only country still defending its borders over there is France. Nobody knows what is happening in Russia."

"We heard some of that," Eliza said. "The evangelical radio station out of Denver claimed that whoever ended up with the Russian nuclear arsenal was going to blow up the Middle East and bring about the Second Coming."

"Not much left to blow up," Gibson said. "In March, the Israelis launched nuclear artillery shells against the Sinai camps. Couple of million Egyptians were trying to storm the country. It was a massacre. By that time there wasn't an Egyptian government left to protest."

"We heard about that," Trost said. "We still had radio then."

"Point is, most of those countries are simply gone. More or less starved to death or descended into anarchy."

"It can't keep getting worse," Eliza said. "Sooner or later the weather will clear and people will come to their senses."

"I wouldn't count on it," Gibson said. "I'll bet a billion people have died already. By the end of the year it will be another billion. Maybe more. For all we know, another nuclear war is going off right this minute. We lost radio contact ourselves about two weeks ago."

"Maybe it really is the end of the world," Trost said. "Maybe only the coming of the Lord will save us."

Eliza didn't want to dwell on that. That thinking pervaded Blister Creek; it was the belief that drove Miriam. The elect, in their desert sanctuary. Waiting for the end, when the wicked would burn like chaff. Jacob urged caution. Prepare for the worst, but don't try to bring it on. She admired how he could maintain his faith in humanity and his doubt in doomsday prophesy against so much evidence. She struggled to do the same.

They fell into silence. Crickets chirped from the darkness around them. Down the hillside, horse hooves clomped on pavement. A gunshot sounded from a few blocks away, up by the foothills to their rear. Eliza hoped it was a hunter in a blind. Not someone shooting at looters—say, at Miriam and Grover. Gibson didn't react. Apparently gunfire was too common to remark on.

The moon rose above the mountains behind the house. It was a deep, ruddy color, full and huge.

"And the moon became as blood," Trost said.

Words from the scripture came to Eliza's lips before she could hold them back. "For the great day of His wrath is come, and who shall be able to stand?"

"Enough of that," Gibson said. "You're creeping me out."

Eliza shook herself. "Never mind the problems on the other side of the world," she said. "What about between here and California?"

He snorted. "Apart from being a war zone? Oh, it's fine. Bandits, starving mobs. Gangs of rapists, murderers, thieves. Preppers living in doomsteads in the middle of the desert who will shoot you and eat you. Major outbreaks of TB, typhoid, and cholera across the West. Medical care and sanitation are like the blasted Middle Ages. The only ones prospering are the goddamn coyotes and vultures."

"If you don't have news for the past two weeks," Trost said, "maybe the fighting is winding down."

"Or, who knows, maybe it's rubble by now. As far as I'm concerned, they can keep killing each other."

"Why?" Eliza asked. "Don't you want the war to end?"

"What do you think is going to happen when the battle of Las Vegas is over?" Gibson asked. "Federal troops will come right up I-15. They'll move into Cedar City."

"What makes you say that?" Eliza asked.

"Think about it. Either they lose Vegas to the rebels and will need a new forward operating base, or they'll have won and will move to secure their supply lines for another push into California. Either way, I-15 is the major artery through Las Vegas, and Cedar City is the only surviving freeway town in southern Utah. Where else would they go?"

She had to admit it made a certain amount of sense. "All the more reason not to want an enemy at your back too."

"Help us out," Trost said. "Don't make us return to Blister Creek and tell them you're hostile."

"So now you're threatening me."

Trost sighed. "Listen, Gibson. We're not asking much. Horses. Food. A rifle for each of us and a couple of hundred rounds. I *know* you have plenty of guns and ammo."

"Yeah, and food and horses. I don't think so. The deal is, you give me your tools and I buy them at a fair price. If you're telling the truth about what you've got, that should get you home."

"What if we promise to pay you when we get back?" Eliza asked. "Give us two weeks and we'll deliver, I promise."

"The promises of fundy kooks aren't worth much these days, if they ever were." Gibson peered down from the deck. "Where's that friend of yours? Shouldn't take her so long."

"Here I am," Miriam called from the darkness below.

Gibson sprang to his feet. "What are you doing down there?"

"Looking for a way up. It's too dark."

Her figure moved through the shadows near the support posts that held up the deck where it hung over the hillside. Moments later she found the stairs and came up. Her hands were dirty and the braid in her hair was falling apart. A scratch marked one cheek.

"It really is dark out there. The road turned and I fell into the scrub oak. Look at my clothes." She let out a bitter laugh. "I found the truck easily enough, but not the tools."

"Someone stole them?" Trost asked.

"Nah, I was just turned around in the dark. I found them eventually."

Eliza's suspicions grew. Miriam was a great actress—it was that acting ability that had brought her into the polygamist communities in the first place, when she infiltrated the Zarahemla cult a few years earlier— but Eliza knew her sister-in-law's moods too well by now. Miriam had been up to something.

"Where's the other one?" Gibson asked. "The kid?"

"I left Grover up there to guard the tools. We really need a light if we're going to hide them any better. You've got to have a flashlight or a kerosene lantern or something."

"Not for you to use, no. Where is he?"

"I'm not telling you that. Not until we've worked out a trade."

"Damn you." Gibson wheeled on Trost. "Get that kid down here or I'll throw you in irons. You'll be on grave-digging duty tomorrow, so help me."

"I'm not in charge." Trost nodded at Eliza. "She is."

Eliza sighed. "We'll go get Grover. Come on. You too, Officer Trost."

Gibson grabbed Trost's arm. "No. He stays here. Sanchez, get out here."

Trost jerked free. "Get your hands off me."

Sanchez came onto the deck. He held a pistol.

"Hold on," Eliza said when she saw the gun. "Everyone calm down. It's fine. We'll get Grover. Trost can stay here. Miriam, you *can* find the truck this time, right?"

"Pretty sure, yeah."

"Okay. The rest of you sit down. Let's not make this a big deal. Miriam and I will be back in a few minutes."

Moments later, the two women were out in the street, picking their way through the darkness, between the blackened mansions overlooking the city. Two men stood on the sidewalk in front of the house, watching them.

"Us again!" Miriam called. "We'll be back in a few minutes." When they reached the end of the street, Miriam said, "Careful with those two. Gibson's thugs. Armed with shotguns."

"Please tell me you didn't do something stupid."

"By stupid, you mean did I figure out how to bust out of this dumb town?"

"Miriam, no."

"God gave me a brain and free will. The FBI gave me training." She let out a little groan. "My boobs are killing me."

"What?"

"They're like concrete and they're leaking like crazy. How long does it take for your milk supply to dry up?"

"I have no idea."

"Can't be much longer. The sooner the better. You know, sometimes it sucks to be a woman."

Miriam said all of this matter-of-factly, as if leaving her baby was no big deal. But Eliza had seen her with the child, tenderly stroking Abigail's head as she nursed, while David beamed down at them both. Miriam was no heartless killing machine; it must have been tearing her up inside to be eighty miles away with no hope of returning anytime soon.

"Stop changing the subject," Eliza said. "What are you up to? And where's Grover?"

"We're almost there. Hurry."

They found the boy at the edge of the cemetery. He had four saddled horses and was stuffing food and supplies into the saddlebag Miriam had hauled from Kemp's school bus into the mountains. Grover had already tied blankets and bulging burlap sacks to the other horses.

"Grover, what the devil?"

"Hi, Sister Eliza." He sounded nervous.

She turned on Miriam. "Where did you get this?"

"We went foraging."

"Stealing, you mean."

"We wouldn't have had to if Gibson had helped us in the first place."

"Now you sound like Joe Kemp. These people don't owe us anything. They're trying to survive, just like we are, and you came in and helped yourself."

"We tried to trade, they wouldn't do it. Anyway, we have no choice, and I didn't take that much, only a few things we needed."

"More justification." Eliza's anger was still burning hot.

"The only thing we're short is firearms," Miriam continued. "I've got two rifles and a few shells, but we'll need to figure that out eventually."

"And what do we do now, flee back through the mountains ahead of an armed posse?"

"We can't go back. We sneak out of town." Again, that nonchalant tone. "It's dark. Cedar City isn't that big. Once we get into the desert . . ."

"We're in the foothills," Eliza said. "The entire town is in front of us. We have to pass through the whole blasted thing just to reach the freeway. And what about Officer Trost? He's still back there."

"He's a good man," Miriam said. "And he knows people around here. I'm sure he'll be fine."

"The devil he will. They'll string him up. We are *not* leaving him, do you understand me?"

"Then we'd better hurry up before someone spots us. Grover, are you finished?"

"Almost. One second."

"No," Eliza said. "I don't know where you got this stuff, but I want it back where it belongs. Horses, food, the rifles—everything."

Miriam cleared her throat. "There's one small problem with that. I, um, had to use harsh measures to get one of the guns."

"You killed someone?" Eliza was so angry she was shaking.

"Of course not. What do you think I am, a monster? But I, uh, well, I kind of bashed some guy over the head with a rock and stole his gun from his hands. He's tied up and gagged. Problem is he got a good view of me. So when he gets untied . . ."

Miriam shrugged.

"So we're backed into a corner."

"You might say that, yes. Sorry."

Eliza wanted to scream. She wanted to snatch one of the weapons and force Miriam at gunpoint to confess her crimes to Gibson. Let the man chain her up with the other criminals.

No, that wouldn't do any good.

"Grover," she said. "Listen to me. Not to Miriam, do you understand?"

"I didn't want to, I—"

"Grover!"

"Yes?"

"If you disobey, so help me I will leave you here, is that understood?"

He bowed his head. "Yes."

"Good. Now give me one of those guns. The ammo too." She loaded rounds into the rifle. "You two stay here. I'm going back for Officer Trost. Be ready, both of you. The moment I return, we ride for our lives."

CHAPTER TWELVE

Eliza came down the hillside toward Hank Gibson's house with the rifle gripped in her hand.

Act confident. Pretend you know what you're doing.

The streets were dark and confusing. At any moment she expected to be challenged by gunmen. If that happened, she would either bluff or run for it. Only if cornered would she shoot to kill.

When she reached the end of Gibson's street, she waited in the shadows until she picked out the two men with shotguns Miriam had warned her about, silhouetted against the bloody moon. They were watching the street for her return. A shotgun was lethal from close range. From this distance, better to have Eliza's rifle, but she couldn't exactly gun them down, could she? Besides, there were at least two more men on the property, counting Gibson.

Maybe Miriam was right about leaving Trost. Surely Gibson wouldn't imprison the man for his companions' crimes. Maybe Trost could even get his job back on the police force. Cedar City would be better served with him in charge instead of Gibson.

You're fooling yourself. Best case, they throw him on the chain gang.

No. Eliza wouldn't abandon him. Member of the church or no, he belonged to Blister Creek now.

And we take care of our own.

She had to think like Miriam and bluff her way in. Why was Miriam's role-playing effective? She chose specific details. She didn't make the story too perfect. That bit about falling into the scrub oak, for example. It wasn't the sort of story that someone typically invented, because it made the teller look foolish and clumsy.

Even so, Gibson had been suspicious. He'd be doubly so now. Eliza's story would have to be better.

She held the gun against her body to conceal it in the darkness, then staggered down the sidewalk as if injured. One of the men spotted her and cried out a challenge. Eliza stumbled and fell to her knees.

Eliza made her voice high, like a younger girl's. "Please, help me."

"Who is that?"

"Kaylee Hatch. Two men, they—" She stopped and let out a sob.

The men approached her cautiously.

"I shouldn't have done it," she said. "They had food and I was so hungry, I couldn't help it. I'm so stupid. No, don't come any closer, don't look at me."

"It's okay," one of them said. "You're safe now. They won't hurt you again, I promise."

"Please, no. There's blood on my face and I—please don't look at me."

As she'd hoped, her act seemed to trigger their paternal instincts. They ignored her pleas and came up to her, slinging their shotguns over their shoulders.

"Who were they?" the other man said. He sounded younger than the first. "We'll find the guys who did this to you."

The older man reached for Eliza's arm. "It's okay. You're safe now. Where do you live? Can we fetch your folks?"

There was genuine kindness in his voice. He didn't sound like a thug, he sounded like a concerned citizen. No, what he most reminded Eliza of was her old LDS bishop in Salt Lake City, the man who had stood up for her against the polygamist men who'd been harassing her. She twinged with shame at the nasty trick she was about to play.

She let him pull her up. As she did, she raised the rifle and chambered a round. She dropped the little-girl talk. "Nobody move. Nobody cry out. I will kill you both."

"What the hell?" the younger man said.

"Drop the guns. Set them down. Now!"

They hesitated, as if they were going to make a charge at her or scream for help. Eliza was not bluffing; her finger was on the trigger. That would take care of one. Could she get off a second shot in time?

Then the older man let the shotgun slide off his shoulder and clatter to the ground. His companion followed suit.

"Hands on your heads. Back up three paces. Do not move."

They obeyed.

"Good, now listen up. I'm from Blister Creek. I have killed tougher men than you. So help me, if one of you makes a move I will turn you into hamburger. Got it?"

"What do you want?" the older man asked. His voice quivered with anger.

"What I *don't* want is bloodshed. I want the two of you to return to your beds tonight, feeling stupid that a girl beat you, but alive. That's what I *want*. What actually happens is up to you."

"You're a fool," he said. "If we let you escape we'll be out of work. That means we starve. That means our families starve."

Eliza ignored this as she frisked them, an awkward move while keeping the rifle trained on them with one hand and searching them with the other. Fortunately, neither made a move. She removed a service pistol in a holster from one and two sets of handcuffs from the other. She made the older man handcuff the younger behind his back, then she cuffed the older man in the same way. She ordered them to a sitting position.

She picked up one of the shotguns, confirmed it was loaded. Pumped the gun to chamber a round. Then she popped the shells out of the second gun, pocketed them, and tossed the empty gun into the brush. She took a step back and put on the holster with one hand, while leveling the remaining shotgun at the men with the other.

"How many men are in the house?" she asked when she'd finished.

The older man shook his head and jabbed his elbow at his companion as if in warning.

Eliza hardened her voice. "Is the secret worth your life?"

"Three," the younger one said.

"Sanchez, Gibson, and who else?"

"Guy named Trost. Used to be a cop."

"Ah."

Gibson had not fully briefed these men. That was to Eliza's advantage.

"Give it up," the older man said. "There's no way you can do this alone. We'll have a posse on you so fast your head will spin."

Eliza gestured with the shotgun. "All right, on your feet. Time to go. And I *will* do it alone, because I'm desperate. Remember that if you're tempted to try something stupid."

She led the two men to Gibson's front porch, then realized she should have waited before cuffing them. She could have fixed them to the railings. She briefly considered messing around with the handcuffs again, but the men were growing surly and likely doubting her resolve to shoot them if they struggled.

So she ordered them to lie on their bellies. They obeyed.

Instead of going through the house, she made her way around the deck as quickly and quietly as she could manage. Trost and Gibson were talking about the New York bread riots when she burst around the corner with the shotgun lowered.

"Hands up!" she shouted.

The men staggered to their feet. "Eliza?" Trost began.

"Take it!" She tossed him her rifle. "Run!"

She turned to flee without waiting. Gibson bellowed for help as Trost pounded after her. They came around the deck to the front of the house as Sanchez burst through the front door. The two handcuffed men had disappeared, apparently running off the moment she'd left them.

Sanchez screamed at them to stop. They didn't. He fired. A bullet whizzed past Eliza's ear. She turned on her heel and fired without aiming. The shotgun roared and the stock kicked her shoulder like an ironshod hoof. It was all she could do to get around and keep running.

Several seconds passed as they fled up the street before more pistol shots chased after them. Footsteps pounded behind them. Shouts sounded. Doors slammed. Gibson screamed orders.

Eliza and Trost ran in the darkness for two or three minutes before Eliza had to stop to figure out the darkened streets leading up into the bench.

"What the hell are you thinking?" Trost said, gasping. "Gibson had just agreed to loan us his shortwave radio. We could have radioed home. Now you've wrecked everything."

"Trust me, Miriam had already wrecked it. I'm just improvising. This way."

They were only halfway to the cemetery when horses came clopping along the road from above. Trost dove for the brush, but Eliza pumped the shotgun, dropped to one knee and waited. Four horses. Two had riders.

"Over here!" she called.

"Where are you?" Miriam called back.

Eliza stood and waved her arms.

Trost emerged from the brush. "Will someone tell me what is going on?"

Eliza climbed into the saddle. "Later. For now we have to get out of here. Hurry."

He grabbed the remaining horse. Below them, torches and flashlights were flickering to life. Eliza turned the horse around and rode in the opposite direction from the lights. The others followed.

★★★

They finally had some luck as they rode along the foothills. Instead of being forced back into the mountains, a second road led down into the town, this one trending north. As they trotted down darkened streets lined with little brick houses, people appeared on porches to watch. Many of them were armed. But nobody challenged them. The pursuit was searching for them back up the mountain highway, but no word appeared to have reached this part of town.

Before long they were on the ranch roads north of town and searching for a way west to cross the freeway and flee into the western desert. Still no challenges.

"Don't they have a way to raise the general alarm?" Grover asked.

"They're idiots," Miriam said. "So no, it appears they don't."

"We could have helped," Eliza said. "If only Gibson hadn't been so blasted unreasonable. We could have shown them how to organize a defense."

"Instead, here we are on stolen horses with stolen food and stolen firearms," Trost said. "Fugitives. Nice work." His voice was heavy with sarcasm.

"We got away, didn't we?" Miriam said.

"Not yet we haven't."

"And with a minimum of bloodshed too. Liz, did you kill that guy?"

"I don't think so. I hope not."

"There you go," Miriam said.

"You think that matters?" he said. "They'll be after us, don't you worry. And plenty of people saw us riding north. Even if we get out of town, we're not in the clear."

"We'll ride all night," Eliza said. "Once we get in the desert, we can hold our own."

"Stop avoiding the issue," he said. "If someone pulled a stunt like this in Blister Creek we'd hunt them to the ends of the earth. You turned us into thieves and bandits. No better than Joe Kemp."

"I'm not trying to avoid it. This is not what I wanted. Miriam is out of control. Believe me, I know."

"Please stop fighting," Grover said.

Miriam snorted. "By out of control you mean pulling our chestnuts out of the fire while everyone else sat around chatting? You're welcome, no thanks necessary."

"I should have known it was your fault," Trost said. "Sorry, Eliza. Of course it was her, not you."

"Please," Grover said. "They're going to catch us."

"Grover's right," Eliza said. "We keep arguing and we'll find nooses around our necks. What do you think, left at the next intersection?"

They picked their way west in silence. They crossed the freeway, dark and empty. On the opposite side, ranch houses gave way to flat dirt roads. Alfalfa fields, grazing land. Finally, sagebrush and rabbit grass, then the flat desert plain. Still they continued.

When morning broke, they'd penetrated the desert hills many miles west of the city. It was dry, barren land, with rattlesnakes underfoot and patient, circling vultures overhead. Finding water for man and beast would be difficult.

But Eliza's heart lifted with the sun as they rode toward the brown, shimmering Indian Peak Range on the other side of the Escalante Desert.

War, famine, disease, bandits, a barren wasteland—nothing could stop her now. Steve was out there and she was going to find him.

CHAPTER THIRTEEN

By the third day after leaving Colorado City, Kemp had climbed into the mountains on the opposite side from Cedar City. He'd entered the dunes on the first night, followed the highway north the following day, then spent another night camping in the desert. On the third afternoon the highway lifted him into cooler elevations. In late afternoon he discovered a luxurious log home next to a crystalline mountain lake. He left his rifle with the horse, drew his Beretta, and approached the house.

There was nothing of value inside. Not that he needed food, thanks to Shepherd and Alacrán, but after two lean years he'd developed the finely tuned senses of a scavenger. People appeared to have squatted in the house over the winter. In a shed around back, he discovered what remained of them, more than a dozen bodies, thin and starved. And stinking. He shut the shed door and turned away, fighting nausea and anger.

What kind of world was this? People starving—children, even—and yet in Blister Creek they sat down every night to dinners of roast chicken, potatoes, and gravy. No, they weren't responsible for this crisis, but maybe if people in general weren't so damn selfish there would be enough for everyone.

Kemp came around to where his two horses were grazing on what remained of the front lawn. Even though he'd been changing mounts, three days of riding had left the animals exhausted. Especially the chestnut mare; she could use a day grazing at the lake and resting. And maybe he could spare it; the roadside campfire he'd spotted earlier in the day was two days cold. Even on foot his quarry had made remarkable strides climbing the mountain road. He didn't think he'd catch them before they got to Cedar City on the other side of the mountains. Better to enter the desert well rested.

He eyed the abandoned vehicles in the driveway. Too bad he couldn't drive out of here. But if the inside of the house was scavenged clean, what chance did he have of finding gas in one of the trucks?

Boot prints.

There they were, stomped in the dirt on the driveway. It hadn't rained in a few days and they were still clear. Kemp measured one of his boots against them. He identified at least three different prints, maybe four, one of which belonged to either a woman or a younger boy. He'd bet anything that it belonged to one of the Christianson women. Could be Jacob's sister, or the one who'd drawn a gun on him when he was standing over his mother's dead body.

He drew his gaze up the driveway, where he made an even more startling discovery: a large rectangle on the pavement. It was a cleaner spot where a missing vehicle had sat without moving for months. The vehicle was now missing.

"You bastards. You grabbed a set of wheels, didn't you?" He took a closer look. The other trucks had their gas caps removed. "And enough gas to drive out of here. Damn."

Kemp came around the truck and drew short in surprise. A man jogged down the highway toward the house, coming from the direction

of Cedar City. He wore a light backpack and carried a rifle. He spotted
Kemp and staggered to a halt. He lifted his rifle and fumbled with the
safety. The two men were no more than forty feet apart.

Kemp dropped to one knee as he drew his Beretta. His opponent
was slow to bring his rifle to bear and this gave Kemp a chance to
aim. He snapped off two shots.

The other man collapsed. As he fell, Kemp got a good look at his
face, now contorting in pain. A stranger.

Kemp approached the man warily. He'd seen all manner of tricks
among Islamist militias in the war. The enemy might have a bulletproof vest, be lying there uninjured and waiting, then produce a gun
and blow off Kemp's head when he got too close.

But when Kemp rolled the man over, he forgot those worries. The
man groaned in pain. His hands clutched at his stomach. Kemp
dropped to his knees and pulled away the hands. The man's guts
looked like hamburger meat stirred up with a jar of strawberry jam.

Kemp let out his breath. "Damn it. Why did you draw? I didn't
want to shoot you."

"I didn't know, I—" The man stopped with a grimace.

The man looked to be in his early thirties, with a receding hair-
line and auburn stubble on his chin. Slender, but with loose skin
around his neck like a man who had once been huskier. Sweat
drenched his clothing as if he'd been jogging for some time.

"It didn't have to go this way," Kemp said. "What were you thinking?"

"Thought you were . . . one of the polygs."

"Why would you think—? Wait, are they still up here?"

"Don't know. Escaped."

"You were hunting them?" Kemp asked. "Did they do something? Tell me, I'm not your enemy."

"Thieves. Gibson wants them dead. Please."

"He sent up one guy?"

"There's a reward." He winced. "Need the food. Others searching desert. I thought . . . *help me.*"

Ah, so this man had set off on his own. No doubt the fundamentalists *had* continued west. Christianson's sister was on her way to Los Angeles. But this particular man thought maybe they'd doubled back to the east to lose the pursuit. Not a crazy idea.

What *was* crazy was thinking he'd take them on his own. And on foot so many miles from town. Kemp was one person and had easily taken this man down. What chance would the man have had against the four from Blister Creek? Zero.

Another groan from the injured man. "Don't let me die. Please."

"I'm sorry, I really am. You came around the corner so fast, and then you were drawing your rifle. What was I supposed to do? Man's got to protect himself."

"Need a doctor." His face was turning white with shock.

"The one doctor I know only takes care of his own. He wouldn't help you. And he's a three-day ride from here anyway." Kemp shook his head sadly. "There's nothing I could do."

"I can't die. My kids, if I don't work—"

Kemp couldn't take any more. Before the man could finish that thought, explain why it was so important that he, in particular, live, he sprang to his feet and paced back toward the horses. Behind him, the man stopped talking and cried out in pain.

Dammit. Why?

When Kemp reached his horses, back to grazing now that they'd calmed from the noise of the gunshots, he turned around and looked at the poor fool writhing on the ground. Kemp was no medic, but he'd seen plenty in the war. The man was as good as dead. His body may not know it, may struggle on for an hour or two, but it was inevitable.

He drew his rifle from its holster on the mare's saddle and pulled back the bolt to chamber a round. The M40 had an effective range of almost one thousand feet, but the injured man was only thirty feet away. Kemp didn't bother fishing out the scope. He lifted the rifle to his shoulder.

It's a mercy. It will save him pain.

The man lifted his head to look for Kemp. When he saw the rifle, he stared.

Kemp squeezed the trigger. The 7.62 mm round took off the man's forehead. The rifle shot rolled through the mountains, echoing for several long seconds. The man lay motionless on the ground in a mess of brains and blood.

It was with a heavy heart that Kemp walked back up the road to squat by the dead man and search his possessions. His bag held a canteen and some homemade fruit leather—apricot by the smell of it. A box of shells and two books of matches. A hunting knife in a sheath. And a wallet.

Inside the wallet Kemp found several hundred dollars (worthless), credit cards (worthless), and a Utah driver's license. Andrew La Salle. Thirty-three years old. Five foot eleven, 220 pounds. Two hundred twenty? Not recently.

La Salle. Kemp had a buddy from the army with that name. He hadn't looked anything like this guy, but the name took Kemp back to Iran. The shelling, the gunfire, the death everywhere. He pocketed the wallet and stood looking down at the dead man. What a waste of life.

After a few minutes of consideration, Kemp hoisted La Salle's body over the back of his spare horse and tied him down. It wasn't sentimentality over the shared name with his army buddy that made him do it, and it wasn't guilt. He'd begun to form a plan.

The horse flared its nostrils and danced around before Kemp could calm it. When he had, he retrieved the dead man's rifle, climbed into the saddle of the other horse, and set off again.

★★★

Kemp crossed the summit after dark and fought his way downhill another two miles before stopping for the night. He slept a few yards from the dead body to keep it safe from scavengers. An animal kept snuffling through camp—maybe a bear—and he slept fitfully, his pistol under his bedroll. When he did sleep, he dreamed about his dead buddies from the war: Bentley, Eibling, Harlow. And La Salle, with his round glasses and the harmonica he'd play at night to calm their nerves. He'd been playing that harmonica at the campfire one night when the mortar rounds came flying into the base. One minute La Salle was there, the next there was nothing. Kemp found the man's glasses the next morning about thirty feet away from their campfire. Not broken, not so much as scratched.

The following morning, Kemp discovered that what he'd taken for the top had only been a false summit, and another climb, this time through snow-covered heights, awaited him. It was midmorning before he reached the true summit and late afternoon before he rode down from the foothills into the outskirts of Cedar City. He rounded a switchback and came upon a cemetery with hundreds of fresh graves. Three men with rifles were lurking in the scrub oak and shouted a challenge as he approached.

He dismounted with his hands held high. When they approached and discovered the dead body, he shared a sad story. Kemp had sent La Salle into an abandoned home to forage for food while he checked out the vehicles to see if they had any salvageable fuel. The polygamists had ambushed them and murdered La Salle in cold blood.

The gunmen listened with their faces hardening into skepticism. La Salle they may know, but who the hell was this guy?

"Name is Joe Kemp. I'm an army scout and sniper. Been watching Blister Creek for a long time. I know where they went. Let me talk to Gibson. You let me see him and I swear to God I'll bring these fundies to justice."

CHAPTER FOURTEEN

Jacob was at the cabin at Yellow Flats, trying to raise St. George or Cedar City on the shortwave, when two men came galloping down the dirt road from the direction of the highway. His wife, Fernie, sat at a card table on the porch, transplanting tomato seedlings. Other women and teenagers worked around the property taking plants out of Sister Rebecca's greenhouse or turning spades in the vegetable garden. It was time to take a risk and do some planting. Other women worked at an old-fashioned loom or dipped tallow candles.

Fernie was the first to spot the men on horseback. "Riders!"

Jacob snatched up his rifle and shouted for the women and children to arm themselves. The Kellen boys came running in from the fields, abandoning their plow and mule team. Within moments, the cabin bristled with weapons. Then Rebecca, binoculars raised, called out that it was two of their own. Safeties clicked and rifles lowered.

The only news that came by galloping horse was bad news, so Jacob turned off the radio, which crackled with static, and came down from the porch. Work resumed behind him. The riders stopped near the creek, their horses lathered and blowing, and waited for him to approach. It was Stephen Paul and Jacob's brother David.

David slid out of the saddle and Stephen Paul followed, but stiffly, with a hand at his back. Yesterday, in surgery, Jacob had removed a splinter of wood from the erector spinae muscles in his lower back.

David wiped sweat and dust from his face. "We tried to signal you from the cliffs. I must have flashed fifty times."

Batteries were scarce and Jacob only used the hand radios in an emergency, but they'd worked out a system for flashing mirrors in the daytime, and blinking electric lights at night. From the Ghost Cliffs you could signal the northern edge of the valley (including Yellow Flats), then to the temple spire in the center of town, and from there anywhere in the valley.

"I wasn't watching," he admitted. "I've been on the shortwave trying to get through to Cedar City. What's going on?"

"There are strangers at the reservoir," David said. "Squatters."

The reservoir? That was above the northern edge of the valley, which Jacob had assumed was still sealed by the quarantine.

"We rode up to check out the dam," David continued. "The smaller turbine has been acting funky. We thought we'd have a ride around the reservoir while we were at it."

"That's when we found the camp," Stephen Paul said.

"How many are we talking about?" Jacob asked. "Like Kemp's group?"

David shrugged. "Maybe twice as big? Hard to say. We didn't stick around to count. Two men whipped out guns the moment they caught sight of us."

"You know the old picnic area on the north side?" Stephen Paul said. "They're dug in pretty good. Fishing, hunting. Pitched tents and lean-tos. Someone is building a cabin out of a couple of turned-over wagons."

Jacob let out his breath. Where had they come from? Panguitch was the nearest town to the north, and it had been abandoned since last fall. So had all the ranching and farming communities throughout south central Utah on this side of the mountains. The nearest population center was—where?—the Green River refugee camp? Suddenly, he had his answer.

"Want me to gather the quorum?" Stephen Paul asked. "Most of the men are in town already. I can fetch the others quick enough. We could meet in the temple this afternoon."

"If we do that, Smoot will agitate to send a raiding party and drive them off."

"I'm sure he would," Stephen Paul said. "And maybe he'd be right. Remember what happened with the school bus? Smoot's son is dead, another son missing."

"That was a drone attack, not the fault of the refugees. We told them to leave and they left."

"You *bribed* them to leave," David said. "We can't do that every time."

"No, we can't," Jacob admitted. "And it seems that the quarantine is lifting or these people wouldn't be so close. This might be only the beginning."

"What is today, May thirty-first?" Stephen Paul asked. "It's been four days since the school bus showed up. These squatters at the reservoir have been there at least a week, based on what I saw. I can't figure out what drew them here. It's the middle of nowhere."

"*We* drew them," Jacob said. "Somehow, word is spreading. It must have reached Green River. Look, maybe they only want safety. They know we've cleared out the bandits. Would it kill us to leave them be? They can have all the fish and game they can take—it won't hurt us any. They haven't approached us, haven't asked to enter Blister Creek. Haven't come begging for food."

Stephen Paul took off his gloves and slapped them over his saddle.

"Or maybe they're waiting for their numbers to grow and then they'll force their way in. Like what the Egyptians did to Israel a few months ago."

"First of all, that was three million refugees. This is a few dozen. Besides, the Egyptians failed."

"They failed because the Israelis obliterated their camps," Stephen Paul said. "And we have a few dozen *now*. What about a year from now?"

"We can't let that happen," David said.

Stephen Paul nodded. "The Lord guided our ancestors here and prepared it for our use. We took the desert and made it bloom. The world mocked us, persecuted us. Even our Mormon brothers abandoned us to scorn. But we persisted. For generations we have prepared for this day."

"Whatever else you believe," David said, "this is our sanctuary and home. Our families, our children. If this isn't the time to defend ourselves, when is?"

They made a compelling argument, but Jacob shrank from the implications. A doctor healed, he didn't raise his fist in anger. Yes, circumstances had forced him to act, and he had taken human life before. But even killing his enemy, Taylor Kimball Junior, had delivered equal parts guilt and peace. This? This would be different. This would be Jacob instigating violence.

He turned to David. "What should we do about it?"

His brother frowned. "I—I need to think. If Miriam were here . . ."

"I want your opinion, not hers."

"Stephen Paul is right. We have to root them out. Drive them away."

"Why? Not his thoughts, yours."

"Because the camp will grow. And then it will be harder."

"Trap one rat in the granary today," Stephen Paul said, "or kill a hundred tomorrow."

"That sounds like something my father would have said," Jacob said.

"Or Elder Smoot," David said. He sounded more confident now.

"Or Miriam, or Sister Rebecca, or any of a hundred other people in Blister Creek. What would a doctor say about stopping cancer?"

"Excise the tumor before it metastasizes."

"Exactly. If you don't, the lump grows and you're forced into more aggressive measures. Double the chemo, throw in radiation treatment, cut out more tissue. Practically kill the patient in order to save him. Isn't that about right?"

"Close enough," Jacob said.

Conceding the point was one thing. Contemplating the logistics was another. Jacob imagined galloping in at night with torches like a mob of Ku Klux Klan. Tearing down tents, bashing people with rifle butts. And if the refugees fought back, what then? A battle. Deaths.

"Then we gather the quorum," Stephen Paul said. "If we make it our idea, not Smoot's, we can make sure it's done with a minimum of bloodshed."

He put on his gloves and prepared to hoist himself into the saddle. His horse had been cropping at the grass and gave him a weary look.

Jacob put a hand on his shoulder. "No, wait."

The two men looked at him.

"Before we start a cycle of violence, we try the gentler path."

Stephen Paul looked doubtful. "What do you mean?"

"We have to give them a chance. We'll ask them to leave, first. And warn them of the consequences."

"I get it," David said. "You're going to politely ask the tumor to recede."

"It's not a tumor, it's a camp of human beings. Let's not forget that."

★★★

Still, Jacob needed a proper show of force. Blister Creek had a reputation, earned with bloodshed during the fight to put down the Kimball clan's violent power play. The outside world knew about the gas attacks, the armed assault. Had probably even heard about Jacob's cousin driving a Winnebago packed with explosives into the army base last fall.

Let them see we are strong. Give them something to fear.

No horses. This was the time to burn some of their precious diesel fuel.

Two years earlier, when Jacob's father died at the hand of the Kimballs, Stephen Paul had shown him the dead prophet's final secret: nine hundred thousand gallons of diesel fuel buried in tanks behind the abandoned service station south of town. Abraham Christianson's last preparation to survive the coming of the Great and Dreadful Day of the Lord.

The three men rode out from Yellow Flats to spread the word. That afternoon, twenty-five armed saints met in front of the temple, arriving on foot and on horse. Jacob, David, and Stephen Paul had lined up pickup trucks in the road.

Elder Smoot was the last to arrive. He looked tired and irritable. He dismounted, pushed back the brim of his hat, and studied the trucks through narrowed eyes. "You've been holding out on me, Christianson? Where did you get the fuel?"

"I've been saving a few gallons for an emergency," Jacob said.

"Oh, yeah? Enough to run the plows? Because it's the devil's work doing it behind a mule team."

"No. Not enough for that."

The irony of the fuel was that Jacob didn't dare use it. Didn't dare admit he had it. Only a handful knew it existed. The instant the army suspected, they would send someone in to confiscate it, quarantine or no.

Smoot grunted. He had three of his surviving sons with him. Yesterday evening these men had lowered Bill Smoot into a grave between Bill's grandfather and a brother who had died as an infant. The remains were too charred to dress him in his temple clothing, so the green apron and white robes lay stacked neatly next to him in a simple pine coffin. Ready to put on when Bill Smoot rose on the morning of the first resurrection.

Which, according to the elder Smoot, could be expected any day now.

But if not, Jacob had dryly noted, Smoot was still young, his loins still fruitful. His wives fertile. He had the tools to forge a dozen more sons before he was done. Oh, and maybe a few daughters too. It was all bravado and stoicism in public, but the bags beneath his bloodshot eyes told a different story.

Jacob was risking his own family. His brothers David, Joshua, and Phillip, plus David's second wife, Lillian. Stephen Paul's wife, Carol, had arrived, together with his oldest son. The Johnsons had sent young men, as had the Youngs, the Griggs, and several other families. It was a solid, if zealous group. Rebecca Cowley had ridden out from Grandma Cowley's cabin at Yellow Flats, making her the third and final woman. The party milled about on the temple lawn, waiting for Jacob to speak.

He raised his voice. "You know why we're here. You know what we're doing."

They drew closer, faces grim in the lengthening shadows. Behind them, the red spires of Witch's Warts glowed flaming red with the light of the dying sun.

There were times when it paid to speak as a prophet. Calculatingly, even somewhat cynically, Jacob did so now.

His voice boomed. "We are armed. Not with guns and grenades, but with the sword of truth and the breastplate of righteousness. The forces of Satan cannot stand before us. If they raise arms against the servants of the Lord, we shall cast them down to hell."

He glanced around the group. Stephen Paul looked proud, Smoot impressed. Lillian and many of the younger men stared in awe. Alone among the group, David looked skeptical, one eyebrow raised a fraction of an inch.

Oh yeah? that look said. *Then why do we have guns? Why not march in there unarmed and drive them out in the name of the Lord?*

Jacob folded his arms and bowed his head. The others followed. "Let me ask the Lord's blessing."

He chose his words carefully. This was the part where he needed faith that he simply did not have. Forget his wife's certainty; he'd have settled for Eliza's hopeful longings.

"Our kind and gracious Eternal Father. Thou hast chosen us since the foundation of the earth. Thou hast saved us to be a remnant. Thou knowest the threats of the adversary that gathers against us. Guide our hands. Soften the hearts of our enemies. Let these people depart our lands in peace, that we shall not raise our hands in righteous anger. In the name of Jesus Christ, amen."

"Amen," murmured the group.

"As we lean on the strength of the Lord," Jacob said, "so shall we be protected only as we obey His will. We shall show force, but we shall not exercise it. Thus sayeth the Lord."

This brought a louder "amen," and a few cries of "thou sayest." They loaded the trucks. David asked Jacob if he could have a word. The two brothers stepped away from the group.

"What is it you always tell me?" David asked. "Something about how God's will conveniently matches the desires of people speaking in His name?"

"What was I supposed to do? Tell them to shoot at will?"

"How about asking for genuine guidance?"

"David, one of two things is true. Either God is leading us, or He isn't. If He's not leading us, I've got to do the best I can. If He is, then He knew what He was getting when He chose me. Some people know, some people believe. And some people doubt. I'm a doubter." Jacob eyed his brother. "What about you? Seems like you're changing."

David shrugged. "Miriam and Lillian are strong in their faith. They've been working on me. And you've got to admit that circumstances seem to indicate it's all true."

"Every doomsday cult from Waco to Tehran is convinced of the same thing. That's human nature."

"Never mind that," David said. "What if the squatters fight back? They're hungry, they're desperate. They're convinced we could feed them all if we weren't so damn selfish. What are you going to do then?"

"If they don't listen, we'll escalate. I understand that. I accept it."

The pickups were ready to go, truck beds filled with rifle-toting men and women. People looked expectantly at the brothers, still standing apart and chatting.

"Then it's settled," David said. "If we have to, we use any means necessary."

Jacob didn't answer.

"So what are we waiting for?" David asked.

"You're pulling away, all of you. The doubters are now believers, and the believers are fundamentalists. The fundamentalists have become fanatics. I've lost Miriam, I'm losing Stephen Paul. My own wife is terrified of the outside world and wants it to hurry and collapse so it will all be over. My children pray for God to burn the wicked so they'll leave us alone. Eliza is gone—I need her back. Until she returns, you're all I have left."

David said, "Before you came for me I was a Lost Boy. A drug addict. Father proclaimed me a failure and I believed it. You brought me home. You saved my life. I would follow you into hell itself."

"I don't want you to follow me to hell. I want you to listen to my doubts. I want you to use reason and not faith. That's how we'll survive this."

"I know you're a man with human weaknesses. Dude, you're my brother—of course you're not perfect." David gripped him by the shoulders. "But God has whispered into my heart. I doubted before. I don't anymore. You are the prophet. You are the One Mighty and Strong."

No, I'm not.

David turned to climb into the back of one of the trucks. All but the first one started up with the familiar, yet by now so rare sound of rumbling diesel engines.

Jacob cast a longing glance at the sandstone maze of fins and spires behind the temple. How easy it would be to walk into Witch's Warts and disappear. Then emerge from the other side and make his way to the mountains. Leave all this behind.

In spite of his lofty words, his attempts to mold the others into a peaceful army, he knew the truth. The moment he climbed behind the wheel, he would set them down a terrible path.

But if he felt unsure, he didn't dare show it. So he straightened his shoulders and walked with long, confident steps until he reached the lead pickup truck. Stephen Paul sat in the passenger side with an assault rifle across his lap. He handed Jacob the keys, which were received without comment. Moments later they were rolling north toward the reservoir.

As they did, Jacob said a silent prayer.

I don't know if you're listening. Chances are, you don't exist. But if you do, if you are listening, please spare us bloodshed.

CHAPTER FIFTEEN

Jacob and his companions drove into the Ghost Cliffs to search for the squatters' camp. The speed of travel stunned him. Over the past year the valley seemed to have grown. The distances, which he'd once measured in minutes—ten minutes to the grain silos, thirty to the Young ranch—had stretched now that those same miles needed to be covered on horseback, foot, or bicycle. You noticed details at those speeds that you never would when zipping along in an air-conditioned cocoon. Colors, smells. The feel of gravel beneath your boot.

And there was time to think.

He had none of that now. Instead, he sat in a truck filled with grim-faced men and women. The other trucks held the same. Give them orders and they would kill and be killed according to his will. His father had relished that sort of power. Jacob feared and mistrusted it.

Long shadows stretched from the cottonwood trees to lean over the reservoir, which was so high that it crept almost to the road.

Clouds of bugs hovered over the water, and leaping trout drew circles across its surface. Jacob felt a pang that he wasn't coming up here with his kids to drop their lines into the water and wait for the telltale tug and the dip of bobbers as fish hit their bait.

Right now the only people fishing these waters were the hungry refugees on the far side.

Let them. Why couldn't they stay, taking what they could from the land, until the crisis passed? Blister Creek didn't need fish and game to survive. So long as these people stayed above the valley, the two sides could live and let live.

By the time they hooked around the reservoir and came upon the squatter camp on the other side, Jacob was calmer and more determined than ever to find a peaceful solution. And so his first glimpse of the camp was a slap across the face.

Occupying a wedge of land maybe five acres in size between the highway and the reservoir, it was bigger than he'd expected, dozens of tents and lean-tos.

The site was an old picnic area, now trashed. They'd chopped down the hundred-year-old cottonwoods that had provided shade. On the other side of the road they'd hacked a gash through the trees a hundred yards into the forest, a wound marked by broken branches and snapped-off pine boughs. Limbs and sticks marked a path across the road. And what a mess: empty cans strewn about, torn tarps flapping in the breeze, strips of corrugated metal, piles of deer bones and hides. They'd dug their latrine too close to the reservoir. When he rolled down the window, he could smell the long, filthy trench.

A bonfire lit either end of the camp, together with half a dozen cookfires that sent smoky trails into the sky. People tossed logs onto the bonfires, which roared eight, ten feet high.

"Blasted fools," Stephen Paul said. "Haven't they ever heard of wildfires?"

Where were the children? Jacob couldn't spot more than a handful. Hiding? Dead of starvation? Abandoned on the road? And if the refugees had brought any animals—horses, chickens, dogs—they were nowhere in sight. Probably devoured, based on the starving look of the squatters. Some of these people must have owned horses at one time, because there were wagons and trailers and no vehicles to tow them.

Jacob parked the truck in the highway. The other vehicles stopped behind him. The people from Blister Creek unloaded. They passed around boxes of shells.

The squatters spotted the newcomers and came streaming toward the highway, shouting, calling for others. More poured out of tents. Soon, a hundred people were descending on them. Fearful murmurs rippled through the saints.

"Steady," Jacob warned. "You!" he shouted as the leading refugees reached him. "Stay back."

A number of the squatters had armed themselves with guns, knives, metal pipes, and branches cut into clubs, but most came running with buckets, empty jugs, and burlap sacks. They were looking for handouts, he realized.

They ignored his orders and pressed in, hands outstretched. Begging, pleading for food. A woman grabbed Jacob's wrist, screeching that she was first. Stephen Paul pushed her back, but not before her long, dirty nails dug a painful scratch into Jacob's skin. The saints formed a tighter and tighter knot around the trucks.

"Is it time?" Smoot said.

"Steady," Jacob warned. He pushed at a man with a bucket. "Get back. Don't touch me."

He drew his pistol and fired twice into the air. The noise died. The squatters drew back onto the shoulder of the highway.

"Listen to me! We have no food for you. We're not here to give handouts."

"You have food, you liar," a woman cried.

He tried to identify the speaker. He thought it came from the woman who'd scratched him. Her light-brown hair was so filthy and matted it had almost become dreadlocks. She glared at him, eyes bloodshot and watering from behind hollow cheekbones.

"That's right," she said when he met her gaze. "Look at you, bunch of greedy bastards. Stuffing your faces while we starve on fish bones and grasshoppers."

"Feed us!" someone cried. The clamor started up again and Jacob lifted his gun skyward. The noise died again.

He whispered to David, who had sidled up to him, "Mark the ones with guns. If it turns violent, they're the ones to worry about."

David nodded and eased through the crowded saints to pass the word.

Had Stephen Paul and David said a hundred squatters? There were at least twice that many packed together, ready to surge at the truck. More lingered at the back. Tension vibrated through the mob. They might go off at any time.

"You can stay at the reservoir," he said. "But the moment you come down those cliffs, you will be shot. Do you understand?"

Murmurs, both from the squatters and from his own side.

"All we want is food!" someone shouted.

"You won't get it. We won't feed you. So if that's what you're expecting, turn around and go back."

"Go back where?"

Jacob didn't answer this question. "But you're welcome to stay up here. Fish, hunt. But I'm warning you, there's only death for you in the valley. We can defend ourselves. And we will."

"*Now* you can," said the woman who'd scratched him. "How about when the rest of us arrive? You can't fight us all off."

"What do you mean, the rest?"

"Don't play dumb. You know where we came from. The Green River camp. Everyone there knows you're hoarding food. You could feed half the country if you weren't so damn selfish."

The shouts started up again. People banged their buckets.

It wasn't the impossible notion that Blister Creek could feed crowds of hungry refugees that caught Jacob. It was the fear that the refugees in Green River thought it could. His wife had spent time at the camps last fall and described the government-run refugee camp as a vast city of plywood and corrugated metal. Tens of thousands strong and growing with every refugee-filled train.

"That's ridiculous. We don't have that kind of food. Who told you we did?"

More shouts of anger, more banging buckets.

"The army stopped feeding the camp," the woman said when the noise died down. "You either starve to death or you go look for food. Most are coming here. We're only the first. The strong ones. The rest will be here soon."

Green River was in the eastern part of the state, across the inhospitable terrain of the Colorado Plateau. Across deserts and mountain ranges that offered little food, and were torn by war and infested with bandits. If what this woman said was true, most of the refugees would die before they came within a hundred miles of Blister Creek. But there were two hundred people standing in front of him that proved it could be done. Even one person in ten getting through was too many. One in a hundred, too many.

"And that's just the start," the woman said. "They'll be coming from Salt Lake, from Denver, from Las Vegas. Everyone knows. You'll have a million people here by the end of the summer. So you have no choice. Either you start feeding us now, or we'll wait until there are enough of us and we overwhelm you."

"I told you—" Jacob began.

"Our numbers are doubling every day," the woman said. "You do the math."

"And a plague of locusts did fall upon the land of Egypt," Stephen Paul murmured.

Jacob looked at his own people. Anger in their eyes. And fear. They were ready. One word from his mouth and it would be a massacre. Kill them all, then burn their camp. Then man the bunkers and hold out against the quarantine, the plague of refugees. Mow them down until they stopped coming.

What choice did he have? He had to protect the valley for his wife, his children, his brothers and sisters, his cousins, uncles, aunts. His people. Every man, woman, and child in Blister Creek counted on him. He had to drive these invaders away, or watch his own people die of disease and starvation.

And he still couldn't do it. He couldn't kill these refugees in cold blood. If that was the will of the Lord, then the Lord had chosen the wrong man. Jacob lifted his hand to order the others back into their trucks.

And that's when his eyes drifted toward the shore of the reservoir. Two yellow pesticide drums sat in the shallows, lapped by the gentle waves. Six more lay side by side higher up the bank. Fish heads and guts sloshed up on shore, where people had been cleaning their catch and tossing the entrails back into the water.

Except they weren't catching the fish so much as poisoning them. That's what the pesticide was. The refugees must have found chemicals at the abandoned farms of central Utah and hauled them south to the reservoir. Where they promptly dumped them into the water to wait for fish to float to the surface.

The same water that circulated through the reservoir. That came down the creek into the valley. That irrigated the fields and replenished the wells throughout the valley. The water they drank. And these people were poisoning it.

Why should they care? They drank from the creek upstream, not the reservoir like Blister Creek. And they were hungry—this was the quickest way to get fish.

Two drums used, six more to go.

This cannot stand. There is no reasoning with these people. There is no compromise.

"Enough," Jacob said. Then, in a louder voice, "Enough!" He glared at the crowd of refugees. "You will clear out of here. All of you. We will return in the morning, and if you are not gone—"

He hadn't fully formed his threat when a gunshot rang out. Suddenly, refugees were screaming and diving for cover. Others surged forward, lifting weapons, fists, hunks of rock, or strips of rubber tires. A bullet whizzed past his head. Another smacked into the side of his truck.

David dragged Jacob back. Then he jumped forward and lowered his assault rifle. He emptied the magazine on full auto. Other saints dropped to one knee or took cover behind truck bumpers. Jacob looked for the enemy who'd fired the shots, but the refugees were already in full retreat, and he couldn't pick out what had happened.

"Hold your fire!" Jacob shouted.

The gunfire ceased. At least a dozen refugees lay bleeding in the dirt. One woman, her jaw shot off, tried to lift herself off the ground. Jacob holstered his pistol and started toward her.

Stephen Paul and David dragged him back.

"Let me go."

"You can't," David said.

"I'm a doctor. I have to. Damn it, let go!"

Elder Smoot tossed his rifle into the back of a truck and came up to lend his aid in holding Jacob's arms; he had almost torn himself free. Smoot threw his arms around Jacob and the three men pinned him against the truck.

"Listen to me," Stephen Paul said. "Brother Jacob, in the name of the Lord, listen!"

Jacob gave up the struggle. He knew what his counselor was going to say. Knew he was right. And couldn't stand it. The sound of men and women crying for help, only yards away . . .

"We have to go," Stephen Paul said, "or there will be more shooting, more deaths."

Jacob looked to David, his brother's face inches from his own. Compassion and sorrow showed in David's eyes. Then he looked to Smoot. Righteous anger there, determination. Smoot must be itching to drive forward, to finish it now. Ten minutes of killing and the camp would be no more. Let it stand as a lesson to others who might come. They would find no sanctuary here.

The squatters down by the shore had broken into two groups. The first kept fleeing, running around the edge of the reservoir for the woods on the far side. They were mostly women and older men, together with a handful of children. The second group was mostly younger men who dove into tents or took refuge behind piles of firewood. Preparing for battle.

A few feet away, David's wife Lillian fired a shot. A man emerging from a tent fell to the ground, a pistol in hand.

Jacob cast a final, anguished look at the injured people on the ground. None of them were his own. Then he gave orders to retreat.

CHAPTER SIXTEEN

Eliza was leading her companions across a desolate salt plain when a dull rumbling disturbed the quiet. It was late on the first full day west of Cedar City. Shallow, briny ponds glittered across the flats, a sight that was unusual for this late in the year. The wind had been moaning over the desert most of the day, but had recently died, leaving an eerie quiet, disturbed only by the muffled steps of the horses. The sun glared overhead and the salt left lips chapped. Nobody talked.

The rumbling sounded at first like the roll of distant thunder, but the sky was clear and still. The ground shook. The horses pranced and snorted.

Grover had been half-dozing in the saddle and the first buck of his horse nearly sent him flying to the ground. He fought to control the animal. "What the devil?"

Eliza ignored him, looking skyward.

Three fighter planes roared overhead. Racing along a few thousand feet above the ground, they kept in formation as they approached the next range, then split as they climbed to clear the mountains. Something whooshed through the air after them. A missile, fired by some unseen foe. There was a tremendous flash, followed several seconds later by a boom that rolled across the salt flats. Something spiraled out of the sky. Nobody saw where it landed.

Later that day they came upon a jet engine half-buried in the salt plain. A scorch mark stretched along the ground like a smudge of ash from a giant's thumb. A hundred yards farther they found a section of fuselage.

Eliza suggested they look for the pilot, thinking he might have escaped.

Miriam narrowed her eyes. "No way are we wasting our water wandering the flats on some foolish search and rescue."

"We have plenty of water," Eliza said. "And there's fresh water in the hills. We're almost across—an hour or two, tops."

"Then there's food. And time. This pilot is probably our enemy anyway."

"I hate to sound callous," Trost said, "but Miriam has a point. What are we looking at, a hundred square miles? You really want to burn a day or two looking for this guy? Is he even alive? I didn't see a parachute."

Reluctantly, Eliza agreed to continue. It was hard to say why she wanted to help the pilot anyway. Maybe only to do something altruistic in a world that had turned red with blood. So much killing. So much suffering.

Or maybe she was harboring delusions that the pilot would help them. She would save his life, and he would in turn lead them to his Air Force base. The general would praise her for saving his best pilot, then radio his contacts. They would find Steve for her, would even fly her in a secret mission across enemy territory. There would be a joyful reunion. Then the Air Force would fly them home to Blister Creek and safety.

Ridiculous.

They escaped from the salt plains around dusk, then found a dirt road that led west over the mountains. When one of the horses almost broke its leg in a cattle guard, Eliza decided it was dark enough to find a camping spot to wait out the night. Dinner was the last of the dried peas stolen from Cedar City, together with a rattlesnake clubbed over the head, stripped of its skin, and roasted on a stick. It didn't taste like chicken.

One of her traps caught a rabbit in the night. Not a cottontail, unfortunately, which were common in the foothills and pretty tasty, but a jackrabbit. By the time the others roused themselves, she'd skinned it, rubbed it with salt gathered the previous day on the flats, and cooked it in the coals. It was muscular, gamey, and frankly disgusting to eat for breakfast. Nobody complained.

When they'd broken camp, saddled the horses, and set off on the dirt road again, Trost caught up with her. The others were twenty or thirty yards back. "I've been thinking."

"Happy thoughts, I hope. I've been dreaming about raspberry pie and homemade ice cream."

A smile touched the corners of his mouth, breaking momentarily the pinched look the others—and Eliza supposed she, as well—had been wearing the past few days. "We're in Nevada, right?"

"Crossed over yesterday, I think," she said. "If not, we will be soon."

"We can't just hoof it across Nevada, then slog our way through Death Valley. I know we've been lucky on water, with how wet it's been, but what about food?"

"What about it?"

"I'm hungry, and I know you are too. We all are. We've got maybe six ounces of powdered milk left and a handful of walnuts. Miriam was raiding a bare cupboard, if you know what I mean."

"I figure we'll scavenge our way across."

"Seriously?"

"What, rabbits and rattlesnakes aren't doing it for you?"

"You got lucky this morning, if you can call eating an oversized jumping rat lucky. And that snake last night wasn't more than a bony mouthful. I'm not putting down your ability to forage, but it's limited."

She felt a little defensive at this and nudged her horse forward. "The Paiute could survive out here. It can be done. My ancestors—"

"Yeah, mine were settlers too. Go back a hundred and fifty years and we're talking about the same people. They knew how to live off the land. But we're not Paiute, and we're not pioneers. Second, we're not staying put long enough to do serious foraging. It's whatever we catch on the run."

"What I'm hoping is to spot a deer or find an abandoned flock of sheep," Eliza said. "One shot, a couple hours butchering and cooking and curing with salt, and we'll have all the meat we need."

"And if we don't find anything?"

Eliza shifted in the saddle to meet his gaze as he caught up again. "I take it you have a suggestion."

"Las Vegas."

"It's a war zone."

"I know."

"Babylon. It is doomed to destruction."

"Eventually, maybe," he said. "Right now it has thousands of refugees, two armies, people coming and going. Total chaos. It's a good place to resupply."

"It's a good place to get killed. That's what 'total chaos' means."

"We don't have to enter the city itself. We only have to join the refugees and take what we need."

"Now you're sounding like Miriam," Eliza said.

"So are you, with that Babylon stuff."

"Touché."

"And maybe she's right," he said. "You have to admit, she got us out of Cedar City. Horses, guns, food. So, Las Vegas?"

Eliza glanced over her shoulder. Miriam and Grover were catching up on their horses, and she didn't want Miriam to jump in on this conversation. This was Eliza's decision to make, not her sister-in-law's.

"I'll think about it. We don't need to decide until we hit Highway 93. Probably tomorrow."

She eyed the next distant, shimmering range, and wondered if they could reach it by sundown, then spurred her horse so she could ride ahead for a stretch, alone in her thoughts.

***

Eliza was tired, and let the miles drift by as she slumped in the saddle. It was hard to maintain attention for hour after hour, day after day. And Gibson and his thugs in Cedar City might be angry, but they'd clearly given up the chase.

They were traveling in the open, right down the highway, and figured that four armed riders would deter casual banditry. And what were the odds of running into the army way out here in the boondocks?

Eliza was hungry. She'd been hungry since Joe Kemp shoved them out of the school bus. At first it wasn't much different than fasting. The first Sunday of the month, members of the church would go without food for twenty-four hours as a spiritual exercise. Accompanied by prayer and scripture study, it was supposed to bring one closer to the spirit.

It never worked for Eliza, not from the time she was baptized at eight and forced to begin fasting with the adults. For those twenty-four hours every month she would obsess over food and feel resentful. Sometimes, as a child, she'd sneak into the pantry when nobody was looking. In a house filled with two dozen kids, that was no easy task. And later, if fast Sunday came during her period, she would grow irritable, her blood sugar low and her energy flagging. This was like that, only day after day.

They had a little bit of food, and it was enough to keep her going, if not to cut the incessant gnawing in her belly. But since trapping the jackrabbit the previous day, she had eaten six prickly pear fruits, a toasted scorpion, and a single bite from a kangaroo rat Grover had dug out of its burrow and roasted on a stick.

Kemp had thrown them from his bus on May 28. It was now the third of June. Hunger was a constant companion. What she wouldn't give for a nice venison steak. But they saw no deer. No sheep. Not even a jackrabbit. Not that she'd fire the deer rifle at a rabbit. In this quiet, thin air, the sound would travel for miles. She'd only risk that for real game.

It was hunger that finally drove her to accept Trost's plan to approach Las Vegas. Miriam was all too happy to agree. Theft? Preying on refugees? Why not?

They'd hooked south on Highway 93, which slid down to Route 317, and then on to Las Vegas. Sagebrush and hillocks blackened with volcanic tuff stretched on either side of the highway. It wasn't great terrain for deer, but food was all she could think about, so she kept scanning the terrain. She was certainly not thinking about security.

Something glinted from one of the ridges ahead of them. It came from straight down the highway several hundred yards, then off to the right maybe a hundred feet. A mirror? A shiny bit of wreckage?

Eliza turned to Miriam. "See that glinting thing? What is that?"

"What do you mean?"

"Right there, on that rise." Eliza lifted her arm to point.

"Sniper!" Miriam screamed. "Everyone off the road."

Even as she said this, the former FBI agent was drawing her rifle with one hand, sliding from the saddle, and diving for the runoff ditch on the side of the highway opposite the hill with the sniper. Eliza had the presence of mind to grab her own rifle before she dropped from the saddle. She shielded herself with her horse as she scrambled after Miriam.

Both Trost and Grover were on the move too, with the older man slightly slower in his reaction. Grover got down and came after the two women. A gunshot split the air.

A horse screamed. It was Trost's, and he'd yet to dismount. He pitched forward over the animal's head as it lurched to its knees and landed awkwardly on the road with his left forearm extended. Eliza and Grover reached up from the ditch and grabbed his ankle, then dragged him back. A bullet slammed into the pavement, then ricocheted over Eliza's head. Just above them, Trost's horse was bleeding from one shoulder and struggled to its feet before running off after the other three animals.

The four companions crouched in the brush, where the raised roadbed shielded them from the sniper. It was quiet.

"Dammit," Trost groaned.

He slumped against the gravel embankment leading up to the shoulder of the highway. His face was pale, and he clutched his left forearm. Eliza crawled over and unbuttoned his shirt at the wrist, then rolled it up. One of the bones between his elbow and wrist bulged out, almost, but not quite breaking the skin.

"Your arm is broken," Grover said.

Trost spoke through clenched teeth. "Thank you, I never would have noticed." He pulled away from Eliza. "Worry about that sniper. I'll be fine."

"You're sure?"

"Time enough later." He swallowed hard. "Not much of a shot, was he?"

"We have no way of knowing," Miriam said. "He was probably waiting for us to get up that rise. The ground is flatter, with nowhere to hide. He could have picked us off one by one as we ran for cover." She looked at Grover. "Where's your shotgun?"

"On the saddle. I didn't have a chance to grab it."

"Oh, that's nice. And there's your horse over there, halfway to the hills. What else have we got?"

"I've got the Glock," Trost said.

He leaned to show the pistol Miriam had lifted from one of Gibson's guards, which was still holstered to his side. Miriam reached over and unbuckled the holster, then put it on herself.

Eliza showed her rifle. "It's loaded."

"Mine is too," Miriam said. "That leaves us a dozen shells and a dozen more bullets in the pistol."

"Not much for a shootout," Eliza said.

"No. I wish we knew what we were dealing with."

Grover pulled something out of the dirt. "Does this help?"

It was a bullet, presumably the one that had ricocheted off the pavement from the sniper's second shot. It was impressive that he'd spotted it among the bits of broken glass, lead wheel weights, and plastic drink rings that had collected in the brush off the side of the road.

"Nice job, Grover," Miriam said. "I knew there was a reason we didn't eat you when the food ran low. Let me see that."

The boy still looked shaken, and his hand trembled as he held out the bullet. Miriam turned it over, then held it up to her eye. Calm and steady. Eliza felt her racing heart slowing.

"It's a 7.62," Miriam said. "Most likely a sniper rifle. Lovely."

"So he's with the army," Trost said. "What's he doing out here?"

"He's got a military rifle," Miriam said. "That's not necessarily the same thing. But these days, I wouldn't rule it out either. Lone sniper might be all they can afford to guard this road."

"How do you know he's alone?" Grover asked.

Miriam pocketed the bullet. "If there were two shooters, we'd be dead. What do you think, six, seven hundred yards?"

Eliza thought about the flash of reflected sunlight. "Seems about right."

"So we're well within his range," Miriam said. "Unfortunately, we can't make the same claim."

Eliza was still thinking about who might be shooting at them. "I don't see how it's the army. Why would they shoot at random travelers?"

"Maybe they wouldn't," Miriam said. "We don't know anything yet. And I don't much care. Whoever it is, I want him dead."

That was all great, but here they were, short on weapons and ammo, and Trost with a broken arm.

"We may be at a tactical disadvantage," Miriam said, "but we're not four random idiots. We know how to shoot, how to defend ourselves. And we are God's chosen people. We wear His garment, which is a shield and a protection."

Had Miriam forgotten Eliza's father, murdered by Elder Kimball? The Lord's own prophet, cut down by his enemy. The undergarments hadn't stopped a bullet then, so why would they now?

But Miriam wasn't speaking for her benefit, Eliza realized as her sister-in-law sized up Grover. "You received your endowments in the temple last month, Brother Grover," Miriam said. "You exchanged covenants with the Lord."

Grover licked his lips. When he spoke, he sounded a little stronger. "Yes, I did. What do you need me to do?"

Miriam examined the two rifles and handed over the 30.06 to Grover. It was a type of gun he must have fired hundreds of times.

"You're going to shoot this gun at that sniper."

"That's a really long shot."

"You don't have to hit him. You probably can't, not from this distance. And he's well concealed—you can count on that. So you have no hope of out-dueling him. Try that, and you'll die. Your head will stick up a little, then he'll fix you in his high-powered scope and blast a gaping hole from one end of your skull to the next."

"Then I don't understand. What am I trying to do?"

"You need to take plausible enough shots that it will draw his attention. While you're doing that, Eliza and I are going to flank him. Send his miserable soul speedily unto hell."

Eliza's stomach dropped.

"And me?" Trost asked.

"You make sure Grover doesn't get killed. Find him some rocks and have him push them onto the shoulder. He can shield his gun. Grover, do not stick your head up. Do not look for the sniper."

"Okay, I won't."

"Trost, are you still wearing that old watch? Good, you keep time. Ten minutes, then Grover fires the first shot. After that, count the minutes. One shot every sixty seconds."

"How about if Grover makes me a rock shield, then keeps time while I do the shooting?" Trost said.

Miriam shook her head. "No. Stick with the plan."

"Eliza, don't you think so? Tell her."

"Listen to Miriam," Eliza said. "She knows what she's talking about."

Trost persisted. "I know I'm injured, but I've got steady nerves. I could do it."

"No," Miriam said. "And that's final. Do you understand?"

He stared back. "Fine."

"Listen to me, both of you," Miriam said. "The man who sticks his head up dies. I cannot emphasize that enough. A fraction of an inch above the road, and it's over. Do not do it."

Miriam pulled out the magazine of the Glock to count the bullets, then returned the pistol to her holster. She looked at Eliza. "Ready?"

"Not really."

"If it makes you feel better, neither am I. Come on."

CHAPTER SEVENTEEN

Eliza felt surprisingly calm as Miriam led her south behind the shoulder of the road, first at a crawl, then at a crouch as the ditch dropped lower below the road surface.

It was training, she supposed. All those hours with Miriam, Lillian, and Rebecca at Yellow Flats. Shooting, running through scenarios. Some of the scenarios were not so different from this one.

Miriam brought her about two hundred yards south of where they'd left Grover and Trost. "Look up ahead. See the culvert? That's how we're getting across."

A pipe about thirty inches in diameter ran beneath the highway, carrying the wash from one side to the other. The spring flooding must have overflowed the culvert, because the asphalt above it slumped and appeared ready to fall away completely.

"How did you know we'd find a culvert?" Eliza asked.

"I scanned the terrain before I dove off the road."

While drawing her rifle and shouting a warning to the others? Sure, why not?

"You're so confident," Eliza said. "I wish I felt the same."

"It doesn't do any good to show fear. Hurts me, hurts my companions. But I do feel pretty good, yeah. Guess you could call it confidence."

"I don't suppose you have any tips, do you?"

"You're like your brother, you know. Jacob is self-deprecating too. It makes me want to tear out my hair, makes me even doubt him. But when the shooting starts, he's cool and collected. So are you. You'll do fine."

"I hope so."

"Do you remember what happened in Colorado City last fall?" Miriam asked.

"I wasn't there, but I heard. You and Steve went up against those bandits."

"Believe me, it was more dire than this. It was dark, which helped, and we had night vision, which our enemies did not. That helped a lot more. But those enemies were a small army. This is one guy. He doesn't know what's about to hit him. He has no idea who we are."

"You have no way of knowing that," Eliza said. "Lots of people know we're out here—Kemp's group, Cedar City, maybe even the guys flying the drones."

"Last fall I was in a bad place," Miriam continued, without addressing Eliza's point. "My confidence was shaken. I think it was the pregnancy. And I was having nightmares about the Kimball cult hiding in those old missile silos. But when I got into action everything fell away. My body did what it was supposed to. It will this time too. So will yours."

They reached the culvert. The flow was no more than a trickle, and didn't make it ten feet from the pipe before disappearing into the sand. The inside of the culvert was damp and cool and just wide enough to squirm into.

Eliza bit down her claustrophobia, slung the rifle over her shoulder, and entered on her belly. She focused on the dim light at the far side and inched forward. Miriam came in behind her. When Eliza reached the end, Miriam grabbed her ankle to hold her up.

"What do you see?" Miriam asked.

"More of the same—brush, rocks, sand."

"Can you see the sniper's hill?"

"No."

"Good, then he can't see us either. Stick your head out. Then tell me what you see."

Eliza leaned out. She could see the hill now, but only the far western shoulder, as the road curved ahead to get around the rocky outcrop. It was about a hundred yards away now. An easy shot for any reasonably competent marksman, if he somehow had a view of this position. She described it to Miriam.

"You'll have to risk it," Miriam said. "Go."

They popped out of the culvert and then hugged up against the highway. After a moment, Miriam proclaimed their position safe. Eliza's knees and shirtsleeves were wet and sand clung to her wet boots. She brushed off the rifle.

"See those boulders at the foot of the hill?" Miriam said. "Look, there's a magpie sitting on the tallest one."

"I see them."

"That's good cover. We'll hide behind there. When you run, pay attention to your surroundings. We'll make another plan when we get there."

"When do we go? Now?"

"Not yet. Wait for Grover's first shot. That'll be what? Three, four more minutes, I think."

This surprised Eliza. She would have guessed that it had already been ten minutes. "What if the sniper spots us running for the rocks?" she asked.

"Most likely he will. But if I'm right, he's got his gun on a tripod. And if Trost did what I asked, Grover has been pushing rocks onto the shoulder. The sniper is watching. By now he's probably had a dozen shots at that kid's hands and arms. He's disciplined. He's held back."

How chilling to imagine a sniper blowing off one of Grover's hands. And chilling to know that Miriam had risked it. All her warnings about sticking one's head above the roadbed held equally for other body parts. What if Miriam had guessed wrong about the man's discipline?

"Most likely, he'll see us running," Miriam continued. "But Grover's shot will force his attention. No way does he get his gun turned around to shoot at us before we've taken cover."

"Assuming there's only one gunman."

"Yes, assuming. I'd better be right about that."

Grover's rifle fired. The two women had been waiting in a crouch, like runners ready to break from the starting blocks, and Miriam was off in an instant. Eliza scrambled to keep up.

The ground between the culvert and the pair of boulders was sandy and gave poor footing. They struggled to build up speed. Eliza tensed herself for an answering shot from the sniper. A sharp, searing pain in the lungs, then she'd go down. The shot never came. Moments later, the two women sat gasping in the cover of the boulders.

"Wait," Miriam said. "Don't do anything. Not yet."

The sun was dipping west and directed its full force against the flat surface of the black volcanic tuff. It radiated heat like a stone plucked from the coals of a fire. Sweat trickled down Eliza's brow. She wished she'd had time to grab a canteen before jumping from her horse.

"The sun is our friend," Miriam said. "It's shining in his eyes. I like our odds better now."

Another gunshot from Grover's rifle. It rolled over the desert. Still no answer from the sniper.

"Is he gone?" Eliza asked.

"I doubt it. Okay, here's what we do. On top of the hill there's a knob that looks like a huge nose. You saw it?"

Eliza shook her head.

"You didn't? I told you to pay attention. What were you doing?"

"Running for my life."

"There's a knob. It's the best feature for a sniper to use as cover."

Another gunshot.

"Next shot we go. The instant Grover fires, you stand up and you shoot at that knob. Keep firing until you empty your magazine. Take your time. Aim."

Eliza swallowed hard.

"Listen to me," Miriam continued. "I'm making a run up that hill and I need that shooter off my butt."

"Got it."

Except Miriam had given a stern warning to Grover to keep his head down. To *not* aim. Eliza would be aiming and shooting, again and again. And closer to the sniper. But at how much greater risk to Miriam, sprinting in the open toward the hill? Not to mention the risk of friendly fire from Grover and Eliza.

But now Eliza understood Miriam's strategy. Two rifles firing at the hill from different angles. They would force the sniper to keep his head down. And while he was ducking, Miriam would overrun his position and put a couple of bullets in his head.

Eliza waited, cooking in the sun. She tightened her grip on the rifle with sweating hands. Miriam squatted beside her with the pistol held firmly in her grip, her breathing slow and fluid. She stared at the ground without blinking. It was like she'd entered a trance.

Grover fired.

Eliza didn't wait to see if Miriam would run, but jumped up with the rifle. It took her a second to identify the nose-like protrusion from among the other rocks, boulders, and humps sprouting along the hill. When she found it, there was nothing to give it away as the sniper's blind, no twinkle of reflected light off a scope, no rifle muzzle jutting out. Trusting Miriam, she fired, her aim a few inches to the right of the knob. A puff of dust rose up where her bullet struck.

A figure raced up the hillside on the right edge of Eliza's peripheral vision. Miriam. Eliza chambered another round, aimed to the left of the knob this time, and fired again. The rifle kicked against her shoulder. No sign of movement. A few seconds longer and she fired again, back to the right. Grover also fired.

Finally, the sniper answered. A hollow thump from his rifle, distinct from the other guns as the fire was suppressed. Not shooting at Eliza; she'd be dead. She fired again. Miriam was straight in front of her now, scrambling up the hillside, but partially shielded from the gunman by the hill itself. Unless the sniper rose to his feet, he'd never get at her. And Eliza saw no movement.

Suddenly, Grover was popping off shots. Eliza looked carefully for movement, then fired again. Miriam disappeared behind the rocky protrusion. Grover kept shooting.

"Hold your fire!" Miriam screamed a moment later. "Eliza, tell that idiot—"

Grover didn't stop.

"Grover!" Eliza shouted. She was midway between Miriam on the hill and Grover and Trost where they'd jumped off the highway. "Stop shooting."

But apparently he couldn't hear. When he finally stopped—most likely because he was out of ammo—Miriam rose from behind the rock, ran to the edge of the hillock, and fired her pistol several times down the highway to the south, out of Eliza's view.

Miriam turned around and shielded her eyes to look against the sun toward Eliza. Even a hundred yards away, her disgust was clear as she shoved her pistol into her holster and came back down the hill.

Behind them, Grover came running down the highway, waving his arms. "Over here! Help."

"Shut up, you idiot," Miriam yelled. "If you hadn't been shooting off your gun—"

"It's Trost. He's hurt."

CHAPTER EIGHTEEN

Trost wasn't hurt. He was dead. He lay on his back in the dirt, with his lifeblood spilling out of a gaping wound in his skull. His body was still twitching, his chest still taking shallow gasps. His fingers clenched and unclenched on the ground. But the light was fading from his open eyes. He was dead already, even if his body hadn't realized it yet.

Eliza couldn't turn away from the horrific sight. Miriam muttered something unintelligible and angry-sounding.

"Aren't you going to do anything?" Grover asked. His voice was pleading, his face stricken and pale. Another moment and Eliza thought he'd be sick.

"Turn away, Grover," she said. She put her hands on his shoulders and flipped him around to stare back toward the highway.

Then she bent, took off Trost's hat, and put it over the man's face. He twitched a few more times and lay still. His body relaxed. It was as if his spirit was visibly taking leave of his body, shucking it off like a glove.

"Say a prayer," Miriam urged.

"Father in heaven," Eliza said. "Into thy hands we commend this man's spirit. He was not of our church, but he was thy true and faithful servant. Welcome Brother Trost into thy arms. Let him stand by your right side, raise him up on the morning of the first resurrection."

"Amen," Miriam murmured.

Grover tried to say the same, but it came out in a shuddering sob. He turned around, but didn't look at the dead body. "Shouldn't it have been me praying? Because, you know, I have the priesthood."

"You've done enough," Miriam said. Her voice was cold enough to freeze the roasting pavement.

"It's not his fault," Eliza said.

"Isn't it? Why is Trost dead, and not Grover? Because Trost was the one shooting the gun, that's why. I gave clear orders. And this coward—"

"I'm not a coward. I was the one shooting at the end. That was me."

"But you weren't at the gun at first, were you? That's what I told you to do. You only got behind the gun when Trost went down."

"He *made* me," Grover said. "I tried to do it, but he pushed me out of the way."

Miriam got in his face. "You could have stood your ground. How about that? You could have followed the orders that I quite clearly gave you. Trost had a broken arm. What was he going to do, fight you for the gun? Dammit, I gave orders. It was your job to carry them out. You didn't and now he's dead."

Grover stared, his eyes wide, his mouth slack.

Looking back and forth, Eliza suddenly understood. Both Miriam and Trost had calculated the odds. Whoever manned the hunting rifle would be the one to face the sniper with his superior arms, his superior position, and his patience. He was likely to die.

"Grover, you stay here," Eliza said.

"Wait, where are you going?"

"To check out the hill. Look for clues. I want you to find the horses. That's your first job. Then cover Brother Trost with stones. If you're not finished when we get back we'll help."

"You won't leave me, right?"

"Don't be silly. We're not going anywhere." When Grover looked unconvinced, Eliza took his trembling arm and stared into his eyes. "Grover Smoot, we are not going to leave you. I give you my word."

When the two women were heading back up the highway, Miriam said, "We may as well. He's no good to us. Now that we've lost Trost, the boy will only be a drag."

"You were going to sacrifice Grover all along, weren't you?"

"Don't make this about me," Miriam said. "If it hadn't been for Grover, that sniper would be dead. But I couldn't stand up and expose myself to Grover's fire, wasting his ammo, blasting away. I said one shot a minute. By the time I got up, our enemy was galloping down the highway. I didn't have a chance of hitting him with the pistol. He was too far away."

"Trost was down," Eliza said. "Grover panicked. But you didn't answer my question."

"No, I did not sacrifice him. Of course that was a risky spot. That sniper had his gun set up and he was waiting for his chance. Grover wasn't the only one in danger. How about when we came out of the culvert and crossed open ground? And then I made a run for the hill. I wasn't asking Grover or anyone to take a risk that I wouldn't take myself."

"Fair enough," Eliza said. "But it wasn't because of Trost's broken arm that you wanted Grover at the rifle."

"You are right."

"I thought so."

"Broken arm or no, Trost was worth ten Grover Smoots. He was a better shot, calmer in a crisis. Better head on his shoulders. And what about navigating in the real world? You know what Grover told me when Kemp dumped us off the bus? Grover said it was his first time out of the Blister Creek Valley since he was thirteen. Five years ago. Never left the valley in five *years*."

"That's hard to believe," Eliza said.

"I'm not the one who said it."

"So you figured he was expendable."

"Nobody is expendable," Miriam said in an irritated tone. "But you tell me who we can more easily spare. Is it the former police officer who keeps his head in a crisis? Or is it the naïve, panicky kid? But hey, if you think Trost and Grover are more or less interchangeable, that's fine with me. Keep telling yourself that. Maybe it will make you feel better."

Eliza was ready to snap. She pulled ahead so she wouldn't say anything she'd regret later. The women left the highway. They kept their guns at the ready in case the sniper had decided to double back and retake his position. He had not. They made it to the top of the hill without incident.

"Right here," Miriam said. "This is where he was dug in."

The digging was quite literal. Using a spade or shovel, he'd excavated the dirt and rocks and sagebrush roots to the right of the knob to make a body-shaped indentation that would shield him from the road. If not for that lucky glint of sunlight off his scope, they'd have never spotted him.

Eliza thought of Trost and the awful way his fingers had grabbed at the dirt while blood and brains gushed out of his skull.

Two empty cans of chicken noodle soup lay to one side. There was a Ziploc bag that smelled like beef jerky, plus two apple cores, munched so deeply into the core that practically all that was left was seeds. An empty plastic water bottle.

Miriam picked up a shell casing and pocketed it. She lay in the indentation with Eliza's rifle to sight it north along the highway, as if she were the sniper.

"He had a decent shot," she said. "Could have taken it earlier if he hadn't been waiting for us to get out from cover. He was greedy—he wanted to kill us all."

Eliza took back the rifle when Miriam stood up again. "It was a lot of work to dig that hole. How long do you figure he was here?"

"Not long. A day, maybe." Miriam walked around, then pointed to a smoothed area in the ground. "Here's where he put his bedroll. I'm guessing he arrived yesterday afternoon. No sign of a fire. Must have eaten his dinner cold. Maybe in the morning he got up and dug himself a little bunker. Yes, I think so. See how the dug-up ground is still clumped from residual moisture? It's in the shade, but it wouldn't take long to turn dry in this heat. He dug it today."

"So his timing was perfect," Eliza said. "And he got in position to attack the road to the north—the open desert—not south toward Las Vegas. Most traffic—if there is such a thing anymore—would come from that direction."

"That's about how I see it, yeah."

"You think he was looking for us in particular?" Eliza asked.

Miriam found another shell casing. She held it up against the dying light, frowned, then fished the other casing out of her pocket. She handed them over to Eliza. "What do you think?"

The sniper had etched letters into the brass bullet casings: "Christianson I" for the first. "Christianson II" for the second.

"What do you bet that he also has bullets that say Christianson III and IV?" Miriam said.

"I don't understand."

"Someone is hunting us."

"I get that part. Why? Who?"

"He's military or former military and is comfortable with a sniper rifle like an M24 or M40." Miriam took the casings back. "These etched shells are just the sort of thing a sniper does while waiting for his prey.

And he knew how to pick his spot. He was patient. Waited to get a good shot on Trost, and wasn't distracted when we ran from the culvert."

"He might not have seen us come out," Eliza said. "He might have been staring down the scope the whole time."

"Which also speaks to his discipline. But I think he did see us. He waited, took one shot, then ran for his horses, which must have been waiting right down there." Miriam pointed down the gentler slope on the south side of the hillock. "He was already in the saddle and galloping away by the time Grover stopped shooting."

"That means he was both hoping to gun us all down on the flats and preparing to run away at the same time," Eliza said. "He's not fearless."

"No, and he makes mistakes. He left these shells. And don't forget the glint you spotted off the sniper scope. Nice catch, by the way."

"That was pure luck."

"You were paying attention. He was not. If he had been, he'd have thought better about the angle of the sun. I'm no sniper, but I did some training in the FBI, and I can tell you that as important as it is to be a good shot, choosing your sniping position is even more critical. He did almost everything right, but not quite."

"He was good enough to escape," Eliza said. "And Trost is still dead."

"There's nothing we can do about Trost. But we can bring this son of Satan to justice. And by that, I mean put a bullet in him."

"Forget that. I have no intention of playing cat-and-mouse games. Or looking for revenge. We're three hundred miles from L.A. We have no food, we're almost out of ammo. Our horses are scattered."

"And?"

"And our job hasn't changed. We're on a mission to rescue Steve, not run around the desert killing people. So let's stay focused on that, and on getting home with him."

"I want to get home too, Liz."

"Are you sure? I'm not convinced."

"Of course I do. My baby is back there, my husband. And my job is to stand by Jacob's side and protect him. Protect our valley."

Eliza softened at this, particularly the part about Miriam's baby. But she was still on edge over everything that Miriam had said and done, actions that had contributed to the tragedy of their dead friend.

"Let's get this on the table," Eliza said. "Grover is not expendable. He wasn't before, and he certainly isn't now. People are not equations. You don't tally them up and decide who is more important and who can be tossed aside."

Miriam didn't respond.

"Either everyone matters," Eliza added, "or nobody matters."

"Even gentiles? Even men trying to kill us?"

"You know what I mean."

"Let me ask you this," Miriam said. "Jacob planned to send you with Lillian and Stephen Paul. Was he or was he not calculating when he made that decision?"

"He was calculating," Eliza admitted.

"He wouldn't send me because of the baby. He wouldn't send himself because he has to lead Blister Creek. He wouldn't have sent Sister Charity because she's old and afraid. He wouldn't have sent Elder Smoot because he doesn't trust the man."

"We didn't have the luxury to choose. And anyway, I'm not Jacob."

"You fought my decision-making in the mountains and in Cedar City. Fine, I gave in, because you agreed that when it came time to fight I'd be in charge. So now it's time to fight and you're arguing. What is it, what do you want me to do?"

"I don't know. I want Trost to still be alive."

"That's not my doing, and it's not yours. It was the sniper's fault, but more than that, it was the will of the Lord. We can't change it. We can only adjust."

Everything Miriam said made sense, but it didn't ease Eliza's dejection as they made their way back to where Grover was stacking stones on Trost's body. Surprisingly, he had managed to retrieve all four horses. He said they'd been frightened and he'd coaxed them to his side with a soothing voice. He'd tied them to clumps of sagebrush while he worked.

Unfortunately, Trost's horse had taken a bullet to the shoulder. Under normal circumstances, it was hardly a fatal wound. It was hobbling, it had lost blood, but it was alive. What the horse needed was a veterinary surgeon to remove the bullet and sew up the wound, then a week or two of recovery time like any injured person or animal. But that was impossible here.

After they finished covering Trost, Eliza came over to where the horse sat on its quarters. She rubbed its trembling neck. It was weak; it could neither handle the road nor survive being turned loose in the desert. Time to make the call.

Why now? Why can't I wait until morning?

Too many blows, too much turmoil. The problem would be the same in the morning, and then she'd have more strength to do what needed to be done.

But that wasn't fair either. Leave the horse suffering all night? No.

Miriam came over to her side. "I know you don't want to hear this, but it will solve the food problem."

"You're right. I don't want to hear it."

"Let me do it," Grover said. "I've put down an injured horse before."

"No, Grover," Eliza said. "My father said that if you have to do something hard, be man enough—well, *woman* enough—to do it yourself. Don't force someone else to do your dirty work."

"I want to, though. I need to do it."

She looked him over. His face was earnest. His motives came into focus. Grover wasn't much good in battle, he had a tender sensibility at a time when the world demanded ruthlessness, but he could do his duty without flinching.

At last she nodded. "Get my rifle."

"We can't spare the bullet," Miriam said. "It will have to be with the knife."

Eliza closed her eyes and put her hand on her forehead. It was too much to bear. And yet Miriam was right. They had two rifle shells left and one more bullet in the pistol.

The horse was weaker than she thought, and didn't struggle as they tied its hooves together with the reins. Miriam led the three able-bodied animals down the highway and around the rock where the two women had taken refuge earlier.

When Miriam returned, the women held the injured horse's head back to expose the neck while Grover took a deep breath and approached with the knife clenched in trembling hands. No more than thirty minutes had passed since they charged the hill, but it seemed like hours.

"Keep your hand steady," Eliza said. "Don't flinch or hesitate. You owe it to the animal to do it confidently and quickly."

Grover nodded grimly. Miraculously, his hand steadied. He found the vein and began. It took too long, involved too much blood and struggling. But at last the awful task was over.

CHAPTER NINETEEN

Jacob entered the Holy of Holies, the innermost sanctum of the temple. The quorum stood, and the dozen men already waiting greeted him with murmurs of "Brother Jacob." It was a solemn meeting and they wore their white robes, white sashes, white hats, and green aprons.

The men looked tense and frightened. From the older men his father's age with their slate-gray beards halfway to their sternums to younger men like David and Stephen Paul, not one of them looked like he'd slept well in days.

David leaned in. "I was at the cliffs all day. Any word?"

Jacob knew he meant Miriam. "No, I'm sorry."

David gave a tired nod.

In fact, there had been nothing from Eliza, Miriam, and the others since they disappeared in the wake of the drone attack a full week earlier. David had a baby in the house without her mother. And his second wife, Lillian, was now pregnant. Or so Fernie had suggested, and Jacob's wife was never wrong about such things.

Jacob turned from his brother to address the group. "You know why I've called you."

"The Blister Creek Legion is ready," Elder Smoot said. "They await your orders."

"Not yet we don't. Everyone sit down."

The men took their seats on the wooden benches. The Holy of Holies was a windowless room beneath the temple spire, with high, cathedral-like ceilings. The brass chandelier overhead had once decorated Joseph Smith's temple in Nauvoo, Illinois, before the prophet died at the hands of a mob. Varnished wainscoting covered the lower half of the wall.

A four-feet-by-six-feet cedar chest sat in the center of the room. It was carved with the compass and square, a moon with a face, all-seeing eyes, and other symbols. Carved wooden cherubim, their wings overlaid with gold leaf, perched on either end of the chest. And what about the contents of the chest? Jacob had never opened it and never heard of anyone who had. His father claimed that among its treasures were the sword and breastplate of Laban, ancient relics mentioned in the Book of Mormon. Some claimed that in the Last Days, the One Mighty and Strong would wield them and lead the saints into battle against the very forces of Satan.

Jacob didn't know much, but he was convinced that part was nonsense, as was much of the other lore surrounding this room. If not for tradition, he'd have held this meeting amidst the rock spires of Witch's Warts instead.

Eight years ago, when Jacob was still a medical student trying to solve his cousin's murder, this room had been the site of horrific violence at the hand of the Kimballs, pursuing their vision of the end of the world. At the time, Jacob had wanted nothing more than to wash his hands of the whole church. Marry Fernie, help his sister Eliza escape the community, and get as far from Blister Creek as possible. Now he was its leader.

The men formed a prayer circle and Jacob offered a plea for divine aid. When he finished praying, he remained standing while the others took their seats.

"Before we move," he said, "we must exhaust all possible alternatives."

"We did," Smoot said. "We warned them, they attacked us, and we warned them again. Four days later they're more numerous than ever. They're digging in for the long haul." Smoot thumped his cane against the floor. "Now it's time to act."

Jacob glared at him. "Elder Smoot, would you like to lead this meeting? In fact, if you can get the votes, I will step down as head of this quorum and you can take my place."

Smoot dropped his eyes. "I apologize, brother."

"I didn't ask for this," Jacob said. "If I could, I'd bring back my father. He would be more confident. He would march you into battle and, Lord willing, lead you to victory. I am not my father."

"You are the man chosen by God," Stephen Paul said. "That is enough for me."

Jacob turned to his counselor. "You need a general. A prophet. I am a doctor and unqualified to lead. My faith is weak, maybe weaker than any other person's in this room. So if you want someone who will lift his sword and call you to war with no doubts, with pure certainty in his righteous calling, you need another man."

"You are Jacob Christianson, the favored son of Abraham Christianson," Stephen Paul said in a calm tone. "He ordained you to step into his shoes. The Lord has confirmed that calling in my heart."

"Mine too," Elder Johnson said, his voice shaky with age. "When you spoke at your father's funeral, I saw your father's visage reflected in your countenance. My bosom burned with the spirit. I knew you were the prophet. I *knew* it."

Murmurs of assent passed among the other men, including Smoot.

"You know my limitations," Jacob said. "If you want me to lead, I will. But if that's the case, you have to let me move at my own pace. We have a hard decision to make and I want to exhaust every possibility. Elder Young?"

Stephen Paul rose. "Yes, brother?"

"Have you and your wife had any luck with the shortwave?"

"Carol reached Durango this morning."

"That sounds promising."

"Colorado is under martial law, but Durango at least still has a mayor. They're flooded with refugees from Green River, and there's a typhoid outbreak. Denver is starving and they're sending out refugees. Some of them are headed in this direction."

"What about Utah?" Jacob asked.

"I raised Salt Lake again. They told me to shove off. Nothing from St. George or Cedar City."

Even more discouraging. "Nevada?"

Stephen Paul shook his head. "We couldn't get Mesquite or Henderson. Didn't try Las Vegas. Whoever is in charge there, it seemed like a bad idea to remind them about Blister Creek."

Jacob didn't know what he'd been hoping. Maybe to find another town like Blister Creek still holding on. Even if it were a hundred miles away it might form a partnership against the collapse. Blister Creek could share its expertise and organization, and a larger town could provide manpower for a mutual defense. From there, an expanding circle of towns, farms, and ranches could form a core of stability as the global mess worked itself out. Hold on for two, three more years and the weather crisis would pass, the wars would die down, and civilization could reassert itself.

Was that a fantasy? What if there was nowhere left to go but down?

"Elder Smoot. Tell me about the south valley."

"We rebuilt the bunker, gave it better earth sheltering. Installed a new machine gun. We're going to mine the road between mile twelve and the old Gunderson ranch, but it will take a couple of weeks. Anyone comes up the highway, the mines will blow them to kingdom come."

"Everyone hear that? Nobody use the road south of mile twelve." Jacob turned back to Smoot. "Where is the new ammo dump?"

"It's three hundred yards north of the bunker. We should have it dug out by Saturday. We'll get about fifty crates in there, good and concealed. Enough to fight a battle or two."

"Good. David? Recon report?"

Smoot sat down and David rose.

"Lillian and I used a few of our remaining batteries last night and infiltrated the reservoir camp with night vision goggles. There was a half-moon, but it was overcast, so I don't think we were spotted."

The other men leaned forward at this. Three days earlier, Jacob had sent a dozen riders into the Ghost Cliffs, only to be met by gunfire. The squatters hadn't abandoned their camp at all, but had reinforced their position. And there seemed to be more of them. After a brief skirmish, the riders retreated to Blister Creek. This was the first new information since then.

"It's bad," David continued. "The camp has grown to several hundred tents, plus overturned carts, lean-tos, and other makeshift shelters. They've whacked up the hillside pretty bad, but they don't seem to be using the trees for much else but firewood. Nobody is building anything with any permanence. They guard the perimeter with bonfires and several dozen armed men."

"Bottom line?" Jacob asked. "How many are we talking?"

"If I had to guess, I'd say a couple of thousand people, maybe more."

"We can't leave them up there," Smoot said.

"They're not planning to stay," David said. "If they were, they'd be building something more permanent."

"That's because they're planning to occupy the valley," Jacob said.

Angry mutters at this. Smoot gave Jacob a hard look and a curt nod.

See, that look said. *There's nothing to discuss. We drive them off or they overwhelm us.*

Was Smoot right? Couldn't Blister Creek maintain its vigil and prevent the mob from descending into town? The cliffs provided the most heavily guarded, easily defended entrance to the valley floor. Jacob had set up gun emplacements at six different locations along the switchbacks. There were two heavy machine guns, automatic and semiautomatic rifles for sniping, and caches of ammo. Whenever the enemy approached, drive them off. Meanwhile, the squatters had no farms, no food except what they could scavenge or hunt. And no shelter. Wait for winter and the problem would solve itself.

Except for those barrels of pesticide. All to kill a few fish. Or maybe the squatters were even deliberately poisoning the water supply. Then there were the latrines right up near the water line, filled to overflowing by a growing camp of sick and dying refugees. How long until cholera swept through Blister Creek?

"Give me ideas, brothers," Jacob said. "Anything we can try that doesn't involve bloodshed, I want to hear it."

Nobody spoke.

"Please. I need suggestions. Even dumb ones. Anything." More silence. "Fine, I'll start. What if we sent riders to Green River? We'll find out who is in charge of the army camp and beg them to take back their refugees."

"Why would they do that?" David said. "The government *wants* the refugees to come here. That's why they let it be known we have food."

"We could pray for the Lord to send them away," Elder Potts

said. He'd been a large man not so long ago, but the creeping ravages of age had left him hunched over, his bones aching with arthritis and with no analgesics to ease the pain. "He will soften their hearts and make them forget about attacking us."

"Is there a man in this room who hasn't prayed for that already?" Stephen Paul said.

"Then we redouble our pleas," Potts said.

"How about sending riders to Salt Lake?" Jacob suggested. "The state government still had a pulse, last we checked."

"You'd ask the McKay brothers for help?" David said.

"We don't know if they're still in charge. Anyway, yes, I would."

"The language the radio operator used when I called would not be fit for polite company," Stephen Paul said. "If we send riders, they'll be arrested or shot."

"How about Cedar City?" Jacob said. "I know they didn't answer the radio, but they were still alive last fall and we haven't seen any refugees from that direction."

"Except Joe Kemp and his crew," David said.

"They didn't pass through Cedar City, they cut across north of St. George."

"Say we go," Smoot said, twisting his hands on his cane. "What do we ask them to do? Take the refugees off our hands? That's the only possible way they could help."

"Could be the army is in charge over there," Jacob said. "Maybe a different division than the Green River people."

"Could be," Stephen Paul said. "We could send someone over the mountain by truck to see. That would take less than a day."

"We're mining the road," Smoot reminded them. "And even then, we'd be admitting to people in Cedar City that we still have fuel enough to drive around town. Which raises the question, do we have fuel?" He shrugged, as if he didn't want to know the answer. "Say we do. The army finds out we have fuel to burn and they'll be far more interested in that than in helping with our refugee problem."

"There's one other option," Jacob began. "Follow the example of Brigham Young."

Scowls deepened. Jaws clenched.

"You mean flee into the wilderness?" Smoot said. "Abandon our farms, our homes, everything?"

"That's right. Look for a sanctuary in the desert."

"This *is* our sanctuary in the desert." Smoot's voice was as tight as a rubber band stretched to the breaking point.

"There are forty-two hundred people living in Blister Creek," David added in a quieter tone. "This isn't the Kimball cult. We can't find a box canyon with a few Anasazi ruins and hide for the next five years."

"Yes, I know."

"And how would we feed them, anyway?" Stephen Paul asked.

"We'll carry as much as we can. Plus seed to plant anew. And our herds. More than enough to live on while we find a new home, lay out homesteads, and clear fields."

"This isn't the Old West," Smoot said. "There's no undiscovered wilderness awaiting us."

"Wherever we go," Stephen Paul said, "we'll simply provide a new target. Those squatters at the reservoir are locusts. They'll come through Blister Creek after we're gone, eat up everything, then look around until they find us."

"Yes, I'm grasping," Jacob said. "But there has to be something that doesn't involve more bloodshed."

"If you think of a solution," David said, "I'm there. Tell me what it is. Convince me. This is the last thing I want."

"The last thing any of us want," Elder Johnson said.

"You can look, Brother Jacob, but you won't find it," Smoot said. "This is our home, this is where we make our stand. It's the End of Days. We're the only thing standing between the forces of Satan and the utter destruction of the earth."

Jacob stared. There were ten million Americans in arms, backed by fighter jets, tanks, artillery, *nuclear weapons,* for heaven's sake, but a few fools in the desert armed with rifles were going to hold the line?

What choice do I have?

"Anyone else? Please, anyone. Any ideas? Anything?"

None of the men answered. There were twelve men in the room, all waiting for him to lead.

The silence thickened until at last Jacob cleared his throat. "Two thousand squatters?"

David nodded. "So far. That's my guess."

"Elder Smoot, how many in the militia?"

"The Blister Creek Legion has two hundred men at arms. The Women's Council offers four hundred more. I'd hold them in reserve, but those ladies know how to shoot if we need them."

"Assuming they agree to the plan," Jacob said.

"You are the prophet. Their priesthood leader. They have covenanted with the Lord to obey."

Smoot had come a long way since last fall, when he'd balked at arming the women and subverted Eliza when Jacob left her in charge of Blister Creek. But he still spoke with absolute certainty of the rights and privileges any male priesthood leader held over any woman. Jacob did not intend to command the women, any more than he had come into this body of men and made demands. But he guessed Smoot was right and they would back him.

Jacob made his decision. He turned to his brother. "Six hundred saints. Is that enough?"

"More than enough," David said. "It's an unorganized mob. Fifty would be enough to drive them into the hills."

"No," Jacob said. "If we're going to do it, this time we don't mess around. They had a warning. This is different. This time we hit them with everything we've got." He raised his voice. "And we don't stop until they are dead or driven from our lands."

Smoot banged his cane to the ground. "Yes!"

And with that, the room erupted in shouts and cries.

Men yelled their frustrations, exclaimed their gratitude. Shouted their joy that the Lord had sent them a prophet. That He would smite their enemies. Elder Heaps raised his arms and babbled in tongues. Tears streamed down his cheeks. David and Stephen Paul clenched their fists and joined in the roar.

Jacob left the room, unable to listen to them carrying on. He shut the door to the Holy of Holies behind him and walked down the hallway, his footsteps heavy and his stomach filled with sand.

It was time to tell his wife of their murderous purpose. The Women's Council would look for peaceful solutions, but in the end what choice would they have? All of Blister Creek must unite or be destroyed.

CHAPTER TWENTY

Kemp had found a receptive audience in Cedar City with Andrew La Salle's body slung over his saddle and a story about polygamists in the mountains. The polygamists were wanted horse thieves. A posse had already chased the four into the western desert before giving up. They were too afraid of bandits, of the army, of the desert itself. The thought of more polygamists in the mountains left them terrified. Cedar City moved to fortify the canyon.

And when Kemp offered to go after the four who'd escaped into the desert, Hank Gibson, the self-proclaimed mayor, police chief, and governor, was eager to help. Gibson swapped him fresh horses in exchange for his tired pair, restocked him with food and ammo, and provided him with an excellent set of maps.

And that's when Kemp got a break. Following his enemies' escape route on the map, he realized that the polygamists had traveled too far north. If Kemp hurried, he had an opportunity to cut them off. So he raced across the western desert, entered Nevada at the

Clover Mountains, then took position on a volcanic hillock to wait. It was the perfect spot for an ambush.

The next day the polygamists came down the road, just as expected. Kemp held his fire, waiting for them to enter a flat stretch without cover. Take his time and he could pick them off one by one, in the open.

Suddenly, one of the women shouted and the four threw themselves from their horses. He fired, hit one of the animals. His enemies reached the safety of the ditch on the far side of the highway.

Dammit. How had he been spotted?

Kemp expected the polygamists to wait for nightfall, then slip away. Instead, they came after him. One person shot from behind a blind of rocks on the edge of the highway, while two others cleverly crossed through a culvert and took refuge behind a boulder at the base of Kemp's hill. He'd spotted the two women running from the culvert, but had resisted the bait. Instead, he'd waited patiently, aiming always at the rifleman, and was rewarded with a glimpse of sandy-gray hair. By then one of the women was charging up the hill with a pistol in hand. He fired a single shot at the rifleman, scooped up his gun, and ran for the horses. By the time the woman reached his position and fired her pistol down the highway after him, he was too far away to hit.

Kemp's horses were already tired and he didn't think he could outrun his enemies, who had been traveling at a slower pace. So he waited for the first opportunity to jump off the road and set up a second ambush. Take advantage of their aggression. But they never showed. He thought about doubling back to search for them, but instead decided to ride on and look for another likely ambush spot.

After consulting the maps, he found one. A ranch road. If the enemies had a map, they might use it to try to loop around him. If not, they'd have to come down the highway itself. So he set up at the junction of the ranch road and the highway. There had been a battle at the spot, and among the wreckage of burned-out, bullet-riddled cars, he found a sedan half-buried in the sand on the shoulder, with its trunk facing up the highway. He hid his horses some distance off. Then he cracked the car trunk, yanked out the backseat so he could stretch out in its interior, and waited with his rifle aimed up the highway. The inside of the burned-out vehicle baked with the heat.

The polygamists never appeared.

Kemp waited until evening before giving up. He packed his gun, retrieved his horses, and set off warily down the highway. A continuous low rumble came from the southwest. He knew that sound from Iran. It was a distant artillery bombardment. A reddish glow stained the horizon—Vegas, burning. When the wind blew from the north, it carried clean desert air. When it stopped, the smell of ash and burning plastic stung his nose and mouth.

For a time he was at a loss. All he knew was that his enemies traveled toward California, probably via Las Vegas, which lay directly to the south. His only hope was to skirt the city and trap them on the other side.

He was exhausted and looking for a secure spot to bed down for the night when he caught a glimpse of reflected firelight maybe a quarter of a mile from the highway. He crept through the darkness until he gained the hillside above what turned out to be a small camp. Three figures stood around a fire, hands out to warm themselves. They had hunkered in a sheltered spot between the hillside and some boulders. There was tall grass for their animals, maybe even a spring.

It would have been a good spot to hide from prying eyes, except the camp was too close to the highway and they hadn't properly shielded their firelight. And now Kemp was in perfect position to kill them all. Easy.

So easy, in fact, that it made him suspicious.

It had taken two days of hard riding to reach Cedar City, followed by six days and a hundred and fifty miles across the deserts of Utah and Nevada in pursuit of his quarry. Kemp was hopeful that he'd killed the older man with his sniper rifle, but the other three had evaded his attempted ambushes since then. Could they really be sitting here in front of him, ready to die?

He set up his sniper rifle on its tripod. Quietly, he fixed the scope, squatted, and took a closer look. Three figures, all right. A rabbit or other small animal roasted on a stick over the fire, and they stared at it as if eagerly anticipating their meal. It was too dark to pick out features.

But were these three the travelers from Blister Creek? Why would they stand around the fire without setting up a defensive perimeter?

He fixed one of the figures in the scope and drew his finger against the trigger.

What if you're killing the wrong people?

He was too far down the path to worry about that now. He'd abandoned the refugees he'd led east from Las Vegas. His mother was dead at the hands of Jacob Christianson. Shepherd and Alacrán had given him the chance to take his revenge. There might be collateral damage. God knows he'd seen enough of that in Iran.

He fired. The gun thumped. One of the figures fell into the fire.

Instead of diving for the shadows, the other two grabbed for their fallen companion to yank the body out of the fire. They let out confused shouts. Kemp chambered another round and fired a second time. Another figure fell. At last the third member of the party seemed to recognize what was happening and turned to run. Too late. Kemp fired again. The last person fell.

No. Wrong.

They hadn't fled. They'd stumbled about and died. The reaction was so different from the hair-trigger flight of the polygamists from the highway yesterday that he knew with absolute certainty he'd killed three innocents.

Dammit.

But just in case, he kept his gun trained on the camp for several long seconds, waiting. If there were others lurking in the shadows, he had to take them down too. He couldn't leave fresh enemies.

"Move and I splatter your brains," a woman's voice said behind him. Kemp froze.

"Good, now lift your hands from the gun and turn slowly. If you drop your hands, I will shoot you. Stay on your knees. Now kick the rifle toward me."

He obeyed. A single figure stood behind him on the hill, about ten feet away, aiming a pistol steadily at his chest. A half-moon hung overhead, providing enough light to see a thick braid hanging over one shoulder. Her face remained in shadows, but there was no doubt who he faced. It was the former FBI agent.

"Who were they?" he asked. "Who did I kill?"

"Refugees, maybe. A family. I didn't get close enough to see. Hands up!"

His hands had been drooping, but now he raised them high again. "Then why—? How—?"

"I spotted three people with a campfire, not far from the road. I knew you'd find them irresistible, think they were us. I didn't think you'd murder them without verifying their identities."

"You killed them as much as I did."

"Nice try, but no."

"You could have warned them. Told them a sniper would be gunning for them. Instead, you used them as bait."

"Who supplied you?" she asked. "When you threw us from the bus you didn't have horses."

"Cedar City."

"I was there. I don't believe it."

"It's true. I came in the day after you ran off with their horses. They were pissed, looking for revenge, and I promised to track you down if they gave me mounts and fresh supplies. They were more than happy to help. Even offered to pay me."

"I see."

"I thought you'd be easy quarry. Look, I see I made a mistake. I'll turn around and go back and you can—"

She shot him in the thigh. He fell over, screaming in pain, his hands digging at the fiery hole several inches above his knee. She came over to him and frisked him, took away his pistol, then put the sniper rifle behind her, well out of his reach.

She checked the magazine of his Beretta, then holstered her own weapon and used his to keep him covered. "Ready to talk?"

"Is that what they teach you in the FBI?" he said between clenched teeth. "To shoot a man when he's not resisting?"

"I'm not an FBI agent anymore. You can call me Sister Miriam."

"Please let me go. I'm sorry about the old man."

"After you threw us onto the highway you drove south in the school bus. Then what?"

"I followed you. Isn't that obvious?"

"Yes, but you didn't drive. If you had, you'd have passed us on the road. But you couldn't have walked either, if you came into town the day after our escape. Somehow, you ditched your refugee friends, picked up horses, and followed us to Cedar City. Who gave you the horses?"

"Army irregulars. Fighting bush wars in the back country while the army puts down the California rebellion."

"Who leads them?"

"Two guys. One named Shepherd—a buddy of mine from the army. The other is named Alacrán."

"Alacrán is not in the army, and never has been. He's a bandit and a criminal. And so are you." Miriam lifted the pistol. "May the Lord have mercy on your soul."

Kemp pitched around for something that would save him from

this religious fanatic. He clawed up memories from his childhood Sunday school. "The Bible says blessed are the merciful. It says turn the other cheek."

"The scriptures also say that it's better for one man to die than for a nation to dwindle in unbelief. You are an enemy of my prophet, and therefore an enemy of God."

"Let me talk to the other girl. Christianson's sister. Please. Have mercy."

"Like the mercy you showed Brother Trost?"

Trost? Was that the man Kemp shot?

"I'm your prisoner. Don't do this."

Miriam hadn't killed him yet. She'd been about to; her posture had tightened, the gun had come up not to guard him, but to fire. He was sure of it.

But now she hesitated. It was one thing to shoot a man in battle, and another to execute him while he lay before you bleeding from a gunshot wound.

"Let your God decide," he said. "You wounded me. You took my guns. Just leave me my food and horses. If God wants me to survive, I'll live. If not, I'll die of this gunshot. And if I live I swear to God I will never bother you again."

He'd spoken this last part out of pure desperation, not expecting it to work. But something changed in her face—she was actually considering it.

"I won't make a wager with the Lord," Miriam said at last. "But very well. His will, not mine, be done. If you survive the bullet and the desert, if you soften your heart against the Lord's anointed, then maybe He will spare your life."

"Thank you!" Kemp gasped.

"Where are your horses?"

He hesitated. She lifted the gun again.

"Down the road a half mile. There's a dry wash. I tied them to a Joshua tree."

"Good. I'm taking your weapons, the horses, and anything else useful. I'll leave you water and enough food for twenty-four hours."

"That's all I had left anyway," he said, bitterly. "How about a knife?"

"No."

"That's not much of a chance."

"Don't push me, Mr. Kemp."

He fell silent.

"You have a choice," she added. "Given not by me, but by God. But I swear to you, if you come after us, you will die."

She gathered his rifle and tripod and slipped into the darkness. He thought briefly about staggering to his feet and hurling himself after her, but quickly gave up that thought. His fingers probed at the gunshot wound. It hurt like hell, and there was a lot of blood. But she hadn't hit the femoral artery, and if the bullet had hit the bone, it had only cracked it, not shattered it. He might have a chance.

What about the campfire below him? There was a rabbit on a stick. And whatever supplies the dead people had been carrying. He waited until he was sure Miriam would be long gone, then scooted painfully down the hill to the campfire.

When he arrived, the rabbit was missing, and if the three travelers had carried any supplies, Miriam had already looted them. They now had nothing of value.

Kemp stared at the empty campsite in growing fury. If there had been any doubt before, it fled now. The hell with letting the polygamists escape into the desert. He would track them down if it cost him his life.

Starting with Miriam. He swore she would die a horrible death.

CHAPTER TWENTY-ONE

Eliza and Grover were waiting down the highway when Miriam returned. She was riding a horse and leading a second. It had been an hour since the gunshots—first three suppressed rifle shots, then a shot from Miriam's pistol—and at least two hours since she'd left the other two hidden in a rocky gully so she could double back to watch the camp. It had been easy to spot. Miriam was certain the sniper would find the camp as well.

That shot from the Glock said she was right, but Eliza was still relieved to hear her sister-in-law calling in a soft voice that she was coming. Miriam slid from the horse. She wore a new hunting knife on a sheath and carried a new rifle tied to her saddle.

"It was Joe Kemp," she said.

"What?"

"I should have guessed. He told Jacob he was a sniper."

Miriam shared the man's story, but it didn't make much sense. Apparently Kemp had met Alacrán, the smuggler turned bandit who'd tried to rob Blister Creek of nine thousand gallons of diesel fuel last fall. The smuggler had armed Kemp and sent him off on horseback to track them down. Kemp resupplied in Cedar City and raced ahead to cut them off on the road.

"And he tracked us all this way, why?" Eliza said. "Because he blames my brother for his mother's death? That's crazy. Jacob tried to save her life."

"Not hard enough, apparently."

"But Kemp is dead now, right?"

"No. I let him live."

Grover stiffened next to Eliza. "You mean he got away?"

"He didn't, so calm down. He's not coming after us." Miriam sighed. "It's dark and I'm cold. I'll explain on the road."

Within a few minutes they were riding south by the light of the moon and the red glow on the horizon. Miriam filled in the missing details as they traveled. Kemp had gunned down the three campers, which allowed her to pinpoint his exact location on the hill and take him prisoner. Instead of killing him, she'd shot him in the leg to force him to surrender the information about Alacrán, then left him with food and water to find his way out of the desert.

"But as long as we're on horse and he's injured," Miriam said, "there's not much chance he'll catch up to us. That's why I felt justified in sparing his life."

"I suppose that executing him wouldn't have helped matters," Eliza said, reluctantly.

She was shaken by the thought that three innocents had died, on top of the haunting image of Trost staring at the sky with his forehead a ruin, but the idea of Kemp still alive to their rear didn't fill her with confidence.

"I am not getting soft, if that's what you're implying."

"She's not implying that," Grover said. "She's saying there's enough killing in the world without you adding to it. Bad enough that you shot him and left him to die."

"And what would you have done?" Miriam said. "Given him a kitten and fluffed his pillows?"

"Leave him alone," Eliza said. "Anyway, that's not what I was saying." "Do *you* think I was too hard?" Miriam asked.

"No," Eliza said. "I think you were too soft. Kemp murdered Trost. He was already our enemy, and now you've shot him, but left him alive. If he survives we're bound to face him again sooner or later."

Miriam looked surprised at this, and a little pleased, as well. "I thought that too. My first instinct was to finish the job. The only tragedy would be the loss of a bullet. But the Lord spoke it in my heart. I had no choice but to obey."

"Spoke what?" Eliza asked, suspicious.

"He told me to let the man live. Kemp will be spared if he leaves us alone. If not, he is sealed unto death."

Eliza had no answer for this, so she fell silent. The others followed her lead. They continued south. Not long now. Another day at most. Steal fresh supplies in Vegas and then make for California.

The blacktop was a ribbon of ink across the desert. The southern horizon burned and the rumble of artillery seemed to redouble in ferocity. About an hour later a jet roared overhead. Soon after it passed, the wind shifted. It suddenly smelled of burning rubber and fuel, and something metallic that left a bitter taste.

"It smells like hell," Miriam said in a flat voice.

★★★

Kemp made himself a leg splint from two straight branches broken from a scrubby tree and strips of fabric chewed off his shirt. He found another branch to use as a cane.

Fueled by his anger, he hobbled down the highway. He should rest, should concentrate on finding food and a source of water so he could camp out for a few days and heal. Instead he continued, one agonizing step after another. Up ahead, he guessed, his enemies would be talking over their plans. Maybe he could catch them before they left. Then they'd be sorry.

He didn't make it more than a half mile before he grew weak and shaky. What was wrong with him? He wasn't bleeding that hard. The wound hurt like hell, but he could handle pain. He stumbled and fell to his knees. His breath came out in a hiss and he ground his teeth together to keep from screaming.

When he put his hand down to his leg, he was terrified to discover that so much blood had streamed out that his pant leg was wet and gummy all the way to his ankle. It hurt so bad it was almost numb and he hadn't noticed that the bleeding had increased. Why? It had only been oozing before.

Of course, you idiot. You didn't give it a chance to clot and scab over.

And all the walking kept tearing it open afresh. His pulse up with the exertion, every beat of his heart had forced more blood from the wound.

Get the straps from the brace. Make a tourniquet.

The fabric was slick with blood and the knots so tight from shifting back and forth as he hobbled that he couldn't get them undone with his shaking fingers. He lay prone on the pavement and tried to regain his strength. He took a swig of water from his canteen, but it turned sour in his stomach and he puked it up. His dizziness spread and the pain eased from his leg.

Now that he was weak and fading, he could only curse at himself. Why hadn't he waited until his leg healed? Why hadn't he given up the whole thing? These polygamists—what did they matter? He was going to die if he didn't stop the bleeding.

He grabbed for his canteen to wash the blood off the knots on the brace. Maybe then he could untie them. Only he'd dropped the canteen when he threw up, and most of the water had spilled onto the road. What was left didn't rinse away enough to matter. And anyway, the blood kept oozing from the wound. Slowing now, but only because he'd lost so much blood. He didn't even have the strength to press his hands against the wound to hold in what blood remained.

As he sank back to the pavement with a moan, he remembered the chilling words Miriam had uttered when she left him on the hillside. *You have a chance. But I swear to you, if you come after us, you will die.*

★★★

When dawn broke, Eliza, Miriam, and Grover found themselves riding across a scorched landscape of toasted juniper bushes surrounded by blackened grass and sagebrush. The hills to the west of the road had burned for miles, while to the east, it looked like the fire had made a couple of attempts to leap the highway but failed to catch. Another mile down, a bomb crater tore a chunk out of the highway. A dead traffic jam of burned semis, twisted family sedans, and motor homes with their roofs peeled off clogged the road south of the crater. All the vehicles faced north, filling both lanes and the shoulders of the road. It stretched for miles.

A caravan of refugees had been fleeing Vegas along this desert highway, only to be stopped by a bomb crater. Then what? Helicopter gunships? Drones? Tanks coming in from the desert? Someone or something had attacked the refugees and annihilated them.

It took almost an hour to pick their way through the sea of wreckage. Even though it had been months, maybe longer, since the attack, the dead lay everywhere. In cars, on the highway. Dead in the ditches on the side of the road, where they'd attempted to flee the fire. Their bodies were too charred to identify gender, and maybe that's why they hadn't been carried off by scavengers. Or maybe they were so numerous that even the greediest vultures and coyotes couldn't eat them all. The companions reached the small town of Caliente, at the junction of Highway 93 and Route 317. It lay in ruins. The dead sprawled in the street outside a gutted casino, their bodies humming with flies. Most were soldiers, but there were civilians among the dead as well, cut down as collateral damage. Burned pickup trucks and army vehicles lay scattered across the pocked road. An LDS church was a pile of blackened beams beneath a single standing wall. Train tracks came into town and promptly turned to twisted, snaking rails, like a scorched piece of modern art. On the south end of Caliente, the devastation was so complete it was impossible to pick out the streets. Then, beyond the town, craters rendered the road impassable. In the desert, more signs of a battle: two downed helicopters, the blackened hulls of armored vehicles, and thousands of brass shell casings littering the hardpan.

"We should back up to Caliente and continue west on 93," Miriam said, when they'd found 317 and were headed due south. "That way we'll bypass Las Vegas to the north."

"What about resupplying in the city?" Eliza asked. She was chewing on horse meat that had started to taste funny.

"I know what Trost was thinking, and it made sense at the time. But if there's nobody to rob, nothing to steal, then it's pointless. We thought we'd run into refugees, but the only ones we've seen have been scorch marks on the highway. Plus those three Kemp killed, I guess. There's no food this way."

"It's not like we're having much luck scavenging the desert," Eliza said.

"We have the extra horses," Grover said. He hooked his thumb back at the two animals Miriam had taken from Joe Kemp.

"You're not sick of horse meat?"

"Makes me want to puke," he said. "And I'm still having nightmares about killing it. But horse meat sounds a lot better than stumbling into that artillery bombardment."

Eliza turned it over. She'd thought to trade the horses in Las Vegas. The military could surely put them to use, if nobody else was willing to pay. That was assuming the army didn't simply seize them. But what if the three of them avoided the city entirely and made for the salt pans of the Nevada desert? Could they find enough water to survive while they salted and smoked horse meat? Maybe the meat of one horse would take them to California, and they could trade Kemp's other horse there, or butcher it if they ran out of food again.

Before she could decide, a thumping roar sounded to their rear. A military helicopter swooped behind them, long and black. It followed the highway, passed overhead, then doubled back to hover some two hundred feet overhead. The horses reared and snorted at the noise and gusting currents of the rotor wash. After several seconds, the helicopter turned and continued south. It soon disappeared.

They didn't know what it meant, but nobody wanted to stick around and find out. So they dug their heels into their tired horses and took them off the road. Before they'd made it a mile across the flat desert plain, two Humvees cut from the highway to give pursuit.

Eliza had pulled ahead. Now she slowed down until her companions caught up. "What do we do?"

"I've got an idea," Miriam said. "Get down from the horses. Leave your guns." When they were down, Miriam drew her hunting knife and handed it to Eliza. She stretched out her braid. "Quick, cut it off."

Eliza took Miriam's braid in her left hand and the knife in her right. She hesitated. Miriam had been growing her hair for the past several years, ever since she'd joined the Zarahemla cult as part of an

FBI infiltration gone wrong. Even as other women in the community had been modernizing their look, shedding prairie dresses, trimming their hair, and even wearing a touch of lipstick in some cases, Miriam had kept her hair growing like a female Samson. Her hair now stretched halfway down her back, a braid as thick and healthy as the faith that sustained it.

The Humvees kept racing toward them, now a half mile distant and closing quickly. Sunlight reflected off the two windshields and made it impossible to pick out details. But Eliza imagined mounted machine guns up top and men with assault rifles inside.

"Do it!" Miriam cried.

Eliza pulled the braid taut and sawed at the hair. The blade was sharp and hairs separated cleanly along the cut. Moments later the braid hung fat and heavy in her hand. Miriam snatched her braid and threw it away. She shoved the knife into the saddlebags. Then she plunged her fingers into her remaining clump of hair and vibrated them rapidly. She was left with a messy mop a few inches long.

Before Eliza had a chance to ask what Miriam was thinking, the Humvees pulled to a stop. Two soldiers jumped out of the lead vehicle, armed with M16s. Eliza and Grover raised their arms. Miriam lifted her hands somewhat more slowly. One of her hands held a badge.

"Haley Kite, FBI," she said.

Eliza tried not to gape. Miriam had never once claimed that name, had even refused to respond when Steve and other FBI agents called her that. She had become Sister Miriam Christianson, first wife of the prophet's brother David. She rarely spoke of her previous life, and seemed to despise everything she had once been. But not only did she still have her FBI badge, she had been carrying it with her all along. How strange was that?

Another soldier stepped out. He was an older man with a weather-lined face and stubble that hadn't seen a razor in several days.

He wore a sergeant's chevrons on the shoulder of his combat uniform. His left arm was in a sling and his uniform was dirty. All these men were filthy.

"Agent Haley Kite," Miriam said to the newcomer, waving her badge again. "You're U.S. Army, right?"

The question was unnecessary. It said "U.S. Army" on the breast of his, and the other men's, uniforms.

"That's right." The man's voice was cool and wary. "I'm Sergeant Ludlow. What are you doing out here?"

"Thank God," Miriam said. "I thought for a minute you were those goddamn rebels. Figured we were done for."

Grover started, perhaps shocked at her profane words. Eliza shot him a look. Miriam was good. She stood with her hands on her hips, sizing up the men as if she expected to be shortly giving them orders.

"You didn't answer my question," Ludlow said.

"Unfortunately, I can't tell you. But my companions are informants from the Green River camp. Where is the line of control?"

"The what?"

"Do you hold Vegas?"

"Most of it. The Californians are still lodged in the northern suburbs and they're shelling the hell out of the Strip. That's them you hear, not us." As if to punctuate his words, the ground shook with a boom that rose above the background rumble.

"Take me to HQ," Miriam said. "I need to phone Washington. Where's your base?"

Ludlow didn't answer. He stared back at Miriam, eyed Eliza and Grover, then gestured with his good hand. "Come here. Tell me what you think of this."

He led the three of them to the rear of the Humvee. One of the soldiers threw open the back doors. Joe Kemp lay inside, dead. His eyes stared blankly skyward and his face hung slack. He wore a makeshift brace on his right leg, made of sticks and blood-soaked strips of cloth. A bloody wound on his thigh. No shirt.

"We found him in the middle of the road about twenty miles back," Ludlow said. "He died of blood loss."

"We've passed several people over the past few days," Miriam said, "but we've kept to ourselves. Although we did hear gunshots last night. Might have been that."

"We dug a nine-millimeter bullet out of his leg. How about I check it against your firearms?"

"You've got a working ballistics lab around here?" Miriam said. "I'd love to see that."

"Don't give me that crap, Agent Kite. You shot him, didn't you?"

"Yeah, I shot him. Then I let him go. Told him not to follow." She cast a pitiless look at Kemp's body. "Seems he didn't listen."

Ludlow yelled for someone named Yancy. One of the young guys going through their saddlebags came over and handed the sergeant a pair of dog tags.

Ludlow read the tags. "Corporal Joe Kemp. First Infantry Division. You killed an American soldier."

"*Former* soldier," Miriam said. "Anyway, the First ID is deployed in the Middle East."

"Not anymore they aren't." He cocked his head. "I'm surprised an FBI agent doesn't know that. Or maybe you've been out in the desert for too long."

Miriam shrugged. "The world has gone crazy. My news isn't always fresh."

Even to Eliza's ears the explanation sounded weak. Her story was faltering.

"She's telling the truth about Kemp," Eliza said. "We had a run-in with him in Utah about a week ago and he came after us. He's not with the army, he's either a deserter or retired, and we think he's taken up with bandits."

"And who the hell are you?" Ludlow asked. Then he looked at Grover. "And this kid. How old are you, boy?"

"Eighteen."

"Draft dodger, huh?"

"What? No!"

"Yeah, right. If you're eighteen, you should be serving somewhere."

"Hey, Sarge, look at this," one of the men called from near the horses. He held up the braid Eliza had sawed from Miriam's hair.

"What the hell?" Ludlow said, eyeing Miriam's short, messy hair. "Nah, forget it, that's above my pay grade." He handed Kemp's dog tags to Yancy. "Cuff these three. We'll take them back to Alpha for interrogation. Moreno, do something with those horses. The colonel will want those too."

Rough hands grabbed Eliza, Miriam, and Grover. Ludlow made for the front of the Humvee.

"Let go of me," Miriam said. "I'm on FBI business. I need to get to California."

Ludlow turned. "Yeah? What for?"

"I've been sent to exfiltrate some agents who are trapped in L.A. These two are desert types who were helping me cross Nevada. But if you can fly or drive me across we can let them go back to their ranch."

"FBI agents? In California?" Ludlow shook his head. "Not anymore. They're either dead or they've turned traitor."

Eliza's mouth turned dry. "What do you mean?"

"We were the last battalion to abandon California. We were tasked with extracting the last U.S. government officials from the state—Department of Agriculture, IRS, ATF. I saw what happened to the FBI. Some traitor ratted them out. Most of them faced the firing squad."

Ludlow gave Miriam another look. "Now we have an agent in the desert, killing U.S. Army personnel, who doesn't seem to know this. Maybe *this* is our traitor. Come on, you slackers. Move it!"

Soldiers cuffed their hands behind their backs with plastic zip-ties and shoved the three of them into the back of the Humvee next to Kemp's dead body. A hot, suffocating closeness settled in when the men shut the door. Moments later, the vehicles rattled across the desert.

"Don't worry," Miriam said in a low voice. "Steve is still alive. The Lord protects His people."

Eliza's throat was so tight she could barely get the words out. "How can you be sure?"

Miriam nodded at Kemp. "That's my evidence. All those who raise a hand against us shall perish."

Which was not the same thing as saying that nothing could happen to Blister Creek and its people. Eliza closed her eyes so she wouldn't have to stare at the dead body, but when she did, all she could see was Steve, together with Agent Fayer and all the rest of them, lined up against a wall, while a firing squad took aim.

CHAPTER TWENTY-TWO

For the past week they'd been pushing their horses, covering up to thirty miles a day. Eliza didn't have her maps, but she figured they'd still been a couple of days north of the city. But zipping along in the Humvees, they crossed the distance in what seemed like a snap of the fingers. This must be what it had felt like for the settlers of the West when the first train service came through. Instead of struggling for weeks in wagons or on horseback, a train crossed the plains and deserts at breathtaking speed.

After about an hour they stopped at a checkpoint, where military police threw open the doors on the back of the Humvee. Eliza squinted against the light until her eyes adjusted.

Sandbag bunkers lined the roads and a pair of tanks sat buried to their turrets. A pair of helicopters thumped overhead. A huge tent with a red cross sat on the east side of the highway, with sloppy rows of smaller tents partially sheltered between a pair of dusty hills. To the west lay a series of trenches and berms with burned beams and twisted metal. Craters marked an earlier battle. This had been the front lines at one point.

More soldiers came in for a closer look. They were filthy and ragged, their uniforms in poor repair and hanging loose on underfed frames. Some of them wore dazed expressions, while others looked hard and dangerous.

An argument broke out between Ludlow, who wanted to foist off his prisoners, and the MPs, who didn't want to take responsibility. One of the MPs poked at Ludlow's injured arm, suggesting that the sling was a fake injury, to shirk combat duty. Ludlow refused to be baited. Instead, he dug in his heels, and the argument continued until someone fetched a major, who ordered the sergeant and his men to carry the prisoners and Kemp's body into Las Vegas. There was another argument about fuel when Ludlow said they didn't have enough to reach the city. Here, the major relented.

While the trucks stopped at a fuel dump a mile or so down the road, Ludlow let the three of them out to stretch their legs while men brought over fuel hoses from a tanker truck. Eliza walked to the edge of the camouflage netting that concealed the dump from the air. Looking south, she got her first glimpse of Las Vegas, now only eight or ten miles distant.

The city sat on a dry plain with a cluster of skyscrapers and towering casino hotels at the core, surrounded by huge swaths of strip malls and subdivisions that metastasized into the desert. One of the tallest buildings was a jagged, twisting mass, while two surrounding towers trickled smoke into the air. Another looked like a frame of steel beams, as if the exterior had simply melted away. A large fire burned across several blocks on the west side of the city. It sent smoke billowing thousands of feet into the air to join the thick blanket smothering the city, where clouds and smoke and haze all joined together.

The west side may have been burning, but the east was taking the brunt of the attack at the moment. A dozen pillars of smoke hung suspended like frozen tornadoes, some thick and angry, others already melting away. The ground shook and a fresh column of smoke billowed skyward. There were no airplanes visible overhead, no tanks or artillery that she could see, but some unseen army was hammering the city.

The men finished fueling the Humvees, and Eliza returned. Ludlow stared at her, as if trying to puzzle who and what she was.

"I should have shot you when I had the chance." His tone made it hard to tell if he was being sardonic or if he really meant it. "My arm is infected again, and I was supposed to go to the field hospital. Now I'm stuck hauling your sorry butts into the city."

"Could you please remove the body?" Eliza asked.

Ludlow fixed her with a stare. "You killed him. You can deal with it."

"We could tie him to the roof," Miriam said. She'd been talking to Grover in a low voice, but now made her way over.

"If you're scared of dead bodies, you'd better get over it. Wait until we get into the city. Then you'll see plenty."

He went around front to talk to his men, who were trying to get a radio report about the state of the highway before they set out. Eliza's shoulders ached with her hands twisted behind her back and cuffed. She turned her wrists to get better blood flow.

"It's not a question of being scared," she said when Ludlow returned. "The body is starting to smell, and it might be carrying disease. It's not just us at risk, but anyone else who comes into contact with it." When Ludlow didn't say anything, she pressed. "I heard there's a TB epidemic in Las Vegas, and we know that Joe Kemp passed through there not too long ago. TB can pass from the dead to the living."

"What, are you a nurse or something?"

"My brother is a doctor. He's taught me a few things to help around the community, given the situation with the hospitals." Eliza stopped, worried she'd said too much.

"I doubt he's got TB," Ludlow said. "He looks clean to me."

"There's no way to know that."

"The TB is mostly gone anyway. We saw some over the winter, but these days cholera is the killer. Meningitis too. Even the flu is more deadly."

"Famine weakens people's immune systems," she said.

"So they say. The city hasn't seen aid supplies in months. There aren't many civvies left. Few thousand, maybe."

"So why do you keep fighting? If there's nobody left, why not pull out?"

"What kind of question is that? We're fighting to stop the rebellion. Who are you people, anyway?"

"My name is Eliza. This is Grover. You already met Agent Kite."

She understood what he was getting at. *Don't you care who wins the war?* But she wasn't prepared to answer that question. What she wanted was for the war to *end.* For peace to return. Every moment it continued, it pushed civilization further over the edge of the cliff.

A little frown had passed over Ludlow's face when she spoke her name. She could see the wheels turning. A generic prisoner had become someone with a name. With a history. Maybe even a future.

"Look," he said. "We're heading out and the road isn't safe." He grabbed a passing soldier by the arm. "Toss some Kevlar in the back for these three." Turning back to the three prisoners, he said, "I'll have someone cut the cuffs, but if you try anything funny, it's a bullet to the head. We're entering the war zone and I can't screw around."

"Why don't you let us go instead?" Miriam said.

He gave her a hard look. "Sure, that's just what I was planning."

"As soon as we get out of camp," Miriam continued, "pull over and let us out. We'll disappear. Nobody will know."

"What we told you is true," Eliza said. "We need to rescue some FBI agents in Los Angeles. We have reason to believe they're alive."

"You'd never make it. Anyway, these agents—assuming they exist—are dead or have been taken prisoner. Trying would be pointless."

"Would it hurt to let us try?" Eliza asked. "Besides, that way you wouldn't have to go all the way into the city. It would be safer for you and your men."

"That wouldn't work. Sooner or later it would come out what I did, and then it would be my head on the block."

"Why, because Agent Kite shot that man who was trying to kill us?"

"It's not just Corporal Kemp. The major wants me to turn over the kid."

"Me?" Grover said.

"Yeah, you. Either you're a deserter or a draft dodger. If you're a deserter, you'll get the firing squad."

"I'm not, I swear."

"In that case, lucky you. Right now, a draft dodger gets thirty lashes, a uniform, and a gun. And you'll get fed. Sort of."

"I don't want to join the army. I want to go back to my family."

"Nobody from the draft ever came to our town," Eliza said. "So there's no way he could be a draft dodger."

"They didn't, huh? Where is this place? Too bad you weren't smart enough to stay put."

"Where are you taking us, anyway?" Eliza asked.

Ludlow ignored her question and yelled for Yancy, who came and cut their cuffs. Relieved to be free, Eliza flexed her wrists and rubbed her hands. Miriam was looking around, and Eliza knew her well enough to know that she was sizing up the men at the fuel dump, wondering if she could grab a gun and fight her way out. Not likely. In addition to Ludlow's platoon, a dozen men guarded the fuel tanker, plus a machine gun nest lurked on the side closest to Las Vegas. Miriam relaxed her posture, apparently coming to the same conclusion.

They climbed in the back of the Humvee and let the soldiers lock them in. They put on the Kevlar vests.

The vehicle returned to the road and crawled toward Las Vegas. With no view of their surroundings, Eliza could only flinch when the ground shook from a heavy artillery shell. A helicopter thumped overhead. A few minutes later, the roof-mounted machine gun let loose a volley at an unseen enemy. The Humvee picked up speed, then slowed again.

Something plinked against the doors. The machine gun opened up again. The Humvee stopped. Men yelled. Assault rifles sounded quick, staccato bursts.

"You idiots," Miriam said. "Why did you stop? Keep driving."

Grover put his face in his hands and took deep breaths.

Then came explosions, like grenades or mortar rounds. The vehicle shuddered, seemed to lift off the ground. A charred smell penetrated the back. Gunfire slapped against the vehicle armor.

A muffled shout rose above the other cries. "Go! Go! Go!"

The Humvee lurched into motion. It picked up speed, more bullets hitting the sides, more answering fire from the machine gun up top. Then it was quiet again, except for the incessant shake and muffled boom of artillery, not quite so distant anymore.

Several minutes passed and Grover cleared his throat. "They're not going to make me join, right? That was a bluff. Don't you think?"

"I doubt they're bluffing," Miriam said.

"Oh."

Eliza wanted to hug him and tell him it would be okay, but she was afraid he'd break down sobbing, and she needed him to be strong.

"We don't know that," she said. "Maybe Ludlow is just trying to scare you."

"I can't join the army," Grover said. "All those gentiles. And fighting in the army of Satan. I need to stay with the church."

"Suck it up," Miriam said.

"Oh, let him be."

"I'm sure you'll find a way to escape," Miriam said. "Then when you get back, you'll have some military training. That'll help."

"If I don't get killed."

"You won't get killed. Trust me. No, trust the Lord. Didn't you get a patriarchal blessing?"

"Well yeah, but—"

"And did it say you'd die fighting for Satan?" Miriam asked. "I didn't think so."

"If the U.S. military is Satan's army," Eliza said, "what does that make the Californians?"

"Also Satan's army," Miriam said, without a moment of hesitation. "The devil's forces are too dumb to be consistent. Whoever wins Las Vegas—whoever storms the gates of Babylon—will be the devil's champion. Mark my words this is—or will be—hell's fortress. From here, the enemy will march forth to assault Blister Creek."

They came under fresh attack, which quieted Miriam's eschatological rant. Gunfire from the Humvees countered the spray of bullets from the other side. It was terrifying to be locked in the back, with no windows, no way to tell what was happening in the battle or ability to affect its outcome.

Moments later, they were moving again, the gunfire dying, but they faced one final attack before reaching their destination. This time, the fire was more intense, and only ended when two heavy explosions sounded to the right. Men cheered from the front of their vehicle. Someone was firing in their support. That gave Eliza hope that they might actually emerge unscathed.

Still, she could hardly believe it when at last the Humvee came to a rest and the doors were flung open. She squinted against the light. Soldiers with M16s ordered them out, then stripped them of their Kevlar vests.

The Humvees had driven into an underground parking garage. The huge open space was empty except for a few old Jeeps, Land Rovers, and pickup trucks—all painted tan or army green—parked in a neat clump nearby. Metal halide lamps cast the interior in harsh white light. A cord as thick as a whip snake stretched from the lights, curved around concrete pillars, and disappeared through a pair of sliding doors with the glass broken out of them. A machine gun squatted outside the doors behind a row of sandbags.

If the men at the base outside the city had looked thin, hungry, and dirty, these seemed almost cadaverous. Their clothes were torn and filthy with dried blood and motor oil. Open sores covered one soldier's cheeks, and another man wore a bloody scarf tied around his head. More blood caked his beard. None of the men had shaved in weeks. And they stank. One skinny guy gave Eliza such a hungry look that she was convinced he was imagining how she tasted.

"You bring any food?" a soldier asked Ludlow.

"No, we've got nothing."

"You look like you been eating plenty," another said. "How about water?"

"Couple of jugs. Not enough to share."

"Thanks, we'll take it. And whatever else you got."

Without waiting to see if Ludlow had been serious in his objections, they opened the backs of the Humvees and helped themselves to several five-gallon containers of water. They dragged out Kemp's body and tossed him casually to one side so they could search for food. One of them emerged from the other vehicle with a first aid kit, and two others tried to make off with crates of ammo before Ludlow and his men shouted them back with a good deal of cursing and threats. For a moment it looked like there'd be a fight between the two sides.

The ground shuddered and men staggered. When the shaking stopped, a quiet stillness took its place.

"Damn, that was close," one of Ludlow's men said. "Let's get out of here."

He was a Hispanic kid who couldn't possibly be old enough to be in the army. He looked no older than Eliza's half-brother Peter, who was only sixteen.

"No way," one of the soldiers from the parking garage said. "You already showed the enemy where we're hiding. Now we're going to take a pounding for the rest of the day. Come inside. The colonel will want to see you."

Ludlow looked nervous. "I have orders from General Minsk. We're to return to base ASAP."

"You're not going anywhere, you lazy slobs," another man said. They didn't appear to have a leader, or at least no one was taking charge. "Not until dark."

"I'm not leaving my vehicles."

"Suit yourself. Sleep on the concrete for all I care."

"Fine," Ludlow said. "All I care about is getting rid of the prisoners. Are the others still here?"

"Yeah, they're in the conference room." A man stepped forward and looked over the three companions. Was this their leader? "Who the hell are they?"

"FBI, I think." Ludlow produced Miriam's FBI badge, which he'd confiscated earlier. The man took it. The sergeant stepped back with a look of undisguised relief.

And then soldiers from the parking garage led Eliza, Miriam, and Grover away at gunpoint. Eliza turned to look at Ludlow, who watched them with a scowl. The look earned her a rifle barrel jab to the kidney. She'd never guessed that she'd be reluctant to leave Ludlow, but she was suddenly terrified to be under control of these filthy, starving men.

Miriam stared straight ahead with her face a rigid mask. Grover's eyes darted from side to side, looking as frantic as a rabbit caught in a snare. A soldier met the boy's gaze with a hard look and he flinched.

Sergeant Ludlow, Eliza realized, had done them a favor. He hadn't said a word about their connection to the dead body. And he hadn't said anything about Grover. If these vermin had been angry with Ludlow's men for having food, water, and security, while they crouched starving and thirsty under artillery bombardment, what would they do to a so-called draft dodger? It wouldn't be pretty. Ludlow might very well have saved their lives.

The filthy soldiers led Eliza, Miriam, and Grover deeper into what turned out to be an enormous hotel and casino. Wires ran up and down the hallways, but there was only enough electricity for the occasional LED light taped to the wall, which cast the hallways in a bluish glow. The elevators were out, and they made their way up three stories via a stairwell of concrete steps. They emerged into a vast room leading past abandoned reception areas and banks of dead video slot machines.

Light streamed in through blown-out windows. Outside were dry fountains and plaster statues of Greek gods pockmarked with bullets or missing heads and limbs. A row of palm trees ran parallel to the street, their fronds shredded and several of them snapped in two. Inside the room, glass shards and metal game tokens sparkled across a burgundy carpet.

The building shuddered with a new explosion and the companions threw themselves to the floor along with the soldiers. Moments later the soldiers were up, ordering the prisoners to keep going. They entered a long, windowless hallway. The LED lights were gone and it was too dark to see, but the soldiers seemed to know their way by feel. A door swung open. It revealed another stairwell and more lights.

They went up four more stories and into another hallway lit with LEDs. Conference rooms lined either side. Two soldiers guarded a pair of padlocked doors at the far end of the hall. One man had a cigarette at his lips and he fumbled with a key to get the lock open. When it opened, the four men who had led the prisoners into the casino pushed into the room, snarling at people on the other side to get out of the way.

It was a conference room about fifty feet long and twenty wide. Blown-out windows on one side overlooked the street several stories down, but a warm breeze failed to cut the stench of human waste and death. Several dozen chairs lay stacked along one side of the room, which was otherwise bare of furniture. Thin figures lay on blankets and sleeping bags, sweating in the heat. A woman in shorts and a tank top, her collarbone jutting out like a brittle stick, slumped against one wall. She let out a dry, barking cough that shook her thin body. There were maybe thirty people in all.

The soldiers shoved Eliza, Miriam, and Grover into the room. The doors closed behind them, followed by the sound of clinking chains and the padlock snicking into place.

"Stick together," Eliza said. "Be careful until we know what's what."

One of the prisoners staggered toward them. He was a tall, frightening scarecrow of a man with hollow eyes and a scraggly beard. His eyes blazed with such intensity that Eliza flinched and closed in with Miriam and Grover, who tensed by her side.

The man drew short. "Eliza?"

"What? Who—?"

"It's you. I can't believe it. Don't you recognize me?"

It was a stranger's face that looked back at her, but the low, gravelly voice was unmistakable and unforgettable.

Eliza stared, trying to wrap her mind around what she'd heard. Trying to convince herself that it was real, that this half-dead man was who she thought he was.

"Is that—" she began, then stopped to catch her breath, which was suddenly short. Her heart pounded. "Is that you?"

A bone-weary smile broke across the man's face and then she was sure. It was Steve. She had found him. They fell into each other's arms.

CHAPTER TWENTY-THREE

Elder Smoot came striding up the sidewalk to the Christianson house, tall and strong, his eyes blazing above his massive beard. No pretense of needing a cane. Not today. Today he was a patriarch in all his righteous anger. Jacob waited on the porch, bracing himself for the coming storm.

Jacob had sent his oldest son to call Smoot to the meeting with the Women's Council. Upon his return, Daniel had described Smoot's thundering reaction with open-eyed awe. Two hours later, Smoot carried that same anger to the porch.

"Where are they?" he demanded.

"In the parlor. But before we go in—"

"Then let's get this blasted farce over with."

"Before we go in," Jacob repeated calmly, "I want all four of us here. I expect David and Stephen Paul any minute."

"Well, where are they?"

"They're coming. They're not late—you and I are early. Even if they were here, we'd wait another few minutes."

"Damn it, Christianson. Let's get on with this. The others can join us when they come."

"I told my wife four thirty. That's when they expect us. Ten minutes."

"Your wife. Your *wife*. Do you hear how preposterous that sounds?" Jacob refused to let Smoot bait him. "Sit down, Elder. Be patient. We won't get anywhere in this meeting by shouting and carrying on."

Smoot yanked over one of the rocking chairs, sat down, and rocked furiously. "This is what comes of giving women their own council. You see now."

Jacob thought about waiting inside, but Smoot might very well barge in after him. So he took his own chair and sat down. Smoot rocked like he wanted to launch his chair from the porch.

Thankfully, the other two men arrived shortly thereafter. It was still a few minutes short of four thirty. The four of them stood in front of the door.

Jacob put his hand on the knob. "This is not a fight. For heaven's sake, don't try to make it one."

"Get it over with," Smoot said.

Jacob expected to find the women in the parlor. Instead, they were in the kitchen and dining room. Not sitting around pontificating, like the Quorum of the Twelve would have done had they been waiting for a meeting, but working. Charity and Ruthie Kimball made bread. Sister Rebecca and Stephen Paul's wife Carol sat at the long table teaching two young girls how to disassemble and clean an AR-15 assault rifle. Lillian sat with David and Miriam's baby, feeding her a bottle. Other women knitted or read old agricultural journals dug out of someone's attic. Jacob's wife, Fernie, sat in her wheelchair, cranking the handle on a wooden ice cream maker. The entire Women's Council was present, minus Eliza and Miriam.

The men entered and took four empty seats at the far end of the table. None of them spoke. Gradually, the women stopped what they were doing. Carol sent the girls from the room while Rebecca finished reassembling the rifle. One of the girls took David's baby with her. Only Fernie kept working, her arms straining to turn the handle.

"Excuse me," she said. "It's getting stiff—I'm almost done."

Smoot snorted.

Fifteen, twenty more cranks, and then Fernie stopped. "There. Peach ice cream. Is anyone hungry?"

"There you go," Smoot said, not to Fernie, but to the other men. "It's a blasted ice cream social."

Fernie fixed him with a look not unlike the one she gave to mouthy children. "There's no need to be rude, Elder Smoot. If you don't want any ice cream, you could simply say 'No thank you.'"

Smoot didn't respond. Lillian took the ice cream maker to the kitchen, where she emptied out the ice and removed the canister. Another woman set out bowls, while someone else found a scoop. When the ice cream was dished up, Lillian passed around the bowls. As she passed David, her hand rested on his. He smiled. She returned a shy smile.

Lillian was an attractive young woman, strongly built, but with a feminine face. Her only flaw was ears that stuck out a little. The ears made her cute, rather than beautiful, but somehow also made her look approachable and friendly. David seemed to legitimately care for her, but there was no disguising that his heart truly belonged to Miriam.

Lillian approached her father and her smile turned wary as she gave him a bowl of peach ice cream.

"Thank you," Smoot grunted. He cleared his throat, then tentatively picked up the spoon.

Jacob took his own bowl. The ice cream was sweet and rich. The peaches gave it tang. It carried him to his childhood, pouring in ice and salt and cranking the handle until it stiffened and his arm trembled with exhaustion. The reward was a heaping bowl of ice cream devoured on the porch at dusk, when the cool air blew in off the desert. Simpler times.

If Fernie had hoped to cut the tension by serving ice cream, she had underestimated Smoot's anger. The church elder ate his in silence, then dropped his spoon with a clank and gave Jacob a hard look.

"So."

Jacob sighed. He looked at Fernie. "You don't like the plan?"

"No."

"I don't either. None of us do. We searched for an alternative and couldn't find one."

"It's an awful situation that defies an easy answer," his wife agreed. "But killing is not the solution."

"Do you have a suggestion?"

"Pray," Fernie said. "Wait for the Lord to send us an answer."

"What if the answer is to kill the squatters and drive them away?"

"It won't be. Anyway, I know you haven't prayed. Not really."

Smoot started. "He's a prophet. Of course he prayed."

"My husband is a prophet when he acts like a prophet. Right now, he's acting like a man. A frightened, panicky man. And that's dangerous." She didn't say this to Smoot, but to Jacob, meeting and holding his gaze.

"Christianson, do you let your wife talk to you like that?"

"Yes," Jacob said.

The elder blinked. "That was meant to be a blasted rhetorical question. Of course you don't let her. Because *you* preside over your family. And that means you are the king and lord of your own house."

"As a general rule, I try not to think of myself as a king. Because my family are not my subjects."

"This is the reason," Smoot said. "This is why a man should never have just one wife. You get a few of them together and they have an outlet for gossip and scheming. Figuring out who has authority, who rules the others. When you've only got one wife, her only outlet is her husband. She tries to rule him instead. You see the problem."

"Do we have to sit and listen to this patriarchal nonsense?" Rebecca asked from the other end of the table.

"Elder Smoot is an elder in Israel," Charity said. "The Lord's anointed."

"The Lord's self-appointed, you mean," Rebecca said.

Charity looked taken aback. "Show respect."

"He's a man with a little authority who thinks the priesthood gives him the right to strut in here crowing like a rooster," Rebecca continued. "We don't have to listen to it."

The women, Jacob realized, had their own internal struggles. Arguments and personality conflicts ready to play out. What had their meeting looked like? How many women agreed with Fernie, and how many agreed with the men?

"Excuse me," he said. "There are fourteen of us in this room. If we all have a turn, we'll never get anywhere."

"Jacob is right," Fernie said. "The women came to a consensus. It took us hours of arguing. We're not going to hash it out again. What we're here for is to come to an agreement between the men and the women."

"Eliza is gone," Jacob said. "And Fernie is her first counselor. She can speak on behalf of the women, and I'll represent the men."

"I will note for the record that she is also your wife," Rebecca said.

"Is that a serious objection?" When Rebecca didn't respond, Jacob looked around the table. "Anyone else? Okay, then. Fernie?"

"Bottom line is, the women don't want war," Fernie said.

"Neither do we," Jacob said. "We don't have a choice."

"We do have a choice. They haven't attacked us, which means your war is preemptive. It's voluntary. So long as they stay in the cliffs, we're going to leave them alone."

"They're poisoning the reservoir. That's a form of attack."

"To catch fish, not to kill us. So no, it's not."

"Same result, in the end."

"Did you ask them to stop?"

"We had a battle, remember?"

"Don't use that tone, please. I know what happened."

"I'm sorry." He took a deep breath. "I don't know who fired first, or how it started, but people died. I warned them, threatened them. They still haven't left."

"Casualties were one-sided, as I recall. I'm sure they feel they're in the right."

"Fernie, what are we supposed to do? They're cutting our timber, their latrines are overflowing into our water supply. They'll eat anything that moves. And they admitted that they're waiting until their numbers grow large enough and then they'll overrun the valley and take what they want. If we let them, we'll all die."

"I say that's a bluff."

"You haven't seen the camp. You don't know what we're facing."

"I haven't, but other women have. Lillian was with David, remember? She gave her report. We're all aware of the grave and growing danger."

"And you're still willing to take that chance? If you're wrong, all of our homes, our land, our town that we built, will be destroyed. People are dying out there. Towns, cities. Entire countries. Starving to death while armies tear each other apart. Our only hope is to preserve our sanctuary and wait for it to end. Surely you agree with that. I know you believe the Lord has prepared Blister Creek as our refuge. So why can't we defend it?"

"I absolutely will defend it. Give me a gun and I will sit out on the porch in my wheelchair and shoot any man who threatens my family. But you're talking about something else. You're talking about killing people because of something that *might* happen. How can that possibly be right?"

"It's necessary. I'd never order an attack if I didn't think so."

"Maybe it's a test," Fernie said. "Have you considered that?"

"How do you mean?" Jacob asked, cautious.

"The Lord has presented you two possibilities. First is violence, bloodshed. Second is peace. Faith that He will guard this sanctuary. That He will soften the hearts of our enemies."

"I don't believe that. If that was the plan, why didn't God turn away the Kimballs when they repeatedly tried to murder their way to power?"

"Different time, different challenge. Those men were working for Satan. These people are hungry, innocent refugees."

"What do you want?" Jacob asked. "Spell it out. What should I do?"

"Refortify the entrances to the valley. If they try to force their way in, drive them off. Until they do, leave them alone. That's my advice."

"While they continue to foul our water supply." Jacob shook his head. "What if I don't do that? What if I order the Blister Creek Legion to attack the squatter camp anyway?"

"Then the men will fight alone."

Stephen Paul cleared his throat. "May I ask a question?"

His tone was reasonable. Jacob nodded.

"Sister Fernie, what would you do if Jacob ordered you to fight, not in his name, but in the name of the Lord?"

She looked Stephen Paul in the eye. "If my husband stood and said that he had prayed to the Lord, and the Lord told him to go to battle, then of course I would sustain him as prophet, seer, and revelator. I would order the women to march forth and utterly annihilate our enemies."

"Do it," Elder Smoot told Jacob. "Raise your arm to the square and order these women to fight. Do it in the name of the Lord of Hosts, the King of Kings."

If Jacob did that, Fernie would know he was lying. He might force her compliance in this one case, but he would damage, perhaps destroy his marriage.

And so Jacob ignored the suggestion. "Fernie, is this truly the consensus of the council, or your own decision?"

"We voted," she said. "Five votes for peace. Four for war. One woman abstained."

"So there wasn't a consensus."

"The consensus was that we would go with the vote."

"But it was close," he pressed. "And if Miriam were here, she'd vote to attack."

"I know."

"Eliza would too. That would make it six to five with one abstention. The motion would carry."

"But they're not here. Anyway, I'm not so sure about Eliza. Probably, yes. She trusts you."

"But you don't."

"Jacob, please. I love you, I support you. I would follow you to the gates of hell. I just . . . my conscience objects. I can't do it."

"A woman," Elder Smoot said in a disgusted tone, "will always vote for short-term safety over long-term security. That's why a woman was never meant to exercise dominion over a man."

Jacob didn't answer. He had no way to counter any of this. And part of him—yes, most of him—wanted to agree with the women. How could he order the deaths of starving refugees? What choice did he have? The squatters were growing in strength, growing bold even as their hunger and desperation spread. Increased numbers meant more fouling of the reservoir too. All too soon he'd be forced into action anyway. Inaction now would mean more killing in the end.

"Thank you for your time, sisters."

"That's it?" David asked. He had remained quiet through all of this, his brow furrowed. "But we haven't agreed on anything."

"Oh, I think we all understand," Smoot said bitterly. "Brother Jacob is going to call another meeting of the quorum. Then he's going to tell the priesthood body, the men chosen by the Lord, that he is bowing to the will of a gaggle of frightened wives and mothers."

"You're wrong," Jacob said. He looked not at Smoot as he said this, but at his wife. "Unfortunately, the reality is unchanged. While we've sat here arguing, more refugees have been streaming south from Green River to join the squatters. They grow more dangerous day by day. We've already wasted valuable time waiting for the Women's Council to render its verdict. Now that we have it, we can't wait any longer."

Fernie looked horrified. "Don't do this, Jacob."

"I suggest you reconvene your meeting after we're gone. If we fail, the men of the church will be dead and refugees will flood into the valley by the thousands. The women will need to mount a final defense of their homes and children. Prepare yourselves."

He thought of Grandma Cowley's diary and the founding of Blister Creek. Wouldn't it be ironic if Blister Creek ended in the same way it had begun? Women and their children, alone in a hostile wilderness.

He rose to his feet and the three other men followed.

"Wait, Jacob," Fernie called. "Please, can we talk alone before you go?"

"Leave him be, woman," Smoot said. "He's got enough weight on his shoulders without you adding to it. Come on, brothers."

"Jacob?"

Jacob continued toward the door, ashamed that he was so frustrated, so twisted up inside that he couldn't stop long enough to defend his wife against Elder Smoot. It was too much. All of it, more than he could bear.

CHAPTER TWENTY-FOUR

For several moments Eliza and Steve stood embracing and she didn't care about the smell, or his filthy clothes, or the fact that he was thin and bony. He was alive. That was enough for now.

"I never expected to find you here."

Steve gave a thin smile. "Where else would we meet? I was heading east, and I assume you were on your way west to look for yours truly. It was either Vegas or nowhere."

His breath came out in a wheeze, and he was wobbly on his feet. The very act of standing and holding her seemed to cost him. What had those monsters done to him? And why?

Steve looked over her shoulder at the other two. "Hey, Miriam. Good to see you again."

"And you. Alive, that's nice to see. I wasn't sure." Miriam looked him over. "Of course you look like hell, you know."

He grinned back. "I've *felt* better too." He took in the third member of the group. "Grover Smoot. Hey." There was an obvious question in this last bit, as in, what the devil was he doing here?

Miriam grabbed Grover's arm and dragged him past Eliza and Steve and deeper into the room.

When they were gone, Eliza looked into Steve's eyes and put a hand on his bearded cheek. "I'm so sorry."

"Not your fault."

"I wanted to look for you, but the drones pinned us in the valley all winter. I only broke out a week ago."

"I figured it was something like that. You should have stayed. I'd be happier if you were safe."

"No way. My place is with you." She felt suddenly shy and dropped her hand. "Do they give you anything to eat?"

"Not since they brought us here, no. Those poor fools with the guns don't even have food."

"Water?"

"Sometimes. Never enough."

She took his hand and led him to the side of the room opposite the staring prisoners, where they sat down with their backs against the wall. Miriam and Grover had already leaned against the wall and slid to seated positions on the floor some distance away. Miriam studied the other prisoners. Grover looked at his hands.

"I didn't expect Miriam," Steve said in a low voice. "Didn't she have a baby? Is it okay?"

"The baby is fine."

"And isn't that one of Lillian Smoot's brothers? Why him?"

Eliza explained what had happened with the refugees and the drone attack. Instead of traveling with Lillian and Stephen Paul, she'd found herself on the road with Miriam, Grover, and Officer Trost. She told how they'd passed through the mountains and down to Cedar

City, where Miriam had stolen horses and weapons. Then, about the flight into the deserts of Utah and Nevada.

Steve chewed on his lip. "And Trost?"

She shook her head. "There was a sniper. Miriam killed him. But not before Trost . . . he didn't make it."

"Ah, crap. He was a good man." He stopped, as if expecting her to fill in more details.

But that was as much as she wanted to tell of the ordeals of the past week. Anyway, they seemed petty compared to the horrors her fiancé must have suffered the past nine months since he'd gone to California to help the FBI and promptly disappeared. Whatever he'd faced had sapped his vitality and left him this starving scarecrow.

A muffled explosion sounded in one of the floors above them. The building shuddered and people curled into balls with their hands on their heads. A pair of acoustic tiles fell from the ceiling, then the building stopped shaking.

"Are they shelling the building?" she asked.

"Yeah, for about three days now. Today is the worst."

"The soldiers seemed to think someone spotted our caravan entering the parking garage."

"Could be. I figure it's only a matter of time."

Until what? Until the building collapsed? Until a shell flew in the open window and vaporized them all?

"Can't the army fight them off?" she asked.

"I don't think they have the fuel for a major offensive. I've been looking out the window when it's quiet, and most of the federal troops are on foot. They used to be coming in and out of this building, but most have moved to the mall across the street. It's taken less damage. I keep hoping they'll move us too."

"You said the shelling has been going on for three days. Were you here long before that?"

"About a week. Before that, we were in Caesars Palace on the Strip. About a half mile from here."

"I've been there," Eliza said, marveling. "That's where one of my brothers worked when he was a Lost Boy."

"It's rubble now. A pair of missiles flattened it. They evacuated us just in time. After that, they kept us in a warehouse for a couple of days, then they captured this building and moved us up here. They gave us each a full MRE when we arrived. Some people gulped theirs and puked them back up. I was lucky. A soldier warned me it would be the last time we ate in a while, so I made it last. He was right. They haven't fed us since."

She was horrified. "Wait, I thought you said that was a week ago."

He gave a weary nod. "You don't miss it after a while. The thirst is another matter."

Miriam rose to her feet a few yards away, apparently having scoped out the conference room to her satisfaction. She made her way over to the prisoners and engaged them in conversation. Grover stayed behind. He met Eliza's gaze, then he looked away.

Poor Grover. Miriam was so hard on him, and then Trost had died under horrific circumstances that may or may not have been the boy's fault. He seemed incapable of pulling himself together.

It hadn't been that many years since Eliza was Grover's age, anxious about finding her place in the community. Uncertain of her future.

Steve lowered his voice. "He looks terrified."

"He is. He has been all along." She took his hand. "What happened in California?"

"I can't remember how much I told you when I called."

"Not much, only that Agent Fayer was in trouble and you needed to go to Los Angeles to help."

"That's right. It's been so long. So much has happened." He shook his head. "We had a couple of traitors. Huang, who was from the Bay Area, and some computer guy by the name of Boggs. They were Californians first, and Americans second. When the state turned, so did they. They blew Fayer's cover and the state arrested her and the rest. The entire L.A. field office was being held as hostages. I came out to negotiate. Then the war broke out and it all went to hell. You remember an agent named Sullivan? Kind of a dick?"

"Fayer's partner?" she said, uncertain. "They were on a stakeout of the California governor, or something like that, right?"

"That's the guy. Anyway, he and Chambers—he was in on that Zarahemla operation a few years back—broke out and liberated one of our helicopters. The rest of us grabbed guns and shot our way to the roof. The helicopter picked us up and we fled for Nevada. Someone else should have taken the stick. Sullivan didn't know what the hell he was doing. But I'd torqued my wrist in the fight, and Sully made up some lie about flight experience. We took small-arms fire and went down in Death Valley. Lost some people."

"Wow, that's terrible. Fayer wasn't one of them, was she?"

"No, she's still with us. That's who Miriam is talking to."

Miriam squatted next to the thin, coughing woman in the shorts and tank top. Eliza stared. The FBI agent from Salt Lake had been strong and athletic before; now she looked about ninety pounds, old, and feeble.

"And the guy with the Yankees cap is Chambers. Don't think you've met him."

"No, but I wouldn't have recognized Fayer either. She looks awful."

"Sullivan died in the fire," Steve continued. "Guess he paid for his BS. Also another agent, who was trying to pull Sully out. Perez."

Eliza started. "Eduardo?"

"That's right, Eduardo Perez. Did you know him? Wait, he was in Blister Creek once, wasn't he?"

Steve went on to describe how the survivors had trekked across the desert on foot. It was winter and cold, but bone-dry.

Eliza's thoughts trailed back to an illicit kiss all those years ago between a teenage girl and a young FBI agent who she'd taken for a Mexican laborer. Eduardo. Now he was dead.

"Here it comes," Steve said, breaking her from her memories.

The thump of artillery shells grew louder, as if the bombardment were following a known pattern through the center of Las Vegas. Then another thundering blast, and the building tottered. More tiles crashed down from the ceiling. Prisoners cried out. Grover covered his head with his hands. His lips moved in a silent prayer. At last the building stabilized.

Steve had paled even further. "That was a bad one."

Eliza's pulse throbbed in her throat. She forced herself to remain calm. "Then what happened?"

"After Death Valley? We crossed the Nevada border into Pahrump. It was a war zone. Loyalists hid us in basements when the Bear Republic troops overran the town. Not much food, though." He let out a bitter laugh. "I thought I was hungry then."

"When was that?"

"Let's see. February, I think. We moved out in early March. About three months ago now, I guess. We made contact with Washington, who ordered us back to L.A. Nobody seemed to care anymore that I'd been fired from the agency. I was back in, as far as they were concerned."

"So you returned to California?"

"Hell no. Fayer wanted to. Chambers and Higgs, no. I was going straight to Blister Creek. Figured I'd get there by Easter."

"Probably better you didn't. The drone quarantine was still in force. They would have bombed you off the road."

"I'd have taken my chances. It would have been better than what came next. We stumbled into a camp outside Vegas just as a cholera epidemic hit. Half a million refugees from the Pacific coast. Most of them died. I caught a nasty bug, had terrible diarrhea for a week—that's when I got skinny. Not this skinny, but skinny. Higgs died. Essentially crapped himself to death."

"I'm sorry."

"The camp got bombed, which finished off what was left. California was winning the war, but then the U.S. pulled out of Iran and shoved a bunch more troops into the conflict. Might have pushed back all the way to the Pacific, but they ran short on fuel. The offensive stalled in Vegas."

"But how did you get here?"

He started to answer, but another shell detonated in the street with a thunderous boom. Eliza braced herself, but the shaking was minimal this time.

"There were five of us left," Steve said. "We ran into a company of irregular army troops hauling around artillery with mules. And a wagon filled with leaking, eighty-year-old mustard gas shells. Like something out of the First World War or something. They'd lost several men in an air strike and forcibly drafted us to fill the ranks. At least we got fed.

"That didn't last long. We met up with another unit run by this insane major with more wagons filled with shells. I was thinking nerve gas or something equally nasty, but no, it was worse than that. Low-yield atomic artillery shells—real Cold War stuff. The kind of thing you launch to keep the Soviet tank army from breaking through. Not the sort of thing you want to blast off and watch detonate."

"That's horrible. Did you fire them?"

"We didn't, no. The colonel was obsessed with security. He interrogated every man in the old company. Threw some kid in front of the firing squad. For what, I never found out. He heard I was from California, and wanted to shoot me too. Didn't care that I was—or had been—FBI. Fayer and Chambers managed to convince him not to. But he had us in confinement when he took a bullet from a sniper. They let us go, but there was apparently another hard case on the way to take charge of the unit. We made a run for it. So here's where it gets weird."

"Weirder than mustard gas and atomic warheads carted around by mules?"

He looked puzzled at this. "That's a good question. The whole world has gone nuts. A few years ago I was an FBI agent looking into doomsday cults. Then somehow I found myself living in one of those cults. And now doomsday is here. I feel like I'm living in a sci-fi movie. Or maybe it's a horror movie—I can't tell. Maybe both."

"Is the Book of Revelation horror or sci-fi?"

Eliza had raised her voice, and now Grover came edging over, as if he wanted to listen.

Steve continued. "So here we are, traveling across the desert on foot when we find a trailer. Beat up, paint sandblasted off, it looks like it's been abandoned for years. But maybe we can find a can of beans or a tin of Spam or something. We try the door and find ourselves facing some naked old dude with a shotgun. His skin looks like leather, and he's got more hair growing out of his ears than on his head. Really crazy guy. I can see guns in his trailer, boxes of ammo. This guy has come here to wait out the end of the world.

"We have a few anxious moments, while we try to back away without shooting the guy or getting shot ourselves. The man says something and we realize he doesn't know. He has no freaking clue that civilization is coughing up blood. That there's a war going on. Never heard of the supervolcano. That the crops have failed around the globe. He noticed the long, weird winter, but that was it."

She marveled at this. "Wow."

"Oh, it gets better. Turns out he's a crazy old prepper who bought a trailer and hid it out on empty BLM land with ten thousand pounds of food and fifty thousand rounds of ammunition. He was worried about all sorts of crap: the president being a socialist, UN helicopters, the Chinese harvesting Americans for their organs, whatever. Out of his freaking mind with paranoia. He moved to the desert because he thought the world was going to end. And he was right."

"That's crazy."

"You know how Elder Smoot is always going on about the End of Days? This guy made Smoot look like the voice of reason." He glanced at Grover. "Sorry, I forgot. That's your dad."

"That's okay," Grover said. "I know how he gets."

"How did you get out of there?" Eliza asked.

"I haven't got to the weird part yet. No, trust me. It's weirder. This old man—I'll call him Methuselah, since we never got his real name—gets all excited. He takes us into the canyon behind his trailer, where he shows us a homemade tank hidden beneath tarps. It's an old Wells Fargo armored car with extra plate-metal armor welded around the sides. Gun ports built into the side and .50-caliber machine guns. Inside, RPGs, boxes of grenades, thousands more rounds of ammo. This thing is out there waiting and all it needs is a tank crew to run it. He'll give it to us on two conditions. First, we take him with us. Second, he wants to drive through Las Vegas on our way east."

"Why?" Eliza asked.

"That's exactly what I ask him. Turns out that Methuselah wants to see his fantasies come to life. He used to live in Las Vegas—had worked as a pit boss there for many years. Then Obama got elected, maybe Methuselah went off his meds, and he put all his savings into a doomstead in the desert. Now he wants to see Las Vegas destroyed. The three of us had a little conference."

"I thought you said there were five survivors."

Steve's face darkened. "I glossed over a few things. When we were in the artillery company we fought several battles. We took casualties."

"Oh. Sorry, go on."

"And we decide—this is crappy, I know—to steal Methuselah's homemade tank and leave him with his trailer and his food. Then we can go wherever we want. Fayer and Chambers are thinking Salt Lake, leaving me in Cedar City to hike over the mountains to Blister Creek.

"Meanwhile, Methuselah goes out to this Cold War–style bunker he has buried behind his place. He has a bunch of stuff he wants to get—gas masks, iodine pills, probably more guns and ammo. You can never have too much. While he's pulling away the boards that hide it, he stirs up a rattler underneath waiting out the heat of the day. Big old diamondback. It bites his hand. All that time hiding in the desert, with the world falling apart around him, and it's a stupid rattlesnake that does him in."

"Did you drive off and leave him?"

"No. We couldn't do that. He was in terrible pain and I knew right away he was going to die, with the hospitals being the way they are. We weren't sure what was waiting around Vegas, if we'd be shot as deserters or if there was a military government who could put us in contact with FBI headquarters, but Methuselah was no threat anymore. What would it hurt to find a field hospital and turn him over?

"We never found a hospital. Methuselah died on the road, and when we stopped to bury him, someone started shooting at us. We drove off in our armored car, got chased into the suburbs of Las Vegas. Where we found ourselves in the middle of a growing battle. We stashed the vehicle in an abandoned air conditioner factory and tried waiting it out in the tunnels. We were safe at first. Three, four days—the bombardment never stopped."

"The tunnels?" Eliza asked.

"There are storm drains beneath the city. Homeless people used to live down there and come up at night to panhandle and Dumpster dive. When it rained, they'd flee like rats. There are still people down there, only now they're refugees from the war. It's pretty miserable." He shrugged, and she could see more ugly details being glossed over.

"The problem is," he continued, "the federal troops were using the tunnels to infiltrate the city. They overran our camp one night. When we realized they weren't Californians, we surrendered and explained who we were. Lot of good it did. They arrested us anyway. That's more or less how we ended up here."

Grover had been listening in silence. "You're either super lucky," he said, "or you've hit one terrible stretch of bad luck. I can't decide."

"Either way, it's a strange story," Eliza said. "One crazy thing after another."

"Only the dead have boring stories these days," Steve said. "Short, boring, and deadly. They got herded into a refugee camp and died of cholera. Bandits shot them. They starved to death while waiting for flour rations. Those of us still around are only alive because of a series of crazy coincidences."

"Maybe you're right," she said. "How long have you been prisoners?"

"About a month. They put us with these others, mostly California-born government officials. Nobody has been charged with any crime. They've moved us around, but always within Las Vegas."

"How many prisoners are there?"

"About thirty now. We had a lot more. Maybe half have died. Every once in a while, new prisoners join us—like you—but nobody ever leaves, except as a dead body."

Eliza let go of Steve's dry, warm hand and rubbed at her scalp, trying to think. They couldn't sit here, waiting for the building to collapse. Starving, dying of thirst.

As if to punctuate her thoughts, fresh artillery shells rained down on the hotel. The building shook and bucked, and more tiles fell from the ceiling. The bombardment continued for several minutes, then faded to the west. When it was over, Eliza went to find Miriam.

She had no intention of waiting here to be killed.

CHAPTER TWENTY-FIVE

Eliza found Miriam near the blown-out windows, taking in the scene. A wrecked armored personnel carrier sat in the street below. Craters pockmarked the road. The strip mall across the street lay in smoking ruins. Papers tumbled down the street. A block down, a slot machine sat in the middle of the intersection, as if carried away from its home by an explosion, then set gently to the ground.

The air blowing in from the street felt like a blast of air from an oven. But the shadows were long and with any luck the evening would bring relief.

"Don't linger," Miriam warned. "There might be snipers."

Eliza stepped back. "Any ideas?"

"No good ones. I didn't realize we were so far up. Seven stories. If you go up to the edge, you can see that a few people have made the jump anyway."

Eliza shuddered. "Steve didn't say anything about that."

"He's probably numb to death. You saw that Fayer and Chambers are here?"

"Steve told me, yes."

"I talked to Fayer. The things she's gone through would curl your toes."

"You mean the part about the helicopter?" Eliza asked.

"I was thinking more about those drugged-up gang members in L.A."

"You mean there's more? I didn't hear about that."

"Let's worry about the here and now," Miriam said. "There's no food, and barely any water. The army either doesn't know what to do with the prisoners, or doesn't care."

"The army can't even feed itself. Question is, what do we do? I'm not going to sit here waiting to die."

"Me either. Maybe we could get the chairs and batter down the doors."

"There are men outside with guns," Eliza reminded her. "What about tearing up the carpet and dangling it out the window? We can lower someone to the next floor."

Miriam raised an eyebrow. "How would we do that? Roll it into a big thirty-foot-long roll?"

"If we had tools we could cut strips and tie them together."

"I've already looked around. There's nothing."

"I didn't come all this way to fall into Steve's arms and die by his side."

"You don't have to tell me, I'm not dying here either. I've got a husband and a baby at home. Did Krantz give you anything to work with?"

"Steve had an escape vehicle at one time. You heard about the tank?"

"The armored car thing built by the old-timer? Wasn't it destroyed?"

"No, they stashed it in an abandoned factory somewhere in Vegas. Might still be there. Of course, we have to get out of here first.

The prisoners have been here a week. I'm sure Steve has given it a lot of thought, but he didn't seem to have any ideas."

"Fayer didn't have anything either. She thinks we're finished. And not from starvation. You know how the building shakes when it gets hit? It didn't used to do that. The foundation is giving way. When that happens, we'll pancake all the way down."

As horrifying as that sounded, it gave Eliza an idea. "Do you think you could take down one of the guards and get his weapon?"

"Maybe. I was looking for an opportunity on the way up, but I was always facing at least two guns. What are you thinking?"

"If Fayer has noticed the shaking, those kids outside have too. You're a good actor, you could convince them the building is about to give way."

"They'll think I'm a panicky woman. What will that get me?"

"No, you're not," Eliza said. "You're a structural engineer. Make stuff up. You infiltrated the Zarahemla cult—surely you can manage this."

"Keep talking," Miriam said. "Then what?"

"Then they'll move. And they'll take us with them."

"Unless they leave us here to die."

"They'll take us," Eliza said, with more confidence then she felt. She couldn't think of any other plan. "When they do that, we'll create a distraction, and you'll take out one of the soldiers."

Miriam looked thoughtful. "Those soldiers are jumpy. Even if I get a gun, the others will start shooting. People will die."

"They're going to die anyway."

A thin smile. "Now who's the ruthless one?"

"I'm desperate," Eliza said. "Aren't you?"

"Getting there." Miriam nodded. "Okay, let's make it happen."

★★★

The prisoners were a starved, ragged bunch, plagued by weak, muddled thinking. Most of them wanted nothing to do with the plan. They wanted to lie down and be left alone. To curl up and die. Eliza imagined what they'd gone through and fought down her frustration. She remembered another time, a pit in the desert outside Las Vegas. A young woman starving on a diet of lettuce. Starvation didn't turn one into a fighter. But at the same time, Eliza's current predicament didn't sound impossible. She'd survived worse situations, or at least equally bad.

Together, Eliza and Miriam coaxed, prodded, pleaded, and threatened. Those who were too far gone they told to stay down and keep their mouths shut when the time came. And then they waited for the next artillery attack. And waited.

The shelling continued to the east, then swept through the center of the city again without passing near their building. The heat was suffocating and Eliza's mouth felt like it had been stuffed with wads of cotton gauze. A woman cried out for water.

Eliza waited with Steve. She was sweating profusely, but his hands were dry and hot. If the soldiers ever delivered water, she'd fight the others if she had to, to get him his share.

When darkness came, gunfire started up in the streets. First a few isolated shots, then back-and-forth chatter. The gunfire grew louder, into angry-sounding bursts. A series of thumping detonations like an enormous bass drum sounded from the direction of the Strip. They were answered by lighter machine guns. A jet roared overhead. A light flashed, followed by a thundering explosion several seconds later.

Finally, the artillery came. Shells rained down on the hotel and its surroundings. Gunfire raged in the streets below. As soon as the building started to shudder, Eliza and Miriam pounded on the conference room doors.

"The building is about to collapse!" Miriam cried. "You have to listen to me—this is what I do for a living. I'm a structural engineer. I'm telling you, the center post of this room is the main load-bearing support of this whole wing. It goes, and we all go down with it—and it *is* going. They do *not* just vibrate like that!"

No answer. A thin blue light seeped beneath the doors, so someone had to be out there still. They kept pounding.

Miriam continued. "Please, for God's sake. The post goes all the way to bedrock. There has to be a stress fracture running right down the center of it for it to shimmy like that. And if the post goes, the entire building pancakes in about ten seconds. You have to let us out." She pounded the flat of her palm against the door. "I was the chief engineer for this building, do you hear me?"

The building lurched and the women grabbed for the wall to steady themselves. And still the artillery kept falling. A particularly heavy blast hit somewhere below them and the floor wobbled like something made of rubber. A beam crashed from the ceiling.

It's real. It's really happening.

Far from a bluff, their ploy was only reflecting reality. Under sustained bombardment, the abandoned hotel and casino was on the verge of collapse. And if there had been soldiers on the other side, those men had already fled.

Eliza grabbed Miriam. "The chairs. We have to batter our way out."

Flashes in the street illuminated the room. The stacked chairs had tipped over. Prisoners were on their feet, staggering to hold their balance on the lurching floor. People screamed and when another light flashed, several had disappeared from the center of the room.

Steve found her. "Watch out. The floor collapsed in the middle."

Another flash and a concussive explosion threw them from their feet. This time the light didn't go out. White flames licked the carpet just inside the windows. A prisoner beat furiously at his legs. Eliza rose to her hands and knees, trying to regain her bearings. The room was shaking, but she didn't know if it was her own swimming head or the building doing its best to collapse.

The hole in the floor was no more than ten feet across. Looking down, she could see the story below them, some sort of lounge with a dark TV screen and couches and easy chairs covered with dust and ceiling tiles and shattered glass. Two people struggled among the debris where they'd fallen. One of them screamed in pain, his arm twisted at an ugly angle. It was fifteen feet or so down to the lounge.

She found Miriam and Steve and they recalibrated their plans.

Choking on smoke, the building threatening to go down at any time, the three of them spread word through the remaining prisoners. Grover, when they found him, was shaking and pale, but didn't cower in a corner awaiting orders. Instead, he was working of his own volition to help the weakened prisoners gather around the hole.

From there, Eliza, Miriam, and Steve lowered prisoners into the hole and dropped them onto a couch in the lounge. Last fall, Steve had been able to pick Eliza up as if she were a child, but now he strained and nearly lost his grip whenever his arms were fully extended into the hole. When they were helping Chambers down, Steve dropped his side. When he did, all of Chambers's weight transferred awkwardly to the two women, and they lost their grip. The man fell with a cry.

"I'm okay!" he called up.

Soon they had everyone down who could move. The blast had killed three prisoners, and the man with the burned legs was so badly injured that he screamed when they tried to move him. He flailed and begged them to leave him alone. Feeling sick, Eliza abandoned the man to the smoldering, smoke-filled room. The air was so thick she had to find the hole again by feel.

With nobody to help them down, Steve and Miriam had made a jump for it. That left Eliza. They urged her down. She lowered herself into the darkness and cried out that she was jumping. Then she let go.

Steve and Miriam broke her fall and the three of them crumpled to the ground. Eliza regained her feet only to stumble when another shell hit the building. She regained her balance and groped for her companions.

All around, prisoners cried out for each other. A few forced their way down the hall, apparently taking their chances solo rather than waiting around for the soldiers to discover they were missing. The burned man could still be heard above them, screaming from the conference room.

"We have to get out of here," Miriam said.

"Where's Grover?" Eliza asked.

"Right here," came his voice from the darkness. "I haven't moved."

"Fayer, are you there?" Steve called. "Chambers?"

They found Fayer coughing, and crying out weakly, but Chambers had disappeared. Nobody knew if he'd staggered off in some random direction, following the fleeing prisoners, or if he was lying in a corner, injured and unable to answer. Nobody had seen him since they'd dropped him through the hole in the floor.

"We have to go," Miriam said. "Now."

By now the other prisoners had dispersed. Gunfire sounded in the building, which shuddered from repeated explosions.

Grover found a doorway down the hall in the opposite direction from that taken by the bulk of the fleeing prisoners. "I think it's a stairwell."

It was, and the companions—Steve, Fayer, Eliza, Miriam, and Grover—found their way down the stairs by feel, hands following metal railings. They had descended two stories when they came upon a head-sized hole in the outer wall. Eliza looked out to see flashes in the street directly below them—a gunfight playing out only yards away. They continued down and soon reached a pair of heavy metal doors.

Beyond lay the main casino. Smoke and tear gas filled the air. Gunfire lashed from one side of the room to the other. Gaping holes opened in the walls to the outside, and men with gas masks poured through them into the building. Phosphorous grenades flashed.

It was a vision of hell itself, and Eliza tried to retreat. Then Miriam pointed to the destroyed plate glass window to their right, away from the firefight. They made a run for it. When Eliza reached the window, she lowered her shoulder and bashed through the hanging shards of glass. She found herself outside, among desiccated flower beds and toppled statuary. Tracer bullets lit up the sky.

When the others were out, they ran in a tight knot for the sidewalk. A helicopter thumped overhead. A missile roared from its underbelly and lit up a building down the block, which disgorged a ball of fire. Gunshots sounded all around.

It wasn't until they reached the street that Eliza hazarded a glance back at the casino-hotel. The main building was burning on three floors, staining the night air red, with smoke pouring from its windows. One of the two hotel towers flanking the casino had a twisted, movie-monster look, while the other sat skeletal against the sky. Another shell came screaming in and a clap of thunder split the air.

The casino shuddered. When it fell, it would take down smaller hotels and strip malls around it.

"Over there," Steve said.

He pointed across a cratered three-lane street. The poles holding the dead traffic lights bent at crazy angles across the road. In the near darkness, she couldn't see what he was pointing at. An underpass of some kind, emerging from beneath the opposite side of the street.

Another explosion hit the hotel. A split second later, something whistled past Eliza's ear. Grover stumbled, crying out in pain.

Eliza and Miriam grabbed his arms and hauled him along. He regained his feet and they raced after Steve and Fayer, now in the lead. Red tracer bullets sliced across the road to their right. They came from a supermarket parking lot, and return fire answered from a brick office building opposite.

They reached the other side of the street, and Eliza found a metal staircase that descended from the sidewalk into the underpass. When they reached the bottom, it turned out not to be a road at all, but a wide, boxy concrete culvert. These must be the storm drains the FBI agents had taken to after abandoning their armored vehicle.

After passing beneath the road, the culvert stretched across the open ground for maybe thirty yards before disappearing into a yawning hole beneath a parking garage. Peeling graffiti colored the concrete walls where they lay exposed to the sky. Bullet holes pocked the surface.

Grover was groaning and clenching his left bicep, so Eliza stopped him just before they plunged into darkness. The tunnel emitted a wet, foul odor, like a cross between a diaper pail and a bag of wet clothes left to mildew.

"Let me look." She made to unbutton his long-sleeved shirt. He flinched away. "Come on, Grover, you've been hit. I'll be careful."

Grover nodded at Steve. "Could he do it instead?"

She stared. They could be killed by a bullet or a stray shell at any moment and Grover was too shy to take off his shirt. But he was insistent, so she looked away while Steve helped him out of his shirt.

Meanwhile, Miriam searched a pair of dead soldiers sprawled at the mouth of the tunnel, apparently looking for weapons. She came up empty-handed.

But the bodies hadn't been completely looted. Fayer took off one man's shirt and buttoned it over her tank top, then tugged off the second, smaller man's boots and socks. She winced as she pulled the socks on over scraped-up feet.

Steve pulled something from Grover's arm. The boy hissed.

"Well, look what we have here," Steve said.

He held something up to the dim light cast from the burning hotel across the street. It was a poker chip, glossy gold and stained around the edges with Grover's blood. Five thousand dollars.

"You're a high-roller now." Steve slapped it into Grover's hand. "Bet there's a bunch of these things back on the road. Want to go back and scavenge up a fortune?"

Grover managed a thin smile. He caught the others looking and hurriedly put his undergarments and shirt back on.

Then the gunfire picked up again and they ducked into the dank tunnel and safety.

CHAPTER TWENTY-SIX

The air grew thicker as they penetrated deeper into the tunnels, first smelling of motor oil, then changing to the stench of rotting bodies. The gunfire grew muffled and then silent after a few corners, but the walls continued to shake as periodic explosions pummeled the ground above them. Steve went first, followed by Eliza, then Fayer, Miriam, and finally Grover. They whispered and touched each other's shoulders to stay in contact.

After a few minutes, they splashed into water up to their ankles, and before Eliza could stop her, Fayer had dropped to her knees and was gulping away. Steve tried to do the same, but Eliza pulled him back and begged him not to.

"I'm so thirsty. Please, just a mouthful."

"Steve, you know it's filthy. You can't."

"She's right," Fayer's voice said hollowly as she rose to her feet. "It tastes awful. I hate to think what's in it."

"Didn't stop you from guzzling like an idiot," Miriam said.

"I couldn't help it."

"What if we filtered it?" Grover suggested. "We could strain it through our shirts like you'd do in the desert."

"That's for clearing out sediment and mosquito larvae," Eliza said. "It won't help with water-borne pathogens."

"Then what do we do?" he asked. "I'm so thirsty."

Yes, so was Eliza. It had become almost unbearable. And that was after less than a day baking in the abandoned hotel conference room. Steve said their last water delivery had come the previous evening, but they'd been thirsty for days. He and Fayer must be suffering from serious dehydration.

But at the same time, cholera had already killed tens of thousands in and around Las Vegas. Any water down here would be swimming in it. Introduced to bodies already weakened with hunger and dehydration, an infection would surely prove fatal.

On the other hand, Steve had already fought off an attack of some sort of intestinal illness. Could you build an immunity to cholera? She had no idea and it wasn't like she could grab her phone and call Jacob to ask.

Steve was edging away as she wrestled with these worries, and she realized just in time that he was heading for the puddle anyway.

She grabbed his arm. "No, not here. I'll find you water, I promise."

"How will you do that?"

"I don't know. I'll go to the surface and look."

"It's impossible."

"If we don't find water by morning, then you can drink the puddles. Can you hold on until then?"

He paused, then said, "Okay. Until morning."

"That goes for all of you," Eliza said. "You too, Agent Fayer."

"Water or no water, we can't stay down here forever," Miriam said. "Does anyone have any ideas?"

"What about Methuselah's tank?" Eliza asked.

"Methuselah's what?" Grover asked.

"An armored car," Steve said. "We got it from some old survivalist. We left it in an abandoned factory."

"Do you remember where?" Eliza asked.

"For all we know, it's buried in rubble," Fayer said. She sounded stronger after her drink, and Eliza wondered if she'd made a mistake denying Steve a mouthful or two.

"Or stolen," he said.

Eliza wasn't so sure. "You said it was an air conditioner factory?"

"That's right," Steve said.

"Nobody is looting AC units these days. And Las Vegas is a big place. Even with all the troops fighting, there's a good chance the factory has been untouched since you took to the storm drains. Could you find it again?"

"Sure, if we're above ground," Steve said. "In the daylight. But if we come up, people will start shooting."

"I agree," Fayer said. "We have to stay down here. It's too dangerous up top."

"*Everything* is dangerous right now," Miriam said. "Even sitting here. Soldiers could come around that corner any minute. Or heck, starving hordes of cannibals might tear us apart."

"Let's not get carried away," Eliza said.

"Point is, we're wasting time. There's nowhere safe, so we may as well start moving."

All five of them agreed with this much, and with no better ideas, they decided to make an attempt to find the abandoned factory via the drainage tunnels. Apparently, the tunnels went on for miles and miles, but it was difficult to navigate them in the dark, so the first step was to find another entrance so they could pop out long enough to get their bearings. They groped their way forward, making slow progress.

There were other survivors in the tunnels. Eliza heard breathing, saw lights snuff out as they came around the corner, smelled a hint of burning kerosene, or saw a wood fire quickly doused. Once, she caught a glimpse of a mattress and several thin, filthy children staring, before someone hastily turned off a lantern.

"I'd feel a lot better with guns and flashlights," Miriam said when they'd put some distance between themselves and the children.

"They're just kids," Eliza said.

"What do you think they've done to stay alive down here? What do you think they've done for food and water?"

At last the tunnel emerged into open air again, emptying into a gravelly wash as it passed beneath the road. The gunfire sounded distant, so Eliza and Steve risked climbing the bank to the street for a better look. Up above, they found more deserted roads, with darkened duplexes, crummy cinder-block houses, and a partially collapsed strip mall across the street. Fires burned to the south and west, and the gun battles continued in those directions as well.

They located the Strip and the burning hotels and office buildings downtown, maybe a mile distant.

"Glad we're out of there," Eliza said.

"Yeah, but in the wrong direction," Steve said. "We've been going east. We need to get west of the Strip and north of Highway 95."

They returned to the edge of the tunnels, where the other three waited. Eliza gave the bad news.

"We passed another culvert about ten minutes ago," Fayer said. "It seemed like one of the main lines. If we took that, it would cut us back under the city and to the west. If we can get under the freeway and then north of 95, we'll be safer."

"I can't go back in there," Grover said. "Not until I get water."

"What choice do we have?" Eliza asked.

"If you have to leave me, I understand."

"We're not leaving anyone," she said.

Fayer bent over with her hands on her knees. Steve leaned against the concrete and slid to the ground. He looked almost fatally exhausted. Miriam put her hands on her hips and started to say something, then turned away with a sigh.

This was no good. Get settled here and they'd never get going again.

Eliza kicked at the rubbish buried in the sediment that had collected on the side of the drainage canal. She pried loose a two-liter soda bottle, tapped it to dump out the sand, then blew into it to pop out the collapsed sides.

Miriam came over. "What have you got?"

"Something to hold water. Stay with the others. I'll see what I can find."

"I'm going too."

Eliza nodded. "Okay. Let's go. The rest of you, go back underground. We'll be back in a few minutes."

Eliza and Miriam climbed out of the culvert and crossed the street to the strip mall Eliza had spotted earlier. Darkened signs advertised a liquor store, payday loans, and a Mexican bodega. The first two stores were collapsed and the bodega had been looted to the floorboards. Cautiously, they made their way onto a side street and into the surrounding subdivisions.

It was a poor, working-class neighborhood, now in ruins. The houses that hadn't burned had suffered from looters. There wasn't a scrap of food or water in any of them. No clothes, no mattresses. The furniture was missing, probably burned for fuel. And the taps were dry. Even the toilet bowls and tanks held no water. With no other options, they continued down the street, house by house.

After nearly an hour of fruitless searching, their luck turned. It started with Miriam spotting a pair of dead soldiers sprawled in the street. Others had stripped their boots, but one of the soldiers, his body nearly cut in two by gunfire, had a pistol holstered at his waist that Miriam discovered when she rolled him over.

She lifted it to the moonlight, then checked the magazine. "Now we're talking. Grab me that holster, will you?"

A few minutes later, a figure slinking down the opposite side of the street sent them scrambling into one of the yards for cover. It was only a coyote, but while still in the yard, Eliza found a concrete cistern for collecting rainwater. Other cisterns they'd spotted had been drained, but this one had somehow remained undetected and was half-full.

The water was warm and tasted of rust. She didn't care. Taking turns with Miriam, Eliza drank until her stomach hurt, then she filled the empty soda bottle. They found a plastic watering can in a backyard shed and filled this too.

The other three practically wept in relief when they returned bearing water. Eliza handed over the watering can to Grover and Fayer, then sat with Steve to force him to take tiny sips from the soda bottle. After he'd downed maybe a third, she made him wait twenty minutes. While he did, she washed his hands and face, and poured some on the back of his neck.

"Don't waste it," he protested.

"There's more where this came from. I only wish I could get you food."

"There's food in the armored car." Fresh optimism warmed his voice. "And it's good stuff too. That crazy survivalist knew what he was doing."

Steve leaned back and sighed as she washed and cooled his neck. He was so thin and dirty, but she relished the feeling of her hands against his skin. So many months without a word and now he was here, by her side. She had despaired of ever seeing him again. It was almost a miracle. Almost enough to heal her wounded faith.

When only a few swallows remained in the soda bottle, she let Steve drink the rest. Fayer and Grover shared out the watering can, drinking some, and running the rest over their heads and hands. When it was empty, Miriam and Eliza went to refill the containers. Upon their return, the group reentered the tunnels.

Their luck continued to improve. After another forty minutes below ground, they emerged to find that they'd hooked north of the airport to the edge of the Strip. The gunfire had diminished to sporadic bursts, although several buildings were still spewing flame. Steve was able to figure out where they were by a pair of intact street signs marking an intersection. Reoriented, they returned to the darkness.

Dawn stained the western horizon by the time they finally picked their way out of the tunnels and emerged in the open air.

Exhausted and dirty, their water gone again, the five companions stood in the open air enjoying a breeze that momentarily washed away the bitter, choking smoke. The FBI agents took their bearings and declared that they were close. When they set off again, Fayer brought up the rear, hands over her belly and frowning as if with discomfort. Eliza dropped back to ask if she was okay, and the woman shrugged and said too much water on an empty stomach had given her cramps. Except nobody else seemed to be suffering the same symptoms.

What about Fayer's moment of weakness, when she'd gulped at the filthy puddle? That had only been seven or eight hours earlier. Even if the water had been contaminated, Eliza doubted the symptoms would have come on so quickly.

A pair of jets rumbled over the city. Flashes of light emerged from their tails, hanging in the air like the dying embers of a fireworks display. Flares, to throw off surface-to-air missiles. More explosions rocked the downtown.

"Keep moving," Steve said. "We're close."

He led them down a wide, vacant boulevard lined with palm trees. At first glance, this part of the city looked untouched, but bullet holes riddled the cement sound barriers, and a few minutes later they came upon a pile of body bags, the dead stacked five deep and extending the length of a city block. They crossed the street to get away from the bodies, and walked past them in silence. The sun rose in the sky, but it was cooler than the previous day, almost chilly, as the northern air masses pushed south again.

Ten minutes later they found the industrial park where the FBI agents had stashed their vehicle. The warehouses, factories, and storage units lay silent. Fire had gutted some of the buildings, while others sat among piles of garbage that had blown against their foundations like so many plastic and paper tumbleweeds.

Steve brought them through an unlocked chain link gate, then to a warehouse next to the main factory building.

"The back way is blocked, so we'll have to go through here."

He drew open a rising bay door with a noisy clank. A dozen or so squatters lay in the middle of the floor or slumped against the walls. They'd made nests of blankets and mattresses. The room reeked of blood and sweat and feces.

Miriam drew her pistol. "FBI. Everybody out of the building."

None of them moved, but simply froze as if too terrified or weak to comply.

Miriam repeated her orders, her voice harsh and demanding. Then she let out a sound halfway between a hacking cough and a groan. "Never mind." She dropped the nose of her gun and moved cautiously into the open bay.

As Eliza entered with the others and her eyes adjusted, she saw what had caused Miriam's reaction. The people hadn't responded because they were dead. Sick or starving, they had found refuge in the loading bay, then simply died where they lay.

Eliza had grown almost immune to death by now, and struggled to see the hollow, dehydrated bodies as humans. She joined Miriam, Steve, and Fayer in going through their possessions. They found several plastic milk jugs filled with water, but no food. No weapons or anything else of value.

"Um, Eliza?" Grover said. "You'd better check this out."

He had backed against one of the empty walls rather than participate in the search and now stood over a big plastic bin with his shirt pulled up over his mouth and nose.

When Eliza came over, the stench greeted her like a wall. She covered her mouth with her hand and forced herself to look. The bin was a latrine. The contents looked like Cream of Wheat.

"Why does it look like that?" he asked.

"Stay back." Eliza turned to the others, who were still checking out the rest of the open warehouse. "Nobody touch those water jugs. These people died of cholera."

"This way," Steve said. "It's through the building and out back."

They continued deeper into the warehouse and then out the other side. The lot and the cluster of buildings beyond were deserted and almost empty of the evidence of battle seen elsewhere in the city: spent casings, bullet-pocked walls, dead bodies, burned-out cars, and wrecked equipment. There was plenty of evidence that refugees had gone through, however, in the form of pried-open doors, cut chain link, and discarded packaging. At last Steve stopped them in front of another bay door, this one open already. A semi parked in front, its tires gone, the hood open, and the engine gutted for parts or motor oil.

"This is the building," he said.

They lifted themselves into the warehouse. The room was a vast space scattered with equipment and debris: empty metal shelves, stacks of shrink-wrapped air-conditioning units everywhere, and abandoned forklifts. Hundreds of pallets packed the gloomy back half of the open room, as if the wheels of commerce had continued turning long after the crisis presented itself. Only there had been nowhere left to ship this stuff and so it had ended up here.

Eliza looked around with growing dismay, thinking the armored car had been stolen, but when she turned, Fayer and Steve were swapping high fives.

"What are we waiting for?" Steve said. "There's food in there and I'm starved."

The agents made their way to the back of the room while the others shared bewildered looks. They attacked the largest stack of pallets. After a few minutes, they exposed a slender passageway that led between pallet towers, deeper into the heap of obsolete equipment. And there, crouching in the dark, sat the armored car. It looked like a giant safe on wheels crossed with one of Leonardo da Vinci's fantasy drawings: iron plates welded around the exterior, with gun slots bristling along the sides. Strange bumps covered the sides like metal blisters or the scale armor of a lumbering dinosaur.

Steve grinned. "Methuselah's tank. And it's untouched."

CHAPTER TWENTY-SEVEN

Later, sitting in relative safety within the armored car, their stomachs blessedly full of dried venison and powdered milk, talking by the light of an LED lamp from among the bountiful supplies prepared by their unfortunate benefactor, Grover voiced what surely they'd all been thinking.

"We could hide in here. If your friend—what's his name?"

"Chambers," Steve said.

"Right, if Agent Chambers shows up, we'll let him in too. But if not, we can restack the pallets and wait for the battle to end."

"And how long would that take?" Eliza said.

"There's food and water enough for weeks if we're careful," Grover said.

"The battle is months old already. That might not be long enough."

"They can't keep fighting forever," he protested. "You saw them. They're starving. And what about guns? Ammo?"

"Keep it down," Miriam said. "We're right here."

Indeed, they were practically sitting on each other's laps. So many crates of ammo and guns, canisters of fuel, boxes of dried food, and jugs of water stuffed the interior that they couldn't move without bumping into each other.

"Weapons aren't the issue," Steve said. "The world is awash in the stuff. Food is another matter, but we have no way of knowing if they're getting resupplied or not."

Eliza was relieved to see him acting more like his old self. Calm, steady. Confident. The food and water had done him good.

"Grover, we can't wait it out," she said. "There are people in Blister Creek who need us."

"They're safe where they are," Grover said. "And they'd want *us* to be safe too, even if it takes us all summer to get home."

"You don't know they're safe. And you don't know how easy it will be to return. Where will the battle lines be in three weeks? Southern Utah, maybe."

"Besides," Steve said. "This warehouse isn't secure. And I'm not talking about hiding the truck. There are bombs, fire. Even crazy army units with atomic artillery shells. What if one side or the other starts in on that? It will turn the city into a radioactive slag heap, with us inside."

As if to punctuate his words, the building rumbled with the force of a distant explosion.

"I feel safer here," Grover persisted.

Miriam passed out handguns and spare magazines. "You can stay behind if you want. The rest of us are going home to Zion, with or without you."

"What about Chambers?" Fayer asked.

"What about him?" Miriam said. "He disappeared. For all we know, he's dead. We can't stick around waiting to see if he shows."

"No," Steve said. He sounded reluctant. "We can't."

"We're stuck here until nightfall," Eliza said. "If he doesn't find us by then, we'll make a run for it."

"I don't want to go," Grover persisted. "What if we don't make it?"

"We'll make it," Steve said.

Grover looked down with his brow furrowed.

Steve, Fayer, and Miriam grabbed flashlights and went out to clear a path through the pallets for the armored car. Eliza stayed behind to treat Grover's arm. The poker chip shrapnel had left a bloody circle on his left bicep, more painful-looking than dangerous, but Eliza didn't want to chance infection. She wiped it with an iodine-dipped cotton ball, then bandaged his arm.

"I'm sorry," Grover said.

"For what?"

"I wish I weren't such a coward. My brothers aren't like this. What's wrong with me?"

"Let me tell you a secret. Everyone is a coward inside. The trick is to keep your mouth shut and stop giving voice to your fears. Act brave and you become brave."

"That's easy for you to say. You're the prophet's sister."

The back door of the armored car opened and Steve appeared, his mouth drawn into a line. "You'd better have a look at this."

Eliza found Fayer sitting outside the wall of pallets, knees drawn to her chest. Her breath came in shallow gasps. Miriam stood a few feet away, staring grimly.

"I'm sorry," Fayer said. "I tried to get farther away, it was just so sudden."

Eliza had no idea what they were talking about. Miriam pointed with her flashlight.

There, on the ground, was the result of Fayer's meal, come out in a stream of diarrhea. Mixed among it were lumps of what looked like brownish hot cereal.

Fayer groaned. "It's that water from the tunnel. I shouldn't have. I knew it."

"You were thirsty," Eliza said. "If I'd been more alert, I would have stopped you."

Fayer staggered to her feet. "Don't look at me!"

She was already dropping her pants as she staggered away. The others turned and went back into the armored car.

Grover held up a lantern as they came in. "What is it?"

"Agent Fayer has cholera," Eliza said.

"What are her chances?" Steve asked.

"And is she contagious?" Miriam added.

"I don't know. I don't understand it. All I know is the signs, how to recognize it. I'm not a doctor."

"You're the closest thing we've got," Miriam said. "What did Jacob tell you?"

"Cholera is water-borne. Fayer is right—she got it from drinking that puddle. Beyond that, I doubt she could pass it easily. But we absolutely can't let her come into contact with our water supplies."

Steve scratched his scalp. "We should use sterilizing tablets just in case. Once we get rolling, she'll have to go to the bathroom in here. You're sure it's cholera? Does it come on that fast?"

Eliza tried to remember what Jacob had taught her. There was so much reading, so many things to learn—there was a reason that medical school took so long, after all. And on top of studying medical stuff, she'd been training with firearms, helping to police the town, plus keeping up with her duties on the farm and ranch. Every day after Steve vanished had been sunup to sundown.

"It does seem fast," she admitted. "I would have guessed a couple of days. It might depend on how much bacteria she ingested."

"So faster would mean a higher dose from the contaminated water?" Steve asked.

"That sounds right."

"Is she doomed?" Miriam asked.

"It doesn't look good. She's starved and dehydrated already. She needs an IV and antibiotics. Maybe if we can get her to Blister Creek."

Grover was going through the first aid kits. "Here are some anti-diarrhea tablets."

He'd found a single box of eight tablets, and the packaging looked ancient. The tablets were a brand Eliza had never heard of. And no doubt meant for a garden-variety stomachache, not a scourge that had killed millions of people throughout history. As a matter of fact, cholera was probably killing millions of people at that exact moment.

The ground shuddered, reminding them of their even more pressing worries. Eliza found a water bottle, scratched it with a knife to mark it as Fayer's, then went out to give the woman the tablets and a drink.

Fayer lay on the ground beyond the barrier of pallets, weeping tearlessly. She had soiled herself, and resisted Eliza's efforts to get her into a sitting position. "I couldn't help it. It came so fast."

"It's okay, it's not your fault."

"Yes it is. All this is my own damn fault."

"Take two of these. They might help."

"No, just let me be. Go on without me. It's too late—I'm going to die like those refugees."

"You're not going to die. We'll get you to Blister Creek and my brother will help you."

"Like he helped that guy's mother?"

"Did Miriam tell you about that? I wish she hadn't. Never mind—that was different. You're one of us now. Come on, open your mouth. Good, now drink this and swallow."

When the pills were down, Eliza brought Fayer within the wall of pallets. She laid the woman down beneath the back bumper of the armored car for privacy, then helped her out of her soiled clothing. She took off Fayer's shirt and laid it across her lap to cover her. Eliza rose.

"I'm scared, please don't leave me."

"I'm going to find you clean clothes."

"I'll just make a mess of them."

"In that case, there's a towel inside. Wrap it around your waist and you'll be able to get it off more quickly next time you have to go."

Fayer groaned and clenched her belly. She crawled away from the bumper on her hands and knees. Her sphincter gave loose, splattering out the water given to her only moments earlier.

Eliza helped her get cleaned up a second time, then brought her a towel plus a bedroll to put under her head. When she'd finished, she went to help Steve and Miriam, working to clear a path through the pallets for the armored car.

After a few more minutes, Steve suggested they stop. "Any more and you'll be able to spot it from the outside. We can finish it up tonight before we head out."

"If we're going to be driving all night," Miriam said, "we should take shifts getting some rest now."

"Good idea," he said. "Why don't you take first shift. Tell Grover and Fayer to get some rest too. I'll take Eliza up to the warehouse roof, see if we can figure out what's going on out there."

Eliza and Steve grabbed binoculars from the armored car, then set out across the warehouse floor for a metal staircase that led up to a catwalk encircling the room.

"I thought we'd never be alone," Steve said as they clanged up the stairs. "Of course I look and smell godawful."

Eliza felt suddenly shy. It seemed like a lifetime since they'd lain on that cold bed in the Bryce Canyon lodge, making out like two horny teenagers.

"You look okay to me."

He turned with a raised eyebrow. "You're a bad liar, Christianson."

"Okay, *Krantz,* I'll shoot straight. You look like walking death. How about that?"

He grinned. "Better."

Steve was steadier on his feet than when she'd found him in the hotel conference room. He was going to be okay.

They made their way around the catwalk, then threw open the metal doors and stepped onto the roof. Feeling exposed, they crouched in the shadow of an evaporative cooler and looked across the factory buildings to the city beyond.

The fires had spread on the west side of the city, sending fresh columns of smoke into the atmosphere. Gunfire crackled in the distance, joined by the steady thump of mortar rounds and artillery. Light flashed to the south, followed by a concussive boom.

"I've never seen anything like this," Steve said.

"Not even in Afghanistan?"

He shook his head. "When they write the history of the twenty-first century, Afghanistan and Iraq won't even make a footnote. Assuming anyone is left to write it down. Might be oral history, the way we're going."

"Or polygamist monks copying manuscripts."

"Polygamist monks," he said. "Wonder how that would work. Is this really the end of everything?"

"I hope not."

"Me too. What does Jacob think? Does he still believe we'll pull it together?"

"He's losing hope. A few weeks ago, he made some comparison to the fall of Rome, then said you'd have to throw in World War III and the Black Death too."

"He's not far off. A billion dead and counting. That's what they're saying."

"That's what they were saying in February," Eliza corrected. "Better double that figure." She thought about the nuclear war on the subcontinent. "Maybe triple."

"It's enough to turn a skeptic into a fundy. So if Jacob admits that it's falling apart, is he still denying he's a prophet?"

"He's trying to, yes."

"And Fernie? How is she?"

"Still paralyzed, but standing tall in her faith. I wouldn't say she and Jacob have been fighting, but it's a stressful time."

Another flash, followed by an ear-splitting boom. The warehouse shook. That one was close.

"Stressful?" Steve said when the building stopped shaking. "Yeah, I'd say so."

"How do we get out of here?" Eliza asked.

"Come on, let's take a look."

They crawled between giant grated fans, meant to circulate long-extinct air-conditioning systems below. An array of solar collectors gleamed on one side—that would be extremely valuable for Blister Creek, if there had been a way of getting them home.

On the edge of the building, Steve lifted the binoculars he'd been carrying. He scanned across the city, then handed them to Eliza and pointed out various pockets of firing.

"We need to get north," he said. "See that road to the west of the burning office tower? What do you think about that?"

"There are soldiers behind those Jersey barriers. They're shooting at someone across the street."

He took the binoculars. "You're right. Okay, so we bypass that street.

The big one running parallel to it is Palms Boulevard. That looks clear. We'll head up a few blocks, then go around."

They stared in that direction in silence for several seconds. Of course it went without saying that the battle lines this afternoon might very well shift by nightfall.

The sun burned orange as it crept toward the western horizon. Sunset was still several hours distant. She didn't want to wait—she wanted to get Fayer to Jacob's clinic before it was too late—but leaving in daylight was suicide and they both knew it.

Steve crawled back to the fans and stopped in front of an enclosed metal water tank that Eliza hadn't noticed before. There was a faucet for draining the tank, and he strained to turn it. In the past, he could have snapped the thing off with his powerful hands, but now he had to crank hard to get it open. A rusty sludge of water came out, then ran clear.

"It's not potable," she warned. "Look, it funnels into the tank from that rainwater catchment system. It was probably used to cool equipment."

"It's got to be cleaner than that slop Fayer drank in the tunnels." He splashed it on his face, but didn't drink.

"Filled with volcanic ash, bomb blast residue, and any other crap coming out of the sky."

"Got any more cheery thoughts?"

The pulverized remains of human beings.

She didn't say this part aloud. But she couldn't help remembering how they'd all drank from the cistern water discovered in the abandoned subdivision.

He turned the tap to a trickle, stripped off his shirt, then splashed more water on his chest and shoulders. He was so thin.

He cast a backward glance. "Sorry, but these pants have got to come off. I'm filthy and they're going to rot clean through if I don't get washed up."

"Then I should probably look away."

He waggled his eyebrows. "It's up to you."

Nevertheless, he turned his back as he stripped out of his pants and underwear. Eliza didn't look away. He ran his head under the water, then let it run through the sweat and dirt along his back.

Steve was more slender than he'd been, but the muscles still rippled along his back and shoulders. She dragged her eyes down his sides to his lean waist, his naked buttocks. Butterflies rose in her stomach.

I'm almost twenty-five and still a virgin.

He was only a few feet away. Would it be the end of the world (so to speak) if she put her hands on him? She could reach around and let her fingernails trail across his chest. Let her hands drift to his stomach and the fine hair that spread from his navel down to his . . .

She flushed, her heart pounding, a warm feeling spreading through her body. He turned and met her gaze.

"You don't know how many times I've regretted waiting," she said.

The words came out before she could consider their potential double meaning. Did she mean waiting to get married, and then it was too late because he'd disappeared in California? Or waiting to be intimate until they were married? The rule in the church was absolute about chastity before marriage. But oh, how her body ached for his touch. Even now, as thin and dirty as he was. As dirty as she herself was.

"Eliza." His voice was husky.

"Steve, I—I—"

"I want you so badly."

She leaned toward him.

"No," he said with visible effort. He held out his hands to stop her. "It's not what you want."

"It *is* what I want."

"Not here, not like this. Soon, I swear to God. We'll get back to Blister Creek. And your brother will say the words. Then we can do it."

"What if we don't make it back?"

"We will."

"Just in case. I don't want to die like this. I want to be your wife. Then we'll be together in the next world. Grover has the priesthood. He could marry us."

"You said we needed to be married in the temple," Steve said. He sounded so calm, but his breath was shallow and he put his hands down to cover his crotch, like there was something happening down there that he didn't want her to see.

Eliza was not *that* naïve. She understood.

She nodded. "To be married in the next world, yes. We need a temple marriage."

"And you believe that?" he asked, bending for his shirt, which he then held in front of him.

She watched his every move, not even trying to keep from staring. "I don't know. Yeah, I guess so. I *hope* so, anyway. Do you?"

"Mostly, no. I think if two people love each other they'll find a way to be together in the next world."

"My father used to say that men were animals," Eliza said. "That girls needed to protect our virtue. Walk down the street underdressed and unescorted and a barbarian is likely to sweep down from the hills, carry you off, and ravage you."

"That sort of bullshit is an excuse for men to control women," Steve said.

"You sound like Jacob. Well, except for the swearing part."

"Sorry. I've fallen into old habits while I was away. I might have to confess to your brother about a few spare cigarettes that came into my hands as well."

Eliza took a deep breath and turned her gaze. "Okay, now that my brother came up, I've suddenly rediscovered my self-control. Better than a cold shower."

Steve laughed. "I always imagine my aunt Hilda when I start to lose control. I accidentally saw her naked when I was twelve. Wrinkles and everything." He grabbed his underwear and pulled it on, then reached for his pants. "But I swear to you that we're driving out of here tonight. And when we get back, I will collar your brother for a shotgun marriage, only I'll be the one with the gun to make sure it happens."

"Oh, yeah? Then what?"

He buttoned his pants. "Then I will carry you off, barbarian-style, for some good old-fashioned ravaging."

"I will hold you to that, Mister Big Shot FBI Agent. Either you ravage me or you will turn in your badge and gun. Got it?"

As they made their way back inside, an unfamiliar emotion stirred in Eliza's breast. For the moment she forgot everything: the drone attack, Trost and the bloody hole in his head, their capture at the hands of Sergeant Ludlow and his men, the horrific escape from the hotel, Fayer's cholera. She wasn't even troubled by the thought of a final, deadly flight from the city.

The emotion was a lifting, rising optimism. It was hope.

CHAPTER TWENTY-EIGHT

Jacob tried to think like a general as he prepared for the fight. This wasn't another drive-by shooting like their first attack on the squatters. The camp had doubled in size, then doubled again. It had suffered one attack; ultimatums had been traded, lines drawn in the sand. Jacob had no illusions; the fighting would start the moment the forces from Blister Creek arrived at the reservoir. It would be a real war.

And so he spent the day after the failed meeting with the Women's Council laying the logistics for the battle to come. He ordered David, Stephen Paul, and a dozen men to the switchbacks to fortify their rear guard positions. Then he loaded a truck with ammunition and weapons and drove up to meet them.

A series of retaining walls protected the switchbacks descending into the valley, and Blister Creek had built concrete bunkers at three of them earlier in the spring. The uppermost one was now a beehive of activity, with men coming and going, while others excavated a series of trenches. They loaded dirt into wheelbarrows, and hauled it across the road to form a dirt berm. David was directing the work and looked up when Jacob parked the truck.

David was already peeling back the tarp from the cargo when Jacob came around. He ran his finger over the barrel of the Browning .50-caliber machine gun that lay beneath.

"I thought you were sending the spare gun to the south bunkers. Did you change your mind? Or did you manage to salvage the one from the drone attack?"

"This isn't that gun," Jacob said. "I swiped this one from the Teancum checkpoint. If there's any part of the valley that's safe, it's the east side."

The two brothers stood aside for men to haul out the crates of ammunition, which they carried toward the trenches.

"We have a machine gun here already," David said with a nod toward the bunker. "Are you sure we need a second?"

"I'm not sure of anything. But I want it here just in case."

Stephen Paul made his way over, a shovel propped over his shoulder. Sweat streaked the dirt at his temples. "I heard what you said. I say we take this gun and mount it on one of the pickups. We could use the extra firepower in the battle."

"We can lose the battle and still recover," Jacob told him, "but if we lose the road to the valley floor we're doomed. If we're forced to retreat, this is where we'll make our stand."

"Have faith, brother," Stephen Paul said. "The Lord of Hosts guides our army. There will be no retreat."

"We could win the larger war," Jacob said, "and still have a rough slog of it in the battle. It might last longer than we think, and if it does, we'll need a strong position for resupplying our forces."

"I guess so," Stephen Paul said, still sounding unconvinced. "We do have the gun mounted on the Humvee. That should be enough."

"How many rounds have you brought me?" David asked.

"For the .50-cal? Ten thousand."

David frowned. "For two guns? That won't last long. I was think-ing thirty."

"If I leave thirty thousand rounds, thirty thousand will be fired."

"How many rounds will the women have at the Moroni check-point?" David asked.

"Twenty."

"So, more. Is that because the women asked for it, or because you're expecting trouble on the south end of the valley?" David frowned. "Wait, you're not preparing to lose, are you?"

"What do you mean?" Stephen Paul asked, his voice sharp.

"I think he is," David said. "He's preparing to flee. In case we're routed, he'll need to hold the south end of the valley long enough for us to evacuate."

"It's only a contingency," Jacob said. "I'm not planning to lose."

"Stop worrying," Stephen Paul said. "We have the initiative. We have the organization. We have the Lord on our side. Now, if you ask me, both the gun and the ammo from Moroni would be better used up here. In the battle itself."

"You're sounding like Elder Smoot," Jacob said. "Both of you."

Stephen Paul carried his shovel back to the trench works. David directed two of the Johnson boys to haul away the machine gun. He watched them go with a scowl, no doubt still wishing he could use it in the upcoming battle instead of here, guarding against an unlikely retreat.

Of course Jacob wished he had more heavy weapons. The Browning machine guns were more or less the same weapon that had killed hun-dreds of thousands of men in the First World War, and the gun's kill-ing power was little changed in the century since.

But more than that, he needed additional ammunition for the four he already owned.

Smaller weapons were less of a problem. The valley was awash in small arms—hunting rifles, pistols, AK-47s, AR-15s, shotguns—but the heavier stuff came courtesy of the occupation forces of the previous summer. First had come armed men under Chip Malloy, when the USDA set up a military administration. Later came the army. When Jacob's cousin Alfred killed General Lacroix in a horrific suicide attack, the army had pulled out. They had failed to secure the USDA's abandoned arsenal before their retreat. None of the equipment would fight off a military offensive, but it would be murderous against bandits, refugees, and other small-scale threats.

At first. In the long run, Jacob doubted they could repel a sustained siege. A valley-wide survey counted more than nine million (declared) rounds of everything from .22 rounds to shotgun shells. Small arms could hold out for years. But for the machine guns, Jacob only had sixty thousand rounds. It sounded like a lot, but with a .50-cal capable of firing six hundred rounds per minute, four guns could blow through that ammo in a hurry. Grenades and mines were in even shorter supply.

Destroy this threat and you won't need to fight again. Everyone will know. Approach Blister Creek and you will die.

Was that true? Or would the refugees keep coming even then, thousands upon thousands? Drawn by starvation and illness to the one remaining source of food, electricity, and civilization for hundreds of miles in any direction. They would come. Year after bloody year as the world tore itself apart. As millions, then billions died. For the huddled remnant in Blister Creek, it would be like waiting out a sandstorm or a plague of locusts that never ended.

He looked up from his thoughts to see his brother studying him. "What are you thinking about?" David asked.

"What else?" Jacob said. "The end of the world."

"I thought maybe Fernie and the women."

"No, not this time. I'm trying not to worry about them."

"You should go to her. Tonight, before the battle."

Jacob sighed. "I wouldn't know what to say. She's angry. I'm angry. We're on opposite sides of a position with no possible compromise."

"You need to say *something*. You never know when—" David stopped, seemed to reconsider his words.

"You never know when you might die? Do you think I'll take a bullet tonight?"

"No, no, I wouldn't say that. Of course not. You're the prophet."

"That didn't save Father."

"All I mean is that the future is uncertain," David said. "I keep thinking about what I would have told Miriam if I'd known she was going to disappear. Last night I was holding the baby, giving her a bottle and thinking how she should be at her mother's breast."

"How is Diego?" Jacob asked.

"He has been crying himself to sleep at night. He's terrified of losing his mother. Can't say I blame him."

"I'll bet having Lillian around helps."

"It does. She's a comfort to all of us. But Lillian didn't come home last night. She stayed up late with Fernie and Rebecca, then spent the night at your place. I don't think she's angry, just busy. I miss her too, you know. Now that Miriam is gone"—his voice caught—"she's all I have."

Jacob threw his arm around David's shoulder. "They'll be okay."

"I keep telling myself that. But the world is dying out there. I'm worried."

"Come on. It's Eliza and Miriam. They can survive anything."

David nodded. "You're right. But I'm going to talk to Lillian tonight anyway. Bring her closer instead of push her away. And you need to talk to Fernie."

"I don't know what to say."

"Who usually ends the fights, you or her?"

"What fights?"

"I'm serious."

"So am I. We've never fought before."

David drew back with a raised eyebrow. "Oh, come on."

"Really. We've squabbled, we've disagreed. Of course we have. But we don't fight. We never have." Jacob smiled. "I think we're what you call soul mates."

"Five generations of polygamists just rolled over in the Blister Creek graveyard and groaned in perfect harmony."

"Some people are wired for polygamy. I am not. Fernie is the only woman I ever wanted. Even when she was married to Elder Kimball, I knew she was the one for me."

"I still call baloney on the never fighting, but if it's true, it's all the more reason you need to go home tonight and see her."

"And talk about what? She's stubborn, I'm stubborn. Neither of us will change our minds about the battle. The moment we start talking, we'll argue, and then the fight will be all the worse."

"Then don't talk. Go home and crawl into bed without saying anything. Put your arm around her and tell her you're sorry and you love her."

"But I haven't changed my mind."

"It's not sorry you made a mistake, it's just sorry. Sorry that you're fighting, that you got angry. That this thing came between you."

"You think that would work?" Jacob asked.

"Maybe. It's hard to say what Fernie will think, but I guarantee *you'll* feel a lot better. I don't care who you are or how many wives you've got, there's nothing more soothing than falling asleep with a warm breast cupped in your hand."

★★★

The truck was going to be used for the dawn attack, so Jacob left it at the switchback instead of burning more fuel returning to the valley.

Instead, he rode home on a borrowed horse. He passed men on horseback, who tipped their hats, or called "Brother Jacob" in gruff voices.

A wagon of women was pulling onto the ranch road at Yellow Flats as he approached. They called to him and he pulled alongside as a woman stopped the team of horses. The driver was Charity Kimball, her hair pulled into a gray bun, with her daughters Helen Pratt and Jessie Lyn Smoot sitting in the back.

They carried a disassembled loom, which Charity had found in a dusty corner of a barn on the Kimball ranch. Charity said she remembered how to operate the loom, if someone could figure out how to put it back together.

Spinning, weaving, candling—the women were reviving old industries. If they could only survive, they had the means to thrive, to reintroduce the old ways to the surrounding communities. Assuming there *were* any surviving communities.

"Do you think Sister Rebecca could figure it out?" Charity asked.

"Probably. And I'll send my brother to help too," Jacob said. "If it's mechanical, David can put it together."

"Thank you, Brother Jacob," Jessie Lyn said, "but we didn't call you over to show you the loom. We would like to pray with you, if you'll let us."

They looked at him with shining eyes and worried expressions.

"Yes, of course," he said. "May I choose someone to say the prayer? Charity, would you please?"

"Thank you," she said in a soft voice. "I would like that."

Charity Kimball was the wife and mother of murderers, her sister wives scattered to other families. Everything she'd known, destroyed. The poor woman lived in fear of being thrown out of Blister Creek, but it was an unnecessary worry. Jacob had no intention of punishing her for the sins of the Kimball men.

Charity's voice was thin and cracked with age and emotion. Her prayer was simple and unadorned, but achingly earnest. Jacob listened, overcome with sorrow that he couldn't share in her faith. These women burned in their convictions, trusted him to lead. At one point he'd dismissed this single-minded devotion as naïve, even dangerous. Like believing in witches or alchemy. Now, faith—whether supported by fact or myth—seemed like a survival mechanism perfectly tailored to outlast the present upheaval. Was that the origin of religion, nothing more than a way to cement group cohesion in the face of existential threats?

The prayer had ended. Belatedly, he opened his eyes to see the women watching him.

"Amen!" he said, as if the delay had been caused by the profundity of his spiritual feelings, and not his distracted mind.

He left the women to their business and continued the long ride through town and to home. When he arrived, his daughter, Leah, stood on the porch ringing the dinner bell. She came running as he slid down from the horse and handed the reins to one of his younger brothers. He swept Leah into his arms and nibbled her neck, making her squeal. When he came inside, a dozen children—his own, his youngest siblings, even cousins being raised in the Christianson compound—came running to greet him. The older children gave him solemn nods and greetings. The younger ones didn't seem to have quite as solid an understanding of the stakes, but they were jumpy and hyper. They must have heard something, felt it even.

Fernie wheeled her chair out of the kitchen when he came in, directing the troops to set tables and carry platters of beans and roasted chicken to the table. She did a double take as Jacob turned from putting his hat on the peg.

"Paul," she said to one of Jacob's half brothers, a boy of about fourteen, "set Jacob a place. Quickly, we're almost ready to bless the food."

"No, it's okay," Jacob said. "I can set my own place."

Fernie wouldn't hear of it, though, and quickly had a place set for him at the head of the main table. She was polite and friendly, but didn't wheel herself down to eat next to him like she usually did. Instead, she stayed at the far end with the youngest children.

Dinner was a buzz of energy from the children, but Jacob settled them by asking about the work. Did the flax get planted? Who was in charge of tying off the tomato plants? Did he need to look at the injured steer after supper, or was it on the mend?

After dinner, Jacob sat on the porch and sharpened axes and garden shears with his two oldest sons while the sun dropped to the west. It was another gorgeous sunset that used every shade of red, purple, and orange. All across the valley, men would be finishing supper with disapproving wives. Were they arguing? Sharing tender embraces? And what of the women who would be widows by this time tomorrow evening? Did they know, sense somewhere in a black hollow of their stomach that tonight was their last night with their husbands?

"Have you changed your mind?" a soft voice asked behind him.

He turned to see that Fernie had wheeled herself quietly onto the porch while he worked.

"Put the tools away, boys," he said. "We'll finish another day." When they were gone, Jacob swallowed his pride and rose to put a hand on her shoulder. "I'm sorry."

"Be safe, please."

Help us. Please, for the love of all that is good.

They would be so much stronger with the women at their side. This is what the saints had been training for, some of them for a year, others all their lives. To fight and defend this valley, this community, this church. Why would the women hold back now? Couldn't they see?

He didn't voice these thoughts. Instead, he nodded. "I will do my best."

"Are you staying here tonight?"

"Until a quarter to five in the morning. Then David and Elder Smoot are picking me up in the Humvee."

"You should go to bed early, then."

"I'm too wired," he said. "I don't know if I can sleep."

"I'll rub your head. That always relaxes you."

★★★

And it did. After twenty minutes in bed, in his pajamas, resting his aching feet, with Fernie massaging his scalp, his eyes felt heavy and he yawned. He wound the clock and set the alarm, but it was an unnecessary precaution; his body would jolt awake in a few hours with or without the alarm.

Before he allowed himself to sleep, Jacob rolled his wife onto her side so her back was facing him. He reached around, unbuttoned the top three buttons of her nightgown, and slid his hand against her breast. She sighed and nestled into his embrace.

"I love you," she said. "Don't forget that, please."

"I love you too."

"There's something I need to tell you before you go to sleep."

"You don't need to say it. I know you haven't changed your mind. I won't push."

"Not that, Jacob. Something else." She took a deep breath, as if tensing herself for some big proclamation.

"Can't it wait for later?"

"No. In case anything happens to you tomorrow—shh, let me say it—in case anything happens, I want you to know."

He knew that whatever she had to say he wouldn't like, but there was apparently no stopping her. "Okay, tell me."

"I'm pregnant again."

Jacob closed his eyes and took his own deep breath. "But we were being so careful."

"It would seem that the rhythm method isn't one hundred percent effective, Dr. Christianson."

It was gentle sarcasm, and as she said it, she lifted his hand and kissed it before putting it back against her breast. But there was also a twinge of worry in her tone. She was afraid of his reaction, he could tell.

"Five children. It sounds like a lot. And on top of everything else."

"This will make three of your own," Fernie said.

"Daniel and Leah are just as much mine as Nephi and Jake."

She rolled over with some effort and put a hand against his cheek. "That's not what I mean. You love those kids and they love you. But I'm happy to have another with you. I'm proud to be carrying on the Christianson line."

Even under the best of circumstances, it would be a high-risk pregnancy. Fernie's paralysis was low enough that she would be able to feel contractions and push, but he wondered if he shouldn't deliver via C-section instead of vaginally, just to be safe.

And what if he wasn't here to perform it?

"Are you okay?" she asked.

"The timing . . ."

"Jacob," she said firmly. "We didn't plan for it, but now it's here. Do you remember last time this happened? You said the same thing."

Of course he remembered. He had been working for the FBI, and had infiltrated the Zarahemla cult to extract their agent. And worse, the hospital had suspended him for his ties to polygamy and he'd lost both his income and his home.

"Is now any worse timing?" she asked.

"Maybe not."

"The Bible says to multiply and replenish the earth."

"It doesn't say we have to do it by ourselves."

"Funny guy." She kissed him. "This gives you one more reason to be careful tomorrow. Now get some sleep."

He didn't think that would be possible, not with this grenade tossed into his lap. On top of all the other emotions boiling inside, he found himself curiously excited. He had three boys, but only one daughter. Maybe it would be another girl.

That was his last conscious thought before his eyes opened several hours later. He grabbed the clock. 4:31. Four minutes before the alarm was set to go off. From outside came the low rumble of a diesel engine. That's what had awakened him.

Fernie rolled over and her breathing changed as he slipped into his clothes and pulled on his boots, but she didn't say anything. He put on his wristwatch.

Jacob paused at the door, and said to her in a soft voice, "Wake Sister Lillian. Tell her to get the clinic ready for trauma cases."

He slipped out of the bedroom. Downstairs, he unlocked the gun safe and strapped on a KA-BAR knife, loaded his pockets with ammunition, then holstered a Glock pistol, grabbed an M16 and a 12-gauge shotgun, and made for the door.

The Humvee waited for him in the street. It was packed with men and the materiel of death and bloodshed.

Elder Smoot sat behind the wheel. As Smoot pulled away, the man prayed aloud, "Thou art my king, O God. Through thee will we push down our enemies. Through thy name will we tread them under that rise against us."

CHAPTER TWENTY-NINE

Eliza had hoped to make a run for it at dusk, but artillery was pounding the north and west side of the city like a thunderstorm rolling in from the desert. The companions hunkered down to wait it out.

Fayer by now was in a bad way. She drank gallons of their precious water, but it was like there was a straight pipe from her mouth to her backside. Every few minutes, while the others looked away, she squatted over a bucket, filling it with a splattering sound like a pissing horse. After she finished, Grover would take the bucket and cart it away to empty elsewhere in the warehouse.

But Eliza wouldn't risk driving out of their hiding spot until the fighting subsided. The artillery rocked the factory again and again. Part of the ceiling collapsed. Twice in the night, vehicles rumbled by outside the factory warehouse. Small-arms fire came and went. Then came quiet that would only last a few minutes.

It was maybe four in the morning when she couldn't wait any longer. The fighting hadn't ended, but it had moved out of their neighborhood. That might be temporary, but she figured they had another hour before dawn caught them in the open. She wanted to put at least fifty miles between themselves and the city before the sun burned over the desert plain.

They'd been waiting outside the claustrophobic interior of the armored car. Eliza called over Steve, Miriam, and Grover. "Correct me if I'm wrong—I don't have military experience—but here's what I'm thinking. I'll drive. Steve and Miriam man the machine guns. Grover, you can snipe with a rifle. If we get in a big firefight, drop your gun and help with ammo." She turned her flashlight in Grover's direction. "You can do that, right?"

He nodded, pale but determined-looking.

"I'm going to plow down anything in our way," she continued. "This thing can take a lot of abuse."

"Depends," Steve said. "Small-arms fire is no problem, and we can muscle aside any standard vehicles blocking our way. But a tank shell will flatten us. You see a tank, or anti-tank guns, you get the hell out of there. As for machine guns, the wrong kind of ammo will punch through our armor, so don't get us in a position where we're slugging it out."

Miriam shone her own flashlight along the exterior of the armored car, as if looking for weaknesses in the plate armor. "Your old prepper did a fine job. Shame he isn't around to see how it performs." She stood off the front bumper. "Look at how the two main guns have almost a 180-degree radius of fire." She looked up at Eliza. "But the right side is better. More range of motion and stronger armor. If we get bogged down, show that side. Like a battleship giving a broadside. You understand?"

"Got it," Eliza said. Give a broadside, don't slug it out—it was inconsistent advice from the two former FBI agents.

"With any luck, we won't get in any firefights," Steve said.

"It will take more than luck to get us home in one piece," Miriam said. She glanced at Fayer, who rested against the front bumper. "It's going to take divine intervention."

"Are we ready?" Eliza asked.

The woman struggled to her feet.

"I was hoping Chambers would show up," Steve said. "Guess he didn't make it."

They helped Fayer inside and tried to fashion her a private corner behind some ammo cans. There she could continue with her miserable rituals. The old survivalist had packed in blankets and they wrapped her in one of them to try to make her more comfortable. Then they went outside and tore down the final flats of equipment to clear a path for the truck. Eliza climbed into the driver's seat.

Steve sat shotgun. "You know how to work this thing, right?"

"Please," she said with considerably more bravado than she felt. "I learned how to drive a tractor before I could ride a bike. This is nothing."

"In that case, let's get going."

She kissed him. "This is going to be easy. What do they call it in the military? A milk run?"

"Great, now quit stalling, kid, and get us out of here."

He went back with the others to man the guns. As Eliza slipped the vehicle through the entry into their hiding place and onto the open warehouse floor, they slid open specially cut slots in the side of the armored car to expose the guns. Eliza's window was a narrow strip of bulletproof glass with limited view. She risked the headlights until she reached the front of the loading bay.

It took all four of the healthy people to drag over the heavy loading ramp and put it in place. When it was done, Eliza eased the truck down it and the others jumped back inside when she had reached the asphalt outside.

It was still dark and she didn't dare use the lights, so she groped her way through the industrial park by the glow of the burning city.

Eliza had almost reached the end of the complex and the open road when a man came sprinting along the right side of the vehicle. He carried a rifle in his hands and it looked like he was trying to get ahead of them so he could shoot them straight on.

Startled by the suicidal attacker, she jerked on the wheel to veer away, but before she could get past, he leaped in front, fumbling with his weapon.

"I got him," Miriam said in a grim tone. The breech bolt snicked back.

"Hold your fire!" Steve yelled. "Stop the truck."

Confused, Eliza hit the brake. With so much weight, the vehicle came to a sluggish halt. Even before it did, Steve was tossing open the back doors and hopping down. He came around to the front of the truck and clapped the man on the shoulders.

Miriam walked up to Eliza and shone her flashlight through the glass. "I don't believe it. It's Chambers."

Chambers was a tall man, almost Steve's height, but so thin and lanky, he looked like a child's drawing of a stick figure with clothes draped over him. After losing his job with the FBI, Steve had developed a cool relationship with his former partners—including Chambers—but there was none of that now as Eliza's fiancé led the man into the back of the armored car.

"Go figure," Chambers said. He sounded gruff, but was grinning wide enough to split his face. Already he was reaching for a water bottle and tearing open one of the boxes with vacuum-sealed beef jerky. "You bozos almost left me, didn't you?"

"What? We'd never do that," Steve said. "We were going to drive around the city hanging lost FBI agent fliers."

Chambers snorted.

"What took you so long?" Miriam asked.

"The usual. Gunfire, missile strikes." His eyes fell on Fayer. "Oh, crap."

Fayer looked up at him through bleary, sunken eyes, her face shrouded monk-like by the blanket. "Crap. Yes, you could say that."

"What happened?"

Eliza didn't wait for the explanations, but returned to her seat and shifted into gear. All her attention fixed on the view through that three-inch-by-twenty-inch portal of bulletproof glass, she pulled onto the road. Steve came up front.

"Chambers has the other machine gun. I thought I'd help you navigate."

"Left here? Then what was it again?"

"Drive to Palms Boulevard and take another left," he said.

"Wish I could risk the headlights. I can't see a blasted thing."

The light was marginally better when she got to Palms. A row of glass offices to her left reflected enough of the burning city to illuminate her path. Palms was a divided, two-lane road with a xeriscaped median, now overgrown with cactus thickets and desert weeds. Most of the palm trees had died, some torn up by gunfire. Abandoned, gutted cars littered their way, and the pavement glittered with thousands of spent casings.

Eliza made it two more blocks before she reached a blocked intersection, so strewn with rubble and wrecked vehicles that she had to go up on the sidewalk and then shove aside an overturned sedan with the machine's nose. This bought her another block, when she came upon a looming black shape in her path. There would be no pushing this aside. It was a battered tank with its treads blown off, surrounded by other dead and smoldering military vehicles, and several wrecked field guns. Dead soldiers littered the ground. Another man lay draped over the tank turret.

"Turn back," Steve said. "We'll cut around that last block."

She didn't like the idea of backtracking, in case they'd been spotted. And when she got there, she liked even less the narrow, apartment-lined street that would get them around the blocked intersection. It was the perfect place for snipers. There were more cars, some of them inconveniently placed. She got around the first several, but had to push aside a little Hyundai that was perfectly positioned to block the entire street. It groaned with metal on metal.

Something clanged against the side of the truck like the sound of a ball-peen hammer striking a metal drum. Then two more shots pinged against the right side. Tentative, probing. Chambers answered with three short bursts through his side gun port. Suddenly, a hailstorm opened up. Small-arms fire rattled them from every side.

Eliza turned on the lights and rumbled to the end of the block. She rounded the corner to get them parallel with Palms Boulevard, then killed the headlights when she got back to Palms and slowed to a crawl.

It was a narrow escape and nobody spoke for several seconds.

Steve turned on a penlight and studied a map. "Get us onto Dwight Eisenhower and then find a place to pull over. I want to ask Chambers about the map. He knows Vegas better than I do."

That was five more blocks. Once onto Dwight Eisenhower, Eliza maneuvered to a place of shelter between a city bus with missing tires and a concrete retaining wall painted over with graffiti. More drainage canals like the ones that had carried them from the hotel lay on the other side of the retaining wall. She killed the engine.

Steve went back to talk to Chambers. Miriam also wanted to know about changing ammo. They had a can of incendiaries that might be useful as they faced vehicles on the highways.

Grover picked his way forward while the others were talking. "The lady agent isn't doing very well."

"Worse than before?" Eliza asked.

"She wouldn't drink any water. I'm not sure she's fully conscious."

Eliza rubbed at her temples. She'd dozed in the stifling heat of the warehouse the previous afternoon, but was now on her second full night without a good, unbroken stretch of sleep. Her mind was too fuzzy to deal with this new information.

"Are all the diarrhea pills gone?"

"There's one left. I don't think they're helping."

"I don't know what else to do. Grind it up and dissolve it in one of the water bottles. See if you can get her to drink a little. Also, while we're stopped, empty her bucket. It stinks, and we don't want it sloshing out and getting the rest of us sick."

"All right." As he rose from the passenger seat, he winced and rubbed at his left arm.

"Are you okay?"

"That stupid poker chip shrapnel. It's nothing—I don't have the right to complain, given the circumstances."

She glanced back at the three agents—former and current—still arguing about the guns. What was taking them so long? And why hadn't they settled it before leaving the factory?

"Here, let me take a look."

Grover wasn't as shy this time. He rolled up his sleeve and she unwound the bandage. It had absorbed a little blood, but not too much. Grover was right; he should count himself lucky. However, the wound itself looked worse than it should. She grabbed the penlight Steve had placed in the coin holder and examined his arm more carefully.

The wound oozed pus and had a sour smell. She chewed her lip.

"What is it?" he asked. "What's wrong?"

"It's infected."

"Is it bad?"

"I don't know. Maybe it's nothing, but it's moving pretty quickly. Like Fayer's cholera. There's a risk of gangrene, of sepsis—I don't want to mess around. Get me iodine from the first aid kit. And some matches. Also, cotton gauze."

He made a sound in the back of his throat. "What are you going to do?"

"Don't worry, it won't be that bad," she lied. "Go on, hurry. Unless you want to lose your arm."

Grover pushed past Steve as the man came back up front.

"Chambers says the 95 is crawling with Bear Republic troops," Steve said. "He thinks they're preparing a push into downtown."

"We don't have a choice—we have to go north. If we can get past that military base, Highway 93 is clear all the way up the east side of Nevada."

"At least it was a couple days ago," Miriam said, also making her way up from the back. "For all we know, the federal troops have sealed the road."

"Why would they bother?" Eliza asked. "There's nothing in that part of the state. Badlands. A few abandoned towns. Any troop movement is flowing east-west. Maybe up from Arizona."

"Chambers thinks there's a gap directly north of the city," Steve said. "A no-man's-land between the two armies. Nothing big—maybe a few hundred yards wide."

"If we find it," Eliza said, "we can shoot the gap."

"That's one heck of a gamble. We could just as well be volunteering for bombardment from both sides." He let out his breath. "But, okay. I don't see much choice. Miriam?"

"I say we go for it."

Grover arrived with the gauze, the matches, and the iodine. Eliza took them and gently tugged him forward. He flinched, like a kid being pushed into the dentist chair. When he was past Miriam and next to Steve, she took his wrist.

"Hold him," she told them.

They grabbed Grover before he could jerk back.

"Listen to me," she said in a firm voice. "This is deadly serious."

Grover trembled. "What are you going to do?"

"What would you do if your lamb had an infected wound and you didn't have any access to antibiotics?"

Eliza rolled up his shirt while Steve held his arm still. Miriam held his other arm behind his back.

"You're going to cauterize it."

"A lamb will kick and scream," Eliza said, "because it doesn't understand. You understand. You won't do that, right?"

"Can't you pour iodine on it and see how it looks in the morning?" Grover's trembling grew more violent, but to his credit, he didn't cry or try to fight free.

"No, Grover. I'm sorry, but it's moving too quickly. I'm not a doctor, but I've learned enough to know there's a better than even chance that if we don't stop this, by tomorrow my brother will be breaking out the bone saw. You'll have a stub instead of an arm."

Eliza tore off a strip of gauze. She struck a match and held it against the cotton. It caught slowly, the flames licking up the sides. Grover watched with his eyes bulging. The firelight reflected off his boyish face. She twisted the gauze to keep the fire from consuming it all at once. Then, when the flames had grown to the point where she only held the bottom part with pinched fingers, she slapped it onto Grover's wound.

He bucked and screamed. The others held him fast. When the burning gauze nipped at her fingers, she used the butt of the penlight to hold it in place. The fire smothered between the end of the flashlight and the flesh of the young man's arm.

When it was out, Steve opened the door and tossed the still-smoking gauze onto the pavement, then waved the door open and closed to get the smoke out of the cabin.

Grover wept silently. "I'm sorry. I tried not to scream."

Steve patted his shoulder. "No worries, man. Any one of us would have done the same thing."

Eliza shone the light on the blackened flesh of the wound. She took some cotton balls and dabbed at it with some iodine. When she had it cleaned off, she took another look, intending to wrap it up and be done with him. What she saw was a job half-finished.

"Grover," she said slowly, reluctantly.

He whipped his head up from the wound to stare at her through watering eyes.

"I'm afraid I have to do it one more time."

CHAPTER THIRTY

A caravan of trucks waited for Jacob on the shoulder of the highway near the base of the Ghost Cliffs. The final vehicle was the military Humvee. Jacob hopped down and approached it slowly, dreading what lay ahead.

This was the same vehicle and weapon used against Blister Creek two summers ago when Taylor Kimball Junior and his cult made one final assault to take over the church. Even with advance notice, the FBI hadn't managed to get field agents in to stop the attack. That had been Jacob's first warning that something was seriously wrong in the outside world.

David was up top with the machine gun. He rose from behind the gun shield and gave Jacob a curt nod. The darkness hid his expression. Was it anxious? Eager? Jacob returned the nod. He climbed in the driver side.

Smoot rode shotgun—quite literally, in this case, with his twelve-gauge across his lap. Two of his sons sat in the back, together with the

Hawthorne brothers. The Hawthornes were sober, middle-aged men, several years older than Jacob, each with two wives and numerous children. Their beards showed the first hints of gray. All four men in the back carried assault rifles and were surrounded by ammo cans.

Jacob pulled into the road. As he did, headlights kicked on all around. Dozens of vehicles pulled in behind him. They carried more than two hundred armed men. Fathers with their sons. Brothers, cousins. White-bearded patriarchs who remembered when Blister Creek lay off the electric grid and who had lived to see those days return. Teenage boys who had been handling firearms since they were five years old, but had never before been asked to gun down a fellow human being.

Jacob feared that many of them would not return.

"We have a lot of trucks," Smoot said. "Plenty of light and noise to warn our enemies."

"It's still faster and safer than attacking on horse," Jacob said. "Anyway, that's part of the plan. A noisy assault up the highway with the main force, while we sneak the Humvee around the reservoir to attack from the rear."

"And a lot of fuel to burn." A note of suspicion tinged Smoot's voice.

"This is what we've been saving it for."

"I counted sixty-two vehicles."

"Sounds about right."

"They all gassed up at your place, from what I hear. Filled the tanks. That's got to be better than a thousand gallons of fuel."

"Do you want to get up there and run out of fuel?"

"But only diesel, that's the funny thing. I've got a good truck I've been working on to make it battle worthy, but it takes ethanol. We distilled some, but you wouldn't let me take ethanol from the bishop's storehouse."

"We need it for other purposes."

"But you can spare diesel?" Smoot pressed. "Why is it so plentiful?"

"Leave it alone, Elder. We have other worries."

"Are you the only one who knows?"

Knows what? Jacob started to ask. He stayed silent instead. His fiction was unraveling.

"Because if something happens to you," Smoot continued, "I don't want the secret to be lost."

Jacob decided to come clean. "Others know."

"Who?"

"David, Miriam, Eliza, and Stephen Paul."

"How much fuel are we talking about?"

"A lot. My father was stockpiling diesel in his last few years."

Smoot nodded. "He was a true prophet. He knew what was coming."

"He also bought a million dollars in U.S. savings bonds six months before his death. That was less prescient. Those bonds are worth nothing."

"No, no, it makes perfect sense. Abraham was preparing for contingencies. He understood when, but only the Lord knew the how. Where is the diesel stored, Brother?"

"I'd rather not say. The fewer people who know, the better."

"But you trust the others. Why not me? I am one of the senior members of the quorum."

Jacob turned from peering out the windshield. "Do I need to answer that?"

Smoot narrowed his lips until they disappeared behind his mustache and beard. "I made mistakes. I learned my lesson."

"Did you?"

"I sustain you as prophet, seer, and revelator. I didn't always trust you—I thought you were young and soft. Weak in testimony, and not worthy to wear your father's boots. And what a time to have a weak leader. That's why I did what I did. That's why I didn't trust the Lord or His prophet. But I have seen you move, Brother Jacob. Cautiously, sometimes too gently, yes. But with conviction. And so I will stand by your side as the mouth of hell yawns before us."

"If that's true, why do you push me so hard?" Jacob asked.

"Do you want a man who bows his head at every word out of your mouth? Is that what you're looking for?"

Of course it wasn't. Jacob didn't want that from his wife, his sister, his brother. And what about Miriam, or Rebecca? Even Stephen Paul could push him back. But it was different coming out of Smoot's mouth.

The elder reminded Jacob of his father. Of an earlier, harder generation. One of Smoot's sons had died in the drone attack, another had gone missing, yet the man didn't complain or carry on. Instead, here he was, ready to sacrifice himself and two more of his boys for Blister Creek.

Meanwhile, Jacob's own family was safe at home. Yes, his children were young, but in three more years Daniel would be as old as some of the kids in this caravan. When that day came, would Jacob shove a rifle into Daniel's hands and drive him into the desert to battle with squatters and bandits?

"No," he said at last. "I'm not looking for blind obedience. Tomorrow—assuming we get out of this thing unscathed—I'll share the details of my father's diesel storage."

The caravan snaked its way up to the cliffs with the Humvee in the lead. Jacob fell under attack the instant he rounded the final turn. Muzzle flashes came from the left and right, with even fiercer fire from the road ahead, where someone had dragged a downed tree across the road. Men stood from behind the tree to shoot. Bullets ricocheted off the Humvee.

From above, David squeezed off bursts from the machine gun. Tracer bullets guided his fire. Smoot and the men in the back stuck their guns out of gun ports and added their fire. In less than a minute they had suppressed the enemy attack and driven the survivors from the road.

Jacob pulled forward to let the rest of the caravan catch up. He hit the floodlight and turned it into the partially hacked-down woods to the left and along the shore of the reservoir. Two bodies lay in the road, and another stretched over the downed tree trunk, almost cut in two. The violence was sickening.

"Easy as shearing sheep," Smoot said. "We get that tree off the road and we could roll straight into camp and end it before dawn."

"No, it could be a trap to lure us in. We stick with the plan."

"All right, then let's go."

Jacob checked his watch. It was now 5:18 a.m. He lifted the CB radio. "Five thirty-five. Over."

Other radios in other trucks would be picking up his message and spreading it. Jacob and the others in the Humvee would split right to creep around the reservoir. In seventeen minutes they would rejoin the battle on the far side of the reservoir. The others had better be ready to move.

He cut his lights and turned the Humvee off the highway to the frontage road that circled the reservoir in a counterclockwise direction. Behind him, men jumped down from pickups and fanned out with guns at the ready. Under their cover, other men connected chains to the downed tree to winch it out of the way.

Using the glint of moonlight off the placid waters of the reservoir as his guide, Jacob crunched along the dirt road at two or three miles per hour. They reached the penstock that led down to their hydro turbines, which provided the largest, steadiest supply of electricity for the valley. The turbines were below, at the base of the cliffs, where the head of water was strongest, but someone could have messed with the penstocks themselves. Destroy them and the cobbled-together electrical grid below would fail. Jacob considered it fortunate that nothing like that had happened.

But if the enemy had failed to consciously harm the valley, their unconscious actions had done plenty of harm. Debris had almost clogged the sluice gate into the penstocks.

Jacob checked his watch. Ten minutes until the scheduled attack. He'd be around the reservoir in less than five. He warned the others in the vehicle, called up to David to alert him of his intentions, then hopped out of the Humvee.

The first thing he noticed was the bodies in the water. There were dozens, mostly naked. They were thin, starved, some rotting and chewed up by fish or scavengers. Others had distended abdomens bloated from expanding intestinal gasses. The squatters must be simply tossing the dead into the reservoir, where they gradually drifted across to pile against the grating. Other refuse floated among the bodies: branches, discarded cloth diapers, a pair of pants, plastic bags, and a battered cooler.

Smoot came out. "Disgusting. My hogs care more about keeping clean."

"These people are starving. They have bigger worries than the integrity of our water supply."

"Maybe so. But we don't. We're damn lucky there hasn't been an outbreak of cholera in the valley. But there will be if we don't stop it now."

Jacob didn't answer. The man was right.

"They shot Clancy Johnson in the leg when he was hunting deer east of the reservoir," Smoot added.

"I know, I treated the wound."

"And someone was up in the cliffs yesterday shooting down at Yellow Flats."

"Sister Rebecca told me that. She also said the range is too great and they're wasting their ammo."

"We should go," Smoot said.

Jacob hesitated. There was still time to radio the others, call it off.

"Brother Jacob, for the love of all that is holy. We have to do it. There's no other choice."

"Five twenty-nine," David called from atop the Humvee. "We have six minutes."

The two men returned to the vehicle and continued to inch around the reservoir. With every roll of the wheels the leaden feeling in Jacob's gut grew heavier. Gunfire sounded on the opposite side of the reservoir. The main Blister Creek force. Muzzle flashes answered from the darkness on the hillside and the lakeshore in what was proving to be a spirited defense. The gunfire from his own forces was stronger, but not overwhelmingly so. Jacob's caravan looked to be bogged down, and was no doubt taking casualties.

Campfires lit his way as he flanked the camp from the east side of the reservoir. True to the boasts of the squatters during the previous confrontation, the camp had metastasized since his last visit. It spread all along the far shore and into the woods to the north. The forest itself was gutted, replaced by hundreds of tents and lean-tos. If the population above the valley hadn't yet outstripped the number of people living down below, it would soon.

The road didn't completely circumnavigate the reservoir, but ended a few hundred yards short of the camp. There had been a dock here once for canoes and small fishing boats, but the decking was gone, the planks apparently pulled up for firewood, leaving only the pilings sticking out of the water. The gentle slope between the missing docks and the camp was a trammeled, muddy meadow.

Jacob checked his watch. One minute.

"Time to go."

One of Bill's sons climbed up above to help David feed ammo

into the .50-cal. When he was secured, Jacob pressed the pedal to the floor and lumbered toward the camp.

For the first few seconds he thought he'd break through undetected. Then a torch waved to his right and the air filled with flashes of light. Most of it missed the dark shape lurching toward the squatters, but a few shots pinged off the front and right side. The Humvee did not yet return fire.

Moments later, they burst into camp. Jacob gritted his teeth and plowed into tents and mowed over lean-tos. People scrambled out of the way or simply cowered. Others stood upright and shot at them with pistols and shotguns.

And now David answered. An arc of tracer bullets cut like a glowing knife in big, sweeping movements. Smoot and the others opened their doors periodically to gun down the closer opposition. Smoot's son tossed grenades into the night, which exploded in flashes of light and ear-splitting booms.

Jacob found a flattened stretch between a line of tents, where he accelerated and swung in a loop through the camp. Gunfire erupted all around them, as if they'd kicked over a giant hive of wasps that darted in, desperate and stinging. Everywhere he looked, more gunfire. Jacob's companions mowed down the shooters without mercy, and anyone else who moved as well.

David stopped shooting and screamed down for more ammo. The Hawthorne brothers passed up fresh ammo cans while the other men—Jacob included—fired out the sides of the Humvee to keep them clear. The enemy took advantage of the quieted machine gun to rush in with guns blazing. Calmly, the men inside the vehicle picked them off.

And by now the trucks from Blister Creek had broken through to the west and the gunfire from that direction was more intense than the slaughter on this side. Jacob turned the Humvee around as David started up the .50-cal again, this time with shorter, more carefully considered bursts. No longer worried about giving away their position, Jacob turned on the spotlight and swung it through the camp as he drove. Every place he illuminated, people were dying. His light caught a woman with a child in her arms and he tried to turn the light away, but not before bullets dropped them to the ground.

Dear Lord, wouldn't it ever stop?

Not until you call them off.

Jacob could finish it now in one final, bloody orgy. Give the orders to go back and forth over the land until there was nothing left but bodies.

What would that accomplish? The dead already numbered in the hundreds. Many more would die from their wounds. People were fleeing north, away from the reservoir, and the enemy gunfire was flagging. Soon the battle would be nothing more than shooting people in the back.

He picked up the radio. "It's over. Pull back. Everyone, back."

"What are you doing?" Smoot shouted. He stood at one of the gun ports with his shotgun shoved out. "We're winning. Don't retreat!"

Jacob barely heard him over the buzzing in his ears. He kept seeing the woman with her child, taking a bullet in the back, sprawling over. What about the child? He wanted to be sick. All those injured people back there—he was a doctor, he belonged in a trauma room, not *causing* trauma.

Smoot kept complaining until Jacob got the Humvee out of the camp and was heading back around the reservoir, then the elder sank to the ground with a long, heavy sigh. David came down from the machine gun and took out the first aid kit. He examined his own arm with a penlight.

Jacob glanced back. "You okay?"

"It's nothing." His tone was bitter.

Then he slammed his fist into the roof and let out a string of oaths that Jacob hadn't heard from his brother since the days when he was a Lost Boy, drug addicted and living in Las Vegas.

Smoot grunted with displeasure. "Remember who you are, brother."

"Leave him alone, Dad," one of Smoot's sons said, his voice raw. "We were all thinking it."

"That woman," David said. "Why did I have to see her face? That look in her eyes. Oh, God."

"Proved one thing, anyway," Smoot said, his own voice flat. "We didn't need the women after all."

"Please, all of you," Jacob said. "Can you be quiet?"

He was so distracted by his own thoughts that he almost forgot to look across the reservoir to see if the others had obeyed his command to retreat. They had. Their lights were on, but the sky was turning gray with the predawn and it was no longer necessary.

Jacob looked at his watch. 5:53. The battle at the camp had lasted less than twenty minutes. And only forty-five minutes had passed since they'd driven into the hills and faced their first opposition. Forty-five minutes, thousands of rounds spent, hundreds dead.

You had to do it. They left you no choice.

Jacob had almost convinced himself of this when the Humvee reached the end of the dirt road and connected with the highway at the top of the cliffs. Some of the other trucks had arrived already and waited, idling, as if wanting him to lead a triumphant procession into Blister Creek. To show the women that their men had protected them. The very thought was ridiculous.

Not to mention dangerous. He could see injured men in the truck beds. They had to be carried to the clinic, where a hellish day of triage and emergency operation awaited. The sooner they brought the wounded to the Christianson compound, the better.

And then he glanced 'down to the valley floor as the sun rose from behind the eastern mountains. The light caught the golden Angel Moroni atop the temple spire, and turned the sandstone columns of Witch's Warts brilliant hues of red and orange. Carpets of neatly laid alfalfa and corn sprouted with hopeful green in those fields Jacob had dared plant in defiance of the crippling late frosts.

It was when his gaze fell on the black ribbon of highway south of the valley that he understood why the trucks had stopped. The reason lay south of the gridded streets at the center of town, past the cemetery on the knoll, past the abandoned service station where he'd hidden his father's hoarded diesel in underground tanks.

Smoke climbed into the air at the south end of the valley. A black trail of ants crawled up the road. It could only be men and equipment entering the valley. A cold, greasy knot formed in the pit of Jacob's stomach.

While Jacob and his men had been at the reservoir battling squatters, an invasion force was thrusting into the valley from the south.

CHAPTER THIRTY-ONE

The second time Eliza cauterized Grover's wound, he didn't scream. He only watched Eliza through those awful, bulging eyes. The smell of charred flesh hung in the air when she finished. At least this time she'd done it properly.

When the ugly business was finished, she got them back on the road. Steve guided her through the streets. The main fighting, judging by flashes of lights and thundering explosions, lay to their east, but the west side was still burning, and whenever they had an open view, pockets of gunfire and explosions flashed throughout the city.

The fighting seemed pointless. What were they fighting for? A ruined ghost town in the desert?

Her worry was that she'd round a corner to find themselves in the midst of a full-scale battle. And if the Californians were making a major push, as Chambers seemed to think, what if they'd completely overrun the highway? There might be no gap to thread.

They crept forward another mile before a foot patrol spotted them and dove for cover behind the wreckage of a downed helicopter, then opened fire. Moments later, more gunfire lashed from windows on either side of the street, all targeting the armored car.

Eliza hit the lights and punched it forward while Steve ducked into the back to help Miriam and Chambers. Their two main guns opened up in sharp bursts. Tracer bullets slammed into the buildings on either side.

"Look out!" Miriam shouted.

Something streaked in from Eliza's left. A rocket-propelled grenade. It hammered into the vehicle with enough force to make it rock off its wheels momentarily.

This is it. This is the end.

The grenade failed to detonate. Chambers let out a string of oaths.

Miriam let loose her gun in a sustained burst that lasted several seconds. "Got you!" Then, to Eliza, she said, "Get us out of here!"

The truck was sluggish to respond. It carried extra armor, water, spare fuel, cans of ammo, boxes of food, and six people. Gunfire rattled against the sides. Most of it was no more effective than a handful of gravel flung against a tin roof. But then a hollow thump-thump-thump started. A fist slammed into them. Tracers lit up the night on either side.

Miriam and Chambers kept firing, while Steve and Grover struggled to keep the guns fed. Eliza was finally picking up speed. She rammed aside two wrecked cars, swerved to get around a burned-out army truck.

At last they rounded the block. The road lay open ahead of them. Gunfire followed, but they shortly outran it. For a long moment there was nothing but heavy breathing and Fayer groaning in the back.

"Thank you, Father in Heaven," Miriam said in a solemn voice, "for sparing our lives this night."

The night may have been ending, but surviving the day would be another matter. They hadn't yet escaped the city, and two hundred and fifty miles lay between them and the safety of Blister Creek.

A block of gutted apartment buildings sat to their right. Dawn's first light streamed through perforated walls and shattered windows, emerging in glowing shafts through the thick smoke. The tang of burning fuel and plastic seeped into the truck.

Steve returned to the passenger seat. He gave Eliza a wan smile. He reached for the map, but there was no point. Block after block of ruined buildings stretched ahead of them, and in some places it was impossible to tell the former street from the general destruction. There certainly were no more road signs in this part of the town to guide their way.

"Look," he said. "There's the highway."

The smoke was especially thick to the north, but the wind was shifting and it cleared a path. Her heart lifted as she caught a glimpse of the long ribbon of cement and its overpasses cutting through the north of the city. Less than a mile to go.

Then the smoke cleared further and what she saw was a punch to the gut.

An army marched east along the highway, cutting across the vehicle's path: trucks, horses, men on foot, mules hauling artillery pieces. Hundreds and hundreds of them. Four tanks rolled along the near flank, creeping along at a few miles an hour. It looked like a major offensive by the rebel forces, pushing toward the federal troops that held the north and east of the city.

Then, to her horror, the trailing tank stopped. It swung its turret in their direction.

"Stop the truck," Steve said.

Eliza hit the brakes. The armored car came to a halt.

"Nobody shoot!" Steve said.

The tank aimed its main gun directly at them. It sat on an overpass, maybe twenty feet above their own road, and five or six blocks distant. The rest of the caravan kept moving while the tank seemed to study them. Eliza braced herself. She would see a flash of light and then it would be over.

The others came up front, with the exception of Agent Fayer.

"One false move and the gunner will blow us to hell," Steve said. "It won't miss."

"Why hasn't he fired?" Eliza asked.

"Look at all the nonstandard equipment in the column. Our armored car wouldn't look out of place up there. That gives us cover while he radios for instructions."

She didn't know what she was looking at, only that the size of the enemy formation filled her with dread. Two foot soldiers stopped and studied them through binoculars, no doubt looking for identifying marks.

"I can't sit here forever."

"They're using smoke as cover to infiltrate the city," Steve said. "And that helps us as much as it helps them. When the wind shifts again, make a run for it."

That made a lot more sense. "Where do I go?"

"Run straight at them," Steve said. "Get under the overpass where they can't see us."

"Are you crazy?" Chambers asked. "Take us back the way we came."

Miriam snorted. "Into that firefight? You think that's safer?"

"We could be killed either way," Steve said. "But they're not securing the road, they're trying to force men and materiel into the city. We can wait it out. And if we have to run, we'll be north of the highway, not south. Eliza, what do you think?"

"I don't want to backtrack."

"Then it's settled," Miriam said.

All the while, the tank kept its gun trained on them. The smoke wasn't rolling back over the freeway; it was clearing in the face of the morning winds that so often blew off the desert as the sun warmed the air. Visibility opened both east and west, all the way to the Strip, where columns of smoke still rose hundreds of feet into the air.

"Get back there, all of you," Steve said. "Get those guns ready."

For what? They sat in the open, with a tank pointing its main gun at them. If the gunner got the orders, there would be no fighting back. No warning, even.

The armored car shook. It sounded at first like another heavy artillery blast, then the freeway erupted in flames and roiling explosions. Two jets thundered over the freeway, their guns spraying down on the troops. They were in view a split second, then were gone.

"Go! Go! Go!" Steve yelled.

Eliza threw the truck into gear and mashed down on the gas. The vehicle rumbled forward. Little by little, she picked up speed as she approached the freeway underpass. In the smoke and fire and general destruction, she could barely keep on the road.

The smoke pouring from the city fires changed direction again. Suddenly, everything was night and her visibility was only a few feet. They reached the freeway. She passed directly underneath.

And to her relief, the aerial assault hadn't collapsed the highway and blocked the underpass. Gaping holes opened in the roadbed overhead, marked with jagged blocks of concrete and twisted rebar.

Bodies clogged the road beneath the holes. Most of the soldiers were dead—long dead, with their boots and weapons scavenged—but several had fallen right through the gaps after the bombing. Some were still alive, and struggled to regain their feet. The smoke and dust was so thick, she couldn't see to avoid them, and the truck tossed them aside, rolling over the dead and dying alike. Nobody attacked them.

The armored car burst out the other side. Eliza plowed through smoke and dust, her visibility terrible for two or three more blocks before the air began to clear.

At last Eliza got a glimpse of the open road. It was a straight shot of double-laned asphalt cutting through squat working-class homes, looted pawnshops, abandoned nail salons, and used-car dealerships. A gutted Pizza Hut sat on one corner, the signage intact but the distinctive red roof blown away.

And the road was clear. No dead bodies, no burned-out vehicles. No tanks. No men at sandbags with machine guns, holding the intersections. Eliza didn't know where the road led and didn't care. Steve was studying the map, muttering, and she counted on him to figure it out before they reached the dry hills ahead.

She continued to accelerate until the vehicle was shaking and the wind whistled in through the jagged holes in the armor cut by enemy machine guns. One hole was right next to her knee. A .50-caliber bullet had passed through there. It could have easily taken off her leg.

A few minutes later the city ended. One block it was strip malls and subdivisions and the next it was a brown desert plain dotted with sagebrush and dry grass.

They had escaped Las Vegas. As far as Eliza cared, it could burn to ash behind them.

CHAPTER THIRTY-TWO

By the time Jacob reached the bunker at the south end of the valley, the women were already in motion. Jacob could see them streaming in on horseback and crammed in the back of pickup trucks. When they reached the battle, they threw themselves into the ditch on the east side of the highway, or crouched behind piles of volcanic tuff. They fired at the enemies who came riding, rolling, and walking down the road toward them.

The bunker itself, so recently rebuilt, was nearly in ruins again. Rocket-propelled grenades streaked from the back of enemy trucks to slam into its side. Gunfire pounded against the concrete, throwing off chips, and tore up the dirt berms piled up around its sides. The noise inside must have been deafening—the conditions suffocating with smoke and fire.

And yet the bunker's main gun chugged away with grim determination, turning the south highway into a slaughterhouse. Men and animals lay dead and dying. The gun swept back and forth, cutting through enemies with every pass. But it was a tenuous position, almost overrun as enemies fanned out to flank the building or set up their own positions.

Jacob had gathered every man in town for the reservoir attack and its aftermath. Neglecting the other main approach into the valley had seemed a safe bet as compared to the risks of waging a half-hearted battle in the cliffs.

But apparently, an enemy had been watching. Waiting for the men to abandon their posts. When that happened, they'd attacked in full force. And if not for the vigilance of the Women's Council, the valley would have been overrun.

All of this went through Jacob's mind as he roared down the highway behind the wheel of the Humvee. Up above, David fired his gun into the sky as a warning, which sent women scattering from their path. A few, caught by surprise, turned and squeezed off a shot or two before their eyes widened in recognition and they threw themselves clear. Others shouted in joy. One woman with gray braids raised an AK-47 overhead and cheered. She looked like a jihadi in a prairie dress.

As soon as the road was clear of women, David let loose. He didn't try to conserve bullets, but let it tear, stopping briefly only as his loader struggled to keep the weapon fed with fresh ammo belts. Smoot and the others fired through gun ports as fast as they could shoot and reload.

The Humvee's arrival broke the back of the enemy attack, or what little remained after it had ground to a halt in the face of the women's furious defense. Within seconds the assault turned into a full-scale retreat. Women rose from behind their hiding places and fired after them.

Jacob waited for a lull from the bunker, then pulled ahead and swung across the highway a few yards short of the first dead enemies.

He jumped down from the Humvee and waved his arms to call a ceasefire.

A caravan of trucks screeched to a stop. Men and women alike shouted at him to continue the pursuit.

"No! We've won. It's over!"

He knew they would disagree. Their bloodlust was up. But enough blood had been shed. If there were any enemies left on either end of the valley, they would surely pause after a pair of crushing defeats.

David climbed down from his gun, and Elder Smoot came out the back of the Humvee. Behind him, Rebecca and Lillian emerged from the bunker and Carol Young followed a moment later. They peeled off earmuffs, staring grimly from blackened faces. Ash coated their hair.

Jacob stared at them. Rebecca, Lillian, and Carol. That was why they'd held on with such tenacity.

Fernie had assigned her three sharpest, most steel-nerved women to the bunker. How long had they held out against withering fire before reinforcements arrived? They were heroes.

Carol spotted Stephen Paul at one of the pickup trucks and they embraced. When he pulled away from his wife, his face was smeared with soot and tears. David and Lillian did the same and just like that the bloodlust faded, almost visibly, from the saints. They hugged and wept. Men clutched wives. Women embraced sister wives.

Jacob ached, knowing that Fernie was home in her wheelchair. She must have been listening to the gunfire, sick with worry. He needed to tell her he was unharmed. And to open the clinic. Men clutched bleeding arms or lay groaning in the backs of pickup trucks. A woman cried for help from the ditch. Already, Jacob was running triage scenarios in his mind.

The time to kill was past. Now it was time to heal.

★★★

Once free of the hell that was Las Vegas, Eliza and the others fought their way gradually north and east, coming under fire three times before they hit the empty road. None of the attacks were serious, although once they blew past a pair of sandbagged bunkers without realizing it. Men watched them from behind anti-tank guns capable of blasting them to pieces, but were perhaps as confused by the armored car as had been the Californians on the highway. Nobody fired a shot. One man stared as they passed, jabbering into a radio. Eliza braced for an attack, but it never came.

Soon they were back on the desert highway the original companions had spent so many days traveling the previous week. By eight o'clock that morning they were hooking east into the desolate western desert of Utah. They stopped by a salt pan shimmering with briny pools long enough to pee and gas up. Fayer took a little water from the jugs, but it passed directly through her. The inside of the armored car smelled like a latrine by now. They'd cracked the gun vents to let fresh air flow through, but it provided minimum benefit. As they started up again, Fayer slipped into a delirious slumber and couldn't be roused.

The four healthy people took turns driving and trying to nap, with limited success. The smell, the heat, and the aftershock of battle kept Eliza dozing in and out of consciousness.

She was driving again a little after ten in the morning when they came east on the dirt road that had taken them away from I-15. They'd covered a stunning amount of ground, more than two hundred miles already, but one final challenge awaited them. Cedar City shimmered against the mountain range on the eastern horizon. Unless something had changed in the past week, Hank Gibson would still be in charge, and nursing his anger about the stolen horses.

Eliza slowed the truck as she filled in Steve and Agent Chambers about what had happened in Cedar City and how they'd bluffed and stolen their way out of town.

"That took guts," Steve said. "Let me guess, Miriam's idea?"

"It got us out of there, didn't it?" Miriam said.

"We could stay west of the freeway, continue north, and try for Parowan," Eliza said. "There's a road that cuts over the mountains. We'd enter the valley through the Ghost Cliffs."

"Is Parowan still occupied?" Steve asked.

"Probably not. If we're lucky, it's deserted."

"How far out of our way?"

"Maybe a hundred miles."

He looked at the gas gauge and frowned. "We'll be coming in on fumes as it is. No way we can squeeze another hundred."

"Cedar City can't stop us," Miriam said. "Gibson and all his deputies could stand in the road blasting away and not penetrate this truck."

"I wouldn't be so sure about that," Eliza said. "With all those army convoys passing through last fall, you've got to bet some heavy weaponry found a home in town."

"Don't provoke them," Steve said. "Drive quietly through Cedar City and make for the canyon road. Do you think they'll attack?"

Eliza chewed on her lip. "Maybe not. They might think it's the army."

"Or bandits," Miriam said. "I say we go for it. If they try to stop us, we make them pay."

"Chambers, what do you think?" Steve asked.

The FBI agent was eating an MRE while sitting atop a flat of bottled water. The smell from Fayer's illness didn't seem to put him off his appetite. "Right now, I don't really care if they attack or not. What I don't want is to run out of gas and spend the next week on foot. The sooner we find your cult, the better."

"The sooner you stop calling it a cult, the better," Miriam said.

Chambers shrugged. "No offense meant. I'm grateful. My point is, I don't want to walk. And I'm sure she doesn't either." He hooked his thumb at Fayer, who lay hunkered in her blanket, shivering, while Grover tried to get her to take sips of water.

Nobody made an argument to bypass Cedar City, so Eliza gritted her teeth and continued straight toward town. About a mile west of the freeway, a rider on a horse paced them for a stretch, trying to keep up. He looked like he wanted to gallop ahead to give warning, but of course Eliza didn't intend to allow anything of the kind. She clattered over the train tracks.

She slowed to thirty when she reached the burned-out box stores on the west side. It was fast enough to outpace the riders who kept appearing and then scattering. Any faster and it would look like she had something to hide. Let them think she was a lost army vehicle and they wouldn't want to risk attacking.

Somehow the word got ahead of them, because they came up past the cemetery and its huge number of fresh graves to find the way blocked with trucks dragged across the road. A dozen riflemen stood behind the vehicles.

"Looks like they figured it out," Steve said.

Chambers and Miriam manned the guns.

"Don't start anything," Eliza said.

"I can take them out in three seconds," Miriam said. "Cut those cars in two as well."

"I mean it, don't fire."

Eliza hit the gas and hurtled toward the barricade. Rifles fired, pocking the window and pinging off the grill. The gunmen scattered just before the armored car hit. Eliza slammed into the barricade and the cars spun out of the way with a shriek of metal. Then they were through. Gunfire followed them up the hill until they rounded the corner.

Eliza let out her breath. So many worries and fears now evaporated that she felt like she was floating. For a moment that feeling cut away the exhaustion, the stress of battle, the horrible memories of men dying. Of Trost, his head blown apart by a sniper's bullet. All she could think was that if the gas held out, she'd be home in ninety minutes.

The numbingly hypnotic drive down empty roads had combined with three days of sleep deprivation to dull Eliza's senses by the time she reached Highway 89. Blister Creek was close now, no more than ten miles away. The others were in back, sleeping. Collapsed in exhaustion, really.

The vehicle was drifting, and she fought that leaden, nodding feeling that threatened to send her into the ditch. Suddenly, she found herself approaching a force of pickup trucks and horsemen traveling south.

Eliza shouted for the others to wake up. As they scrambled to their feet, she acted on pure instinct, hitting the gas instead of the brake. Men raised guns. Some threw themselves from the road or swerved their trucks to the shoulders. In an instant she was tearing down the middle of them.

Some of the men wore fatigues, others jeans and T-shirts. They were filthy, bloodstained, and thin. Haggard faces and scraggly beards. Young men, mostly white, but with a few darker faces. The remnant of an army or maybe bandits—she couldn't be sure which. But they were retreating from Blister Creek, either driven off or having just plundered and murdered its citizens.

No, not the latter. This was a defeated force. An army in retreat. She could see it in their drooping expressions and the sheer exhaustion of their movements.

Whoever they were expecting, it was not Eliza. She was in the heart of the force before the first shots went off. She swerved around trucks, but forced aside men on foot or horse. One man bounced off the hood and went flying.

As they passed, the enemy gunfire picked up strength, attacking their retreat. Miriam and Steve got their guns working. But it was only a few seconds and then Eliza had them out of range.

A mile north of the caravan, they passed two men lying in the middle of the road. Their companions had taken their boots, but they were still alive. One man lifted a bloody face from the pavement and waved feebly for her to stop. She hardened her heart and swerved around him.

"Damn," Steve muttered.

"You know we can't."

"I know. There's about thirty reasons why not. But it's a hard world where you can't stop for a wounded man begging for help."

She started to catch familiar sights: hillocks of volcanic rock and sagebrush, a sandy wash, the old gravel quarry. When she reached the flapping sheet-metal sign for the Blister Creek city limits, she pulled to a stop.

"We drive in there, we'll get the same welcome as those poor jerks behind us," Eliza said. "Blister Creek will see the armored car and think it's another attack."

"Hmm," Steve said. "Good point. So what do we do?"

"There's a flare gun back here," Miriam said. "What if we fire it down the road to signal?"

"Signal what?" Eliza said. "That could mean anything."

Grover spoke up from the back. "The lady FBI agent is wrapped in a white blanket. We could wave it out the windows."

"I like that idea," Steve said. He went back to help the others get the blanket off the sick woman. "Come on, Fayer, let go. The sooner we get into town, the sooner we get you help."

Eliza searched the road ahead. Someone might be studying them even now, lining up for a shot with a heavy gun. The others were murmuring to Fayer, who seemed to be uncooperative. Then they fell silent.

Steve returned to sit next to Eliza, his face a gray mask. He stared down at the blanket clenched between his two big hands. "I got the blanket." He swallowed hard. "But Fayer is dead."

CHAPTER THIRTY-THREE

"Hand me a 3-0 Vicryl on a PS-2," Jacob said. He held a clamp in one bloody, latex-gloved hand and held out the other for the needle with suture attached. A woman placed it in his palm.

He'd been working for so long without looking that he was no longer sure who was assisting. Not Lillian; she and Jessie Lyn Smoot were at the other table, plucking buckshot with forceps from the gluteal muscles of Jacob's younger brother Joshua. It was a job that should be done by a doctor, not his nurses, no matter how game. But he had already treated twenty-two patients and had at least six more to go. They were through the critical cases—two had died on the operating table and another when Jacob didn't get to him soon enough—and into the merely serious.

At least a dozen different assistants had come through since he'd started operating. Only Lillian had remained throughout, working tirelessly and efficiently. The others came and went, a succession of young women who had received medical training in the clinic over the past year. He made do.

Clancy Johnson lay unconscious on the table under Jacob's home-brewed ether, synthesized from ethanol. Jacob sewed up the bowel, then called for the 4-0 sutures to stitch up the skin and muscle. He should probably use a smaller size, but he was running short. This would leave an unpleasant scar. He was so exhausted, he was mostly relieved he hadn't botched the operation. How long had he been going? Thirty hours? He'd stopped only to visit the bathroom and to choke down a few bites of food Fernie had shoveled into his mouth.

He straightened with a groan and peeled off his gloves, which he dropped into a bucket of syringes, needles, vials, clamps, and forceps at his feet. Later, all of this would be sterilized for reuse. He couldn't afford to throw out so much as a used strip of gauze.

"Okay, who is next?" Jacob asked as he made his way to the sink to scrub down with a bar of lye soap.

Lillian looked up. She wore a curiously amused expression. "That's all."

"Really? I thought you said six more."

"Sprains, greenstick fractures, abrasions, and the like. All stuff the nurses can handle. But no more surgery."

He let out his breath. "Thank goodness for small miracles. I'm going to catch a few minutes of sleep, then I'll do rounds."

"You might thank your nurses before you go." Again, that funny little smile.

"Of course, I'm sorry. Thank you." Jacob glanced around the garage-turned-clinic and was surprised to see how many young women were working around him. He'd been in a zone for so long that he'd scarcely noticed them coming and going. "And you, Sister Sarah. Sister Jessie Lyn, Sister Nell. Sister—"

Jacob gaped. His sister Eliza stood over the prone body of Clancy Johnson, where she had been bandaging the incision in his abdomen.

"Something the matter, doctor?"

"You!"

He swept her in his arms, laughing.

"I swear," she said, when they broke their embrace, "seventy minutes of surgery and you never once looked up. I was attending the whole time."

"When did you arrive?"

"Yesterday morning, from the south. Right after your battle. We saw the aftermath. Sister Rebecca almost blasted us off the road. I'd have come in, but we were so exhausted we just collapsed." Another smile. "And some of us hadn't had a home-cooked meal all year. That big lug of mine is all skin and bones."

Jacob stared. "Does this mean what I think it means?"

"We found him, Jacob. Steve is home."

Eliza was glowing. It was a beautiful thing to behold and he thought he would burst with joy.

He hugged her again. "I'm so happy for you."

Then Eliza's face fell as she sketched in the details of her trip to Las Vegas and the harrowing escape. There had been dark moments: Trost, killed on the road. Agent Fayer—no real friend of Blister Creek, even though Jacob respected her—dead of cholera.

He was especially sorry to hear about Trost. He was a good man and a friend of the saints. Later, no doubt, Jacob would feel that loss more deeply. For now, he was so relieved that Eliza was safe, and Steve and Miriam too, that he couldn't give Trost's death the attention it deserved.

Eliza also explained how she had cauterized Grover's wound. Jacob listened, chewing on his lower lip.

"Was that the right thing?" she said. "Please don't tell me I caused him unnecessary pain."

"Well, I wasn't there."

"Jacob, give it to me straight. I screwed up, didn't I?"

"Truthfully? I don't know. They don't generally recommend cauterizing infected wounds. The damaged tissue is often more at risk than it was before. But that's presupposing modern antibiotics. And it must have been spreading awfully fast." He put a hand on her arm. "You used your best judgment. That's all you could do."

She let out her breath.

"All the same," he added, "I'd better take a look. Where is he now?"

"Digging graves at the cemetery, last I heard."

"Better send him in."

"Lillian and I treated him earlier. It's going to leave an ugly scar, but it looks clean."

"Good. Then I'm going to bed. What time is it?"

"Almost midnight." Lillian spoke up from the other side of the room, where she and her assistant were finishing up with Joshua.

Jacob had operated all through the night and through the next day and into the evening. It had been like one of the hellacious rotations at Sanpete when he was a resident, only following a short night of sleep and a bloody battle. He yawned and made for the door into the house.

"How long do you need?" Eliza asked.

"About two days."

"I need you awake by ten."

"Tomorrow morning? Are you kidding? I am not getting up before noon."

Eliza fixed him with a serious look. "I've already waited a day and half. And I wouldn't have done that either, if I hadn't collapsed in exhaustion. I'm not waiting another day. If you're asleep, fine—I'll ask David to do it."

Jacob stared. "Ask him to do what?"

She raised an eyebrow. "Let's see. I didn't leave the valley, venturing life and limb, to go on a joyride through the desert."

"Wait, you're talking about getting married?"

The women in the room laughed, and he felt foolish.

"Wow, you *are* tired," Eliza said. She leaned and kissed him on the cheek. "See you in the morning, big brother."

★★★

It took Jacob fifteen minutes just to get upstairs. Everybody wanted to stop him and chat. Why weren't they in bed already? He was at the bottom of the stairs, one hand on the railing, when his mother caught up to him, wringing her hands about Joshua's surgery. He wasn't going to die, was he?

"He has buckshot in his butt, Mom. He'll be fine." His tone was sharp, and he regretted it at once. "Sorry, I'm just—please, it will have to wait."

Upstairs, he collapsed on the bed, too tired to even take off his boots. Fernie wheeled herself in a few minutes later. "Come on, off with the boots."

She tugged them off and set them to one side. "Now the rest of it. Do you know what a hassle it is to wash blood out of sheets these days? Get them off, mister. You're not going to force me out of this wheelchair, are you?"

He groaned and undressed to his undergarments, then climbed under the covers. "Don't let me sleep through the wedding."

"Not a chance. I promised Eliza you'd be at the temple at ten or I'd do it myself."

"Oh, so you've given yourself the priesthood now? This I would like to see."

Fernie turned her chair so she could stroke his face. It was the first time they'd been alone since he'd left her in bed forty hours earlier. "I'm glad you're safe," she said.

"Me too. And thank you. We'd have been overrun if you hadn't been vigilant."

"It was Rebecca's idea. She suggested that the best time to attack Blister Creek would be when the men were fighting at the reservoir. I put my best women at the bunker and had everyone else on standby."

"They said no women died. Is that true?"

"Yes," she said. "I wish the same could be said for the men."

"We lost three at the clinic. I don't know if others didn't make it to me. Nobody would tell me a thing."

"You didn't need the distraction. That's why I kept Eliza out until you were almost finished."

"Well?"

Her voice dropped. "Eight more fell. Eleven dead in total."

Eleven. A sick feeling settled into his gut. "Who?"

She named them. Three were teenage boys. Eight were men with families.

"Elder Potts had five wives," Jacob said. His throat was so tight he could barely get the words out. "Twenty children still living at home."

"There are ninety-two fresh orphans today. Nineteen widows. If you count Bill Smoot from last week, twenty-one women have lost their husbands."

"We'll take care of them."

"We held a joint meeting of the Quorum of the Twelve and the Women's Council this morning," Fernie said. "Of course, the decision is awaiting your approval, but Elder Stephen Paul and I have put together a plan for the care of widows and orphaned children."

"That's good," he started to say, then caught something in her tone. "Wait, why do I suddenly have the feeling I'm not going to like this?"

"Shh, we'll discuss it later." She pulled her hand from his cheek. "Get some rest. I'll wake you in a few hours."

★★★

Jacob was half-dressed on the side of the bed while Fernie was putting on his white shirt before he realized that he was out of the covers and sitting up. Daylight streamed through the window.

"You are not making this easy," she said. "Come on, you big baby, give me a hand."

"Sorry." He buttoned up the shirt, yawning. "What time is it?"

"Quarter to ten. If I know Eliza, she's pacing back and forth in the temple lobby. Steve has already received his endowments, so any time you show up, they're ready."

Jacob dressed in his temple whites and then helped his wife down the stairs, where David and his two wives waited with the wheelchair. Miriam and Lillian were freshly scrubbed and looked sweet and pretty in their long white dresses. Lillian looked especially young, with her hair drawn back and her ears sticking out a fraction too far. Miriam held her baby close, wearing a look of devoted motherhood. It was hard to believe he was looking at a cool, calculating killer. Blister Creek's own lioness.

Jacob eyed her short hair, cropped above the shoulder. She'd previously worn a braid that had stretched halfway down her back.

Miriam caught his look and shrugged. "Had to pass myself as an FBI agent."

"Do I dare ask why? And if it worked?"

David shook his head. "I would recommend, no."

While they walked the few blocks to the church, David filled him in on the developments of the past day. The bodies were in the icehouse, the funerals scheduled for that afternoon. Stephen Paul had accompanied David in the Humvee back up to the reservoir—not another punitive expedition, David assured Jacob—but reconnaissance. There were still squatters at the lake, although they were down to a few hundred, not thousands. The rest were either dead or had fled north.

"We can deal with a few hundred," Jacob said, relieved. He glanced at his watch as they reached the steps to the temple and its doors rebuilt from the previous fall. "Perfect, we're right on time."

"You three go ahead," Fernie told David and the other two women. "Tell Eliza we'll be there in a second."

Jacob stepped around Fernie's wheelchair so he could speak to her face-to-face. "Is this about what you told me last night?"

"Yes, about our plan for the widows and orphans."

"I think I know what you're planning, and I don't like it."

Fernie met his gaze with a serious expression. "And I know what you're going to say. You're going to say they don't need to remarry, that we can take care of them anyway."

"That's exactly what I'm going to say." He made his voice light. "See, we don't even need to have the conversation."

"Don't get sidetracked. Eliza is going to strangle us if we don't hurry."

"Then what's the rush? We'll talk later."

"I need you to hear it from me, and not someone else."

"Fine, you say your piece and I'll say mine."

"You can make the case that they don't need to remarry, and in some circumstances you would be right," Fernie said. "But civilization has collapsed. We need to keep our wagons circled. A home isn't just a way to support a family, it's also for mutual protection. And a man is needed for priesthood authority."

"So you say."

"So we all say. The Second Coming is at hand, and those women want the power of the priesthood in their houses." She held up her hand. "No, don't interrupt. I know how you feel—we all do, really. And we still decided this is for the best."

"Be that as it may, you can't just give away the widows. At the very least you need to—"

"To ask them? We did."

"Already? Their husbands died *yesterday*. And except for Bill, they're not even in the ground."

"No man—or woman—knows the day or hour of the Lord's coming. Nobody wanted to wait. But I promise, we gave the women a choice. Every one of them is free to remarry or to live as a widow. Two of the twenty-one women have chosen to move in with Sister Rebecca and Sister Charity at Yellow Flats instead of remarrying."

"It's a dying institution," Jacob said. "I'm going to rid this community of polygamy. We no longer kick out the excess boys, and there's no more underage marriage or swapping of daughters. It's only a matter of time."

"Yes, I know. Your goals are transparent to one and all. But it's not going to happen overnight. In the meantime, this is what the widows want."

He sighed. "You're telling me this is what the women want? To be traded like cattle?"

"It isn't like that. The nineteen who will remarry have chosen their husbands, not the other way around."

Jacob was taken aback. "Well, that's something. My quorum agreed to that?"

"More or less. That is, some more, some less. Again, they're awaiting your judgment."

"And you can promise me that the women are making this choice freely? That there's no coercion of any kind? Other than the usual religious kind, of course."

"Don't be so cynical. But yes, all of them. Of course we didn't just let any woman choose any man. There was a lot of back and forth with existing sister wives. In the end, we gave each of the widows three options, based on the deliberations of the council and in consultation with the quorum. David will be marrying a third wife. Your brother Joshua will be marrying Bill's youngest widow. She doesn't have any children yet, so it seemed a good pick for Joshua's first."

"Joshua is not ready for marriage."

"He's twenty-five. Time to get ready. Stephen Paul is taking two new wives. Elder Smoot is marrying Elder Potts's two oldest. One of Smoot's sons is taking one of his brother's widows."

"Okay, I don't need all of it right now. First, I want to speak with the quorum and the council and chat with a few of these widows. I'm not convinced."

"You'll want to start with Jessie Lyn," Fernie said.

"Yes?" He shrugged. "Okay."

"What do you think of her?"

"Think of Jessie Lyn?" Another shrug. "Nice young woman. Seems to be a good mother. She was a big help in the clinic. Oh, she's one of Potts's widows. I didn't even think of that. She didn't say a word."

"You almost married her once, remember? When your father was trying to maneuver Eliza into an alliance with the Kimballs, they offered you Jessie Lyn Kimball in trade."

"Yes, I remember. Thank goodness I—" He stopped. "Wait. No."

"Jacob, listen to me."

"I have a wife. I don't want another. We settled that a long time ago."

She held his gaze. "And how is that fair? Do you think David wants another wife, when he's already struggling to incorporate Lillian into his family? Do you think any of these women and children want to make this change? Wouldn't they all choose to be with their own husbands and fathers?"

"I can't do it."

"Jessie Lyn is a Kimball. They are still a vital part of the church. This would finally end the conflict between the Christiansons and the Kimballs."

"It wouldn't be fair to Jessie Lyn."

"You would grow to love her."

"I promise you I would not. I'm not wired that way. I can only love one woman and that's you."

"You would, because you would try. And because you're a good man and sincere, you would succeed. Maybe it would be different. I don't know. Of course I want to be special in your heart, but it's a big heart and I can share it."

"Fernie, please." Jacob shot a desperate glance at the temple. "Eliza and Steve are waiting."

"It was Jessie Lyn's idea, not mine. None of the other widows asked, though I know that several were thinking it. They know what kind of man you are."

"Jessie Lyn came to you specifically?"

"She said she'd had a dream that she would be your wife."

"I dreamed once that I was a Roman emperor," Jacob said. "When I woke up, I was not wearing a toga."

"You made the call, Jacob. You sent those men into battle. Hundreds of people died and some of them were your own followers. They trusted you, and their wives and children trusted you too. Jessie Lyn put her husband's life in your hands. Now Elder Potts is dead and she has asked if you will marry her. If you will be a father to her daughter, and give her more children, so that she can raise a righteous seed as her patriarchal blessing has promised. Are you going to tell her no?"

Jacob didn't have an answer. Only a sick memory of the dead, either by his hand or by his orders. Twenty-one widows and ninety-two orphans. One of those widows was Jessie Lyn; one of the orphans was her daughter.

The temple doors swung open. A tall, skinny stranger in white appeared and started down the stairs. Only when the man had reached the bottom and was greeting them with a familiar deep voice did Jacob recognize him.

"Steve, what the devil happened to you?"

"Crash diet," Steve said. "But don't worry, I've been doing nothing but eating and sleeping since I got home. I'll be in fighting trim before long. Now, are you going to come marry us or do I have to send a posse to drag you in?"

Jacob's troubles momentarily forgotten, he pushed Fernie up the side ramp, then had Steve help ease her chair over the threshold and into the lobby of the temple. More guests lingered there—siblings, cousins, uncles, and aunts. Only a few would fit into the sealing room itself. While Fernie rolled up to Eliza, who was chatting nervously with Miriam and Lillian, Jacob looked through the crowd, searching for someone.

"You believe all this stuff?" Steve whispered.

"I take it you did the endowment?"

"Yes. Handshakes and moving robes and sashes around and all that. It was all I could do not to run screaming for the door."

"It helps if you think of it as symbolic," Jacob said. "And to remember that if you don't do it, Eliza won't marry you."

"In that case, lay it on me. What other crazy stuff do I have to do?"

"Nah, you're through the worst of it."

Where is she? Jacob wondered as he picked his way through the crowd toward the sealing rooms down the hall. Several others pulled in behind him.

It was then that he realized who he'd been searching for. Jessie Lyn Potts, née Kimball. The young woman who would be his second wife. Subconsciously, he'd been expecting to see her, not because she was family, but because he'd been worrying that the marriage was a fait accompli. That she was already here with her temple robes, ready to marry him.

She was not present. He was grateful for that much, at least.

CHAPTER THIRTY-FOUR

Eliza knelt at the altar with Steve by her side. They wore their temple robes. Jacob stood above them. Her family crowded the room, which was no more than a dozen feet square. Jacob was speaking words of advice, as was customary for the officiator. No doubt he had put some thought into them, was pouring out his deepest philosophies on marriage. They were a buzz in her ears.

Seven years. That's how long it had been since Gideon Kimball had tried to forcibly marry her. She had been a teenager still, young and afraid. Father had been willing to trade her to the Kimballs in order to elevate his favorite son into the quorum. Only Jacob's courage had stood between Eliza and a life of servitude and misery.

No, I did it too. I stood up to them. I stood up for myself.

Jacob instructed the couple to take each other by the hand in the patriarchal grip. They did so.

So many struggles since those days. Eliza had tried to leave the church, had joined the mainstream LDS and even served for a time as a missionary at Temple Square in Salt Lake. She'd returned home to aid Jacob in rescuing David from his drug addiction in Las Vegas. Had defied her father again, then seen him buried next to Grandma Cowley. Had fought off the Kimballs again. Had defended the valley as the country collapsed into chaos. And finally, Eliza had set out across the blasted landscape to rescue her beloved and bring him home.

I am no longer a child. I am a woman and an adult.

Eliza didn't kneel next to Steve as chattel, but as an equal.

She squeezed his hand. He returned a thin smile. The marriage ceremony may have been bewildering for him, but if he harbored any thoughts of backing out, he'd better think again. She wasn't going to let go of him now.

He must have caught her grin, because he met her gaze and mouthed, "What?"

She gave a tiny shake of the head and her smile broadened.

And then it was time.

"Brother Steve," Jacob said, "do you take Sister Eliza by the right hand and receive her unto yourself to be your lawful and wedded wife for time and all eternity, with a covenant and promise that you will observe and keep all the laws, rites, and ordinances pertaining to this Holy Order of Matrimony in the New and Everlasting Covenant, and this you do in the presence of God, angels, and these witnesses of your own free will and choice?"

"I do."

Nervous laughter passed around the room. Jacob raised his eyebrows and gave Eliza a wink.

"You're supposed to say 'yes,'" Eliza whispered.

Steve blushed. "Oh, um, yes."

"Sister Eliza, do you take Brother Steve by the right hand and give yourself to him to be his lawful and wedded wife, and for him to be your lawful and wedded husband, for time and all eternity, with a covenant and promise that you will observe and keep all the laws, rites, and ordinances pertaining to this Holy Order of Matrimony in the New and Everlasting Covenant, and this you do in the presence of God, angels, and these witnesses of your own free will and choice?" Eliza's heart pounded. "Yes."

And then Jacob was buzzing again, something about marriage for time and all eternity, multiplying and replenishing the earth and all that, blah, blah, blah. He seemed to be milking it.

Get on with it!

And then he pronounced them married and Eliza floated to her feet. Steve was grinning like an idiot and so were Jacob and Fernie and Miriam and David. It was all Eliza could do not to swoon.

They made their way out of the sealing room and fought through the crush of people in the front rooms of the temple. Everyone seemed to have a reason for delaying the new couple. It was all rather transparent.

Fernie caught up with Eliza and tugged on her sleeve. "Hey, hold up."

"I see what you're doing," Eliza said with a raised eyebrow. "I was there when we trashed David's car. I know the wagon—or whatever is waiting—is going to be decorated like a clown car."

"No, it's not that. I mean yes, of course. But that's not what I'm talking about."

Fernie handed over a small leather bag with a drawstring, then gestured for Eliza to lean down so she could whisper in her ear.

"You're commanded to multiply and replenish the earth," Fernie whispered in her ear, "but you don't need to do it on your honeymoon, if you know what I mean."

Eliza's face felt hot. She took the bag. Some sort of natural birth control. A folk remedy? No, Fernie was married to a doctor. Whatever it was would offer some efficacy.

"For after you're done," Fernie added. "To prevent fertilization. Read the instructions."

Steve had been vigorously pumping hands with all manner of well-wishers and his eyes widened when the doors of the temple swung open to cheers from an even greater throng on the stairs and sidewalk outside. And there it was, their wagon and team of horses, decorated with strips of colored cloth, tin cans on strings, and ribbons. The horses wore bonnets decorated with wildflowers.

Jacob stood at the doorway and beckoned theatrically. "Off you go! Happy honeymooning."

★★★

Even before the collapse, honeymoons in Blister Creek had not been celebrated by jaunts to Disney World or the Bahamas. If the husband was the type to consider a new wife as a piece of his eternal inheritance, the woman would be lucky if he took her hunting in the mountains for the weekend. The more romantic had honeymooned in the beautiful, otherworldly national parks of the southwest: the Grand Canyon, Zion, Arches, Bryce Canyon. But even these locations were off-limits at the moment, and might be for years to come.

Instead, Eliza's family had cleaned out a little brick farmhouse at the far northeast corner of the valley, in the green foothills two miles north of Stephen Paul Young's compound. With a little extra elevation, it was a cold place in winter, but in summer it was beautiful, with green meadows and wildflowers, and a bubbling spring that ran to join the creek on the valley floor. Aspens stretched up the mountainside behind the home.

One of Stephen Paul's brothers had lived out here until last year, before relocating to the safety of the central valley. Because of its exposed location, Grover and Henry Smoot rode ahead of the wagon as a precaution, and were already patrolling the perimeter when the couple arrived. They stayed at a discreet distance.

Eliza paused in front of the door and glanced back at Steve, who was coming up behind with a suitcase. "You still look pretty feeble," she said. "Maybe I should be the one doing the carrying over the threshold."

"No way. I feel great. Ready to run a marathon, in fact."

"Oh yeah? We'll see about that."

He swept her up and carried her across, then acted like he'd hurt his back when he got her inside. The act stopped when he looked around. Vases with cut flowers sat around the room and a bowl of strawberries waited in the middle of the table. The curtains were fresh and clean and the floors swept. The room smelled of rose water.

"Did you do all this?"

"It sure wasn't the Smoot boys."

"It's wonderful. What time did you get up this morning?"

"Early. I had to scout it out. Make sure it was suitable for my man. I can't always be bashing skulls, you know. Sometimes I have to show my gentle side." She shrugged. "I had some help."

Steve pulled her in and kissed her long and hard. A flood of warmth washed through her body. This time she didn't fight it. She was married now. Such a simple observation, but it filled her with a thrill.

At last she pulled away. "You're stubbly again. Why don't you shave while I get ready? There's no running water, so you'll have to go out to the pump."

"And leave you?" He sighed.

"Go on. I'll be waiting in the bedroom when you come back."

Eliza went into the bedroom and closed the door. In the drawers she found a green silk nightie wrapped in paper. A gift from Fernie. She undressed and put her clothes in the closet, slipped into the nightie, pulled her braids out to spread her hair, then lay back and waited. She didn't feel embarrassed or underdressed. She was too aroused.

When Steve came in he gaped. "Oh, my G—" He stopped himself. "My *goodness*." He shook his head. "That doesn't have the same ring to it."

"Go ahead and say it. Just this once."

"Oh, my God. You are hot."

"Am I?"

She sat up and leaned forward, coquettishly, she hoped, but since she didn't have much experience, was worried that it looked silly. From his heavy breathing and flushed look, maybe not. Eliza grabbed his shirt and pulled him forward. He fell down on top of her.

"Do you remember the first time we met?" she asked.

"Of course." His voice was husky. "You were a missionary at Temple Square. So young and chaste and virtuous."

"I saw you looking."

"Good thing you couldn't read my thoughts."

"No, I couldn't," she said. "You'd better tell me."

"I was thinking how luscious your breasts looked. They begged to be liberated from all those clothes."

"You're a patient man. You waited four years to find out. So? Now is your chance."

He slid his hand up the side of her body, fingers gliding over the silky fabric. His first touch against her breast was electric, and when his thumb brushed her nipple she gasped. His hand pulled away.

"No, don't stop," she begged.

He ignored her and drew the spaghetti strap down over her shoulder to expose her white breast and her pink nipple, now standing rockhard. Steve lowered his mouth, kissing first at her neck and then moving to her breast. When his lips touched her nipple she arched her back and moaned. He pulled at it slightly. Her body ached all over. She kissed him hungrily. His body pressed down on her and his leg was between hers. He moved to one side and slid his hand along the inside of her thigh. His fingers traced higher and higher until they touched the warm dampness between her legs. She thought she would hyperventilate.

"Can you—" she began.

"Tell me."

"Take your clothes off. I want to touch you too."

"Are you ready?"

"I have been ready for so long." Her voice trembled. "But slowly, please. I'm a little nervous."

"Of course."

Steve was gentle and patient. They kissed for a while and he touched her everywhere. She touched him too, tentatively at first, anxious. Not knowing what she was doing. He guided her hand and showed her.

And then it was time. He lay above her with his body pressed slightly against hers. Their faces were inches apart. His breath was hot against her face. Perspiration beaded his brow.

"Thank you for rescuing me, Eliza Christianson."

She looked into his beautiful brown eyes. "I would have torn down the gates of hell to bring you back."

"I know. I love you for it."

He closed his eyes and leaned forward. She clenched him tight and surrendered her body. And then he was inside her.

It hurt a little, but it also felt good.

★★★

Several hours later, in the evening, after they cooked dinner and ate by candlelight, Eliza put on her nightie and stepped onto the porch. Steve pulled on his underwear and followed her outside. It was the first time either of them had been dressed since that morning.

Crickets chirped their nightly chorus. The breeze shook the leaves in the quaking aspen on the hillside behind them. Shivering, she took Steve's arm and wrapped it around her. To the west and below them, the candles and lanterns of Blister Creek shimmered from windows. The occasional electric light lit the main entrances into town.

"We could stay out here," Steve said. "Bring the land back into production."

"We're police officers now," she said. "And valley security. Who has time to farm?"

"A garden, then. And some chickens. Maybe a couple of goats."

"I'd like that. But there's a reason the Smoot brothers are camped down by the creek with loaded guns." She spotted something up in the Ghost Cliffs to their right. "Look."

A flashlight moved along the edge of the cliff, maybe a mile away and several hundred feet above the valley floor. Scouts from the refugee camp. Watching. Waiting.

"Why can't they leave us alone?" Steve said.

"You were out there. You know the answer to that."

"It won't do any good. If they come, we'll fight them off. Again and again if we have to. We have no choice."

"I know," she said. She wrapped her arms around Steve's waist and leaned her head against his chest. "The rest of the valley is worrying about that. Let them, just for tonight."

He lifted her chin and kissed her. And then he pulled her toward the door to go back inside.

Outside the valley, the world was burning to ash. Cities turning to dust. Millions dying from starvation and disease. The desperate survivors knew about this sanctuary and were descending upon it like clouds of locusts.

But for tonight, that was not their concern. Steve barred the front door and led Eliza toward their bed.

ACKNOWLEDGMENTS

I would like to thank my agent, Katherine Boyle, for her help and advice. Thanks also to my great team at Thomas & Mercer, with a special mention to Anh Schluep, Terry Goodman, Jacque Ben-Zekry, and David Downing.

ABOUT THE AUTHOR

Michael Wallace was born in California and raised in a small religious community in Utah, eventually heading east to live in Rhode Island and Vermont. An experienced world traveler, he has trekked through the Andes, ventured into the Sahara on camel, and traveled through Thailand by elephant. In addition to working as a literary agent and innkeeper, he previously worked as a software engineer for a Department of Defense contractor, programming simulators for nuclear submarines. He is the author of more than a dozen novels.